RELUCTANT DEAD

RELUCTANT DEAD

A Quin and Morgan Mystery

John Moss

DUNDURN
TORONTO

Copyright © John Moss, 2011

All rights reserved. No part of this publication may be reproduced, stored in a retrieval system, or transmitted in any form or by any means, electronic, mechanical, photocopying, recording, or otherwise (except for brief passages for purposes of review) without the prior permission of Dundurn Press. Permission to photocopy should be requested from Access Copyright.

Editor: Shannon Whibbs
Design: Jennifer Scott
Printer: Webcom

Library and Archives Canada Cataloguing in Publication

Moss, John, 1940-
    Reluctant dead / John Moss.

(A Castle Street mystery)
(A Quin and Morgan mystery)
Issued also in electronic format.
ISBN 978-1-55488-856-6

    I. Title. II. Series: Moss, John, 1940- . A Quin and Morgan mystery. III. Series: Castle Street mystery

PS8576.O7863R45 2011   C813'.6   C2010-905996-4

1 2 3 4 5   15 14 13 12 11

We acknowledge the support of the **Canada Council for the Arts** and the **Ontario Arts Council** for our publishing program. We also acknowledge the financial support of the **Government of Canada** through the **Canada Book Fund** and **Livres Canada Books**, and the **Government of Ontario** through the **Ontario Book Publishing Tax Credit** and the **Ontario Media Development Corporation**.

Care has been taken to trace the ownership of copyright material used in this book. The author and the publisher welcome any information enabling them to rectify any references or credits in subsequent editions.

J. Kirk Howard, President

Printed and bound in Canada.
www.dundurn.com

Dundurn	Gazelle Book Services Limited	Dundurn
3 Church Street, Suite 500	White Cross Mills	2250 Military Road
Toronto, Ontario, Canada	High Town, Lancaster, England	Tonawanda, NY
M5E 1M2	LA1 4XS	U.S.A. 14150

1

Crimes of the Early Morning

Miranda Quin wondered how many of her fellow passengers on the Boeing 747 were contemplating murder. Before the shuddering rush of takeoff had fully subsided, she noticed that people around her had cracked open mystery novels that would mostly begin with gushing blood or gruesome dismemberment. A few sat with eyes closed, strained at the corners, perhaps thinking of adversaries they might prefer dead. One or two, possibly, thought about victims they had safely interred in secret places.

David Morgan, outside the parking garage at Pearson International, scanned the overcast sky, wondering which sound reverberating through the fog signified his partner's escape. He was sympathetic to her need to get away, but he was puzzled, amused, and a little concerned that she was going off to the South Pacific to try her hand at writing a mystery. At least she was travelling business class. She had been saving Aeroplan points for years, waiting for the appropriate occasion. As he wheeled out onto the throughway, Morgan took a deep breath and exhaled slowly. After more than a decade working homicide together, having faced death in so many ways, they were closer than lovers. He would miss her.

He swerved to avoid a truck. When Miranda was around, she did the driving. Either an unmarked police car or her 1959 Jaguar XK 150. Morgan was a bad driver, too easily distracted. A sixteen-wheeler pressed him to speed up. He accelerated, moved into the slower lane, and slowed to a comfortable speed. She had taken a night course on crafting the mystery novel at Sir Adam Beck College. Mostly, she skipped classes because they were immersed in actual murders. He tried to focus. She had trusted that he would get her car back to the parking garage and avoid it until her return.

As the plane slipped above the fog into dazzling blue, the cabin flooded with evening light. Miranda loosened her seat belt, leaned forward, and gazed out the window for a while at the illusion of a receding horizon, then drew down her shade, and, closing her eyes, drifted into an uneasy sleep.

She woke up with a start when the hush was shattered by a voice instructing passengers on how to conduct themselves should the plane crash on water. In three languages. She imagined that by now Morgan had tucked her away in the back of his mind and was intent on other things. She felt a moment of panic. He was always there, for ten years he had been the defining witness to her life.

A year ago Morgan had gone to Easter Island for a holiday and he had come back filled with unbridled enthusiasm. His rambling narrative about the authenticity of his own experiences in the most isolated and exoticized destination in the world translated in her mind into a haven of dreams, where the tropical sun warmed ragged grasslands and towering palms, where the saltwater breeze cooled the dreamer in the verandah's shade while local people lived ordinary lives amidst the thronging of their ancestral past. Shadows of the giant *moai* loomed over everything on her imagined island, making her daydreams tantalizing and dangerous.

She planned to stay for three months. The isolation would give her perspective and she would write mysteries with a Toronto setting because that was the locale she knew best. She had never been anywhere so remote from the centre of her world, thousands of kilometres from its nearest neighbours. She would be able to look back and envision Canada as a whole; she would be able to see around the edges, she would understand for the first time where she came from. And, of course, she would write about murder.

After she had started talking about her plans to colleagues and friends, by a curious form of cultural osmosis the news of her adventure reached a publisher who offered an advance payment for her novel large enough to cover a good part of her expenses. Taggart and Foulds were based in New York with a branch in Toronto. Morgan had thought it was unusual to invest so much in a new writer, a Canadian at that, but she took their offer in stride. It wasn't that much, really, relative to her investment of time. A few thousand dollars and an upgrade to business class. A little embarrassed by her good fortune, she had told Morgan she had upgraded with Aeroplan points.

Miranda raised her window shade and was staring down into the darkness that seemed to be rising from below when a steward leaned over and said something to her that seemed exotic, but was unintelligible. She was flattered. The first leg of her journey was to São Paulo and she had obviously been taken for a cosmopolitan Brazilian returning home. That pleased her. She did not want to appear as if she were from Toronto. She knew this was a trait shared with many of her countrymen, who were vaguely embarrassed to be recognized as Canadians abroad, although if pressed they were righteously proud.

She smiled and nodded in the affirmative.

"You just agreed to exchange your window seat for an aisle seat with that unhappy fellow several rows back," said the man beside her in perfect English.

"Did I?" she said. "Of course I did."

"I hope it wasn't on my account," he said and smiled with an insouciant Errol Flynn/Johnny Depp radiance.

"No. My Spanish is a little rusty, I thought she was asking me if I wanted a blanket."

"She was speaking Portuguese."

"My Portuguese is also rusty," said Miranda, rising to her feet and gathering her travelling paraphernalia, which consisted of a horseshoe-shaped inflatable pillow, a large handbag, a notebook, a P.D. James mystery novel, a book called *Inventing Easter Island* by Beverley Haun, a book by Thor Heyerdahl, and a small sheaf of vintage comics that Morgan had presented to her at the airport, the top one featuring Scrooge McDuck on Easter Island.

"Excuse me," she said. "It's not personal. I prefer the aisle. The negative ions are highest if you're close to the window."

"Exactly," he said. "That's why I didn't offer to trade places."

She disliked him immensely. He was far too comfortable being outrageously handsome, too casual with his wit, too indifferent as to whether she liked him or not.

Edging around the elderly gentleman who was displacing her, she leaned down and whispered to her erstwhile seatmate with all the condescension she could muster: "You speak very good English."

"Thank you." He smiled and his teeth glistened. "Sloane Square, Jesus College Oxford, Washington, my life in six words, five if you don't count Square. English comes rather naturally."

"Final disposition?"

"Of my mortal remains? At present, unknown. Have a safe flight."

"You, too," she said, puzzled, since they were on the same plane.

Later, when Miranda walked forward to the washroom, she noticed he was the only one awake in the entire business-class section, reading by the focused light beaming down from overhead. She slipped past in the gloom, apparently unnoticed. For some reason the notion that he would know where she had been made her feel exposed and vaguely improper.

He, of course, looked up upon her return and smiled directly at her as she tried to pass by in the semi-darkness.

"Couldn't sleep," she said, mouthing the words to indicate she did not wish to wake the other passengers. Suggesting she had merely been for a brief stroll.

"Nor me," he mouthed in return and nodded in the direction of his book.

She smiled in the affirmative, as if there were something conspiratorial about them both reading in their isolated cones of light. Then, as she was about to move on, she realized he was reading the same book as she was; it was open at a photograph of the author confronting a giant stone head on Easter Island.

She paused, then knelt down in the aisle at the elbow of the insufferably good-looking Englishman. Since he had admitted to being posted in Washington, he must be a diplomat. He was too attractive to be a spy. She wondered if London had spies in Washington? Most likely they did. It was more important to keep up with the covert activities of your friends than your enemies.

"You're reading Thor Heyerdahl," she whispered. "*Aku-Aku.*"

"Yes," he whispered back. "I am."

Nothing evasive about that, she thought. *Probably a spy.*

"We are defined by our enemies," he said.

"I beg your pardon!" She was alarmed that he had been inside her head.

"I thought you were trying to read the note —"

"No."

"In my book, there, it says, '*We are defined by our enemies.*'"

"Heyerdahl said that?"

"No. This is an American first edition, Rand McNally, 1958, it was inscribed by a previous owner. It sounds very Oscar Wilde."

Someone else might have said, "used book," she thought. *Someone else might have forgone the allusion to Wilde so early in a relationship.*

"The scribbling of a bibliophobe — someone who dislikes books," he clarified, with the relaxed authority of a person used to explaining his own vocabulary.

"It looks quite deliberate," she said, suppressing her annoyance as she leaned over to get a better look at the angular script, then, aware of the awkward intimacy of her posture, she edged away.

"It doesn't seem to bear any relationship to the text," he said, smiling at her self-consciousness. "You recognized the book?"

"I'm reading it, too," she said.

"What an uncanny coincidence."

"I write in all my books," she said. "There's nothing wrong with writing in books if you own them. It's a sign of engagement, the bibliophile's prerogative."

She winced at her own words. She sounded like Morgan. She stood up abruptly, smiled coldly, and walked back to her seat, where she picked up her own copy of *Aku-Aku*, which was a later printing of the same Rand McNally edition belonging to the Englishman. Morgan had given it to her, passing it on from Alex Rufalo, their boss, who received it from an acquaintance of his wife. When she turned it over she realized it had been splayed open at the same page as his, but there was, of course, no note in the margin. *Coincidences do happen*, she thought. She stared at the photograph of the Norwegian adventurer and the enigmatic stone face of the *moai* that appeared to be gazing right through him, despite the empty eyes. Leaving the book open on her flight table, she leaned back and let her mind wander.

When she woke up the plane was circling São Paulo. She vaguely remembered dismissing the steward when she had been offered breakfast, even though she knew it was sure to be excellent fare. She was travelling business class for the comfort, not the food, and preferred to sleep through. She had a six hour layover in São Paulo and would eat in the lounge at the airport.

She looked ahead to see if her companion of the dark hours had read through the night but his seat was empty.

The seatbelt signs were on. The plane banked in rapid descent. He must have moved to a window seat for the landing. Thinking about him was unsettling and she censured herself for the sensations that were coalescing at the edge of her mind. Miranda knew she was an attractive woman, but this guy wasn't travelling on points. He was the kind of man who hung out on the pages of *Vanity Fair* and romanced women a dozen years younger than herself who had record contracts, runway experience, or doctorates in psychology.

Morgan woke early, gradually, and the layers of sleep peeled away until he found himself staring at the framed poster from Rapa Nui, as Easter Island is called by the people who live there. The tinted line drawings of *moai* caught the morning light that drifted up through the open blinds on the lower level of his two-storey front window. The upper blinds had been jammed shut from the day he moved in, casting his sleeping loft in welcome gloom.

The telephone jangled, snapping him out of his morose reverie about monuments and mortality and the absence of Miranda. He missed her, it felt like being in the house of a dead relative after the funeral.

"Morgan?"

"Yeah. Alex?"

Since Alex Rufalo had become superintendent, Morgan usually addressed him by his title. It was early.

"I've got a murder for you, something you can handle on your own."

Morgan said nothing.

"Over on Toronto Island," Rufalo continued.

"You know who it is?"

"Yeah." He did not elaborate.

"You know who did it?"

"No."

"So, I go to the islands and look for a dead woman." From the tone of Rufalo's voice, Morgan somehow knew the victim was a woman.

"She was found on her husband's yacht, a forty-two-foot sloop, wood hull, a classic, Lion Class, moored at the Royal Toronto Yacht Club. I'd start with him, he called it in."

"You a sailor?" He was surprised by the superintendent's ease with nautical terminology.

"No, I like boats. You'd better get going. Look for the *Pemberly*."

Rufalo described it as the man's yacht. The wife must be younger. Rufalo was curiously evasive. Morgan decided not to ask for clarification.

He hung up. The best bet would be to call a cab, but instead, after he washed up and got dressed, he walked over to University Avenue and took the subway to Union Station, then walked down to what was officially known as Harbourfront. There was a police boat waiting, but he decided on the club ferry.

"I'm sorry, sir, but you must be properly attired," said a boat attendant dressed in grey flannels and a blue blazer.

"It's seven-thirty," said Morgan. "In the morning," he added with emphasis. "What do you expect, pajamas?"

"Jacket and tie, sir."

Morgan looked at the young man shrewdly, waiting for him to smile. When he realized the humourlessness of the situation, he flashed his police identity card and the young man backed off. Morgan regretted not carrying his Glock. There was nothing like a gun to test the esoteric traditions of the pampered class.

From halfway across the harbour he could see the top of the Gibraltar Point lighthouse through a cleft in the trees, poised on the southernmost side of the big island. He had never been there. As a kid growing up among the tenements of Cabbagetown, he thought of Toronto Island, the islands, as distant outposts, like Florida in winter or Muskoka in summer. Places other people visited.

He found the Lion easily enough, moored bow-out in an open slip within hailing distance of the clubhouse, which hovered like a stately ghoul behind a sweeping facade of columns and verandahs. The name *Pemberly* was embossed across the transom in block letters, black with gold edges. And, of course, the woman's body exposed to the morning air, propped up in the open cockpit, left him in no doubt that he was in the right place. Curiously, the few people moving about — a couple of groundskeepers, staff from the clubhouse preparing for breakfast, several deckhands of indeterminate age and gender — were completely ignoring the murder scene, although the unnatural stillness of the woman proclaimed she was dead to even the most casual observer.

Perhaps it is a matter of maintaining decorum, he thought, gazing across the manicured lawn at the Toronto skyline in the distance. How close to the city, and how very far. Another world, other times, crystallized in an institution as oppressively charming as a gangland funeral.

The body was not quite warm, but that may have been because she was dressed only in a bikini, and the air was cool, even for August. Raven hair, golden skin, lithe physique. If a corpse could be described as elegant, this was an elegant corpse.

There were no marks. As a courtesy, Morgan pressed his fingers to her jugular to confirm that she was dead. Then he turned to the man with the clipped grey moustache and jaunty cravat who was sitting across the cockpit, scrutinizing his every move as if committing Morgan's actions to memory for future reference. *He must be a lawyer*, Morgan thought.

Morgan looked around, expecting to see a forensics team and medics or someone from the coroner's office. There were only the two of them, three, if you counted the dead woman.

"You called Rufalo, yourself," Morgan observed.

"Yes. My name is D'Arcy. Harrington D'Arcy."

"Well, Mr. D'Arcy," said Morgan. Given the name of the boat, he almost expected the corpse to be Elizabeth Bennett. "Your friend seems quite dead." Sometimes using the wrong word to describe a relationship revealed the unexpected.

"She is not my friend, she was my wife." It struck Morgan as interesting how precisely the man shifted her into the past tense. In Jane Austen, marriage is forever. "I asked Rufalo to have you come ahead," said Harrington D'Arcy. "Your backup will be here on the next ferry."

"If properly attired," said Morgan.

"Quite," said Mr. D'Arcy, failing to see the humour.

"You asked for me, personally?" Morgan wondered if the term 'backup,' was meant to be manipulative. The man was a lawyer. He wondered why his "backup" would take the club ferry, not the police launch?

"You have a sound reputation."

"No, that would be my partner. I simply have a reputation. And why do I not know you, Mr. D'Arcy, if you are so well connected?"

"Because I am successful enough to afford the luxury of remaining anonymous. I do not need to be known."

"Corporate law, hostile takeovers?"

"Indeed. Venture capital. Acquisitions. We try to keep the hostility minimal."

"Would you care to explain what happened?"

"I would if I could. That is why I requested you, because I cannot. And I do realize how compromising this all might appear."

"By *all*, you mean the death of your wife?"

"And the facts, Detective Morgan. There are no witnesses to her death, I have no alibi, I do have a motive — several, in fact. It was a September-December affair. She's younger than I am, but not as young as she looks. We were tiresomely unhappy. She was promiscuous, I am bisexual, when I bother at all. Quite unsuited. She was generally well liked, very kind to the less fortunate and a generous patron of the arts — and I am regarded as ruthless. By my friends in the profession. My enemies are not so charitable."

"Did you?"

"Kill her? Good Lord, no. I don't even know how she died. I woke up at dawn, came up for a morning's pee over the side, it is always quite satisfying to piss publicly in such an august place as the Royal Toronto. And there she was. I slept on board alone through the night. God knows where she came from. I called in to your superintendent immediately, of course."

"Did you touch her?"

"Well, yes, obviously. I thought she was sleeping off a binge, I shook her damned hard and I dressed her. Apart from that, no I did not touch her."

"But you dressed her?" Morgan asked, looking at the string bikini and noting that the top, such as it was, was green and the bottom was tropical blue. "She was naked when you found her?"

"No, of course not. She had on her bottom piece, but her top was absent."

"You heard nothing. It must have been light when she was —" Morgan paused. He could see no harm in allowing D'Arcy's story veracity, for the time being, "— when she was brought on board. You heard nothing?"

"No mystery there. I sleep with ear plugs."

Morgan gazed at the man. *Yes, perhaps*, he thought. But when he had first stepped onto the boat it rolled under his weight and halyards rattled against the mast. You'd have thought someone carrying a corpse would waken a sleeper below. You would have thought a distraught husband wouldn't have the detachment to shave. Mr. D'Arcy, aboard the *Pemberly* in the lee of the stately RTYC mansion, seemed quite in control and very well groomed.

* * *

Miranda looked around for the handsome Englishman when she disembarked at São Paulo and was ushered to the business-class lounge with a crush of other transients. Perhaps he had remained sitting and she had missed him in the bustle of baggage retrieval from overhead bins and the thronging masses moving up from steerage. She settled in with a gourmet breakfast of croissants, Swiss cheese, and prosciutto on a linen napkin and picked up her Heyerdahl book.

It had occurred to her that the Englishman might be going to Easter Island, as well. She was restless. She put the book back in her travel bag and pulled out the comics Morgan had given her. *Scrooge McDuck* from January 1988 was on top. She opened to the panels on the first page and was immediately engrossed, the way she used to be as a child reading *Archie*, with the voices inside her head.

The storyline was predictably silly, but there were a few brief passages referring sympathetically to the tragic past of the Rapanui people and there was a jarring reference to the brief visit of Captain Cook in 1774. It was like the cartoonists were using an elaborate code to deliver intimations of another story, not about ducks and their dog-faced adversaries, but about actual people in an actual place.

She turned to *Batman*, September 2003. Far from Gotham, the Caped Crusader was locked fist and fang with nefarious nasties among the *moai* when, suddenly and arbitrarily, there was an historical reference to the terrible plight of the Rapanui following their island's fate at the farthest edge of Empire. The drawings in *Batman*, while bleak and sinister, detailed an array of hillside statues similar to their cheerfully pastel representation in Uncle Scrooge's realm. The genre was different, the artwork was different, the setting in *Batman* was grim and austere while in *Scrooge McDuck* it was opulently tropical, and yet the *moai* gazing with sightless eyes from the volcanic quarry on the side of Rano Raraku were uncannily alike.

Miranda thumbed through the April 1954 issue of *Wonder Woman* — it was a prize, a decade older than she was. She then skimmed the April 1982 issue of *The Mighty Thor* and several other comics Morgan had tracked down for her during his exploratory forays on eBay. Each one delivered, in the midst of mayhem and fantasy, a brief homily about the horrors of a remote Eden corrupted by outsiders, all subversively inviting the reader to identify with the people of the *moai* rather than with the degenerate interlopers from the reader's own world.

She recognized the Rano Raraku site in its various colourfully hued manifestations from photographs in Hyerdahl and other books, the same sources undoubtedly used by the comic-book artists. She had taken the trouble to memorize a few of the key names on the island. She knew the solitary town was called Hanga Roa and that the only beach, which was eight miles away on the other side, was called Anakena. She knew that the people of Rapa Nui speak Rapanui, and that *moai* rest upright on stone platforms called *ahu*, or at least that was their intended destination and the place where they received eyes carved from pale coral with red stone pupils, and where many, but not all, were given top hats of the same red scoria.

Deciding a cartoonist conspiracy to undermine established American values was in her own mind, Miranda pulled out *Aku-Aku* and began to read, but it seemed tiresomely indulgent, a kind of comic-book anthropology. Setting the book down on the glass table beside her, it bumped against her coffee cup and, in an attempt to avert catastrophe, she wrenched the book back and it tumbled onto the floor.

As she bent to retrieve the splayed book, Miranda noticed the scrawl in the margin beside a page of photographs. The Englishman! He must have exchanged books. How? While she was asleep. Why? She was wary. Why would he do that? She examined the book more closely. He had. And then he had disappeared.

She opened the book to the flyleaf and was surprised to find an autograph that was difficult to decipher, but might have been the author's signature. There was no accompanying message or salutation, but low on the same page was a curiously enigmatic equation written in a clear script: $4/5 = 00$. Four over five equals zero-zero. Linked zeroes equal infinity. Nothing more.

She thumbed through the pages, knowing intuitively that there would be a further revelation among them, but not expecting something so obvious as the neatly folded note she found near the back. She opened the note slowly and held it to the light to decipher penmanship that was sufficiently elegant to appear incongruous in ballpoint.

The missive started casually enough: "I regret we did not have the opportunity to pursue our conversation about Mr. Heyerdahl's island." It quickly shifted in tone: "You are with the police, I am quite sure of that. We are kindred, Miss Quin. (Your name is on your hand luggage, Miranda Quin)." The tone shifted again, from invasive to casually plaintive: "I seem to be in a spot of trouble. Perhaps as a fellow in the constabulary, you could help me out. Would you mind terribly if we leave the plane together? They will not risk making a fuss if there are two of us. Thank you. T.E."

She read the note through again, carefully, trying not to be distracted by his precise and flowing hand. His message seemed almost nonchalant, yet it candidly implied distress. He was a cop, then, or a government agent. *"A fellow in the constabulary." How charmingly pretentious*, she thought. She looked around the lounge, but of course he was nowhere to be seen. If he was not flying through, there would have been no reason to remain at the airport. If he did not get off the plane ... well, he must have, dead or alive. She shuddered, and for a moment was ashamed because she had thought what a pity, if such an attractive man was now dead.

At the service desk she had trouble making herself understood. The young woman spoke fluent school-English, but seemed to find Miranda's request for a passenger manifest of the flight she had come in on to be an inordinately complex one. Finally, politely, she declared she could be of no help in Miranda's quest for the handsome stranger.

Miranda sat down again, feeling oddly vulnerable.

In spite of his note, the man was little more than a face in the crowd. They had exchanged a few words, then he had passed on, leaving only a hazy feeling of erotic regret for a connection unmade, an opportunity missed. There was nothing she could do. She was a detective sergeant in homicide with the Toronto Police Service, a former RCMP officer, and far outside her jurisdiction. She tucked the note back among the pages of *Aku-Aku*, found some old copies of *People* magazine, and tried to read the captions.

She looked up occasionally and surveyed the bland, good quality furnishings in the business-class lounge and she felt a brief surge of claustrophobia, as if the walls had closed in while the world outside had fallen away. Miranda was not a world traveller. She had flown south to the Cayman Islands to scuba dive, had been around Canada and the States a few times as a Mountie during her training period in Saskatchewan and then with the prime minister's office, where her police function had been to appear in scarlet uniform for photo ops. She had felt like a stuffed moose and left the force after three years for Toronto. This probably meant missing theopportunity for advancement to become a static Canadian icon on international missions.

After an interminable wait through undifferentiated minutes and hours, she boarded her plane for Chile and landed at dusk in Santiago, only a little apprehensive that she was in the country notorious for its thousands of *disparu*. She had to wait overnight for her flight to Rapa Nui — she was trying hard to think of her destination by the Polynesian name, not as Easter Island or Isla de Pasqua.

She settled back in the taxi driving in from the airport as they passed by a parade of decrepit buildings covered with graffiti and scruffy tropical vegetation. South America had always seemed unreal; it was only now, away from airports, that it was coming alive. She felt dread and a strange elation, driving into the centre of a city haunted with ghosts of political dissidents, but also with the ghosts of Incan emperors and the righteous conquistadors who destroyed them. She gazed out the window of the taxi at the people milling about in the evening light, trying to pick out individual faces. The driver, in whom she had put her trust to deliver her unscathed to her hotel, spoke occasionally in Spanish and shrugged amiably at her confused responses.

The Best Western was above expectations evoked by her travel agent, who had little sympathy with anything Latin. It was late, she skipped dinner, she would be on the move again at dawn.

She tried to read the Heyerdahl book, but ended up thumbing through, gazing at the photographs. They seemed to have no relationship to her destination. Everything was reduced to archaeological sites and artifacts. Here and there she found handwritten snippets of potted wisdom like the one about the importance of enemies she had discussed with the Englishman. They were inscribed in ink, the letters formed with a rigid evenness that suggested careful deliberation, not the zealous spontaneity their sentiments implied. Several more were about the ambiguity of enemies:

"*It is not our foes we must fear but our friends.*"

"*Forgive friends, they will hate you. Forgive enemies, they are in your debt forever.*"

And there were as many whose positive sentiments in such an arbitrary context seemed almost as chilling.

Miranda shuddered at the incipient paranoia of the writer, which eerily conveyed an anonymous, but distinct personality. She set the book aside and fell immediately into a deep sleep, surrounded by wailing throngs of the *disparu*, with ominous *moai* looming in the background. She had no idea of the time when she was awakened by the noxious smell of burning cigarettes. Motionless and silent, Miranda stared into the gloom, for a moment suspecting she was dreaming. Two hulking figures, featureless in the dark, stood smoking at the end of her bed.

After a curiously relaxed breakfast as Harrington D'Arcy's guest on the sweeping verandah of the RTYC mansion — since the exchange of currency was not allowed, this was the only way to get food, except for a few discreet vending machines in the men's locker room — Morgan had wandered aimlessly among the docked boats, admiring the simple complexity of the spars and rigging. The Royal Toronto was not a club that took kindly to power boats unless the owners were inordinately influential. When he walked back toward the *Pemberly*, he noticed among the flurry of police activities that no one had thought to cover the body — perhaps because she was wearing a bikini and exposure seemed natural, even in death.

Gazing intently at the corpse as he approached, Morgan had to do a quick sidestep to avoid colliding with Ellen Ravenscroft, the medical examiner from the coroner's office.

"Quite distracting, isn't she!"

"G'morning," said Morgan.

"You've been here awhile?"

"Arrived by invitation at dawn."

"That sounds sinister."

"The husband's connected. He called Rufalo at home and requested me."

"Where's your intrepid partner?"

"She'll be in Santiago about now."

"Good God, she really did want to get away from you. That's in Chile."

"I know it's in Chile. She's on leave."

"Well, good for her, love. She's been through a lot. She needs to put murder behind her."

"She's writing a murder mystery. On Easter Island."

"Lovely! I hope in the arms of a comely young Polynesian."

"She's not that way inclined."

"You're telling me 'comely' refers only to women? You never know, Morgan. She's on holiday. So, I'm comely, and you're not?"

He smiled. He found her amusing and wearing. She was Miranda's age, late thirties, and one of those people who was very attractive until you analyzed their features and realized it was all in the personality. You ignored the features and concentrated on the personality, which could be dangerously seductive.

He had no idea why he thought of Ellen Ravenscroft as dangerous.

"Is she really writing a mystery?"

"Yeah."

"Well good for her. So you're available, then?"

"That's not determined by the whereabouts of my partner."

"Morgan, Morgan, Morgan. I could have had my way with you years ago, if I'd wanted." She paused. "So tell me about the bikini, which is mismatched, by the way."

They were still on the dock, waiting for the forensics people to stand aside.

He shrugged.

"She's rather voluptuous."

"Apparently."

"Vivacious."

"It's hard to be vivacious and dead."

"She's stunning."

"On the surface," he muttered, stupidly.

"Is there another way, love?"

Morgan braced himself on the wire shrouds and eased Ellen aboard. He watched her examine the corpse, first very close without touching, then gently shifting and prodding.

"No bruises. Minor abrasions around her upper arms — you can see by the discolouration from her blood settling, pale side up, it confirms her posture, she probably died right here."

"Of what?"

"Suffocation … an overdose … poison …"

"What about natural causes?"

"Morgan, you're very unromantic."

"But could it be?"

"Yes. That's a possibility."

"Then why does the husband prefer murder? He set up the scene, he called us. We're here on the presumption of murder."

"*The presumption of murder*, I like that. Good title for what's-her-name's mystery."

"Yeah," said Morgan. He wondered what sordid scheme the widower could possibly need to conceal by using murder as an alibi.

"Morgan, look closer at her face. Serene expression. Make-up, a perfect mask. Except for the eyes — look at the creases. This woman was crying when she died. Someone has done her make-up after death, someone who knows what she's doing."

"She?"

"Could be a professional, a mortician. Make-up artist with a film crew."

"At sunrise?"

"Time and a half for overtime."

"When did she die? The husband told me he tried to shake her alive — that would be the abrasions on her arms — but he claims to have been down below until dawn."

"It's after ten, now. I'd say four, five hours ago.

Whatever I find, you'll be the first to know."

"Yeah, call me. I'm going to wander around here for awhile."

"For sure, might as well take advantage. It really is a world apart, isn't it?"

"Yeah," said Morgan, looking across the harbour at the city, which seemed to be floating like an island of towering facades between water and the late summer sky.

"You take care, love. I'll call."

Morgan stepped over onto the dock and felt the gentle sway of the Lion as his weight shifted, and heard rasping high in the shrouds where the mainsail halyard slapped against the mast. He liked the sounds of sailing, although they were not part of his personal history. Perhaps in another life.

Morgan spent the rest of the day wandering around the RTYC, admiring boats, sidestepping guano deposited by innumerable seagulls, ducking overhanging branches of ancient willows, his mind skipping back and forth from the dead woman in the bikini to Miranda, on her way to a wind-swept island in the South Pacific. After lunch, back in the city, digging through files of old newspapers, financial papers and journals, scoping out Harrington D'Arcy. The dead woman's name was Maria. A Brazilian heiress. The details were vague, the wealth implied. The D'Arcy wedding had been so exclusive even the *Globe and Mail* was uncertain of the guest list, although it received restrained coverage in the *Financial Times* and a paparazzi photograph in *Vanity Fair*.

The few photographs of Maria D'Arcy were difficult to read. It was as if each had caught a separate aspect of her personality, although she was identifiably the same person. Like a signature, he thought; always the same and invariably different — too much the same, and it was fake. *She was certainly not fake,* he thought. *Intriguing, yes, and from her pictures somehow inscrutable.* He found himself liking her, she was familiar and exotic at the same time. Her pictures invoked the scent of wildflowers and sun-drenched pebbles — the lingering smell of her perfume that was caught in the air around her corpse although he had not focused on it at the time.

In the dark and brutal instant it took for Miranda to assimilate the unknowns, her mind swarmed with facts, as it often did when she needed to dissociate from raw feeling. President Salvador Allende was an elected Marxist. Augusto Pinochet was the general who overthrew him. Pinochet brought relative prosperity, he established a totalitarian reign of terror, it lasted two decades, the *disparu* numbered over four thousand. The coup took place on September 11; another September 11. Allende shot himself in his office, within walking distance of this room. It was an act either of desperation or martyrdom. The fascist Pinochet was now out of power, but he was alive. He presently lived within walking distance of this room.

The two figures looming at the foot of her bed smoked in silence, cigarettes illuminating their distorted features with each inhalation in a macabre gleam. They did not know she was awake. Or perhaps they did. She kept her breathing even. They said nothing.

Miranda mentally reached for her Glock semi-automatic, which was secure in her gun locker at Police Headquarters in Toronto.

She wanted to laugh at the absurdity, she wanted to scream, she wanted to absorb every detail: muted light pushing against her curtains from the quiet street outside, the smells of a tropical city at dawn, of American tobacco, and the sound of her own breathing. She wanted to be calm, fully present at her own execution. She tried to suppress fear; fear breeds futility. She suppressed rage; rage would make her more vulnerable. She wanted to cry. She could do nothing, feel everything. She waited.

A cigarette arced onto the carpet, was ground into the fibres in a small conflagration of sparks. A hand touched her foot through the sheet. Gently, like a lover, trying not to startle. She flinched involuntarily and drew herself up against the headboard, with the sheet wrapped around her. Contact had been established. In a moment, pressing their advantage, they would turn on a bedside light so that they could see her better than she could see them.

"*Hola*," said a man's voice, surprisingly high-pitched and cheerful.

Miranda said nothing.

The bedside light flicked on.

"You are Mrs. Miranda Quin?" He spoke English.

She said nothing.

"We regret this intrusion, Miranda Quin, we must do what is necessary." In spite of his soothing voice, this sounded ominous.

"You are naked beneath your cover, is it true?"

Miranda's sense of her own vulnerability ratcheted up by several degrees.

"We must ask you to get dressed. We will watch."

She pulled the sheet closer, then realized this might seem enticing and fluffed it away so the contours of her body disappeared in oblique planes of shadow and light.

"We must watch, Mrs. Quin. You are a policeman, yes? You might have the gun. You might be well trained in the martial arts, you might be hazardous. Possibly you would run away."

"Naked?"

"Please. You get dressed in your clothes."

"Where are you taking me?"

"Nowhere, Mrs. Quin. We wish to talk."

"Can't you talk to me like this?"

"No, Mrs. Quin. You are naked."

His courtesy puzzled her, given that they had broken into her room in the dead of night. The man who spoke English handed her the clothes she had left in a neat pile on a chair for dressing in the early morning. He waited until she had squirmed into her panties and then he withdrew the sheet. Awkwardly, she continued to dress, wavering for balance on the soft bed as her weight shifted, feeling unutterably vulnerable.

Their thinking: it would be easier to explain away a fully clothed corpse than a naked one. They must be police of some sort. Gangsters or revolutionaries would simply kill her, dressed or not. There seemed no threat of rape, which upset her because it implied something more complex, even more sinister.

Morgan had finished out his day watching bad television. Usually he read, but he was feeling uneasy. His eyes were sore from researching Harrington D'Arcy. He wondered how Miranda was doing in Santiago. She was staying at the same Best Western where he had spent the night a year ago. The beds were excessively soft, but it was a clean, well-lit place. When he turned in, he thought of her asleep, and when he awoke in the morning, it felt as if they had spent the night together, but she had left early.

2

Easter Island Cryptic

To Miranda's surprise, she was still alive. The city stirred outside her window and she was not a corpse, she had not been molested, she had not been tortured. So far, she had been treated with a kind of deferential civility calculated to invoke terror. The acrid smell of burned synthetic fabric made her nauseous. The smoking man who did the talking frightened her more than the man who was silent, even though his voice was amiable. He had absolute power in a room swarming with ghosts of the *disparu*, because in the dead hours of early morning he was responsible to no one. He smiled politely as she arranged herself against the headboard, drawing her knees up to her body.

"You are ready now to talk?" he said.

"About what?"

"This is not a social visit, Mrs. Quin. You know why we are here."

"It's Ms. Quin."

"Yes. That is good. You will tell us, please, where is that man?"

His high-pitched voice was smooth and she thought of drowning in oil, suffocating.

"No," she said. She had no idea who they were talking about, but it seemed a good idea to answer in the negative.

He moved close to the side of the bed. The other man moved close on the other side. She felt squeezed, twisted inside, like meat in a grinder.

"Mr. Harrington D'Arcy. You know Mr. D'Arcy?"

"I've never heard of him." The name sounded vaguely familiar. "Are you with the police? I assume you are armed."

"It is not necessary, Miss Quin."

The implication was that the two men could kill her with their bare hands, although his tone was conciliatory. The feeling of drowning in warm oil.

"Strange," she said. "In Canada, we need warrants."

"There are police you do not know, Miss Quin, even in your country, they do not need warrants. Public police, you serve the law. *Carabinaros*, we serve the state. We do as we do." He paused, savouring the idea, and as he repeated the words they took on an aura of menace she felt to the bone. "We do as we do."

"Really," she said. "I have never heard of Harrington D'Arcy."

The man leaned forward so that the circle of light from her bedside lamp washed over his distorted features, making him look for a moment like he was wearing a death mask. He picked up a book and leaned back into the shadows.

"You are reader of Mr. Thor Heyerdahl, yes?"

She shrugged noncommittally, suddenly realizing they must be after the handsome Englishman, annoyed that it had only now occurred to her.

"This is not your book."

"Yes," she said. "No, it was a gift."

"From Mr. Harrington D'Arcy?"

"From my partner."

"Sexual?"

"What! No, professional. What business is it of yours?"

He smiled.

"Mr. Harrington D'Arcy gave you this book. On the airplane from Toronto to São Paulo."

Nothing makes you so vulnerable as knowing you have been watched unobserved.

He reached into a leather satchel the size of a human head. She had not noticed it before, as it was resting on the floor by his feet. She flinched at the macabre possibilities. He withdrew a book and handed it to her. She let it slip through her fingers onto the bed. She half-expected it to leave a bloodstain.

"He left this book behind. It has your name inscribed in it. Open, you will see, it is your name."

She reached down and tentatively folded back the cover. On the flyleaf were the words "Miranda Quin." They were written in ballpoint, in an elegant script that was unnervingly familiar.

"Yes," she said. "That's my book, and this, the one

in your hands, that's his, the man's. I didn't know his name. I've never seen him before, I haven't seen him since the plane from Toronto. I know nothing about him." She remembered wondering if he was a spy. She almost forgot finding his note, where he virtually declared his covert and endangered status.

The Englishman had asked for help. She was police. These men were menacing and possibly murderous. Miranda stood up, forcing the smoking man to back deeper into the shadows. She decided to take the position that she was no longer afraid. The man turned and flipped on the overhead light, and in the brightly illuminated room, Miranda felt a rising sense of control.

"I do not know the man," she said. "I have to go to the bathroom."

"No," said the man.

"I have to pee."

"No pissing."

"That's easy for you to say," said Miranda. "There will be pissing, one way or another. You can watch, if you want, but I am now going to pee."

She moved past him into the bathroom.

"No," he said. "I do not watch lady piss."

He reached out and pulled the bathroom door shut as she began to slip the waistband of her slacks down over her hips. She sat down amid shadows cast from the dim light that seeped under the door. The door then opened a crack and a hand reached in, scraped along the wall, and switched on the overhead before rapidly withdrawing. *Superstitious*, she thought. *Afraid I'll disappear in the dark.*

She really did have to pee and it gave her time to think. As she rearranged her clothes, she decided the best strategy was to be volatile. Not grace under pressure, but explosive. She banged her forehead a couple of times with the heels of her hands, re-channelling the adrenaline from roiling to rush, and, swinging open the door, she strode out into the bleak light of the room.

They were gone.

She held her breath, then gasped, shivering, walked over to the window and looked out on the street. A few people were trudging to work; it was too early for traffic. Behind her, the carpet smelled like smouldering brimstone. She turned and surveyed the room. She coughed and it echoed. They had left both copies of the Heyerdahl book discarded on the bed. The note from the Englishman lay open on the bedside table.

Whoever he was, the man who signed himself T.E., was not Harrington D'Arcy. Miranda had seen Harrington D'Arcy once. She had been leaving Alex Rufalo's place after a staff party. Rufalo's wife, Caroline, was a high-powered lawyer, a colleague of D'Arcy's who was dropping her off before the last guests had departed. Curiosity compelled Miranda to peer into the shadows of the limousine when the car door swung open. D'Arcy was sitting back against black leather, washed in the pale light seeping through the tinted glass. Her endangered Englishman with the flashing eyes and irritating self-assurance looked nothing at all like Harrington D'Arcy. She admired his wit and panache for having chosen the name as a *nom de guerre*. The real D'Arcy was exceptionally wealthy, very influential, but competely unknown beyond a rarified world defined by his own corporate interests.

In the morning, Morgan went directly to the morgue after a brief stop at The Columbian Connection on the edge of the Annex, a new place that made him think of a Starbucks made over by Tim Hortons, a place of such compromised authenticity he found it unnerving. He doubted he would become a regular patron.

Coffee and bagel in hand, he flagged a taxi. The driver had no idea where the city morgue was located. Morgan was surprised. He did not often take cabs, but he trusted that the cabbies would be familiar with notable locations.

Morgan preferred to walk or take public transit — the subway, never buses. Together, they usually took Miranda's XK 150, her consolation for a sordid episode in the recent past, something to remind her she was a survivor. She was a better driver; he liked her car, but not driving.

Although it was early, Ellen Ravenscroft was already at work. Morgan apologized for not bringing her a coffee. He offered her part of his unfinished bagel, but she declined. He nodded in the direction of the shrouded cadaver. "What's the verdict? Was it murder?"

"You tell me, love. Did someone want her dead?"

"Wanting a person dead doesn't make it murder. Possibly a gruesome coincidence. Of course, there is no such thing as coincidence," he said, mouthing a cliché he didn't believe.

They approached the stainless-steel table isolated in a pool of light. Ellen pulled back a plasticized sheet, revealing Maria D'Arcy's face. It was empty, now, the personality vanished. Death was not unkind, only indifferent.

"You don't want to see the rest of her, not until I've done some tidying up."

"No," Morgan agreed, leaning down so close to the dead woman, in another context he might have been her prince, come to kiss her awake.

"What are you looking for, love?"

"Perfume."

"Very expensive. With all she's been through, it lingers, doesn't it?"

"No. That's the point," said Morgan. "It doesn't. Yesterday morning, it was distinct, the smell of sunlight and pebbles. But there's nothing, now."

Ellen Ravenscroft leaned over so that their heads almost collided. "You're right," said the medical examiner. She stood upright and tilted her head back, with nostrils flared, gazing slowly around the room. "How very strange. There's still a bit lingering in the air."

"Did you wash her down?"

"Not the parts you're sniffing." The ME pulled the sheet back all the way. Her normally animated features congealed into a mask of stunned disbelief. "Apparently someone has given her a right good clean-up."

"Is that possible?"

"It's ridiculous. An embarrassing, offensive, outrageous, ridiculous comical absurdity. Oh God, I'll have to get to the bottom of this. When I left her last night she was scented with money, the way the good Lord intended. And I was the first in, this morning. The universe is not unfolding as it should, David, no one breaks into a morgue."

Morgan was aware she had used his first name. The only person to use his first name had been his wife of brief duration — and occasionally Miranda, but only in exceptional circumstances. "Someone apparently did," he said. "Unlikely as it seems. Security's light."

"That's an explanation, not an excuse." Ellen Ravenscroft drew in a deep breath and exhaled slowly. "Damn it! Damn it, I was pretty much done with the autopsy part, moving on to analysis. So, God damn it, I don't think anything's been compromised except my dignity. And hers, of course." She took in another deep breath and exhaled with a warming smile, searching for equilibrium in morbid good humour. "Bloody ghouls, if you ask me. Necrophiles. Hapless vampires — the blood's already been drained. Necromancers, social pariahs, royal creeps. Generally the dead don't make very good company, you know. Well, they do, sometimes. But they don't issue invitations."

"Invited or not, she had visitors. So why is she here?"

"She's dead. Oh, you mean *why* is she dead?" Ellen Ravenscroft grimaced. "From causes yet to be determined. I'd say what killed her was generalized hypoxia brought on by acute respiratory distress. She died from asphyxiation. Exactly what caused the asphyxia, I just don't know."

"She could have been smothered. I don't see any strangulation marks."

"There aren't any. It might be self-induced hypocapnia."

"Suicide?"

"Death by hyperventilation, which could be a possible response to the symptoms of hypothermia. A side effect from exposure."

"In the middle of summer."

"It's August, Morgan. The nights are cold."

"Cool."

"It doesn't have to be freezing for hypothermia. And she had a fair bit of alcohol in her system. French champagne, I believe. And not much on in the way of clothes."

"Can you check out the champagne for me?"

"Yes, of course. And before you say it, I know *French* champagne is redundant. If it's real champagne, it's French, *n'est ce pas?*"

"Could someone else have done it?"

"Exposed her, yes — misadventure, or at the worst, manslaughter. Asphyxiated her, yes, but damned if I know how. I'll keep trying. No evidence of a man lurking about down there in the nether region. Maybe a bit of messing about, but gently, perhaps on her own. I'll let you know. I'd say the bikini top was put on by a man post-mortem — he cupped her breasts in it, before struggling to secure the clasp. Left a few abrasions. A woman would have done it up at her waist, then slid it around."

"Her husband did it."

"That's quite a revelation! He's confessed, has he?"

"To covering her breasts, not to murder. Bared breasts may be commonplace these days, but not at the RTYC."

"You think it's about owning her boobies, Morgan?" She looked down at the body and smiled capriciously. "He doesn't own them anymore."

"Yeah, he does. He'll be along to collect the remains. Don't let her go?"

"What?"

"Her body, don't let her go."

"Of course not. Her remains remain."

"Good. Now all we have to figure out is why her husband wants a murder investigation, what nefarious crimes is he trying to obscure through misdirection? And what's with the perfume?"

She looked up at him. "Listen to you," she said. "Morgan, you need me. Without your partner, you've got no one to talk to."

"I'll manage."

"Off you go, then, love. I've got work to do." She did her best in the circumstances to shrug coquettishly, then turned back to peruse the exposed corpse. "I'll call if the lady reveals anything more."

Morgan edged back into the shadows that circled the autopsy tables, casting each in a separate cone of light. "Yeah," he said in a casual voice as he turned and sauntered out the door, irritated that she might be right. About Miranda.

She would be in the air over the Pacific by now, landing about the same time as he reached headquarters if he walked slowly and didn't stop along the way.

Hanga Roa, the only community on Rapa Nui, surprised Miranda. She had expected something more exotic. This was a small town not unlike Waldron, the village where she had grown up, an hour west of Toronto on the banks of the Grand River. There were a few streets, mostly unpaved, a few palm trees, a scattering of shops and restaurants nestled casually among stucco and cinderblock houses, an open-walled market and a closed-in market, two scuba-dive shops in the tiny open harbour, and there was one bank. There was an imposing church, fronted by carvings of saints with bird heads. The people seemed to be a mixture of Spanish and Polynesian. Teenage boys rode island horses among occasional taxis and the odd delivery van. Girls wore full skirts or school uniforms. Tourists were few, and stood out as much for their vaguely furtive demeanour as for their wash-and-wear clothes. Dogs and chickens ranged freely along the sidewalks, haphazardly chasing each other.

It's nothing at all like home, she thought, changing her mind as the taxi pulled up a gentle incline to the Hotel Victoria. While she unpacked in the simple room with white plaster walls and a window opening west toward Tahiti and New Zealand, she wondered where such a notion had come from. Perhaps the island was not lush like the background in a Gauguin painting, nor wondrously strange, despite the giant statues for which it is known throughout the world, but it was definitely alien territory.

Miranda realized she was standing by the open window, staring into the empty distance, thinking about times lost and about home, feeling lonely.

There was a faint knock on the door.

"Come in," she said, assuming it was the elderly gentleman who had let her the room.

She turned as the door swung open, but no one was there. Although it was midday, the corridor was dark and cool and she could feel the gentle rush of air. She walked to the doorway. On the floor of the corridor to the side of the door, a man's body was slumped in deep shadow. A pool of blood, drained of colour in the murky light, spread out from the body on the smooth cement floor.

She knew he was alive from the stillness of the body in its awkward posture, the muscles not yet settled into their final grip on his contorted frame.

It was the Englishman.

She squatted beside him and gently rolled him over. His eyes were open.

"Hang on, there," she said. "You're not dead yet."

She thought she detected the glimmer of a smile. In his eyes. They searched her face.

"How'd you get here?" she said. She did not expect an answer. She had seen enough of violent death to recognize someone at the precarious edge. He tried to focus on her, his eyes widened, he nodded assent, as if claiming he had got there himself, as if he were declaring he was not about to slip over.

"You've been shot," she said.

His eyes closed, then opened again.

"No? You've been stabbed. A knife. Let's see. Under the ribs." She probed gently beneath his blood-soaked shirt. "Good," she said. "Only once. It's not sucking. You're not spitting blood. It missed your lungs. In broad daylight. Drying blood, you opened the wound getting here. Where from? Not far. Down the hall —"

She slipped away from him and instinctively strode down the hall to an open door, forgetting she was unarmed, and swung into a room, the duplicate of her own except for the unmade bed and congealing blood on the floor.

Satisfied his attacker was gone, she returned to the Englishman. He seemed to have rallied and was trying unsuccessfully to turn onto his side.

"I wasn't trying to catch him, you know," she said as she lifted under his shoulders and began to drag him out of the corridor. "I just wanted to know he wasn't lurking around to attack me, too."

"So," he coughed. "Preemptive," he said. "Bad strategy."

"Hush," she said. She forced him to lie back, then hauled him across the floor, and, with great difficulty, onto her bed.

"We're going to owe the Hotel Victoria for clean sheets," she said.

"Honeymoon suite," he murmured.

"What? Oh, quaint," she said. "God," she added, "you do attract trouble. But I doubt you're going to die, not today. Let's get a doctor in here."

"No," he said, and passed out.

Usually, when Morgan entered the granite edifice that was Police Headquarters, he felt soothed by its vast public spaces that led to a warren of offices, calmed by the pink of the stone and the jet transparency of the glass slabs that mirrored the city. Today he felt stifled and claustrophobic at his desk. After lunch with colleagues in the food court across the street, where he tried to be congenial and failed, he returned to his paperwork, out of sorts.

The telephone rang and he ignored it.

The telephone persisted. He picked up without saying anything.

"Morgan?"

"Yeah, it's me," he said.

"It's Miranda."

"Sounds like you're in the next room." He was suddenly cheerful. "So how's Easter Island? You found a suitable distraction, yet?"

"Well, I do have a strange man in my bed."

"Good for you," he said with what he knew was excessive good cheer.

"And he's unconscious."

"Not good."

"And bleeding."

"Not good at all."

"And I think he's a spy."

"A spy?"

"Yes."

"Is he dying?"

"Probably not. I dressed the wound. Morgan, talk to me."

"Have you called the police?"

"The Chilean police do not inspire confidence. They paid me a visit in Santiago. In the middle of the night, Morgan. I thought they would kill me."

He was alarmed.

"And they didn't?"

"Hilarious. It was scary. They were looking for him."

"Who?"

"This guy in my bed. They say he's Harrington D'Arcy."

"Who's they?"

"The Chilean cops. *Carabinaros*."

"Miranda."

"Yes."

"He's not."

"I didn't think so."

"You know who Harrington D'Arcy is, don't you? His wife has just been murdered — she's dead and her husband thinks it was murder, or he wants *us* to think it was murder. He might be the murderer. I think he might want us to think that, too. It's my case. And you could help. What's that perfume you used to wear, the expensive one?"

"Rare, not so expensive. It was Fleurs de Rocaille. Morgan, what on earth are you talking about?"

"Fleurs de Rocaille, yeah. Someone broke into the morgue and washed it off her body."

"Whose body? Broke into the morgue? To steal her perfume? Morgan, you are making no sense."

"You've got a guy on the verge of expiring in your bed and the only thing you know for certain is that he is *not* Harrington D'Arcy."

"Yeah."

"And you're making sense but I'm not? Sorry I can't help, I don't know who he is, either. Otherwise, how's it going down there?"

"It was good talking to you, Morgan."

"You, too."

"Bye."

"You're alright?"

"Yeah, it's a good place to be."

"That's it, then?"

"Take care, Morgan."

"Bye."

Morgan's ebullient mood wavered on the brink of collapse. Miranda in his life made him feel good. He had never felt as close to anyone else, not even his former wife. Especially not her. Perhaps to a girlfriend, the year he lived in England half a lifetime ago, Susan with the copper-red hair. He was fine now. Miranda was still in the world. People got on planes, went away, and you didn't know if they were real anymore. But hearing her voice, she was still real.

But what the hell had they been talking about?

It was like they had caught brief glimpses of each other across an abyss between parallel worlds. He felt himself slipping into a funk. He envied her having an adventure. A fake Harrington D'Arcy bleeding in your bed at the Hotel Victoria. She had slipped into a story by Somerset Maugham. A spy? Not likely, if he was using the name of an establishment lawyer. He was attractive, though. He could tell by her voice. And dangerous.

Miranda sat on the only chair in the room, gazing at her unconscious companion with something approaching affection. He had roused while she was talking to Morgan, then slipped off into a deep sleep, which projected, as it does among even the most dangerous, an innocent vulnerability that she found disconcerting. They had been through a lot together. So it seemed. Really, he had been through a lot, and so had she, but separately. She would let him sleep and heal. Then she would try to sort things out. It was good talking to Morgan. She had not crossed over into another dimension after all.

She had gone out and gotten medical supplies from a pharmaceutical and curio shop on the main street and picked up a few ready-to-eat groceries from a small grocery and curio store next to it. She had noticed very few tourists in Hanga Roa, but every retail outlet in town seemed to have rows of table-top *moai* replicas, gaping *maki-maki* ashtrays fashioned after an open-mouthed god of the island, and a stack of T-shirts emblazoned with *moai* or birdmen or heroic images of Hoto Matua, the island's first leader when the people of Rapa Nui arrived from the sea, about the time ancient Rome fell to the invading Vandals.

Cruise ships, she reasoned. At random intervals, a sudden influx of exotic visitors would no doubt arrive, take photographs of themselves standing in front of a scowling *moai* to prove they had been there, pick up a few souvenirs on the run, and sail away. *There can't be too many*, she thought. The nearest port for their next stop would be more than two thousand kilometres away. Curiously, she did not feel isolated, or that the rest of the world was remote. She knew her loneliness was something carried within, not imposed from outside. This would be a good place to write mysteries, if she could just step away from the one she was in.

When she returned to her room, she dressed the man's wound. He shuddered from pain, without fully awakening, and when she was finished he mumbled something and fell back into sleep. After the interlude with Morgan on the phone, she squirmed down in the room's only chair and watched as the hours went by, until the room grew suddenly dark when the subtropical sun plunged into the western ocean. She got up and went to the bathroom, leaving the door open in case the Englishman stirred. When she came back, he was awake. He had turned on the bedside light. Even in pain, he was insufferably handsome.

"Hey, how are you doing?" she said.

"Good, a lot better."

"You just lie easy."

He boosted himself up against the headboard.

"I'm all right," he said. "I'm a fast healer."

"You lost blood."

"I've got a lot. Was it blue?"

"Was it, oh yes, very blue. Sloane Square and Oxford, right? And before that, Eton or Harrow, no doubt."

"Eton."

"And what name are you going by today?"

"Tonight? Shaw, Thomas Edward Shaw."

"You're lying."

"Am I? Yes, I suppose I am." He hunched a bit to the side, to relieve pressure on his wound. "What about Ross," he said, "could my name be Ross?"

"I suspect your name is Lawrence — T.E. Lawrence of Arabia, he used both Ross and Shaw as pseudonyms."

"Quite so. You must be very good at crossword puzzles."

"Yes I am."

"Did you read his very pretentious book, *Seven Pillars of Wisdom*? Are you a Middle-Eastern history buff? Or was it the film with Peter O'Toole? An excellent film."

"Where on earth did you get the energy? You were dying a few hours ago. I read the abridged version; *Revolt in the Desert*. Didn't finish it. And what's your connection with Harrington D'Arcy?"

"I am of stern stuff, my mother habitually proclaimed. Heal or die, my father would say. I had a

Victorian childhood, generations too late. My parents were really quite evil, in their own charming way. I have never met Harrington D'Arcy. It's just a name with a history, powerful, but obscure. Makes it easier to take on another identity if there's an identity to take on, so to speak. For now, I need to be Ross. I believe I am carrying papers that will establish I am Thomas Edward Ross."

"And are you?"

"Yes, certainly. Did you know when Lawrence was Ross he was John Hume Ross. He was only T.E. as himself and as Shaw. If there was an *himself*. I prefer my own version. Do you know Mr. D'Arcy?"

"Intimately. From a distance. His wife was just murdered — died."

"Which is it, Miss Quin?" He was trying for a quip, but he seemed, for a moment, confused. "How could you know that?" he said. He glanced around, then looked at the telephone.

"And how would you know she was not?" said Miranda.

The Englishman who had decided to call himself Ross shifted his weight against the headboard.

"I think perhaps we should clean up the blood," he said.

"I'll do it later. I bought cleanser and some wiper-uppers."

"Were you out?"

"I don't carry dressings for a knife wound when I travel," she said, gesturing toward his bandaged abdomen.

"Yes, of course. Thank you. Why are you being so helpful? Thank you for not calling the police."

"I reserve the option. At this point, though, I'd rather keep the so-called authorities as far away as possible. I had some midnight callers in Santiago. They claimed to be police. *Carabineros*. They were looking for you. They did not inspire confidence."

"And do I?"

"Inspire confidence? Anything but. You seem like a dangerous man to know." She paused, then smiled. "I doubt you're a cop, but I do think you're one of the good guys. That could just be part of your disguise, of course."

"Disguise?"

Come on, Thomas Edward Ross, she thought. *No one wears good looks so casually without something to hide.*

"Yeah," she said.

He smiled with roguish insouciance. "I have no idea what you are talking about, Miss Quin. I will confess, I am not actually a member of the constabulary, although I might have been, had life gone in a somewhat different direction. I am a wounded man and vulnerable. Have we anything to eat?"

"And I might have been Pope," she said. "We eat after you fill me in the mysteries of life, Mr. Ross. You disappeared on the plane to São Paulo. Then what? Begin there. Conclude with what you know about the death of Mrs. D'Arcy."

"Nothing, I know absolutely nothing about her death."

"The plane, you disappeared. You left me a note."

"Right. Well, I did, yes. It didn't do me much good."

"Nor much harm, apparently. You're here."

"Somewhat harmed."

"Yes, well…. Let's start with, who do you work for?"

"Myself, mostly. In the end, we all do."

"Oh really?"

"The age of spies and spying isn't what it used to be."

"If it ever was."

"Point taken, Miss Quin."

"Would you stop calling me that."

"Certainly. Calling you what?"

"Miss — Miranda Quin, yes. Detective Quin, or Ms. Quin, if you feel compelled to give me a title. Not Miss Quin. My great-aunt Maude was Miss Quin."

"Indeed, Ms. Quin. Or might I presume and call you Miranda? Detective, next question?"

"Your employer?"

"Would it be enough to say I am associated with a certain large entity that does not wish to be compromised by being associated with me?"

"That's a start, if it's the truth — which I doubt."

"Quite wisely. But it's something like that. I'm more of an agent than a spy. You really do not need to know more. You are alive because you know so little."

"You think my visitors in Santiago might have killed me?"

"Of course. They are professionals. And skilled

enough to know you could lead them to me — which you have."

"Hardly. You got here first."

"Yes, I came in on an American freight plane yesterday afternoon."

"And coincidentally ended up in a room down the hall."

"Hanga Roa is small. You are travelling under your own name. It was easy to find you, even before you arrived."

"And they knew you'd find me?"

"Apparently."

"Why?"

"Why what?"

"Why find me?"

"Because you are a very attractive woman."

"Thank you."

"And to check out the status of my book."

"You're kidding. They had them, you know. In Santiago. Both copies."

"That is a shame. It belonged to Maria D'Arcy."

Miranda sat upright. Until now, she had felt surrounded by terrors so absurd they were laughable, because sooner or later she knew she'd wake up. Suddenly, she was awake.

"I have it, again," she said. "Your copy and mine. They apparently don't like Heyerdahl. I thought you didn't know D'Arcy."

"I don't. I know his wife — I knew her."

"And you just picked her husband's name at random. Now that is quite a coincidence."

"I've lost a lot of blood, Ms. Quin, is that better? Do be kind. I have been quite careless — "

"With your lies."

"With the truth."

"Same thing."

"Yes, I suppose it is," he said.

The connection between them was the death of Mrs. D'Arcy. Miranda felt like she had plunged into a Hitchcock film, the victim of forces beyond her control.

"I assure you," said Ross, as if despite the revelation nothing had changed, "I did not know that Maria D'Arcy was dead. I had a private dinner with her near the airport, only hours before I met you. She was very much alive."

"What is a private dinner, may I ask?"

"Private."

"Gotcha. Word had it she was adventurous."

He smiled ambiguously.

"In my business, you do what you do."

She had heard that expression before. *We do as we do*, said the smoking man in Santiago. She realized she should be afraid of the handsome Englishman. He was in the same business as her midnight callers, but with polished manners. That made him more difficult to read, and perhaps even more treacherous.

The afternoon dwindled into ennui and Morgan went home early. Maria D'Arcy's death puzzled him, but he was distracted by the feeling that it was incidental to something bigger — as to what that was, he had no idea. He nuked a frozen dinner and opened a bottle of Ontario merlot.

Alex Rufalo had called him in after lunch for a progress report.

"The medical examiner thinks probably misadventure," Morgan had explained. "That means a coroner's inquest."

"I know what it means, Detective Sergeant. But until we get a definitive report, it's an open case, so keep at it."

"Yeah, sure," Morgan had said, wandering back to his desk. He spent the rest of the afternoon on the computer, trying to find a connection between his boss and Harrington D'Arcy.

Before going home, he had made an appointment to see D'Arcy in the morning. *You don't make appointments with suspects*, he thought. *Only with witnesses.* He realized D'Arcy had somehow positioned himself as an innocent by insisting on murder. He also realized sticking to protocol was his response not to the crime, but to his feelings of being played when he didn't know the the game, let alone the rules.

For the most part, Morgan was a procedural maverick. He and Miranda were very good at their jobs, bent rules, or overlooked them, and got things done. Nothing illegal — they were both so straight their shadows wouldn't bend on a bicycle — but sometimes they cut corners, ignored protocol, overrode bureaucratic niceties. And because they were good, they got away with it.

He did not always get along with senior administration, but he assumed they were on the same side. Right now, he wasn't so sure.

He forgot about his dinner in the microwave and the open bottle of wine. With CNN on in the background, he slouched on the sofa, and distractedly sorted through a stack of books on Easter Island, not looking for anything in particular. He picked up a hackneyed guide to the island featuring the inevitable *moai* on the cover and thumbed through its pages. The book was overflowing with unfiltered ephemera; it was trite, amateur, and soulless. He tossed in on the floor.

The telephone rang. It was Ellen Ravenscroft.

"Sorry to bother you so late," she said, "but I thought you'd want to know."

"Yeah, sure. What?"

"Maria D'Arcy —"

"Murdered."

"Yes, Morgan. You never doubted it?"

"It was your voice, and the hour. You've been working late."

"No, love, I'm at home, with the heat turned up and nothing on but the radio. Yes, I'm at work. I'm standing in front of the lady's naked cadaver as we speak."

"Murdered."

"Unequivocally."

"How?"

"I thought you'd never ask. It's the perfume, Morgan — why would anyone risk being caught breaking into a morgue? There had to be something in the perfume. And if the perfume was gone, there had to be traces of whatever it was masking — or, was the perfume a delivery system? Either way, it got me to thinking."

"That's always good. Do you want to finish this conversation over dinner?"

"You haven't eaten yet? It's nearly midnight."

"I forgot."

"You forgot to eat. I never thought I'd be saying this, but no."

"Okay."

"No, really, it's a lovely idea, but I'm still at the 'office,' and tomorrow's a heavy day. They've been bringing in the dead all evening, accidents and executions. Toronto's getting to be a lethal place. I'm going to sleep here."

"Okay."

"Okay, so there were minute traces of poison absorbed through the skin on her neck. The details will be on your desk in the morning."

Morgan went to bed on an empty stomach and lay awake for a long time. He listened to the darkness, excited, then calm, until a rush filled his mind and he drifted to sleep.

Miranda and her companion talked deep into the night, huddled over a light supper of sliced Spam with crackers, cheese, green grapes, and a Chilean cabernet to wash it all down. At ease with each other and yet wary in the ambient gloom of the bedside lamp, they might have been lovers in a dangerous time.

She changed the dressing on his wound, sluicing the ragged flesh with alcohol until he proclaimed he'd rather die from blood poisoning than painful benevolence. There was an urgency to their playfulness that heightened the intensity of being together. But even had the Englishman been up to it, Miranda thought herself unlikely to have sex with such a man. There were too many unknowns, too many evasions. Being in the midst of a conspiracy, when she was not even sure who the players were, was not supposed to be erotic.

But of course it was. It crossed her mind that intrigue was an aphrodisiac, better than oils and roses. It was infuriating because he looked so astonishingly handsome, his body taut and hard, suppressing pain like a great muscle ready to spring, the strain enhancing his face by making each feature more sculptural. His dishevelled hair and stubbled beard, the bared chest and bloodied bandage, the quiet but resonant voice and elusive accent, made him almost irresistible.

Bad news, naturally. She gazed at him and realized that the danger and confusion surrounding him were a natural state of affairs. The rational side of her mind found this intolerable, while, strangely, a small part of her wanted no resolution, but for things to go on as they were, one mystery rolling into another, each adding layers of complexity, like a snowball caught in an avalanche.

Looking at herself in the mirror, Miranda had never been so aware of herself as a woman. She decided to turn this to her advantage. She suspected Thomas Edward Ross could out-manoeuvre her in the manipulation of truths, but in the oppressive intimacy of their situation, perhaps she had the upper hand.

She led him on, playing on his urge to define himself. He talked. He had abandoned her book on the plane to São Paulo, he told her. That's where the smoking man must have found it. Ross had spotted the Chilean travelling in the tourist section, that's when he exchanged books and asked for Miranda's help. But when he realized his pursuer knew he had been seen, he changed plans. Instead of leaving with Miranda, he slipped out through the baggage hold, leaving a few dollars in his wake.

What is odd, she thought, *is that this seems improbable, but not impossible.* She asked questions.

Why were they after him, whoever *they* were?

Why was he concerned about the Heyerdahl book?

How did she fit in?

Had she been part of his plans from the beginning?

What was special about Maria D'Arcy's copy of the book?

Did it have something to do with the handwritten notations?

Was there a connection between the book and Maria D'Arcy's death?

Who attacked him here in the Hotel Victoria? Was it the smoking man?

Why did they follow him to Easter Island?

Or did they follow *her*?

He repeatedly responded without answering, leaving her enthralled by his artful evasions when she should have been infuriated or frightened.

They both flinched at the sound of a gentle knock on the door. She recognized the voice of the concierge — perhaps he was also the owner — but could not make out his words.

She looked to Ross, and he shrugged, indicating that the inevitable could not be avoided. She slipped the lock on the door and opened it a crack.

The door slapped against her, pushing her backward into the room. A man came in, and the concierge stood behind him. The man walked directly to Ross and wrenched him to his feet. Another man entered the room. He imposed himself between Miranda and the door. When she moved, he slapped her hard and she fell to the floor. The first man hauled Ross out of the room. The second man snapped off the bedside lamp, then followed, drawing the door closed sharply behind him. Both men had worn kerchiefs pulled up over their faces; only the concierge was recognizable.

No words had been spoken. Miranda's head throbbed. The scene had played out like a black-and-white movie, with the sound muted. *Film noir*, she thought, aware she was lying alone in the dark, with the taste of blood in her mouth. She had slipped into a screenplay written by Dashiell Hammett in league with John le Carré.

3

Murder Becomes Us

Miranda telephoned Morgan again, in the early morning after she got back from her interview with the Isla de Pasqua Police, but he was already out. She did not leave a message. Despite being half a world away in the southern hemisphere, she was only an hour west of him, so he would be working. She tried the office, but he was not there, either. The bland inflection in the Canadian voice at Toronto headquarters struck a chord of empathy, and she longed to be home. She wanted to solve mysteries, she realized, not invent them. And not inhabit them from the inside looking out. She sat down on the edge of the bed and saw that one of the two Heyerdahl books was missing. Her mind was muddled, searching for a metaphor to describe the panic swelling inside her; the feeling that Kafka was in charge of the world.

***

When Morgan arrived at Harrington D'Arcy's office, high in a bank tower near the intersection of King and Bay Streets, he was surprised to find that D'Arcy had vanished.

"I had an appointment with him at nine," Morgan explained to the receptionist, then to a secretary, then to an administrative assistant, and finally to an associate executive, each of them dressed in expensive clothes, surrounded by the lavish accoutrements of their relative positions, all in a warren of offices so tastefully appointed that the excess seemed somehow an aspect of corporate efficiency. There was nothing to indicate what kind of work was done there, but the place reeked of success.

Each person he talked to declared that they had no idea of their employer's whereabouts. He was assured Harrington D'Arcy was unlikely to take off for a sail, to work out at his club, or to attend a secret meeting, without his entire office staff being made fully aware. There were apparently no clandestine moments or covert affairs in the life of Harrington D'Arcy. His very private business activities and reclusive social life were apparently tracked and controlled by his staff.

And yet he had disappeared the day after his wife was found dead, when he was wanted to assist in a police investigation into the possibility of her murder.

There was nothing in the office to indicate tragedy; no sign of grief, no particular interest in being interviewed by a homicide detective. No one professed to knowing Maria D'Arcy on a personal basis. She was apparently no more than a rumour in their glass-walled garrison high above the city streets.

As Morgan stood facing the polished marble of the elevator wall, waiting for one of two ornate metallic doors to slide open, and distracted by the emptiness of his experience in D'Arcy's office, the reflection of a woman moving down the length of the opposite corridor caught his eye. The apparition came into focus beside him as if the woman herself were caught in the cool surface of the marble walls.

When she said nothing, he turned toward her and was immediately struck by the sculptural radiance of her appearance. The austerity of her demeanour could not suppress the astonishing beauty of her features and figure and carriage. At first he thought she was waiting for the elevator. She stood slightly turned, however, so that when he shifted to look at her they were nearly facing each other, eye to eye. In heels, she was almost as tall as he was. Without them, she would still be several inches taller than Miranda. Her presence made him intensely aware of his own physical being.

"I'm told you are a policeman," she said, her voice as cool and crisp as January.

"Yeah," said Morgan, shifting his weight. The elevator door opened and neither of them got on. Several people moved past them and the door closed.

"Your name is Morgan, am I right?"

"Yeah, and you are Ms. …?"

"Simmons."

"First name?"

"Yes." She did not volunteer to tell him what it was.

"What can I do for you, Ms. Simmons?"

"Mr. D'Arcy was called away on business."

"And you are the only one here who knows about it?"

"Yes."

"Why is that?"

"I am his partner."

He looked at her closely, moving so that she had to back into the full light of the corridor. It was impossible to tell her age. She wore makeup so well it appeared to be minimal. She was groomed exquisitely; her eyebrows arched with a natural grace and the style of her hair seemed somehow inevitable. She could be in her late twenties, she could be in her early forties. His chest constricted and he gazed past her, catching his breath.

"You want to ask Mr. D'Arcy about Maria?"

"Isn't it an odd time for a business trip, Ms. Simmons? His wife is on a slab at the morgue — what about grief?"

"What about grief, Mr. Morgan?"

"Detective."

"Detective Morgan. Is there a protocol for grief required by the police?"

"No, but there are conventions and needs. My goodness," he declared, using his favoured expression and a little nonplussed by her cool civility, "the man is implicated in murder! Even he seems to think so."

"I doubt it was murder."

"You favour the suicide theory."

"People die, Detective. Sometimes by accident."

"But there's always a cause."

"Death can be a creative force, Detective Morgan."

"Did I hear you correctly, Ms. Simmons?"

"Possibly not."

The woman offered a depthless smile, the lawyerly equivalent of a dismissive shrug, he supposed. She proceeded with a rhetorical shift that he found amusing, but only because he recognized what she was doing. "I can assure you, Detective, Mr. D'Arcy has not left the country."

"It's a big country."

"I received a call. If you would step into my office, it's on my machine. I can't tell you any more than he told me."

Her office had the same impersonal opulence as its surroundings. The paintings on the walls were originals; they seemed familiar, but there was nothing Morgan actually recognized. There were several pieces of Inuit sculpture, industrial size, several Inuit prints, and a woven wall-hanging.

D'Arcy's message was simple. "Ms. Simmons. There is a matter of some urgency, I need to be away. If a Detective Morgan calls, assure him I will return."

Morgan stared intently into the woman's eyes; they were deep brown. Like eyes in a painting by Vermeer, they revealed so much and nothing at all, they gave no indication of the soul within. Her partner had addressed her as Miss.

"How do you know he hasn't left the country?"

"I would know if he had."

"You know where he is, then."

"I suspect he is in the Arctic, but I do not know that as a fact."

"The Arctic?"

"Baffin Island. We are putting something together." She paused. This was a woman unused to explaining herself and certainly unaccustomed to sharing her company's secrets. Confidentiality was their stock in trade. She was also a woman who recognized priorities.

He waited.

"Zinc and copper on Baffin Island, problems of sovereignty. The Arctic and problems of sovereignty can be quite pressing."

"Enough, apparently, to leave his wife on ice." He smiled at the droll connection between ice and the Arctic, but she showed no emotion. "Can you track him down?"

"No."

"Surely there is no place in the world where a man like Harrington D'Arcy cannot be reached."

"There is, and he is there."

"That sounds sinister."

"Not yet. Now if you will excuse me. If I hear from him, I will call."

"Promise?"

"What? Oh, yes, Detective, I promise. I am glad you like your job; you find it amusing."

"Yes," said Morgan and walked back to the elevator on his own. Her most memorable trait was her hair, which draped in a honey-blonde cascade to her shoulders and shimmered when she moved as if it were constantly under studio lights.

He went straight to the D'Arcy home in Rosedale. It was a charming stone cottage tucked away on a curving side street, reminiscent of a small seigneurial manor along one of the more remote rivers of Quebec. Only when he was up close did it seem imposing — from the street it made neighbouring houses appear pretentious and ill at ease.

He had expected something more lavish from a Brazilian heiress and a lawyer legendary for his success managing corporate takeovers. Discreetly legendary; an heiress of what?

The woman who answered the door was older, and she had evidently been crying.

"I don't suppose Mr. D'Arcy is here?" Morgan asked after introducing himself.

The woman looked at him warily.

"I am here only. The *señora*, she is deceased. Mr. D'Arcy, he is not at home at this time."

"Was he here last night?"

"Last night, yes. This morning no. He is go."

"Do you know where?"

"I do not know where to. There have been calls from his office, looking for Mr. D'Arcy."

"Could I come in, do you think?" asked Morgan.

"You are police? You have the warrant?"

Morgan was startled by her confidence; she was certainly not an illegal immigrant.

"No, I do not," he said. "I'm trying to discover

what happened to Mrs. D'Arcy. I am trying to help find her husband."

"She was not murdered by Mr. D'Arcy."

"No, you're quite possibly right. And he may be in danger himself." That thought had not occurred to him before, that the wife's murder might presage the husband's, assuming he hadn't killed her.

"You may come in. What do you wish?"

Morgan simply asked to look around. He was not sure what he was looking for, just something, whatever, an entry into the labyrinth.

In the library, there were photographs on the mantle in silver frames, some of the *Pemberly* under full sail and at anchor. In the centre of the mantle, there was a piece of wood the shape of a paddle blade, inscribed with hieroglyphs. Morgan immediately recognized *Rongorongo*, a script devised by the people of Easter Island, which they reproduced for the tourist trade although, now, sadly, no one was able to read it. *This example is particularly good*, he thought. The wood was riddled with wormholes and the surface appeared very old, not weather-worn, but had a powdery sheen, creating an illusion of authenticity. He reached out and touched it. The surface was surprisingly hard. He traced a line of glyphs with his fingertip.

This was the second time he had touched an original piece of *Rongorongo*. Only the previous year he had come across another in private ownership that was peripheral to a murder investigation. It belonged to the original owner of Miranda's Jaguar, a nasty man capable of unspeakable crimes; a low-profile lawyer like

D'Arcy, but unremarkable as a consequence of limited achievement, not professional strategy.

Morgan surveyed the room until his eyes came to rest on a stone carving sitting in the shadows, also from Easter Island. The ubiquitous *moai* with furrowed brow, pursed lips, and eyes gazing vacantly into the emptiness. He marvelled at how such a remote place, so distant from the Western world, could have had such an impact on cultural consciousness. He guessed that Miranda would bring him either a smaller replica of *Rongorongo* or a diminutive *moai*, modest enough to be carried in her hand luggage.

The library seemed, like the rest of the house, to be without gender and with no indication of children, although there was ambient warmth to the furnishings. It was clearly a room frequented by the D'Arcys. In addition to books, there were magazine and newspaper racks, a small stack of the *Guardian Weekly* and *The Economist*, a tray with decanters of madeira and port, and kindling to start a good fire once autumn set in.

Wandering into a study off the library, he saw an answering machine blinking and touched the play button. There were calls from a nail salon, a dry cleaner, and two from Maria D'Arcy's husband, asking her to call him, without saying where. The office was hers. It was more distinctively an expression of personality than the library, not feminine in any recognizable way, yet it clearly bore the imprint of a woman. *For one thing, there is the faint scent of Fleurs de Rocaille*, Morgan thought. Also stacked neatly, were back issues of *Vogue, Architectural Digest, The Walrus,* and *Vanity Fair*.

He played the machine again, this time he focused on her own message. It was warm but precise, first in English then repeated in her native language — he assumed it was the same greeting as he did not speak Portuguese.

He slipped the tape from the machine and put it in his pocket.

When the woman he had described to himself as *older* let him out, he wondered, older than what?

He walked out of Rosedale past the subway station and turned south on Yonge Street. Morgan walked everywhere when he could. He knew the D'Arcys better now, enough to know how little he knew of them. The lives of strangers were simple to understand, summed up by an item of clothing, a vocal inflection, the twist of a smile, incongruous movement — but the more someone was revealed, the more impenetrably complex they became. At the death scene, the D'Arcys were stereotypes; in their empty study, they became real.

Wherever Harrington D'Arcy was, it was not illegal to grieve in seclusion. Unless, of course, being a widower was a self-inflicted condition.

When Morgan got back to headquarters, he took the tape to a technician and they listened together until the technician got bored. Morgan wrote down what Maria said in English. He checked out the nail salon — she had missed her appointment, and the dry cleaners, who wanted him to pass on the message that the stain on her cashmere sweater would not come out. He listened to her voice over and over, and the more he listened the more empathy he felt for her, although he couldn't determine why, exactly, except that she had been alive.

He asked a colleague with the surname Gonzales to come in. "Manuela, could you listen to this? See if it's a word-for-word translation."

She listened intently.

"It's not a translation, I mean, it's her own language she's speaking. The statements are equal, but not quite the same. And it's not Portuguese."

"No?"

"It's Spanish. I know Portuguese, Morgan. My grandmother and my father speak it at home. This is Spanish. I don't really speak either but I understand both."

"She's from Brazil, it should be Portuguese."

"Who? Is this the woman who died?"

"Yeah, Maria D'Arcy."

"I think she is not from Brazil. Perhaps from Chile, maybe Peru. She speaks like a South American, and not Portuguese, not on this tape. Maybe she had Spanish friends, maybe it's for them."

"Yeah, thanks," he said, retreating to his desk to think things over.

Morgan decided that when the errant Mr. D'Arcy turned up, he could straighten this out. He would have to come in from the cold on his own, though. His employees weren't going to turn him over. Under a glossy veneer of professionalism, D'Arcy's staff had given an ominous impression of loyalty, as if, from the receptionist on up, they had sworn a blood oath of some sort, or belonged to a cult.

Sitting back with his feet on the desk, he perused the medical examiner's report. As Ellen had said, a skin swab turned up traces of poison: coniine and pancuronium, along with a blend of talcum powder, and minute particles of ground glass. She had appended a note explaining that the mixture would be rapid acting, the symptoms post-mortem would indicate death by asphyxia, the talc was an adherent and would bind with the the glass to create nearly invisible lacerations to allow the poison a subcutaneous entry into the system. A similar concoction had been used over the last decade or so in Papua New Guinea, on Madagascar, and also in Dublin, according to her research. No probable connection.

No mention was made of the break-in or of the body being washed down by ghoulish intruders. That was speculation, based on the scent of wildflowers that was no longer there. But the report was unequivocal: Maria D'Arcy had been murdered.

Morgan walked to the door marked Superintendent of Detectives and pushed it open.

"Come on in."

"No," said Morgan. "Not here."

"What do you mean, not here?"

"I need to talk to you about Harrington D'Arcy."

"Yes."

"I need to interview you."

"You what?"

"Could we go somewhere else?"

Morgan turned and led the way to an interrogation room. Rufalo followed like an animal in pursuit.

As soon as Morgan closed the door, Rufalo wheeled on him. "What the hell!"

"Easy, sir. I need to ask a few questions."

Perhaps it was Morgan's ironic deference or his own ingrained respect for procedure, but Rufalo became immediately conciliatory.

"Of course," he said. "Whatever I can do."

"Let's sit down," said Morgan.

"I'm not a suspect, am I?" said the superintendent cheerfully, trying to relieve the tension.

Morgan did not smile. "No," he said. He paused. "But you might be an accessory."

"Good God, Morgan. The man called me. He told me his wife had been murdered. I am a policeman, that was a reasonable thing for him to do."

"He was sure it was murder?"

"There was no doubt at all."

"He called you at home? You called me from your place?"

"Yes ..." Rufalo gazed around the room for a moment, seeming to see it for the first time as an unfamiliar and oppressive place. "He and my wife are business associates, both lawyers. The legal community at their level is small. We've met a few times. He wasn't asking for favours."

"One favour?"

"He did ask specifically for you, yes."

"Didn't that strike you as odd, a murder suspect determining who should investigate the crime?"

"He *suggested*, Morgan. *I determined*. And it did not cross my mind that he was a suspect. Is he?"

"Yes. He virtually insisted on it." Morgan grimaced at his own break with procedural decorum as he confessed: "We had breakfast together."

"He can be charming, can't he?"

"Dangerously so, it appears. And yes, I do have my doubts, but at this point he is the only suspect we have."

"Fill me in."

"I'd rather not, Alex. Right now, I'd like to keep you out of the loop, for your own sake. He's disappeared."

"D'Arcy! Disappeared?"

"Like the Cheshire Cat." Inappropriate: he left no smile in his wake.

"You want me to stand down?"

"From your job? Heavens, no. The accessory bit was just to get your attention. Why do you think he asked for us?"

"You and Miranda? Because you're the best. That was his assumption, not mine. It was my decision, though, not his."

"Let's put modesty aside and assume he's right — about us — that means he wants to get caught."

"If he did it, Morgan."

"Yeah." Morgan was thoughtful. "Or it could mean the opposite: a back-handed compliment. If we can't crack the case, no one can. Get by us and he's home free. Or, of course, it could mean he's innocent."

"Anything else? No? Good. And by the way, you keep saying *us*. Your partner is out of the country."

"Yeah."

"Let me know if there's anything you think I should …" He didn't finish his sentence.

As Alex Rufalo left the room he looked back. Morgan was still lost in thought. Rufalo closed the door firmly behind him.

Morgan sat slouched at the interrogation table for more than an hour, letting facts and impressions swirl in his mind. He felt like he was caught at the edge of a whirlpool, unable either to break free or plunge through. This was a case where Miranda's capacity for deduction would be invaluable. Revising his water imagery, he thought of pebbles tossed in a pond, their ripples confusing the surface — she was good at inferring who threw them from their intersecting patterns.

But she was busy by now on her novel. Her story about the man bleeding in her bed who claimed to be Harrington D'Arcy had faded from his mind. This was not a failure of imagination on his part, but submission to the power of hers. The bleeding man was well on his way to becoming fiction. Apart from a general sense of apprehension, Morgan felt worrying about Miranda was a response too personal, too intimate, for comfort.

It was only her first full day there, so perhaps she was still getting her bearings. He had suggested renting a Jeep and driving out to Rano Raraku, the volcano quarry. It was not far — the whole island was a tiny triangle in the vast Pacific, six miles by eight by twelve. Morgan did not think in metric. His idea had been for Miranda to counter the strangeness of such an amazing place by starting with the familiar. The cover of every book about the vaunted mysteries of Easter Island, every appropriation of images to sell credit cards and cosmetics, featured shots of *moai* on the outside slopes of the quarry where they stood, inexplicably abandoned, while over the centuries silt had built up to their shoulders. They gazed, pensively, incomplete, over the savannah to their intended platforms bordering the sea.

Morgan would like to have been there. The disjunction, particularly at Rano Raraku, between the powerful presence of the past and a full understanding of how it had all come about, had created in Morgan an oddly intense feeling of serenity. If he were a religious man, he might have described the feeling as mystical. He was moved, literally, beyond words. He hoped Miranda wouldn't reduce it all to historical hypotheses. Sometimes it was better to live with mysteries than to resolve them.

Perhaps she was still asleep, washed by the westerly breeze through an open window, dreaming of being exactly where she was. Morgan was surprised that he found the image of Miranda in the tranquil embrace of the Hotel Victoria vaguely erotic. Quite suddenly, he got up and strode out of the interrogation room, out of Police Headquarters, into the midday Toronto sun.

An hour later, he was meandering across the manicured grass in front of the clubhouse at the Royal Toronto Yacht Club, which yesterday had seemed so imposing and now struck him as an embarrassingly misplaced anachronism. Perhaps it was being here on his own, without the mediating effect of Harrington D'Arcy, but the antebellum enclave of privilege now seemed a little sad, like a fat man who smokes.

He made his way past the colonnaded portico to the *Pemberly*. It was still cordoned off with yellow tape strung across the pilings, but no one had thought to post an officer to keep watch. It was assumed the entire premises were secured. And they were: from ethnic interlopers, class jumpers, women of a certain sort, but not from murderers, embezzlers, politicians and lawyers, or world-class sailors.

Morgan had the heart of an anarchist, but the mind of a cop.

He did not want to change anything because that wasn't his job. The world worked the way it worked, and when it didn't, then it was up to people like him to get it working again. He stepped on board the *Pemberly* and felt it rock gently against its moorings. Morgan's knowledge of boats, particularly yachts, was from books. You don't grow up among the working poor in old Cabbagetown familiar with halyards and spinnakers, bowsprits, and transoms. Sheets and shrouds were to cover the living and the dead, not to catch the wind.

When he stood on the foredeck and gazed down at the hatch, something seemed askew. The hatch was locked from the outside. Under him was the fo'c'sle locker; why wouldn't it be secured from within? He went below and made his way past the head and a large locker into the forward hold. There were no bunks, as he had expected, only a stowage area.

He realized he was wrong about the lock. The hatch was used for passing things through, probably sails, so an outside lock was appropriate. Still, as he ran his fingers around the mahogany combing beneath the hatch, he felt dents in the wood and by shifting his position he could see gouges that a screwdriver might have left in an attempt to pry the hatch open. Flecks of varnish came off on his fingers. The damage was very recent.

Someone, a woman, he suspected, had been forcibly confined down here. D'Arcy would know his own boat; he would know how much force it would take to smash through the fo'c's'le or companionway hatches. They were wood, thick enough to withstand the forces of water lashing the boat in a storm — but they were *only* wood, mahogany, and they could be broken from inside with a few sharp blows from a winch handle, an elbow, or even the blunt end of a screwdriver. Most places can be broken out of, if you are willing to break things. A woman is less likely than a man to resolve the dilemma of her confinement through violence. It is not about the nature of women, but how they are taught restricting conventions as absolutes. The truth is, wood breaks, glass breaks, it would not have been difficult to escape from the belly of the Lion.

Miranda would be irritated by the sexist assumption. She would counter with a statement of resonant ambiguity: *we live in an age, thank God, when even absolutes are uncertain*. She would conclude that the person locked below, without deference to gender, was either incapacitated or lacking imagination, or both. The autopsy indicated Maria had consumed alcohol. She might have been up to no more than a haphazard effort. She likely anticipated a hangover, not death, or she would have tried harder. He could hear Miranda's words in her own voice.

Morgan looked around for the screwdriver and found it against the foot of a berth in the main cabin. As he leaned over to pick it up he smelled Fleurs de Rocaille. She had certainly been there, lying on this berth, not long before dying. He touched where she had been, and withdrew his hand with an instinctive rush; the mattress was still warm. But of course it was not; it was his own body heat reflected from the Ultrasuede cover.

Morgan was seized by a sense of connection with the dead woman. The rich gleam of highly finished mahogany brightwork, the blue mattress covers on the three berths, the brightly coloured cushions and small pillows, the diminutive curtains drawn away from the portholes, the gleaming brass fittings, polished chrome instruments, and spotless galley with a stainless-steel stove on gimbals and woven tea towels folded neatly in a slot, all signified a distinctive taste. The confined space of the cabin was an expression of personality and Morgan felt certain it was not the work of a nautical designer, nor that of Harrington D'Arcy.

There was a gallery of framed photographs screwed into the forward bulkhead. Morgan had noticed them before. What seemed to be generic sailing pictures now resonated, since he had seen duplicates in the D'Arcy home. There were expected shots of the *Pemberly* under full sail, heeling perilously close to the wind, with canvas taut, the skipper's hand on the tiller with an iron grip; and of the *Pemberly* moored against a series of familiar and exotic backdrops.

In one of the action shots, professionally dramatic in black and white, there were two people in the cockpit. Harrington D'Arcy could be identified, braced against the combing on the high side. Morgan peered this way and that until he confirmed that the other figure, wearing the skipper's cap with her hand on the tiller, was Maria.

He recalled thinking of D'Arcy as the sole owner. If the *Pemberly* had been moored at the Port Credit Yacht Club down the lake, he might have assumed it was a family boat. In fact, he recognized the Port Credit clubhouse in the background of one of the pictures. He had been there a few years ago on a case that proved to be a suicide masking a murder. There was something familiar, if generic, about the tropical setting of another picture. Then he realized it was not the *Pemberly* in the foreground, but a two-masted ketch, a small ocean sailor of about the same size. Both D'Arcys were in the cockpit. Behind the ketch was the semblance of a harbour, little more than a bay, edged by a few buildings and a sparse scattering of palms. And, indistinctly, near the centre, a shadowy rectangle, the back of a *moai* facing a soccer field across the gravel road. He could not see the road or the field in the photograph, but he knew they were there.

Easter Island, the village of Hanga Roa. The *Rongorongo* on the mantle was a souvenir, not an auction-house acquisition. The D'Arcys had sailed there in the ketch, probably east from Tahiti. They would have stopped at Pitcairn along the way, before the long haul to the most isolated island in the world. He had not thought of it as remote when he was there last year, but in the context of small-boat sailing, the open sea surrounding it seemed limitless.

They sailed together. He was slowly assimilating the fact that Harrington D'Arcy and Maria D'Arcy must have been a very close couple, who handled intimacy as discreetly as if they were having an affair.

And she had died here, he thought, *on this berth. Perhaps her husband found her, he was sure it was murder but had no proof. He carried her above to the cockpit and placed her in a nonchalant pose. He went back down below to wait for dawn. Why wait?*

Apparently to be sure he got Morgan involved with the case. Why the disinterested attitude? As a boardroom lawyer, he was used to planning strategically, guiding events to a desired end. But each move along the way was a controlled response. That was tactics. The difference was subtle: the attitude was strategic, manipulating Rufalo to bring Morgan on board, that was tactical. And disappearing into the Arctic, what was that?

Ellen Ravenscroft said Maria D'Arcy had died where she was found, verified by the way blood had settled in the corpse. But if her husband had attended her closely, and moved her carefully within a short time of her death, lifting her up through the narrow companionway, she might have died below decks. Could he have done it by himself? Perhaps someone else was involved. Someone who knew where he was now. Ms. Simmons, perhaps.

Morgan walked back to the clubhouse and found an attendant in the men's locker room, a lithe sunburned man in his forties.

"Were you working yesterday?" Morgan asked him.

"Are you here about the murder?" said the man, running his fingers through a shock of sun-bleached hair. "Yes, I was working. I saw you talking to Mr. D'Arcy on the *Pemberly*, and Mrs. D'Arcy. You had breakfast with him on the verandah."

"Mrs. D'Arcy was dead," said Morgan, a little taken aback at having been so closely observed.

"Well yes, but she was there. You must have arrived just after seven, you caught the first ferry, I caught the second."

"How'd you know I didn't come on a police boat?"

"You didn't. He didn't kill her."

"You figure not."

"I'm certain of it."

"What makes you so sure?"

"Look out there, that window, it looks straight down the channel, the third boat along, I can see the *Pemberly* from here while I'm working."

"And?"

"And sometimes they'd spend the whole evening by themselves, without going out on the lake, just reading, talking when the sun went down. They were very private, very together. The kind of people you like from a distance. You don't want to know them, just watch them."

"Do you know many of the members — personally?"

"Ah, the class thing. The service thing. Yes, yes I do. I sail. I've sailed quite a lot over the years. I'm available whenever anyone's a hand short. I've sailed most of these boats and, trust me, the minute we cast off I'm as good as the best of them. I can see the wind, Detective, and there's not a sailor here who doesn't respect that."

Morgan couldn't help but warm to this man, who struck him as his own mirror opposite. The man tilted his head forward and looked up. The corners of his eyes were creased from years of squinting into the maritime sun. His eyes glittered like an ancient mariner who was kept young by his passion for the sea.

"You sailed with the D'Arcys in the South Pacific, didn't you?"

"How'd you know?" There was a glint in his eyes, but no wariness.

"You skippered a ketch from Tahiti to Easter Island."

"Rapa Nui, yes. From Hawaii down and across. They flew in, joined us in Papeete, Tahiti. They flew home from Rapa Nui. Several years ago. How do you know what a ketch is?"

"How do you know they were a good couple? Not looking out your window. You said you wouldn't want to know them close up, but you did."

"No mystery there. One felt intrusive, being with them. It was just the way they were. How'd you know about the Pacific thing?"

"I'm a detective," said Morgan, who had made a lucky guess. "When you say they joined 'us' in Tahiti, you mean you and your boat. You sailed single-handed down from Hawaii."

"Yes I did. And how'd you know that? I suppose because you're a detective?"

"Because you work at a menial job and have the skills of a man born to privilege. Spells renegade to me, an authentic loner, rising to the challenge of a lonely voyage."

"Yes," said the man. "Sorry I can't help with the murder."

"With solving it?" said Morgan, wondering exactly how his regret was directed. "Perhaps you've helped already —"

"I don't think so. I never saw them quarrel, I don't know their problems, or their enemies, their business interests, their politics, their religion."

"What about their sex lives?"

"What about their sex lives?" said the man, shifting the emphasis.

"I understand D'Arcy was ..." Morgan paused, then recalling it was D'Arcy himself who had made the assertion, he continued, "... that he was bisexual."

"Oh, come now, Detective, aren't we all? I'm no help to you there."

"Morgan," he said. "Detective Morgan."

"Rove," said the man.

"First name or last."

"McMan. Rove McMan, sailor at large."

"Let's hope it stays that way."

"What? Oh yes, you're being ironic. No, Detective Morgan, I am not a murderer. I adore the cramped quarters of an ocean voyage, but I would not fare well in a cell. I would prefer to remain free, as it were, and a sailor."

"As it were," Morgan repeated, turning the phrase

over in his mind. *A strangely effete expression for a seaman*, he thought.

"Upper Canada College," said Rove McMan, reading Morgan's response. "A first in philosophy at Oxford. Rowed, you know. But chose not to affect the Oxonian accent. Sailed dinghies as a child, have sailed ever since. Poor by choice."

"And is Rove short for something?"

"Yes it is."

"What?"

"Yes, it is short for something."

Morgan smiled, and he walked away without saying anything more, as if he had other business more pressing. When he reached the front door under the portico of the main building, he turned to see if he was being watched, but the attendant had apparently gone back to work.

When the club ferry pulled in, he recognized the same officious young man who had accosted him the day before for not dressing to code, assisting passengers ashore. Morgan waited on the return crossing until they were in the middle of the harbour and the RTYC was obscured behind a shoreline frieze of staggering willows. As Morgan approached him, the young man glanced around furtively; the ferry was nothing but a glorified launch and there was no place to hide.

"Where were you when I came over around noon?" Morgan asked him, closing in as the young man edged against the rail.

"Right here, sir."

"No," said Morgan.

"You weren't looking for me. I stayed in the wheelhouse."

"And why would that be?"

"I don't know, sir."

Morgan gazed into the young man's eyes. What he saw there was familiar, not the sullen defiance of an ex-con, or the horror of an illegal dreading exposure, and it was not the fear of a man guilty of crime. It was the suppressed panic of someone cowed by the power of a gun in the hands of authority. Morgan was used to this, the fear of police. Here was a young man at the service of people who could bring down governments, who could buy and sell entire nations, and he was comfortable in their aura of privilege and power because he knew his place in their scheme of things. But a cop, one of his own, terrified him.

"You know Mr. and Mrs. D'Arcy?" Morgan asked. The young man nodded affirmative. "The day before yesterday, did you bring them over?"

"I worked the evening shift. I brought Mr. D'Arcy over, not her. She didn't come."

"Well, she did. She was murdered over there." Morgan nodded in the direction of the yacht club.

"Not on this boat, sir. I would have seen her. Sailors know each other."

"You're a sailor?"

"I aspire to be a sailor, sir. I read *Yachting* magazines my passengers leave behind. I have made a study of sailing, although I have not actually sailed, yet."

"And what about Rove McMan, do you know him?"

"Yes, sir, of course."

"Did he come over yesterday."

"Yes sir, the run after yours."

"No, I mean the evening before?"

"Sunday. No sir. He was already there. I think he'd been out on the lake for a couple of days. I took him back Sunday morning."

"You worked a double shift? And how do you know McMan?"

"It's a seasonal job, I often work double. Everyone knows Rove McMan."

The locker room attendant was someone the young man admired, Morgan could tell by the way he spoke his name. Working the ferry was the closest he could come to emulating the lifestyle of an itinerant world-class sailor. Morgan felt sorry for him.

He gave the young man his card. It was an old card with writing on the back. It was only his number at home.

"If there's anything you can think of, give me a call," he said.

The young man brightened. He was an ally, a police accomplice.

"Oh, I will for sure. If I see or think of anything unusual."

"Thank you," said Morgan, wondering what the young man might think was unusual.

Back at headquarters, Morgan ran a search on Rove McMan. The locker-room attendant and world sailor had anticipated any question of criminal involvement by declaring his arrival at the club subsequent to Morgan himself. The ferryman would seem to have cleared him, as well. Still, anyone who had sailed in a small boat for weeks on end with a couple he claimed hardly to know must have been concealing a great deal of himself, or about them.

McMan checked out. RTYC, dinghy races as a kid, with distinction. Upper Canada College. Father bankrupt, a Rosedale suicide, mother remarried. One sibling, a sister, resident until death at 999 Queen Street, the public asylum; no further record. Oxford, full scholarship. No tax or employment records. Never married. Round the world twice, once non-stop single-handed in a borrowed boat. Wrote a book, *Random Wake*. Good title, poor sales.

All this from public archives, newspapers, and the Internet. No criminal record, not even a parking ticket. No car, a rented apartment.

He is a man living his own life to the fullest, which is more, than most of us so, Morgan thought. *Of course many of us live a number of lives simultaneously.* Rufalo walked by his desk several times and Morgan ignored him, but late in the afternoon he looked up and saw Rufalo watching from his office. In that moment it occurred to Morgan that there was the link. He wanted to rush in, but instead sauntered into the superintendent's office without knocking. Rufalo looked wary.

"Any word on D'Arcy?" Rufalo asked.

"Nothing. The guy walked off the face of the earth."

"I'm getting calls. Polite inquiries, so far. I've been vague, and there's not a news editor in the city willing to risk the wrath of Harrington D'Arcy by speculating murder, suicide, misadventure, or sudden poor health without the word from us. Once they find he's missing, though, they're going to go wild."

"Why bother," said Morgan. "He's not a celebrity."

"No, but he's exceptionally powerful. Your corporate lawyer could be turned into bloody good copy. If he killed her, Morgan, it will be news, I guarantee it. Missing, that makes him fair game, I'm afraid."

"But I don't think he did it."

"Good."

"Good?"

Rufalo shrugged noncommittally.

"What I wanted to ask, did you ever talk to D'Arcy about Miranda?"

"Good God, no. About Miranda. No, not at all. I don't know D'Arcy, not like that."

"What about his wife?"

"What about her?"

"Did you talk to her about Miranda going to Easter Island?"

"No, of course not. I've only spoken to the woman a few times in my life."

"But Caroline knows them both, and she knew about Miranda's sabbatical project."

"Yes, I suppose she did, but no, Morgan, I —"

"And she might have mentioned it?"

"To D'Arcy, I don't think so. Perhaps to his wife, it's possible. There was nothing confidential about it. In fact, yes, of course, that book I passed on for Miranda. It would have been from D'Arcy's wife. It's quite possible Caroline told her. She must have, I suppose."

"Alex, I'm not accusing you. I just need to know."
"Why? What's the connection?"
"I'm not sure, but there is one. Thanks."

Morgan walked back to his desk. He sat down, he stood up. It was after six; he left for the day.

He picked up smoked meat on rye and coleslaw from a deli on the way home. The air smelled of August as he walked along Harbord Street. The heat of the day was draining away and the cool of the evening was rising from the lengthening shadows. He had been tempted to eat in the restaurant, but decided that he wasn't all that hungry and would rather change first and crack open a beer and watch some TV or read the paper.

As soon as he approached the door of his condo, one segment of a rambling Victorian house subdivided into a postmodern architectural puzzle, like those three-dimensional intelligence tests where no two pieces are the same, he realized he was already rehearsing his conversation with Miranda. At the door he hesitated for a moment, discerning his spectral reflection in the paint he had applied, layer after layer, when he had first moved in more than a decade earlier. He had been trying to emulate the magic depth on the Georgian doors of Dublin, where he had spent several months half a lifetime before.

He picked up his mail without looking at it and dropped it on an end table beside his answering machine, which registered no calls. He set down his deli parcel on the ottoman, slumped back into the blue sofa, and dialed the very long number of the Hotel Victoria in Hanga Roa. After two rings, someone spoke to him in Spanish. He tried to explain what he wanted, but got nowhere. He hung up and called a Bell Canada operator and asked her to make the connection, person to person. After an interminable wait, during which he could hear voices in Spanish and English negotiating, the operator informed him there was no one registered at the Hotel Victoria by that name.

"Miranda Quin," he said. "One *n*."

"There's no one there by that name."

"Did she move out?"

"I don't know, sir. They said no one by that name has been registered there. She must be staying somewhere else. Is it a big place?"

"What?"

"Isla de Pasqua?"

"No, it's a very small place. Could you connect me to the police?"

"The Toronto police?"

"I am the Toronto police; to the police on Easter Island."

"Where, sir?"

"Isla de Pasqua!"

"One moment, sir."

She came back on the line.

"There is no number for police on Isla de Pasqua. Would you like me to try Santiago. That is also in Chile."

"Try Carabinaros. Isla de Pasqua *Carabinaros*."

"Is that a person or business, sir?"

"Try *Guardia Civil*."

"I'm sorry sir, is *Guardia* the first name or last?"

"Uh, try *Policía*."

"*Policía*. Thank you, sir."

She came back on the line again. "To whom did you wish to speak?"

"The Isla de Pasqua *Policía*!"

"This is a person-to-person call, sir."

"Anyone. Please."

He could hear muffled voices in the background and then the operator returned. "I will connect you now."

"Thank you."

"Thank you for using Bell Canada."

"*Si?*" a new voice inquired.

"*Carabinaros?*"

"No *Carabinaros*. Policía."

"*Habla Inglés?*"

"No, *poco*. A little."

"I am looking for Señorita Miranda Quin," said Morgan in a very slow and deliberate voice. "I am calling from Canada. She is a police officer, she is staying at the Hotel Victoria."

"I am police, *Señor*. There is no Miss Quin at Hanga Roa."

"How do you know?"

"I know, we are a little place."

"And you know everyone?"

"*Señor*, it is my job."

"You know everyone there?"

"*Si*. I know Rapa Nui. Señorita Miss Quin, she has never arrive. Thank you for your call. Goodbye."

The line went dead.

She'll phone, Morgan thought. *She's moved to another hotel. She'll call this evening. It's only mid-afternoon in the South Pacific. She's out exploring at*

Rano Raraku. He was annoyed that she was inaccessible, irritated by her lack of consideration. He was worried, too. It was not like Miranda to disappear. A pang of fear ran through him, but he shook it loose. She knew how to look after herself.

The telephone rang. Morgan jumped, then took a deep breath and relaxed.

"Miranda?"

"It is Edwin Block."

"Who?" said Morgan, his anxiety about Miranda rising.

"Eddie, you gave me your card."

"When?"

"Today on the ferry. I called the office number, but you weren't there so I called this number."

"Yes, Eddie, what can I do for you?" said Morgan. He wanted to get off the phone in case Miranda was trying to get through.

"Well, you know, you wanted to know things," he stopped.

"Yes?"

"Well, you know, it's not difficult to get over to the RTYC lots of other ways."

"Such as?"

"Well, you know Toronto Island is just one of the islands, it's actually called Centre Island, but most people call it Toronto Island, but anyway, the islands are connected, you can take a ferry to Centre Island Park or to the airport, you can hire a water taxi."

"You're a good man, Eddie, you're thinking outside the box."

"I am?"

"You are. Now, I'm expecting an important call so we'll have to cut this short. If you think of anything else, you call me. At the office." Without waiting for a response, Morgan clicked off. He held the phone in his palm, staring at it, but it remained silent.

He set the telephone on the ottoman beside the uneaten sandwich, and sat back and waited, while darkness slowly filled the room. He felt something vaguely like homesickness. She would be fine. If it were him, he'd be out at the quarry among the *moai*. The sun would be low on the Pacific by now, poised to fall into the sea.

A sharp knock on the door startled him.

He opened it, framed by the darkness behind him and blinded by the light from the street which cast his caller in a stark silhouette.

"Yeah," he said.

"Morgan. You all right? It's me."

"Oh," he said. "Sorry. I must have fallen asleep. Come in, let's turn on some lights. There. Well, now, this is a surprise."

Ellen Ravenscroft gazed around the room. It was not what she had expected. In her mind she had furnished Morgan's home with oriental carpets and Inuit carvings, time-battered tables and chairs glazed with layers of paint, original prints by Canadian artists, a pair of old skis or antique snowshoes leaning against a back wall. There were lots of books, as she assumed there would be, and there was an aura, a masculine warmth that probably came from the smoked meat in the delicatessen bag on the ottoman. The place was distinctive, but dishevelled. Like Morgan. She would have preferred enchanting, exotic, or ominously seductive.

"So this is it?" she said, indicating the entire place with a slow pirouette.

"Yeah," said Morgan. He turned off the overhead, but left the lamps on at either end of the sofa. "My sanctuary. What brings you here?"

"A predatory impulse."

"Can I get you a drink?"

"Do you have any wine?"

"Pouilly Fuissé in the fridge."

"White?"

"Pouilly — yes, white."

"A good year?"

"Vintage."

"Lovely."

All years are vintage, Morgan thought as he opened the wine. He could be giving her plonk and save the difference. Still, class serves the establishment, mumble mumble, he was nattering to himself. Maybe she would go away.

He brought two glasses of pale, lustrous wine back into the living room, each filled precisely half way. She was sitting on the sofa, comfortable as an old friend.

"How are you managing without Miranda?" she asked.

"What?"

"What's happening with the D'Arcy file?"

"He's missing."

"Who? D'Arcy? Come on, he's too famous."

"No, he's not famous at all."

"You know what I mean, he's too important. Important people can't go missing. They get missed. Is he dead?"

"If I knew, he wouldn't be missing."

"Don't be testy, love. I was just asking."

"I don't think he's dead."

"This is a lovely wine. I've seen it in the stores. It's very generous of you to share a bottle."

"A bottle?"

"We don't have to drink it all now, love. Save some for the morning."

"Ellen, why are you here?"

"Maria D'Arcy …"

"Yeah?"

"It bothered me, the poison, even a concentrate should have left something in her blood. I went back to the report I sent to you. Re-reading it — funny how one notices in words what one didn't pick up in real life, even when the words are your own."

Morgan immediately knew what she was going to say.

"There was a turn of phrase, Morgan —"

"Yeah, I missed it, too. *The swab* —"

"Exactly. If she was cleaned down so thoroughly even her perfume was washed away, how is it I found no trace in her blood, but the poison powder concoction appeared on a swab?"

"On the nape of her neck?"

"No, the front, just above the clavicle. It was easy to miss the ground glass abrasions because it was applied after death. Whoever broke into the morgue interfered with the corpse in a most unusual way. I've never heard of poisoning a corpse before. The poison, it was meant to be found. So there you are. Someone wanted us to think she was murdered. I was working late. When I realized what happened, I needed to tell you."

Morgan recognized the desire to share a discovery; that somehow telling someone else made it real. He felt a warm sense of kinship with Ellen Ravenscroft, and empathy, realizing she had no one in her life to share things with. He at least had his partner. He and Miranda sometimes called back and forth in the dead of night to exchange nocturnal revelations about work. It was a kind of intimacy he missed terribly with her being away, knowing she would be gone until well into winter, if winter came early.

"So what do you think, love? I mean, apart from the fact I screwed up."

"No, you didn't screw up. You found poison, it's in your report. I'm the detective, I missed the implications."

"But I declared the death homicide. I should have seen the anomaly. I got distracted."

"Yeah, we both focused on the absence of Fleurs de Rocaille."

"My, my, Fleurs de Rocaille. You do your research."

"So we're back to square one. This doesn't mean that she wasn't murdered. We just don't know if, for sure, or how, or by whom."

"Sorry, love. If it's any consolation, the champagne in her gut was Dom Perignon. Very classy, very expensive. I've only had it once. It did the trick."

Morgan needed time to assimilate the shifting patterns — same events, different perceptions. He looked at Ellen Ravenscroft, sitting languidly against the cushions of the blue sofa, the stem of the heavy crystal poised in her fingers, the glass empty now except for a few drops that she swirled lazily against the sides. It was difficult to tell if she was embarrassed by the error or amused. She seemed to be enjoying herself.

He went to the kitchen and brought the bottle back out into the living room and poured more into her glass without asking. She accepted with a smile. He poured more for himself and sat down facing her. She drew her legs up to the side on the sofa, shifting her weight, and her skirt revealed more of her legs than he could actually see in the shadows.

Neither of them spoke. She seemed comfortable with silence. It was nice, just to sit, to be together for a while.

Finally, she got up and went into the bathroom. When she came out she walked by him and started up the steps to his sleeping loft. She paused halfway, shrugged out of her blouse, and, letting it drop behind her, disappeared into the shadows.

Morgan watched, feeling vulnerable on her behalf, admiring her willingness to risk rejection. He rose, turned off the lamp, and, leaving the remainder of the Pouilly Fuissé open on the table, he followed her.

In the soft light of the city drifting up from the open blinds of the living room, he could see that she lay naked in the centre of the bed, arms by her sides and knees modestly together, like a doll waiting to be animated, or a sleeping princess. He stepped over her clothes on the floor, and, removing his own, placed them neatly on their chair in the corner. He turned to her and saw she had rolled onto her side to make room for him. He settled his weight gently on the bed beside her, so close he could feel the body heat between them, and they lay still, listening to the sounds of Toronto seeping through the walls and to the sounds of their own breathing.

Gradually, their bodies drifted together. At first they touched so imperceptibly, it was like a tingling, and then they touched with a lightness that sent shivers running over the surface of their bodies, enveloping them and pressing against them, and then they touched with deliberate pressure, not yet with hands or lips, letting their skin merge in common sensation, then, tentatively, they kissed, they caressed, their bodies entangled, and they became fierce in their lovemaking, like creatures intent on devouring each other, each drawing satisfaction and finally being sated by attention to their own separate needs. When it was finished they edged apart, staying close enough they could still feel their body heat warming the air between them.

Morgan realized three or four hours had gone by. It must be well after midnight on Rapa Nui. He listened to Ellen breathing. She was awake. He was pleasantly depleted, but lonely. He got up.

"Thanks," she said into the darkness.

"You too," he said. "Why don't you sleep? I'll be back in a bit."

He picked up a robe that was draped over the balustrade, surprised at how difficult it was to put on in the dark, and descended into the living room. Both of them were aware he would not be coming back up. She would sleep soundly for a few hours. He would read through the rest of the night. She would get dressed and leave in the morning as if she had just popped by for a chat. They would never talk about what had happened; it would remain in their minds as the most uninhibited and generous sex each had experienced, but they would remember only themselves making love and the other would fade like a dream.

4

Till Death Do Us Part

Morgan woke to find himself slumped against the side cushions of the sofa. Someone had placed a light cover over him and turned off the lamp. He had not heard her leave. He swung his legs over and sat up, trying to focus on yesterday's mail beside the answering machine. Poking out from a small pile of bills and flyers was the upper edge of a vellum envelope bearing a monogram with the letters *D* and A intertwined, and the return address of the seigneurial cottage in Rosedale. The note inside was not from Harrington D'Arcy, but from his wife, Maria. It was addressed to Detective Sergeant Morgan. It was a suicide note.

"*Kai i te au.*" That was the answer Miranda had received to every question she asked of the Isla de Pasqua police. She had gone straight to their office after

Ross had been dragged away, but they were closed for the night. She had returned in the early morning and talked with a man identified by a name tag as Te Ave Teao — at least she assumed that was his name — a man who, by his uniform, was part of the island constabulary. He did not seem interested when she gave her own name, although it registered when she said she was a police officer.

He was cheerful. He seemed unperturbed by her report of violent abduction, as if such a thing were not possible on Rapa Nui, and by implication was more likely the product of a hysterical imagination.

"How do you think I got this bruise on my face?" she demanded.

"*Kai i te au*," he said. "It is not a very big bruise."

No, she thought, *I don't suppose it is*. That was hardly the point.

"Do you have any record of a man called Thomas Edward Ross?"

"*Señor* Ross? No, I do not know him."

"Do you know where he is?" she persisted.

"*Señora*, how I can know where this man is if I do not know him?"

"But you know who I mean?"

"*Kai i te au*. I do not know anything." Behind him, another officer, sitting at a desk with his back to her, chuckled as if she were a bit of a fool.

"Thank you for your help," she said.

"You will be staying for long?" asked her interlocutor amiably.

Miranda smiled. "*Kai i te au*." If she understood

the phrase correctly, it meant, *I don't know and it doesn't matter*. "*Kai i te au*," she repeated.

The policemen with his back to her turned his head and smiled, not at her but at the man called Te Ave Teao; perhaps conspiratorially, or in derision, she didn't care which.

Miranda had walked back along the dusty street and up the small incline to the Hotel Victoria. She tried unsuccessfully to call Morgan from her room. Sitting on the edge of her bed, her mind was a jumble of brutal images and fragmented thoughts. She could feel the panic swelling inside her, but she refused to let herself cry. *Kafka*, she thought — *I wonder if you know when you've turned into a cockroach*. After a while she walked down the corridor to Ross's room. The blood had been cleaned up. There was no evidence that he had ever been there, or that the room had been occupied recently.

She found the old concierge puttering outside the house next door and asked if he knew where Ross had been taken. His response was not unexpected.

"*Kai i te au*," he said, shrugging.

"*Kai i te au*," she repeated, then asked again, "Mr. Ross, *Señor* Ross, you know *Señor* Ross?"

"No, *señora*."

"He was here."

"No *señora*, never."

"Are you afraid?"

"I am afraid nothing, *señorita*. No Mr. Ross."

Señorita. He had shifted to the title for a young woman, perhaps trying to appease her with flattery.

Or perhaps her obvious bewilderment made her seem younger. She looked the old man straight in the eye until he averted his gaze, glancing around as if he were trying to find something to capture his interest, then he shrugged and walked away.

Miranda was annoyed with herself for allowing anxiety to get the upper hand. It was being in a strange place and surrounded by languages she did not understand. It was the mystique of Easter Island; she had been seduced by the stories she had read and the stories she had not read. This was a place of tangible unknowns, huge statues whose origins and significance were subjects of the wildest speculation, rocks and gates and walls bearing inscriptions that could not be read. She knew about the *moai*, there were over nine hundred, ranging from the size of a small child to at least one over sixty feet tall if it were standing erect. She knew about the hieroglyphic inscriptions on stone and wood that no one could decipher. She had read of curses, and, that beneath the Catholic veneer, powerful forces shaped lives on the island, because people believed in their power. She had already experienced the capacity of the island to absorb violence and close over it as if nothing had happened.

She changed into a light sundress and sandals, then walked down to a cottage on the main street decorated with travel posters that housed the office of Lan Chile, the national airlines.

"A man came in on Monday," she explained. "I am trying to find him."

A young woman in crisp, white blouse and ironed slacks, a uniform that seemed quaint and incongruous in what was little more than a hut, answered in excellent English.

"What is the gentleman's name, please?"

"Thomas Edward Ross."

"No," she responded with casual authority, not bothering to look anything up. "There is no Mr. Ross."

"Perhaps he was travelling by another name?"

"No," she repeated. A brief shadow crossed her features. "That would not be possible," she said. "If his name is Mr. Ross, he must travel as Mr. Ross. It is not legal in Chile to be some other person."

Miranda caught a glimpse of life under Pinochet, with memories of thugs in the night and the *disparu*. The terrors of the past were buried in a shallow grave.

"I believe Mr. Ross is a policeman," she said, meaning to reassure the young woman, but of course this declaration only increased her apparent anxiety.

"No Mr. Ross," the woman declared. "You are policeman?" she asked. Without waiting for an answer, she made it clear she was in no doubt by responding as if to interrogation. "I am not from Isla de Pasqua, not Rapa Nui. I am born in Valparaiso, I am …"

"You know nothing, correct?"

"I know nothing."

"*Kai i te au.*" The young woman looked bewildered by the phrase, confirming her off-island origins. "Please look," Miranda said. Using the woman's nervousness to her advantage, she gestured toward papers on the desk with an air of authority.

The woman shuffled the papers without even pretending to look at them. "On Monday, *señora*, there was no airplane."

Miranda momentarily blanched. "A freight plane?" she asked. "Maybe American."

"No, *señora*. We have no freight plane. No American freight plane. Maybe military. All planes come on Tuesday, you came on Tuesday. All other days, sometimes, but not Monday. There is no Mr. Ross, I am sorry."

She seemed apologetic, now, more out of courtesy than fear.

"Thank you."

Miranda paused at the door. She was a little thrown by the instant return of the woman's composure. "I may come back," she said.

The woman smiled, her teeth gleaming like an image on one of the travel posters.

As Miranda stepped out into the humid sunlight, she caught the scent of the ocean on a cooling breeze; it brushed sensuously across her exposed skin and for a moment the terrors of the previous night might have happened to someone else. This dissociation was not reassuring. She walked down to the harbour, which was really no more than a small sandy break in the ragged volcanic shoreline, and sat on the windward side of a *moai*, letting the breeze wash over her. Like the statue at the airport, this one was apparently authentic, but obviously displaced from its original site, perhaps to affirm for the incoming armies of anthropologists that their dreams of glory had already begun. She tried to remember what arcane pursuit had brought her so far from home.

Eating lunch in a restaurant overlooking the bay, she thought about what Morgan had told her. Maria D'Arcy was found dead under ambiguous circumstances. She was relatively young; inevitably her death would be considered ambiguous. It was a relief for Miranda to think about murder in a context she knew.

By the time she began sipping a postprandial Chilean chardonnay, her thoughts had swung back to her immediate circumstances and the bewildering disappearance of Thomas Edward Ross. It was like he had never been there, like he never existed. She caught her own reflection in the picture window, spectral against the dazzling ocean, and shuddered at the perverse reassurance she felt to see she hadn't disappeared, as well.

She stood up abruptly and her chair fell over, rattling against the floor. Her nerves jumped, making her gasp for air. A man appeared out of the shadows, silhouetted and featureless against the brilliant sunlight filling the windows. She paid too much and hurried out. The harbour was alive again. A dog and a chicken rooted in the dust near the lone *moai*, a couple of divers came out of their shop and loaded a small boat with gear, two boys and a girl began kicking a ball around the field, and a couple of older boys on horseback, with T-shirts wrapped decorously around their heads, cantered past, nodding solemnly to her as they went by. A covey of girls in school uniforms strolled down a side street, preceded by giggles, and when they came abreast of Miranda they lapsed into silence and smiled shyly, but squealed with delight after they were distant enough they would not seem rude.

Good God, she thought. *I'm paranoid*. For one moment, the area was empty, that doesn't signify evil, it doesn't portend a catastrophe, invite the apocalypse, it was just an eerie coincidence. *Everything is as it should be in paradise*, she thought, and absently rubbed the bruise on her cheek.

Miranda ruminated as she walked toward her hotel. Mr. Ross will turn up or he won't. It was not her concern. Being insufferably handsome with an elusive identity and surrounded by intrigue, possibly malevolence, made him interesting, but dangerous. Whoever said evil was banal? But that was nonsense, of course. Evil was seductively interesting and highly contagious.

By the time she had walked up the sloping drive to the Hotel Victoria she had overcome any fears she might have had for herself and was wholly enthralled with the fortunes of the missing man. Was he alive? Whose side was he on? She didn't even know who the combatants were or what was at stake. The fear had gone, but she felt uneasy, so far out of her own jurisdiction, so removed from the social parameters within which she normally lived. She thought of the Robert Heinlein novel, *Stranger in a Strange Land*. She had never read the book but the title described her situation perfectly.

She nodded to the concierge as she passed him on the lawn of the house next to the hotel, but he ignored her. Walking down the corridor into a tunnel of light streaming in from the west, she did not notice that all the room doors were ajar. When she got to her own door and found it open she was taken aback. She was further disconcerted by the tidiness of the room, by its emptiness. Then she realized her things were gone. Even the Heyerdahl book was missing. She stepped out into the corridor and looked at the room number. This was her room. She strode into the bathroom, hoping her belongings were there. Nothing. She must have been moved to another room. She hurried from room to room, peering through the open doors. They were all empty. The hotel was deserted.

Kafka, she thought. She was dreaming in real time. Her passport, her laptop, clothes, books, money, credit cards, police ID, proof of who she was, proof she was here, all gone. Good God, what was happening? She gazed into the hall; someone was coming, the concierge, he must have circled around from the back. No, it was a bigger man, a man with a weapon, a pistol, walking into his own shadow, walking toward her. There was nowhere to flee. She stood transfixed, waiting to see what he would do. Her fear was swallowed by anger — if only she could see over the walls of the labyrinth.

The man inhaled deeply on a nearly dead cigarette hanging from his lips and for a moment his familiar features glistened in a fiery light. He was close enough for her to breathe the rank smell of tobacco. Suddenly she kicked out at his head, twisting when she kicked so that as he reeled backward from the blow she landed on all fours. *Damn it*, she thought, *I'm too old for this*. She smoothed her dress down over her legs at the same time as she grasped for the fallen man's gun. He squirmed around, but she was faster. Holding the gun at his head she motioned him to stand up.

"You will not do this, *señorita*, I am policeman. *Carabinaros*."

She struck him sharply across the cheek with the gun barrel.

"Do not, *señora*," he said in a firm voice, while framing his face with his hands to ward off further blows.

Waving the pistol, she motioned for him to back into the clear light of the lounge where she could get a good look at him.

"We've met," she said.

"*Si*. We have met. I did not hurt you, *señora*, *señorita*."

He looked grotesque. The smashed stub of his cigarette was stuck to his lower lip but her kick had smeared ashes across one cheek, while the other cheek was livid with a gash of blood running from ear to chin. She motioned for him to sit and when he hesitated, she lashed out with her open hand and pushed him down. He missed the chair and sprawled at her feet. She planted her sandalled foot across his neck and pressed. She glared into his eyes. He was looking up the skirt of her dress. She rolled her sandal across his neck and stepped back.

He rose slowly to his feet, backed up a pace and sank into an easy chair. He was smiling.

"You will not kill me," he said. "I am policeman."

"From Santiago."

"*Si*, you remember, from your hotel, I was not alone, *señorita*. You should give me the gun. It is a nice gun, no? Like you have in Canada? No, this is revolver like in United States of America, yes? You should give me the gun. My friend, he will shoot you, no problem. I will not shoot you."

Miranda felt at an impasse. The man smiled; she could see tobacco stains on his teeth. Behind her, she could sense someone approaching along the corridor. She heard the clicking action of a semi-automatic. She set the revolver down on a table.

"*Gracias*," said the man, leaning forward to reach his gun.

A shot like a sharp sneeze pierced the air. The man sat back abruptly, as if he had been thrown. His eyes opened wide, he tried to smile but his features collapsed, he sat bolt upright for a moment, as Miranda took several deep breaths, then he slumped sideways on the chair. She stood absolutely still.

Slowly, a man edged by her into the light. The first thing illuminated was his nametag, Te Ave Teao; she saw this even before his face or his gun. He kept his gun trained on her, not her head but her body. He was not about to execute her, but it seemed likely he would shoot if she did not co-operate.

"There is another," she said.

"No, he is dead."

"You shot him?" She was surprised because she had heard nothing.

"He is dead," said Te Ave Teao, opening the palm of his free hand and spreading his fingers in a gesture that somehow indicated he had strangled the smoking man's accomplice.

"Are they police?" she asked, trying to conceal the flinching inside.

"Yes, they are very bad police. Now they are dead. Tonight, they will be buried; tomorrow, they were not ever here."

"What about me?" said Miranda "What do you intend?"

"What do you intend, yourself, *señora*?"

"You have the gun."

He leaned over and placed his semi-automatic on the table beside the dead man's revolver, and turned his back to her, gazing out over the dazzling Pacific. She did not move. He turned to face her.

"We will talk," he said, spreading both hands open, which, despite the conciliatory gesture, made her shudder.

They sat down on chairs facing each other, with the dead man slouched in the chair to the side.

"You are here to write romance," he said, as if he were explaining something to her.

"I am a detective sergeant with the Toronto Police in Canada."

"But you will write a fiction, no?"

"Yes."

"You are here because Maria sent you."

"Maria? Maria D'Arcy."

"Yes, she sent you to Rapa Nui."

"No, she did not. I do not know the woman."

"She knows you, *Señora* Quin*.*"

"Not any longer. She's dead," said Miranda.

A rage of emotion stormed over Te Ave Teao's

face and immediately disappeared behind a mask of inscrutability.

"Oh my God, I am sorry," she said. "She was from this island! She was, wasn't she?"

"She was my friend."

And? Miranda wondered. *And? And? And?*

"You will come with me," he said, rising to his feet. Clearly, she had no alternative.

"My clothes?" she asked, meaning, in fact, her passport and money.

"You will not need them."

Oh God, she thought, *either his side in this bunfight has a wardrobe department or I am about to be murdered.* She thought of Morgan, who at the oddest moments blurted out snippets of nonsense. *I see England, I see France, for God's sake, Morgan, you cannot see my underpants.* As she walked down the corridor to a waiting car, she was surprised by the feelings of nostalgia for her partner that crowded out surges of panic.

When she was shoved into the back of the police car and her head unceremoniously jammed down against the seat so she could not be seen through the windows, she felt strangely sad, as if she were feeling sympathy for someone else, not herself. It was all a case of mistaken identity and she was not who she thought she was.

The car lurched forward and rolled along, making its way among potholes and chickens, then picked up speed. It did not seem opportune to be taken hostage in the middle of the day. The seat smelled of old vomit and urine. She twisted and looked up; all she could see through the windows was open sky. They must be outside Hanga Roa. She thought she could hear the ocean through the passenger-side window over the complaints of the engine. She twisted further. There was no passenger, only a driver. It was not Te Ave Teao. She slowly sat up, apprehensive that the driver's arm might swing around and clout her down. When she was upright and could see his eyes in the mirror, she was surprised that he smiled, his eyes crinkling at the edges.

"*Hola!*" he said.

"Hello. Am I your prisoner?"

He did not answer. Perhaps that was not a smile, but sun-lines around his eyes.

"Well, of course, I'm your prisoner," she said.

He said nothing, but turned in half profile and she could see he really was smiling. He slapped the passenger seat with amiable vigour, indicating she should move up front, but he made no gesture to slow the car down as they careened along the coastal road, on and off stretches of pavement and gravel. To clamber over the seat, she thought, would mean a certain loss of decorum, given she was wearing a sundress. It would also make the situation seem like less of an abduction. That was obviously his intent. She climbed into the front, noticing with appreciation how extravagantly he diverted his eyes.

"*Hola!*" she said as she settled into the seat.

"*Hola!*" he responded. "*Bella señorita, hola.*"

She thought perhaps she had received a compliment.

She looked him over and he was good to look at. In the police office earlier, he had stayed in the background and she had hardly noticed him. Like Te Ave Teao, he appeared Polynesian, not from mainland Chile. He was her age, perhaps a year or two younger, it was difficult to tell. Gauguin was a racial imperialist.

Miranda realized her mind was strolling, that she was inappropriately relaxed. None of this was real. She gazed out the open window and the wind blew in her face.

Gauguin's paintings distorted Polynesian features, erased their individuality, made them stolidly exotic, but drawing from her observation of the native people on Rapa Nui, they were lithe and quick, with radiant complexions. *Like this man, they were beautiful,* she thought. *A sort of golden mean among races; the best of us all if we merged and became one.*

"What is your name?" she asked, turning to her abductor. "Te Ave Teao? Your name?"

"Matteo."

"Well, Matteo, where are you taking me?"

He said nothing. He apparently spoke no English. But he gestured toward fallen *moai* and crumbled huts of stone as they passed, as if he were giving her a silent tour of the island. They passed a small signpost reading "Rano Raraku."

"Matteo," she exclaimed. "Go back, can we go there? I know about Rano Raraku, it's the quarry. Please, go back." What a ridiculous request! She was being abducted.

To her surprise, he slowed the car, jockeyed it

around, and proceeded back to the ragged lane leading to a parking lot at the base of Rano Raraku.

She leaned low to look past him at the steep slopes of the volcanic quarry. The sun was still high and the *moai* cast brief shadows that made them shimmer in the light as if they were straining against the land, trying to move from the quarry, perhaps to the shore, where they would be given eyes and souls of the ancestors, and she felt sad for their bondage.

They got out and walked side by side, then single file, along the narrowing paths that forked and intersected like a maze, some routes leading to *moai* buried deep and fallen over, with only their noses showing, others seeming to go nowhere, just providing alternate footholds in the rough terrain, while others led to splendid isolated statues, their features exaggerated by the overhead sun, solemnly gazing into the distance with blind eyes.

When they reached the brink of the volcano, they stared down into the centre. It seemed to Miranda a magical place. The lake at the bottom was lined with reeds and glistened in the sunlight. *Moai* in various stages of completion hovered along the slopes all around, some resting on the grassy surface, some lying awkwardly prone, some partially embedded in rocky cliffs with their features cut only roughly into the stone.

She and her companion moved down among shadows into the lee of an overhanging wall that bore evidence of work by a thousand hands over innumerable generations, when the island was a world unto itself. A few tourists in the distance carefully walked the western rim.

It did not occur to her to signal for help. She and Matteo sat down close together in the shade of a *moai* they were examining, one of the minority with big ears draped close against the side of the head. They sat silently, observing the birds flying over the reeds and the bright water in the heart of the crater below them. After a long and comfortable silence, Miranda rose and ambled into the privacy of lengthening shadows cast by another *moai* close by. When she finished and was walking back, it occurred to her she could try to escape.

But from what, and to what? You cannot resolve the complexity of a labyrinth in haste. You'll run smack up against walls or into the jaws of the minotaur.

Matteo seemed in no hurry to go anywhere. She stood over him, against the sun. He looked up to her, then boldly let his gaze run down the length of her body and she realized he could see her in clear silhouette through the thin cloth of her dress. She stood perfectly still, like a statue, and watched his eyes, knowing he could not see hers against the sun. She smiled, and he could not see her smile, but he could see her perfect body, and this made her smile run deep inside.

There was for a brief time no past and no future, no inexplicable violence, no spiriting her off to God knows what. There was only the moment. If Matteo had made any gesture inviting her, she would have slipped down onto him as openly as if they were in love. The fact that he did nothing made him more endearing. But when he moved, only slightly, time began again and she no longer felt safe. They had already left two dead men in their wake, admittedly bad men, but very dead.

Where would he take her? Not back to Hanga Roa. She had seen a few small farmhouses set back from the road as they were driving along; maybe one of those, where she would be kept prisoner. Tortured? Ravaged? Executed? Entertained? She had no idea; there was nothing in her situation she could decipher. It was like staring at a panel of *Rongorongo*, the characters inscribed with deliberate precision, knowing they must mean something, a sequence of sounds in another language, a message in pictures, perhaps a complex grammar, a profound philosophical treatise, or perhaps little more than a listing of properties, ancestors, attributes, perhaps only an aid in the recitation of prayers. The problem was, no one alive could read *Rongorongo*.

That was how it all seemed to Miranda. Like *Rongorongo*. She said the word aloud. Matteo rose to his feet, rising into the sun, and strangely, his features looked hard, even menacing, as if she had said something terrible.

He took her roughly by the hand and they scrambled up a sequence of paths and over the rim of the volcano and then he released her hand and strode ahead down to the car, and she walked at a purposeful distance, making it clear she was in no way following meekly behind.

Surprisingly, he greeted her with a canteen of lemonade extended as a peace offering. She took it, but defiantly repeated the rhythmic syllables, *rongo-rongo*.

"*Si*," he said, shrugging affably. "*Rongorongo*." He wiggled his fingers, as if he were tracing invisible hieroglyphs in the air, and nodded his head in the affirmative. She had no idea what he was affirming. Was he being coy, playing the fool? Or was he genuinely conciliatory, forgiving her for some unknown violation? Was he covering for revelations of pain or sorrow even he couldn't explain?

They drove to Anakena, the only real beach on Rapa Nui. The sun was setting on the other side of the island, casting brilliant skeins of fire across the sky. The two little refreshment kiosks had been abandoned for the night; only a line of *moai* raised on a terraced *ahu* beyond the grove of towering palms were witnesses.

He helped her over the low stone wall where they had parked, and, instead of releasing her hand this time, he turned and let it slide along his arm so they were facing the same direction, and he guided her quite formally down the slope to the edge of the trees. They sat on a grassy clump, watching the light dance over the water until darkness spread through the air and glistened as the full moon slid from behind thin clouds above the *moai*, casting the surf in a filigree of silver.

Sometimes it happens this way, Miranda thought.

They listened to the water and the *moai* seemed to breathe behind them as a wide sky slowly wheeled overhead.

Miranda had no idea how much time had passed before she stood up.

"You want to swim?" she asked. Not waiting for a response, she stripped in the moonlight, dropping her clothes on the pebbled beach in a neat clump. She stood facing him. He rose to his feet, slowly removed his own clothing, never taking his eyes off hers, and when they were both naked, they joined hands and walked together into the low surf of the broad lagoon.

They swam languidly, not frolicking, but with sweet fluid motions, staying close as they circled round and around each other, their eyes locked now in an embrace that seemed to Miranda the spiritual equivalent of making love. As they touched bottom, wading into the shallows, she took his hand and drew him close to her. "His name is Matteo," she said to herself.

Standing beside their clothes, they kissed and the lengths of their bodies touched gently and firmly.

She tilted her head back and smiled. His eyes seemed filled with tears.

"You are very beautiful," she said.

He ran the back of his hand across her forehead to lift a damp lock of her hair away from her eyes.

"You are very beautiful," he repeated, his accent smoothing the words into a kind of lament.

There was a huge silence that seemed to swallow them whole. She did not move.

"I like you," she said.

"I like you, too."

Too!

She whirled away. She grabbed her clothes in a single motion and strode up onto the grass. She had never felt more vulnerable in her life.

"You speak English, you bastard!"

He scrambled after her.

"Bastard!" she repeated.

"What? Why am I a bastard? I speak English. It is an uncivilized language, in spite of Shakespeare, but that does not make me a bastard, Miranda Quin."

"Don't call me by name. Don't you dare." She held her clothes awkwardly in front of her. He held his in front of himself, as well.

"Why not, that is your name."

"Damn you. Have you any idea how stupid I feel?"

"Because I speak English.

"Because I'm stark naked on a beach with a total stranger."

"But I was not a stranger — if I did not speak English?"

"Yes! No! You don't understand a damn thing about romance."

"Maybe in Spanish, maybe in Rapanui. Apparently not in English."

"Don't use *apparently*."

"What?"

"The least you could do is speak broken English. You don't have to use words like *apparently*."

"Apparently not. I have an accent, does that help?"

"Shut your eyes, Matteo — if your name really is Matteo and not Bill or Roger or Bob."

"Bill?"

"Turn around, damn you, don't look at me naked."

"You or me?"

"What?"

"Naked. I don't look at you being naked, or being naked, I shouldn't look? If I get dressed first, is it okay to look?"

"Me, damn it. I don't care if you're naked or not."

"Well, that's a promising start to our relationship."

"We don't have a relationship."

"I think I'll get dressed, too."

Both of them struggled to get into their clothes. Both refused to turn their backs.

"There is no relationship."

"Even if we're dressed?"

"I'm going."

"Where? You have no place to go."

"The Hotel Victoria."

"You are not registered there, ever, since yesterday. It is on the other side of the island."

"Give me my passport, take me to the hotel."

"Your passport? And that will make you Miranda Quin! Now, do you think you are nobody? You look lovely in clothes, *bella señorita*."

"You look better naked."

"Is that a comment on my body or on my tailor?"

"Tailor! Nobody refers to their tailor."

They were both fully dressed, both a little bedraggled from donning clothes over wet skin. He held out his arm.

"Miranda."

She glowered, but took it.

They walked back to the police car under the whispering palms like old friends. Or, as an observer might have assumed, like brand-new lovers.

Now Matteo seemed to be driving with a purpose. He sensed her apprehension and flashed a grin, which, in the lights of the dashboard, unfortunately looked macabre, like a mask of death. She sighed, not frightened, but resigned.

"Was that you who smacked me?"

"Where, in your room? Possibly. If it was me, it would have been because we did not know if you could be trusted."

"And now you're all sweetness and light. What's made the difference? Seeing me naked?"

"Yes." He smiled into the darkness. "And finding we have enemies in common."

"The secret police from Santiago, the ones you killed?"

"The *Carabinaros*, they are dead, yes. You know the old saying."

"'The enemy of my enemy is my friend.' But why was I their enemy?"

"Because you are my friend. The friend of their enemy is the enemy, too."

"You're rescuing me, then, not abducting me. It's hard to tell."

"For me, too. We need you."

"Why did you trick me?" she said.

"About what?"

"About speaking English."

"You made the assumption."

"Bullroar," she said. "We spent hours together."

"In which you never once asked if I spoke English."

"It was sneaky, despicable, and cowardly."

"All that, for not speaking your language. What if I don't speak Swedish and Russian? How bad is that?"

Miranda laughed.

"*How bad is that?*" she said, giving the phrase an adolescent inflection. "Shuddup. Where'd you learn English?"

"UCLA?"

"Really?"

"Really."

"Okay, now I'm confused. Who are you, really? How did I get here? Come on, Matteo."

"Maria D'Arcy sent you." He did not try to explain who she was. He assumed Miranda was familiar with the name.

"No, Maria D'Arcy did not send me." He didn't seem to know; he had not talked to his friend when they exchanged drivers. "I came here to write a book. No one sent me." She paused. "Maria D'Arcy is dead."

The car veered, his eyes filled with moonlight, then went black. "You think no one sent you?" he said, ominously taking his foot from the gas peddle so they slowed to a crawl. "You are wrong."

"Damn it," she responded, she wrenched the steering wheel from his grasp so the car swerved around on the gravel. It came to a jolting halt against a low bank of earth under the doleful gaze of a small herd of shaggy island horses in the nearby grass who flared their nostrils, shook out their manes, and went back to grazing. "This is not funny," she said. He had not said anything to make her think that it was.

"No, it is not funny. It is dangerous," he responded.

"What is dangerous?"

"For you, being with us."

"Who is 'us'?"

"People. Some people on Rapa Nui. Not everyone."

"What? Is this a political movement? Have I floundered into a revolution?"

"Yes."

"Oh for God's sake!"

He said nothing.

"You're serious?"

"Yes."

"How can you have a revolution; there are only three thousand people on the island."

"Four thousand. Revolutions have started with less —"

"Fewer —"

"With fewer — did you just correct my grammar?"

"Diction — my partner says it's what I do, use pedantry to cover confusion."

"You are very confused."

"Yes."

"This is our ancestral home, you understand that. Some of us were born in Chile, or came back from Chile, but most have always lived here. We are Rapanui. When the Romans ruled Britain, Hoto Matua came here with his two canoes and landed on the beach at Anakana. Maybe it was not until Charlemagne and the Holy Roman Empire. We do not measure our lives and our generations by what happened in Europe.

"This became our whole world without end. *Te Pito o Te Henua* we described it, the navel of the universe. That is not a name. It is a statement. *Rapa Nui* means big paddle; this name was given to us by Polynesians from Mangareva in the nineteenth century, during the days of slavery. We did not need a name before that."

"But you are Polynesian, right?"

"That's like saying Englishmen are Angles and Jutes. We are a people and we are a continent — you think about that, we are a continent. It is not a geographical term, it is a statement of being. Like the rest of the world we have suffered through rises and falls in fortune, especially after those distant descendents of the Romans *discovered* us. Your ancestors. We were ten thousand strong and they wrote us into their history, and, as they did this, from the early seventeen hundreds, we dwindled, and when all our men were taken into servitude in South America, and the handful who returned brought back smallpox, we were reduced to a hundred and eleven. Then Chile annexed us, and those few of us who survived were imprisoned within the village limits of Hanga Roa for a few generations while the rest of the island was turned over to sheep."

She listened intently. In the glow of the dashboard and the light streaming in from the moon his features had taken on a messianic aura of solemn and resolute conviction. She felt humble. She reached over and turned off the ignition and the car lights faded and his face softened.

"Chile and the Church, they belong to the past. Americans in some ways have defined our present, they built the great runway for jet planes, for strategic purposes. Now tourists fly in and fly out, and we have *discovered* in the mirror of their eyes, and in the notebooks of scientific entrepreneurs, the past we had almost forgotten. This is the early morning of a new era. We want to possess our own future. It is not an unreasonable thing to wish for."

"Then secede," she said, knowing it was not that simple.

"Chile has a naval base here."

"Chile has a navy?"

"The base is important, as Gibraltar was important to the British, as Guam was important to the Americans. Strategically, not in military terms, but geopolitically —"

"Okay, please, you're overwhelming me with rhetoric."

"It is not rhetoric, Miranda."

"No, I didn't mean it that way. I just need to catch up."

"You have questions?"

"I have questions. First of all, about you. We nearly became intimate, my silent lover, my abductor, guardian, whatever you are — are you my friend?" She paused, looking at him quizzically. Asking the question made her feel vulnerable. "Okay," she said, "let's start with UCLA, what is that all about?"

"I received a scholarship, I studied in Valparaiso, I received another scholarship and with help from the Van Routenberg Fund and the Sebastian Englert Foundation I went to California."

"And studied what?"

"Medicine."

"You've got to be kidding."

"Why? What is wrong with medicine?"

"Nothing, nothing at all. It just seems an unlikely beginning for a career as a terrorist."

"Terrorist?"

"Freedom fighter," she amended.

"Che was a doctor, many revolutionaries are doctors — although, proportionally, not many doctors are revolutionaries. You want to help people, you want to cure their bodies, then you want to cure the conditions of their lives, their political souls."

"Political souls? And did you graduate?"

"In my last year I came home for a visit. I married and did not go back."

Miranda was stunned by the revelation of a domestic life, but she remained silent, attentive.

"My wife disappeared. We never found her body."

A profound spasm of sadness ran through Miranda's heart. She wished they had been lovers at the beach so that now she could comfort him or share his sorrow. "I'm so sorry," she said.

He said nothing for a lingering moment, gathering his resources. Then he continued, "In the last days of Pinochet, we were a nuisance. Nuisances are not to be tolerated. We kept a low profile and waited. It was not until after his fascist regime collapsed that his people discovered how useful we could be. The junta, regrouping in the shadows, now supports us. We represent a threat to the stability of the present government."

"The Pinochet bunch, were they brought in by the CIA?"

"It is not the first time American covert operations have backfired."

"Doing right for the wrong reasons?"

"Doing wrong for the right reasons. Look at Afghanistan, look at Iraq, even Cuba. Pinochet and his cohort were known as the Chicago Boys! The chiefs of the military and the *Carabinaros* under Pinochet deposed Allende, a democratically elected Marxist, with help from their American friends. Pinochet, himself, is finished, of course, a discredited old man, but the junta remains in the wings. Still fascist to the core."

"And what about you?"

"Fascist? No, of course not. But politics makes strange bedfellows, Miranda."

"So I've been told. If the present government of Chile goes down, you prevail. If you prevail, the government goes down. Either way, the fascist junta wins. Unless things stay as they are."

"The trick is to be Hitler's ally without being Hitler's apprentice."

"Sometimes it's better to sleep alone."

"The present government — their agents were going to eliminate you, my friend. And it was not the junta in charge when my wife disappeared."

"And have I disappeared, Matteo? And Mr. Ross, has he disappeared?"

"On a small island, to disappear is to die. You are here." He smiled. "I see you."

"And if you witness my life, I exist?"

"In this place I am your witness, yes."

"How does Maria D'Arcy fit into all this? If she was from Rapa Nui, why did she represent herself as a Brazilian heiress?"

"That was gossip of the nattering class, of no consequence."

"And did her husband know?"

"That she was Rapanui? Of course."

"And what's the connection with me?"

"As I said."

"No. She did not send me."

"Your colleague, he was here a year ago. Detective David Morgan."

"Yes?" She was wary now. "You aren't going to tell me he manipulated me into coming?"

"Possibly."

"No, if there is one person in the world I trust, it's Morgan."

"Good. That is a good thing to know."

Miranda sat back in her seat, feeling that somehow she had betrayed her partner.

"He told me about this place, how much he loved it."

"I know."

"You know?"

"He would not remember me, but we talked several times. One evening we talked by the harbour for a few minutes. Another time, in a restaurant, from adjoining tables. I was part of the background. But I know him, I studied him, I researched Mr. Morgan. And through him, I know you."

"He talked about me?"

"Not at all. But later, in Toronto, Maria opened a file on you. We like your mind."

"You what? Get serious."

"I am deadly serious, Miranda Quin."

Yes, he was, this strange man who spoke in passing of his wife's murder, who seemed both profoundly engaged with a political cause, and a grim observer of the forces at play. "Perhaps we should now drive on and meet with our friends," he said.

"Our friends?"

"Yes."

He backed off the low bank of earth that marked the edge of the road and began to drive without turning on the lights. Even in the fullness of the moon she could see the road only as a premonition. She felt a surge of relief, with each turn and twist, that he had managed to avoid slamming against remnants of ancient walls or smashing into wandering horses or crashing into the more indecipherable mysteries of the night. He negotiated the ragged terrain the same way she walked through her apartment in the darkness and knew where everything was, the way she had heard Inuit could trek through a snowstorm and read the landscape with all of their senses working together.

Looking up through her window, she recognized a sheer edge of Rano Raraku receding in the darkness. Then nothing was familiar, not even the stars in their strange configurations. The Earth was different in the southern hemisphere from the planet she knew. Just as she was about to tell Matteo she would be happier if he slowed down, he wheeled the car into a long laneway, and, after edging around gaping potholes, pulled up beside a squat farmhouse, stuccoed in moonlight.

When they got out of the car, Matteo drew his revolver and clicked off the safety. He motioned her to walk behind him, so that he was between her and the house. They approached the door slowly, and suddenly it swung open. A man's silhouette loomed against the flickering glow of a lantern. He too held a gun in his hand, but casually, pointed off to the side.

"Matteo?" he said, peering into the darkness. It was the voice of Thomas Edward Ross.

Miranda was astonished at how vulnerable Ross made himself, back-lit and framed in the doorway. Then she heard a shuffling in the darkness beside them and turned to see the shadowy figure of Te Ave Teao glide into view, the glint of a rifle barrel preceding him. She had witnessed the policeman's deadly efficiency at the hotel. Had they been enemies he would not have hesitated to shoot them.

Ross welcomed them in without fanfare. He did not seem surprised to see Miranda and she suppressed any show of astonishment on finding him unapologetically safe. It was best to maintain an air of detachment, as it suggested she had not ceded control. The four of them settled around a table in the middle of the low-ceilinged room that took up the first floor of the house. There was a ladder leading up to a loft and a doorway opening at the back into a lean-to kitchen. The furnishings were sparse and the walls showed years of smoke from kerosene lamps, but the air was fresh, the place was untidy, but clean, the way places are when men live without women, or women without men.

Te Ave Teao poured them each a shot of Scotch in coffee mugs. She looked from Ross to Matteo. She felt a cultural kinship with Ross that she found disconcerting; he was far more of a mystery to her than the islanders and probably more dangerous. Matteo clinked his mug against hers and raised it high before taking a gulp. He was welcoming her. She liked him best.

They talked very little. Miranda felt no urgency to understand her situation. Time was on her side; sooner or later they would have to explain. An hour passed and another and after several more Scotches the men dispersed to bunks against the walls, directing Miranda to sleep in the loft. She made a brief foray outside with the only lamp, then climbed the ladder, and, removing her sundress, sprawled out on a fresh sheet spread over a comfortable mattress that seemed to float in the moonlight. They would talk in the morning. She knew something of what these men were involved in, but they would clarify why she was part of it. She may not have been sent by a woman she'd never met, but she wasn't here by accident.

She heard someone moving around, the metallic click of a rifle, then nothing, just silence. After an interminable wait, she heard another click as the rifle was disarmed, then more silence, heavy like the dark shadows surrounding her in the loft of this strange little house, in the midst of this strange little war.

She slept, dreaming furiously, and awakened at dawn.

Feeling thick-headed from the Scotch and the confusion of the last few days, Miranda gingerly dressed and descended the ladder with extra care to avoid waking the others. She needed to go outside and then, if they were still asleep, she thought she might return to the comfort of the loft for another hour or two. She was feeling grubby, still in her underwear and sundress from the day before. At the bottom of the ladder she peered around into the shadows, and, not unexpectedly, saw her belongings from the hotel in a far corner, including a rather forlorn sheaf of comic books. It had not occurred to the men to offer her the opportunity to change before going to bed, and, oddly enough, it had not crossed her mind as a possibility.

Still standing at the base of the ladder, she realized the room was ominously quiet. She walked closer to each of the three bunks in turn and discovered them empty. She opened the front door to let in some light and the brilliance of the rising sun startled her so that she stepped back a pace before venturing out into the yard amidst a scattering of irritated chickens.

Well, at least I know we're facing east, she thought. *Unless dawn is different in the southern hemisphere.* She hurried off to the outhouse beside a small driveshed, but after being assailed by a wall of stale odour when she opened the door she slipped into the long shadow cast by the shed and peed in the open air, close to the spot she had used the night before.

The car was still there, so they must have walked, or someone picked them up. The car was not locked, but there were no keys in the ignition, nor under the seat or in the glove compartment. Even if she could cross the wires, she had no idea where she would go. At this point, her role was to wait.

Back inside the house she found coffee in a canister and with water from a large plastic thermos in the lean-to kitchen she brewed up a pot on the kerosene stove. As the small house filled with the aroma of fresh coffee, she sponged herself down at the kitchen sink, using brackish water from a hand-pump, and changed into a fresh outfit. She settled at the table with a mug of coffee and her makeup kit. There was bread on the table, but she was not hungry. Beside the bread there was a book. She hardly noticed it at first, it seemed so familiar. Then curiosity got the better of her and she picked it up, deciding she wanted to know whether this was the copy she got from Morgan, or was it the copy with the scribbled notes? It was the latter. She settled back and sipped her coffee and began to thumb through the book, looking for messages.

5

Te Pito O Te Henua

Morgan read Maria D'Arcy's suicide note over and over, trying to find an opening, some anomaly that would allow him into her mind. On the surface it was a characteristic blend of banality and despair. Her words expressed the self-absorbed anxieties of a person embracing death because she could think of no better alternative. The angular handwriting suggested strength of character; the message, vanity. He thought that suicides were victims of absolute solipsism. In the sad and contradictory rationale of self-annihilation, the world might be a better place when the suicide was gone because the world would cease to exist.

The only peculiar thing about the note was that it was addressed to him personally. They had never met while Maria D'Arcy was alive. How could she anticipate his involvement in the investigation of her death? She must have known that it would be perceived as murder. If she were actually murdered, though, the note only proved that she saw it coming and felt some moral imperative to exonerate her killer.

As he walked from the Annex over to Rosedale, Morgan ruminated about moral imperatives. Police work was invariably about morals. Lawyers and judges transcended morality, or slipped beneath it in the service of justice. Cops, however, even traffic cops, made moral decisions dozens of times a day. Sometimes foolish ones, sometimes kindly ones, sometimes wise.

Morgan stood on the stoop of the seigneurial house in Rosedale with his back to the door. He stared out through the shrubbery, past the well-coiffed garden, beyond the red-brick sidewalk edging the quiet street that ran through the winding tunnel of shade stretching under a canopy of towering silver maples. This would be a good place to live if you had the money. Maybe the dead woman was happy. Maybe that was why she died.

Morgan was still puzzling that one out when the door opened behind him.

"Mister Detective, I see you through glass, you are waiting?"

"*Señora*, yes, I was thinking." He had taken her to be staff on his first visit. "Do you live here?"

"I have my apartment over carriage house. It is at the garage, upstairs." She evidently was not certain he would know what she meant by "carriage house." The woman stepped back to let him in. She was dressed in black, not in a service uniform. She was wearing pearls. The strain on her face showed grief, but she was quite radiant.

"You have found him?" she asked.

"No, not yet."

"You have found what has happened to Maria?"

"No," Morgan repeated. "Not yet. I received a note. I would like something she has written to make a comparison. Perhaps we could go to her study."

"Of course, follow me. How you have received a note, she is dead?"

"That is part of the problem, *señora*."

"Maria Pilar Akarikitea"

"*Señora aka-riki-te-a*." He broke down the syllables, then let their melody embed in his mind.

There was nothing deferential about her as she turned and walked ahead of Morgan through the library into the study, but she did not object when he went through the drawers of a desk and fished out a small packet of letters tied with a faded blue ribbon. While she watched from the doorway, he compared the suicide note with one of the letters. The note was in English and the letter was written in what he assumed was Spanish or Portuguese. Each language asserted certain protocols of style: the Spanish, or Portuguese, had elegant flourishes, the English showed angular dips and rises. But they were in the same hand. He would take the letters with him, to be sure, but he felt a handwriting analyst would concur.

"I will bring you some tea," said the woman and vanished.

Morgan sat down at the desk. Three revelations had occurred to him simultaneously, vying with each other for primacy. The woman was a member of the family. The letters conveyed a story of personal loss or estrangement simply by being in the desk of the person who wrote them. The suicide note was a fake.

Back at his own desk, Morgan toyed with the note. It was clearly a fine sample of Maria's handwriting. But the message was too perfect, in precisely the words one would expect if the writer had studied the genre in a forensic manual and then written in exact imitation. And the handwriting was very deliberate. The penmanship in suicide notes usually revealed the traumatized psyche by slanting askew.

He picked up the letters and carefully slipped off the worn blue ribbon which had evidently been tied and untied many times. Maria Pilar had readily given her permission for him to take them downtown, but with tears in her eyes she asked for their safe return. It was then Morgan realized she was the murdered woman's mother, information she had not offered on her own, but confirmed when he asked her. Each letter was in an envelope, but as he shuffled through them, he noticed they all bore Canadian stamps that had never been franked. The escalating denominations of the stamps indicated the letters had been written over a period of years. They had been sealed in envelopes ready to mail, then torn open, probably re-read, and stacked with their predecessors. They were all addressed to the same person on Isla de Pasqua, someone called Te Ave Teao.

The telephone rang. It was Edwin Block.

"Mr. Morgan?" he said. He wanted reassurance.

"Yes."

"It's Eddie. From the ferry. How's everything going?"

"Couldn't be better."

"Keeping busy?"

"Can't complain."

"Can't ask for more than that."

"No, I can't ask for more than that."

"You're staying out of trouble? I guess in your job you would be. Dumb question."

"Yes, on all counts."

"Everything's going fine?"

"You asked that."

"Okay, then."

"Eddie?"

"Yeah?"

"What is it?"

"What?"

"What did you call for?"

"Well, they have a really good criminology course at Sir Adam Beck."

"So I hear."

"I was just wondering if you could, you know, write a letter for me? It's too late to apply, sort of, but if I had a letter from you I could probably get in."

"Eddie, I don't know you."

"Edwin Block. I work on the yacht club ferry. We've talked; I phoned you yesterday."

"I know who you are, Eddie, but I don't know anything about you."

"That's okay." He paused. "I can still get into funeral directing. They have openings." He paused again. "Could you write me a letter for that?"

"I'd have to write a letter saying I don't know you."

"That's okay. I don't think you have to know me. They need a character reference. Like, people aren't dying to be a mortician."

"Good joke, Eddie."

"Yeah, like, people are dying to get into cemeteries."

"I've heard that one, too. Is there anything else?"

"No."

"Goodbye, then, Eddie."

"Do I get the letter? Whoa, there goes the *Tangata Manu*."

"Pardon? Where are you calling from?"

"Cellphone. I'm working. The *T.M.* crossed right in front of us."

"*Tangata Manu*?"

"Yeah, it's a boat."

"Is it a ketch?"

"A ketch or a yawl. I can't see for sure."

"Where's the wheel?"

"Not a wheel, it's a tiller. Behind the mizzen. It's a ketch."

"And Rove McMan is at the tiller."

"He is, Mr. Morgan. How'd you know that?"

"I'm a detective, Eddie. Is the boat on the way in or on the way out?"

"Just arriving, I'd say. Must have come in the Eastern Gap."

"Good, I'll see you in half an hour. I'll bring you a letter on police stationary, vague enough you can use it for criminology or undertaking or cooking school."

"I hadn't thought about cooking school."

"Goodbye, Eddie."

Morgan hung up and jotted a quick note recommending Edwin Block for his adherence to rules, his initiative, and his persistence. *Tangata manu*, of course, was the name of Morgan's tattoo. When he had visited Easter Island he had had a small bird-man figure etched into his upper arm. The Rapanui call the stylized image *tangata manu*. Similar figures were abundantly displayed throughout the island, sometimes as pairs in balanced opposition. They were an expression of what anthropologists call the bird-man cult, which was really, as Morgan understood it, a form of governance with theological underpinnings, not much different from the British parliamentary system in relation to the Church of England, but more egalitarian, and much more efficient.

Tangata manu and *komari*, they were everywhere on the island, wherever there was a surface of exposed rock, a mound of stone, a rare slab of wood. *Komari* were stylized female genitalia, they looked like clamshells poised to spring open. It was a word, Morgan thought, less likely to be used to name a boat than *tangata manu*, although, God knows, boats were considered generically female.

The *Tangata Manu* was the ketch in the photographs off Rapa Nui, the boat Rove McMan sailed home through the Panama, Morgan was sure of that.

Miranda had laughed at Morgan's tattoo. *How James Dean*, she had said, although neither of them associated Dean with tattoos. It was precisely because Morgan was so unlikely a person to decorate his flesh that he had done it. His father sported a crown and anchor on his forearm from his stint in the merchant marine during the war. She thought the innocuous perversity of Morgan's rebellion was endearing.

Just as he was about to leave for the Harbourfront, his phone rang again. He was tempted to ignore it, but it might be Miranda, explaining where she was and why she had changed hotels.

"Morgan, here," he said, expecting her to say, "yeah, I recognized the voice," or some other hackneyed quip.

"Detective Morgan, it is Gloria Simmons."

For a moment, Morgan was at a loss. "What can I do for you?" he said.

"I've heard from Mr. D'Arcy."

"Oh, it's Ms. Simmons. You do have a first name."

"I don't know where he is, exactly."

"But you've heard from him."

"He's on Baffin Island."

"You already told me that, Ms. Simmons. He's working out the details of a mining deal. Zinc and copper, I think you said. The only zinc mine on Baffin is at Nanisivik on the shore of Lancaster Sound. At the very north end."

"You've obviously checked?"

"Rumour is, Nanisivik is closing down. Not much incentive for wheeling and dealing with an international consortium."

"No. But they've discovered another lode, a few hundred kilometres to the southeast. That's why Mr. D'Arcy was out of reach. They went in by helicopter.

It's very secret at this stage. No radio contact. There are billions of dollar at stake."

"Billions! And that's why he left his wife on ice. Does he normally go into the trenches?"

"Meaning?"

"He's a suit, a boardroom guy, he wears a cravat, does he usually work on site?"

"Mr. D'Arcy does what he has to do, whatever it takes."

"Whatever it takes? Do you always call him *Mister* D'Arcy? Seems rather formal."

The curious enunciation of D'Arcy's name, so precise and carefully non-sexual, he found both intriguing and oddly disturbing.

"I received a call," she said, after a polite silence that made it clear she was ignoring his invitation to discuss their relationship.

"From him?"

"No. That's what is puzzling. It was from an Inuk guide named Simonie Ipellie. He said Mr. D'Arcy and two other men were picked up along the coast on Baffin Strait by small boat. That was yesterday. They never returned. There's some rough weather out there, but they're getting together a search party when it breaks. Mr. D'Arcy left instructions with Simonie Ipellie, he was to call me. And ask for you."

"For me?"

"Yes."

"About what?"

"I assumed you would know. I was just to make the connection."

"Well, at this point, I don't know what I can do," said Morgan. Harrington D'Arcy was accustomed to manipulating others. Usually people in business are more covert, using experts in public relations, or more crass, buying co-operation. It annoyed him that D'Arcy did not bother with subtlety, making the assumption that Morgan could be deployed like a piece in a chess game. "If you hear from him again, let me know."

"Detective Morgan, I'm flying north in a couple of hours."

"To Baffin?"

"Yes. Do you want to come?"

"Why?"

"Because Mr. D'Arcy is missing. And you want him for murder."

"I thought you favoured the suicide theory."

"If she *was* murdered, I don't think Mr. D'Arcy killed her. But I do think you will only find out who did through him."

"Not if he's dead."

"Dead?"

"He's missing somewhere between Baffin Island and Greenland, he could easily be dead."

"I doubt he is dead, Mr. Morgan, but I believe he is in need of assistance."

"You're very close, are you? You can sense his needs."

"Will you be joining me? The plane leaves from the Island Airport at noon on the dot."

"On the dot. Company plane?"

"Yes."

"A jet?"

"Yes."

"At noon?"

"Yes."

"Have a safe flight, Ms. Simmons."

Morgan gave Eddie Block his letter on the ferry going across to the RTYC and chatted with him about the relative merits of careers in police work and undertaking, but not as a chef. Eddie had no idea where the *Tangata Manu* would be moored. He had never been ashore at the club, not beyond the landing dock. Morgan inquired at the porter's desk in the main building and was directed to an obscure site along a system of docks and dykes reserved for the less affluent or, perhaps, for those wishing a low profile.

Rove McMan was sitting in the cockpit when Morgan approached, working loose the knots in a tangle of rope with a marlin spike.

McMan waved the spike in an ambiguous salutation when he saw Morgan, and invited him aboard.

"Your boat?" Morgan asked.

"Yes," said Rove McMan. "She's a nice old thing."

"It actually belongs to D'Arcy, though?"

"She's registered in his name. She's not much for speed, but she's comfortable."

"You live on board?"

"Yes. You want to see below? It's quite homey."

"This is the boat in the Easter Island pictures."

"There's no secret about that, Detective. Its name is Rapanui —"

"For bird-man, I know."

"Well done, Detective."

Irritated, Morgan turned and backed down the companionway steps into a beamy cabin that seemed more like an indulgent bachelor's den than the austere quarters he had expected. The space was richly appointed with deep blue Ultrasuede and bright mahogany. There were various chrome and copper instruments and a stainless-steel galley. Morgan quelled a pang of envy that anyone might feel for the life of a wanderer, and moved forward beyond the head and sail-locker into the fo'c's'le, which was cluttered with gear.

When he turned back into the main cabin, Rove McMan was peering down at him through the companionway hatch. "Everything all right down there, mate?" he asked.

Morgan was looking for something, but he was not sure what.

"Yeah," he responded, sitting down on one of the bunks.

"You got time for a sail?"

"No. Thanks. You were just out."

"Right. But I can always go for another."

"You sailed this back from Easter Island yourself?"

"Through the Panama and up the inland waterway."

"Around Cape Hatteras?"

"Yes, that's the only difficult part. You're on open water there. Apart from a couple thousand kilometres on the Pacific."

"You need to carry a lot of ballast for stability."

"No, Detective. A boat like this has all the ballast she needs built into the keel."

"Then what's under here?"

"Where?"

"Under the floorboards."

"Storage tanks. For water. Farther aft, for fuel."

"You mind if I look?"

"I don't see why."

"You don't mind?"

"I don't see why you'd bother."

"But I'd like to. Of course, I can get a warrant."

Rove McMan gazed at him, with the light shimmering behind so that Morgan could not see his features. But his voice suggested forbearance. He was not pleased, but he was resigned to whatever was about to happen.

"It's up to you, mate."

Morgan lifted back the sisal floor-covering and raised a large wood panel to reveal a fibreglass tank the size of a child's coffin, with the lid bolted in place.

"Satisfied, Detective? It's a freshwater tank."

"With a removable top. Could you hand me a wrench?"

McMan descended into the cabin and retrieved a large wrench from a toolbox behind the companionway steps. He raised it, as he had the marlin spike, in an ambiguous gesture, then turned it innocuously to the side and handed it to Morgan.

When the bolts were removed, Morgan grasped the lid with his fingertips and wiggled it loose while McMan watched impassively.

Whether he expected to find treasure or a mummified corpse, Morgan wasn't sure. Whatever would be revealed, he knew it was important. At first it seemed like packets of heroin or cocaine, neatly wrapped in airtight plastic, taped meticulously against contamination. But the shapes were unusually long and thin, like paddle blades or embalmed forearms, stacked neatly to fill the casket to the brim. He lifted one, it was surprisingly light.

"You know what's in here," he said to McMan.

"Of course."

"Hand me a knife."

"Be careful," said McMan, handing him his knife.

Morgan slit open the plastic wrap around one of the packets. A funerary odour of old wood and oils seeped into the air. He unrolled the covering on his lap until a flat slab of ancient wood emerged in the dull cabin light, gleaming with a patina of tiny carved symbols. He held it up. Despite its obvious age, it did not seem brittle.

"You know about *Rongorongo*?" asked McMan in a curiously conciliatory voice.

"Yeah," said Morgan. "This is quite a treasure."

"There's another tank up forward, maybe two dozen altogether."

"All old?"

"Well, the wood is, for sure."

"How do you know that?"

"That's *toromiro*. Exceptionally rare. Most of the tablets extant are *mako'i*, some people call it *miro*, but it's not the same." He seemed quite pleased to be able to elucidate. "In the sixties, Thor Heyerdahl took seeds from the last *toromiro* tree back to a botanical garden in Sweden. I don't know why, since he was Norwegian. On Rapa Nui, *toromiro* had all but disappeared by the seventeenth century, before Europeans arrived."

"Why you?" said Morgan.

"What, why am I the keeper of the island coffers? Good question. It just happened that way. I lived there for five or six years."

"You're not sure?"

"I'm not much for calendars. Months and years are useful for predicting currents and weather, that's about it. I sail by dead reckoning: you're where you're at today based on where you think you were yesterday and where you hope to be tomorrow. It's all about trade winds for me."

"There must be a fortune here," said Morgan, ignoring the lesson in navigation and lifestyle. "There are only a few of these known to exist in all the museums of the world. Do you know what they're worth?"

"To whom, Detective?" He shrugged amiably.

"Several million, maybe more."

"But only if they were released a few at a time. Otherwise you'd saturate the market."

"You're on the wrong tack there, I'm afraid. These *Rongorongo* have more value than anything you'd get at Sotheby's."

"Explain."

"Well," said McMan, his voice dropping an octave for added authority, "written here is the Rapa Nui Declaration of Independence, Detective Morgan. This is their political legacy. You ever heard of the *Domesday Book*, when William the Conqueror surveyed his offshore domain and turned British geography into history, fixing forever the rules and roles of Britain in print. These are their *Domesday Book*. This is their history, their link with the ancestral past, when they were *Te Pito o Te Henua*, the only place in the world."

"Even if no one can read it?"

"It will be deciphered."

"You seem certain. By whom?"

"Maria was working on it."

Morgan's head reeled with improbable connections. "That's why Miranda is there," he said. He had the feeling she had been sent.

"I don't know about that. I don't know Miranda."

"Miranda Quin?"

"No, I've never met Miranda Quin. I knew someone called Miranda, once. On Ibiza. We were young and, well, you know, we didn't have last names back then. I doubt it was Quin. She wasn't Irish. On Ibiza, it was …"

As McMan prattled on, Morgan decided he was a peripheral character in the complex scenario, playing his role without even knowing he was inside a play. Or else. Or else he was Prospero, controlling the entire illusion, including his own desultory appearance. It was possible. He was not stupid.

"… and of course, there was Miranda in *The Tempest*, Prospero's daughter, but …"

If he was a master illusionist, he was letting the machinery show from the wings. Almost certainly, he was the guardian of the trove only because it was stored on a boat, and in return he got to treat the boat like his own.

"There is nothing illegal, here, Detective Morgan. There's no law that says *Rongorongo* cannot be hoarded."

"The Chilean government might not be happy to have it in circulation."

"I really don't think they care."

"On the contrary," said Morgan. "If these are historical artifacts representing the sovereignty of the island, I suspect the Chileans would be vitally interested."

"I suppose you're right. The truth is, I haven't given a great deal of thought to all this, not until Maria died. I've been waiting to speak to Harrington. We'll have to sort out what is to happen — sooner or later, something has to be done with old things like this."

"Old things like the *Rongorongo*, or the boat, or you?"

"Ah. All three, I suppose. But wither we go, that's up to Mr. D'Arcy."

"You might be waiting a while, my friend."

"Are we friends? Isn't that pleasant. And are you suggesting Mr. D'Arcy is no longer in charge of the world?"

"He seems to be missing."

"Just because you don't know where he is? Detective Morgan, Mr. D'Arcy is where Mr. D'Arcy is."

"Well, Mr. D'Arcy seems to be adrift in Baffin Strait, somewhere off the coast of Greenland."

"Really? That seems unlikely."

"That he's in the Arctic or that he is adrift?" If Harrington D'Arcy was not adrift, then he was dead in the water. "What is Maria D'Arcy's connection with Easter Island?" The two of them secured the top to the fibreglass casket and replaced the floorboards and sisal carpet. "Do you know someone on the island called Te Ave Teao?"

The sailor looked into his eyes, flashed a thin smile, and shrugged noncommittally.

"Te Ave Teao," Morgan repeated. "Were they lovers?"

Again the man flashed the thin smile. "I couldn't say, Detective. The only passions that catch my interest have to do with strong winds and billowing sails."

Morgan shrugged in turn and gave strict instructions that the Rapa Nui treasury was to remain undisturbed until he returned. Then he went back to the clubhouse and telephoned his superintendent. His cellphone was as usual in a drawer in his office desk, his Glock semi-automatic in the gun locker. He preferred to travel light.

Rufalo was no more surprised than Morgan himself that he was flying north in a private jet to interview Harrison D'Arcy, especially since the man was no longer unavailable but actually missing. Morgan didn't explain his conviction that the mystery surrounding Maria D'Arcy's death was linked to a murky connection between Baffin Island and Easter Island. Harrington D'Arcy seemed the most likely person to clarify that connection. He mumbled something about Mohammed and mountains, while denying he was the Prophet or that D'Arcy was a mountain. But he was going. Morgan's standing joke was that for him, *North*, the concept so revered by Canadians who haven't been there, began at Highway 401, running across the top of Toronto. Yet on the vaguest of premonitions, the fuzziest of speculations, he was on his way to the Arctic.

When he emerged from the clubhouse, McMan was waiting for him at the bottom of the steps in front of the sweeping verandah. He held an old-fashioned Raleigh bicycle leaning away in a gesture of offering. "Just leave it at the terminal," he said.

Morgan took the bicycle from him testily. He did not like being subject to the initiative of others, as if his own free agency were only an illusion. He did not like someone else knowing what he intended to do before he did. He listened as McMan gave him instructions on which route among the forking paths would lead to the Island Airport. If he went straightaway, he could be there before noon.

Setting off on the bike into an avenue of shrubbery and trees, he felt mildly embarrassed about his own petulance and gave McMan a backward wave over his shoulder. He was sure the sailor would be watching. The laneway broke into the open and skirted down almost to Gibraltar Point before tucking back in toward the airstrip. In other circumstances, it might have seemed a charming ride.

Leaning the borrowed bicycle against a security fence that he scaled with no trouble, Morgan strode across a sward of grass onto the tarmac. From a distance, he recognized Gloria Simmons approaching an executive jet positioned for takeoff. She walked with her head tilted forward like someone wearing glasses in the rain, only she wasn't wearing glasses and it wasn't raining. The wind blew her skirt taut against her thighs and her open jacket flapped around her shoulders, accentuating the thrust of her breasts in a thin cotton blouse. Morgan nodded, surprised at his response, and aware that she wasn't dressed for the Arctic. She nodded back, showing no surprise that he was there, nor at his strange arrival.

By mid-morning, none of the men had reappeared. Miranda was apprehensive and restless. She could see the occasional rooster-tail of dust rising from vehicles passing beyond her line of vision in the sullen heat and she realized that she was not a prisoner, had perhaps never been a prisoner, and was free to leave. But how? Where to? She washed yesterday's sundress and underwear using dish detergent and hung them outside to dry. Although it was the tail end of the rainy season, the weather had been inordinately dry, verging on a drought, and surprisingly hot. The sundress was all she needed, although she had been told the evenings could turn suddenly cool. She had packed according to her desire for a semi-tropical climate.

She could always buy cold-weather gear if she needed it.

She walked to the edge of the property marked by a low stone wall, beyond which the grasses were only a little longer and more tangled, the rubble only a little less orderly. She wondered if there was a boulder, a rock, a pebble, a grain of sand, on the entire island that had not been arranged and rearranged by human hands? Ten thousand people for a thousand years on an island the size of Manhattan. Were there pockets of earth and grit and gravel that did not contain the granular fragments of human bone?

She settled into the shade of the crude latticed portico and nursed the brackish dregs of coffee in her cup, still lukewarm from the ambient heat. She stared at the Heyerdahl book on the raw wood table as if it were a distant relative, familiar but inscrutable, then picked it up, leaned back in her rickety chair, opened it to the flyleaf where she scrutinized the autograph, trying by sheer force of mind to decide whether or not it was real. Not that it mattered. In any case, the equation below it was in a different hand, written with great deliberation. *Four over five equals two zeros. Or was it infinity?* Probably infinity, since two zeros on their own are pointlessly redundant. So four over five equals infinity. Infinity or eternity? Boundless space or illimitable time, each was the measure of the other. She proceeded to thumb through the book, front to back, then back to front, and front to back, again and again, waiting for the revelation that, surely, she felt, was at hand.

And slowly an idea began to coalesce in her mind. She could see her reflection in the glass chimney of the kerosene lantern hanging over the table. In this age of instant communication, when coded messages could be embedded in the most innocuous email, why use something as cumbersome and fragile as a book to convey dark secrets? Either the book was just a book or this particular book was imbued with hidden meaning before the advent of electronics and the person who sent it from Toronto had been unable to break into its elusive cache.

Miranda stood up, prepared to let out a whoop, or the Canadian version, a fist pumped to shoulder height followed by a cadenced "*Yeah!*" but her triumphant exclamation was squelched as she caught sight of a roiling fantail of dust moving up from the main road. As the red Land Rover lurched into view she clutched the book in her hand and receded among the shadows of the portico, backed through the door into the house, wheeled and stumbled across the ground floor, and ventured out again into the light at the rear. Keeping the building between herself and the new arrivals, she scurried through the low underbrush, then made her way to the side in a running crouch ,and burrowed under a pile of volcanic boulders where she was completely hidden, but had a good vantage on the grounds of the house.

The Land Rover was new, the red paint, the colour of congealed blood, hardly grazed enough to give the accumulating grime a purchase, the fenders only a little dented by flying gravel. Miranda had seen it parked outside what she now understood was a Chilean Naval Base. Even before spotting it coming up the lane, she could tell by the thumping roar of the engine and the aggressive swirl of dust in its wake that it was a government vehicle and that had made her wary, so she was surprised when the first two people out of the vehicle were Matteo and Te Ave Teao. For a moment they stood squared off in front of the house as if they had never seen it before. Then three other men in uniform got out of the Land Rover. Two of them carried what looked like Kalashnikov AK-47s slung at the ready. Could be Colt M4 Carbines, but whatever, they were lethal. Miranda pressed down into the coarse grit on the floor of her shallow lair, then lifted her head and came face to face with a human skull.

She had taken refuge in what appeared to be a makeshift grave. She squirmed around so that she could reach out and touch the skull with her finger tips. The bone felt smooth and porous, brittle around the eye sockets, suggesting her host in this shadowy cavern, while not ancient, had been there awhile. Miranda realized she was still clutching the Heyerdahl book in her hands and she set it close to the skull, then twisted onto her side so she could look upwards, and, as she had begun to suspect, the scowering visage of a *moai* pressed down on her. The forehead and chin formed the edges of her lair, while the nose crumbled into rubble from which shards and slivers of human bone protruded. The pursed lips leered directly above her head. This must have been a statue that had fallen in transit, or had been attacked or abandoned and pushed over. The head was severed from the torso, and the body segments must have been levered into position against the head to form a burial chamber for ensuing generations.

When Miranda looked back into the light, the five men were in exactly the same position, no one had moved. The ominous stillness was suddenly shattered by the staccato burst of sustained gunfire. Instinctively, Miranda ducked her head low against the ground and her body went rigid. She heard shouts and looked up again. The walls of the house were peppered with bullet holes. Silent wisps of dust drifted away from each hole as threads of debris dribbled down. Matteo was walking toward the house, past Te Ave Teao. One of the armed men in uniform was waving his weapon to indicate direction or to ensure compliance. Te Ave Teao glanced in her direction or past her, at the quarry.

Matteo stepped into the dappled shadows of the portico and a moment later Miranda heard breaking glass, then plumes of smoke pushed at him from behind as he walked back out of the shadows and into the clear, with rising cascades of flame shimmering behind him that built quickly into a raging smokeless inferno.

One of the inscriptions in the book, taken from Wilfred Owen's vision of Hell, burned through her mind: *I am the enemy you killed, my friend.* Or vice versa.

She was meant to be inside.

6

The Dying Light

Gazing down from a cloudless sky as the sprawling Toronto cityscape gave way to settled landscape striated by road-lines that gathered here and there into town grids and then petered out into endless wilderness, Morgan was restless. They talked very little. Gloria Simmons seemed to feel her partner was in need of assistance, as she put it. He was missing, for goodness' sake, in the Arctic, a long way from the office towers that seemed to define her. And Morgan was playing a hunch: despite the coroner's report, he was certain he was dealing with murder and D'Arcy had virtually chosen to be a suspect, he wanted Morgan to come after him.

And Morgan had. He settled back and tried to make himself comfortable in the plush leather seat. He thumbed through a magazine and a couple of brochures. He asked how long it would be until they got there.

"It's about the same as flying from Toronto to Dublin," Gloria Simmons explained. "We're a big country."

She was sitting opposite, her long legs folded one over the other so that he self-consciously closed his eyes. She had the alluring qualities of an ice sculpture, but none of the transparency. More like the stillness of a flame caught in a photograph, shaped like a woman by an accident of light. He drifted into reverie about women, about love, about making love. Miranda was on Easter Island, he thought about her. He thought about Easter Island. He thought about his affair there that had seemed, until now, an isolated episode in his life.

Why did he think of it as an *affair*, he wondered? There was no guilt involved. He had violated no commitment. When he had been with her, with the other woman, there was something about their relationship that made him think of Miranda, but when he returned home, Miranda, his partner and friend, mirrored only herself. Why *the other woman*? They had met, they spent a few days together, they fell briefly in love. And, oddly enough, they were never actually lovers.

Iqaluit loomed through the overcast sky as the Hawker 800 banked steeply and sliced down toward the runway, straightening at the last moment so the earth seemed to pitch upwards before levelling off. *Good landing*, Morgan thought. He had never flown in a corporate jet before. He had been astonished at the burled walnut woodwork and the plushness of the leather seats. He was irritated by his pleasure in the opulence. Through the entire flight he had felt comfortable, but not relaxed, not the way the immaculate Ms. Simmons was, from the moment she stepped inside. This was her world. He was an outsider.

He gazed through a window as the jet taxied across the asphalt. There was more activity than he had expected for Baffin Island, even though this was the territorial capital. Helicopters and Twin Otters flanked the access pavement. Another executive jet painted with a sinister black sheen, no doubt to intimidate competitors and clients, was tucked in beside the green and grey storage sheds that blocked his view of the townsite. What had seemed from the air like a children's toy, a clump of brilliant yellow plastic rectangles, turned out to be a brilliant yellow plastic modular airport terminal. Seldom had he seen a work of architecture so fully unsympathetic to its environment, which, from his limited vantage, looked austere and monochromatic. *Perhaps that is the point*, he thought. *It's comical, a cheering edifice in the bleakness of the North.*

Hearing a commotion behind him, Morgan turned to locate Ms. Simmons amid the white leather, stainless steel, and dark wood, but she was apparently behind closed doors in the back cabin. The doors to the back cabin opened with just a touch of drama and an entirely different woman walked out. Gone were the heels, replaced by heavy leather Vasques, and the skirt had given way to coarse twill kakis, the pristine blouse to a plaid work shirt with a stylish touch of leather at the collar tabs, and the impenetrable look on her face now seemed neither sullen nor superior but, rather, an expression of grace and forbearance.

Striding across the tarmac and up the steel steps into the terminal, Morgan kept pace, but there was no question about who was in charge. This was fine with him. Gloria Simmons spoke to a man who looked like he'd rather be out hunting than hanging about in an airport, presumably about her bags — Morgan was travelling exceedingly light — and then they passed through the yellow cubist building, down another set of metal stairs, and slid into one of two waiting taxis.

"The Frobisher Inn," Gloria Simmons said to the driver, and as he started up he chortled and said something to her in a brief rhapsody of breathy and meaningless sounds, to which she answered in an equal flurry of noises from deep in her mouth, without moving her lips except to shape a smile of unutterable beauty. Morgan was stunned.

She glanced at him. "Inuktitut, the Inuit language. I am an Eskimo, Mr. Morgan. An Inuk. If there were two of me, I'd be Inuuk."

Morgan followed her into the small lobby of the hotel apartment complex on the hill overlooking Iqaluit. There was apparently a suite set aside for D'Arcy Enterprises. She seemed entirely at home here, among casually dressed business travellers and overdressed visiting civil servants and roughly dressed men passing through, hunters, perhaps, and anthropologists, almost all of them male. But she had seemed equally at home in an office tower at King and Bay. Morgan watched as she arranged for their rooms adjoining the suite which was technically still occupied by Harrington D'Arcy.

Later, after he had picked up toiletries and a few clothes and some boots in the store off the lobby, they met for dinner in the hotel dining room. Sitting by a window with Frobisher Bay spread out below them, still brilliant with daylight although by now night would have enclosed Toronto in its turgid grip, Morgan took the initiative.

"I take it your boss hasn't turned up," he said, wondering if Miranda had. Baffin seemed like a parallel universe, just out of reach. He glanced at the candle flickering between them, a concession to convention during a high summer evening in the land of the midnight sun.

"No, he seems to have disappeared."

"Which is not a good sign."

"Not if he wants to be found."

"Where do you think he is?"

"That's a good question."

"And?"

"It's a good question."

"Are you from …" It seemed absurd to say, *from around here.*

"From here. Yes, born in Apex."

"Which is where?"

"Down the road. It's a suburb of Iqaluit."

"Really, Iqaluit has suburbs?"

"Suburb — singular. It's called Apex."

Morgan was determined he wasn't going to say, *you don't look Inuit.*

"My father was Norwegian," she said, anticipating the question he wouldn't ask. "Or so I've been told."

"An anthropologist? Using Baffin as a base camp for a run at the Pole? Movie star?"

"Laplander, here to advise on making caribou behave like reindeer."

"And to make Inuit behave like Laps? I take it he failed."

"He fathered several children. By different women. I never met him."

"Would you want to?"

"Why?"

Morgan shrugged. Her personal history was beyond his imagination. She was a white Inuit, beautiful beyond words, a highly successful lawyer. She was the child of a brief liaison, brought up between cultures at odds with one another.

Reading his thoughts once again, she said, "I was born into benevolent poverty, surrounded by love and squalor. My mother froze to death walking home after a binge when I was seven. My aunts and grannies and sisters and cousins brought me up and pushed me out when I was old enough to look after myself. Shipped south with tuberculosis, finished high school in Ottawa. University, honours chemistry, an ideal prelude for law school. Articled for D'Arcy. This is my first time back without an executive entourage. It's just you and me, Morgan, and the Great White North."

He wondered how many stories her story concealed? It was eloquent in its simplicity and fairly humming with what she'd left out. Her eyes were deep brown, but in the flickering candlelight they seemed hazel, like Miranda's. Her blond hair, pale with amber highlights, like sunlight through honey, was nothing at all like his partner's. He felt strangely drawn to this woman, in part because he knew her so little — he had never met anyone who seemed to exist so completely in the moment, her personality revealing nothing, concealing nothing. She simply was who she was.

"Are Laplanders blonde?" he asked.

"Yes," she said, smiling. This was the first time she had smiled at him directly, although he had seen her smile occasionally for the benefit of others. "Herders on one side, hunters on the other. Sounds like a lawyer with political ambitions, doesn't it?"

"Do you have political ambitions?"

"Political? No."

"Are you a hunter?"

"Not at all. But I'm sure if I had wanted to learn I would have been very good." She didn't seem to be joking. This struck Morgan as quite endearing.

They lapsed into comfortable silence and focused on the thick, rare slabs of peppered caribou that had been served to them surrounded by garden vegetables sautéed in butter. It was more than Morgan could eat, but his slender companion devoured hers and eyed the blood-red portion that remained on his plate.

"No," she answered to his unasked question. "I'll need room for dessert."

Over coffee, the quality of silence between them thickened so that Morgan became aware there were things that needed to be said. He wasn't sure, though, which of them was suppressing the need to speak. She was gazing outside and he followed her gaze. Frobisher

Bay had taken on the patina of burnished pewter, while the rugged land reaching away on either side had lapsed into shadow. Where the water met the sky a shimmering band of yellow tracked the hidden sun's movement as it swooped low on the horizon behind them. Above, a massive grey cumulous cluster pressing down promised rain.

What he had seen as monochromatic when he arrived, he now saw as the expression of "God's grandeur" — a phrase from a poem that filled him with pleasure because the right words trumped his habitual denial of supernatural powers. Morgan's favourite poet at school had been Gerard Manley Hopkins, not for his irrepressible devotion, but for the passion infused in his language that caught the reader's innermost yearning to transcend. Transcend what? Whatever. He couldn't remember.

Morgan caught in the window the reflection of a tall lean man approaching the table and turned at the same time as Gloria Simmons to face him. Even before registering that the man was in uniform, Morgan recognized by the casual precision of his movement that he was a Mountie. *No one else carries authority with that disconcerting mixture of humility and self-assurance*, he thought. He could still see the residual effect in Miranda's confident demeanour of her three years with the corps.

The constable nodded to Morgan, but leaned down and spoke privately to his companion. She turned away so that their conversation was nothing more than a buzz. Several times, Gloria Simmons flinched, but her voice never rose to an audible level.

After what seemed an interminable lapse, the Mountie straightened to his full height, nodded again in Morgan's direction, and moved away. Other diners glanced up as he passed their tables.

Morgan waited patiently for her to speak.

"They have found him. Or at least they have found where he isn't."

"D'Arcy?" he asked, but he had no doubt.

"They found one survivor."

"Where?"

"Between Aberdeen Island and Baffin Island. He was wearing a survival suit. The Inuk guide. The RCMP say the boat was smashed by a pod of whales."

"What kind of whales?"

"What difference does it make? Bowhead, I imagine. Three others are presumed dead."

"Did they recover the bodies?"

"Life jackets, no bodies. One survival suit and it was on the hunter. It was his boat. He was floating near the wreckage. He managed to call in before they went down."

"What do *you* think?"

"I think we head north as fast as we can."

"Do you think he's alive?"

She stared at him as if she were trying to fathom how much he understood from what she had said, how much didn't add up. As they rose from the table, the pallid fringe of light across the outer edge of Frobisher Bay faded to black. Morning would not show for an hour or two, depending on the weather. Morning farther north of Iqaluit had already begun.

***

Miranda gazed at the skull, into the empty sockets that had once held living eyes. It was curious there was only one intact skull other than her own in their shared grave. Fragments of at least one other that seemed relatively recent revealed themselves when she ran her hand through the rubble beneath her. She looked back at the whole skull. It was leaning toward the Heyerdahl book in a grim tableau that made of its emptiness a mockery of knowledge contained in books. She closed her eyes and the skull remained in her vision, a *memento mori* demanding she accept its dictum, *remember, you too will die*. The exact translation from Latin: *have to die, must, will? Remember*. Death is inescapable, mortality is a terminal condition.

"No!" she said in a whisper. *Think Descartes: I think, therefore I'm not dead yet*. She took a deep breath and rolled onto her back. The ghastly roar of the fire was beginning to subside. She could hear the insistent rhythm of her blood beating against the inside her skull. *Memento vivere. Remember to live*.

When she was sure that the red Land Rover had left, and the fiery pillar had died to a pulsing flicker, she edged out of her burial chamber. The police car was gone as well. It was dusk and night would fall suddenly. She wanted to think clearly and that meant getting out into the open, even if it made her vulnerable. She clambered over the wall and was almost at the smouldering ruins when she realized she was not alone. A man was standing perfectly still with his back to her, his head tilted, staring into the embers.

He didn't turn when she approached, but when she was almost beside him, he said: "I'm glad you're okay."

"You looking for me or your book?"

T.E. Ross turned slowly and the sinking sun caught fleeting signs of concern on his face that softened immediately to a cheerful grin.

"Both," he said, glancing at the book clasped against her like an inadequate breastplate.

She looked down. At this point, it was her only possession, it gave her security; she tightened her grip, pressing it into her chest.

"That's mine, of course," he said, reaching out for it.

"I know," she said, and irrationally held it closer.

"Okay," he said. "Let's go. We'll have to walk."

Miranda followed him as he led the way down the lane toward the coast and into the blackness that swallowed the sun.

She clutched the book like some sort of talisman until they got to the main road and she could hear the low surf shredding itself against the ragged volcanic shoreline and the stars suddenly appeared in the great southern firmament as if an invisible hand had turned on the lights. It was bright enough that she could see nuances in Ross's face suggesting he was confident, wary, and concerned perhaps for her. She held the book out to him. Without saying anything, he took it and turned along the road, picking up a quicker pace, his body language an invitation for her to stay sociably close.

Over the next two hours, only one car came by, a Jeep, its single intact headlight giving them plenty of warning. They crouched low behind a small bit of scrub brush while it passed, leaning into each other as if somehow as a tight clump they'd be less visible. They walked on, then cut down an overgrown side road, then another and another, traversing what seemed to Miranda an invisible maze.

"We're nearly there," he said as they veered onto a ragged path toward the sea. When they got to the edge, Miranda marvelled at how the vast Pacific was brought into a more human perspective by the infinite canopy of dazzling stars, despite the roiling surge of water grinding against the rocks beneath them. She leaned forward. The rocks were far below. She realized they must have been climbing for much of their walk and were now poised at the edge of a precipice.

Ross took her by the hand and eased forward. She hesitated, he drew her on, she pulled back.

"Trust me," he said.

"Why?"

"You really don't have an alternative."

Well, she thought, *I could push you over and walk away. Or be dragged to my death by your side.* "No," she said, "I suppose I don't."

"Follow my footsteps precisely. Is there sufficient light?"

"Sufficient," she said. "Quite." She was mocking his formality, his Oxford accent, his gallantry, and concern. Since he was shuffling an inch at a time, and since she was following so closely, holding one of his hands in an iron grip while sinking the fingers of her other hand deep into his opposite shoulder, keeping their bodies so near that her breasts repeatedly grazed his shoulder blades, apprehension about her overall predicament, her terror at plunging to her imminent death, seemed strangely amusing.

Suddenly he pulled away. Struggling motionless against vertigo, she waited for logic to kick in. He hadn't fallen, so he must have moved into the shadows of the cliff face. She reached out toward the rock and there was nothing but darkness. Just as she was about to take a tentative step forward she felt a finger on her lips. It wasn't her own. She smiled to herself.

She heard a shuffling descend away from her, then felt a hand grasp her ankle. *Strange*, she thought. The hand rose to her calf and pressed firmly against her skin. She waited for logic to kick in again. She reached out and her fingers landed in a rather unkempt thatch of hair. She squeezed and pulled and she heard a muted whimper. He had crouched low, he was drawing her down, he was urging her to be silent, he was sliding his hand up her leg under her sundress as he drew her into a niche in the scarred face of the precipice wall.

She manoeuvered around until she found herself secure, straddling his outstretched leg, which was braced to prevent them both from plummeting backward into the abyss. She could feel his breath on her face and instinctively her lips softened. Instead of kissing him she exhaled gently and edged her body over his, moving deeper into what seemed to be a wound gouged out of the volcanic rock.

Ross pressed his open lips close against Miranda's ear. She turned to where she imagined his face to be in the dark and said in a barely audible whisper, "There are proprieties, Mr. Ross."

More shuffling sounds and his fingers squeezed gently on her bare thigh. Instantly he pulled away as if her flesh were fire. A moment of absolute stillness, then he placed a hand on either side of her head and turned her so that his lips were again brushing against one ear. She stayed very quiet, holding the pose, even pressing back a little. She was apparently caught up in a fetishist version of a Jane Austen parody, but instead of the tongue she had half-expected, only a few words entered her ear.

"We are caught, Ms. Quin, between a rock and a very hard place."

She felt reassured.

"I was not joking," he whispered, having sensed her response.

Miranda was not disappointed. The best wit was born deep inside, that's why it often accompanied terror and fear. He would have enjoyed Austen's *Northanger Abbey*. Maybe he had read it at Eton. If he didn't appreciate his own sense of humour at the moment, that in no way diminished its impact. He was a man to be trusted. Especially, as he had observed, since there was no alternative.

She pressed her ear against his lips, urging him to continue, although she wasn't sure why they hadn't had this conversation up on the road.

"Above us," he whispered. "Soldiers. They are waiting for my return."

Miranda felt a wave of reality wash over her. She nodded acknowledgement to his warning. He released her skull from his grasp.

"Stay close," he whispered. "There is another way in."

He inched along a ledge, then crawled on his belly under a fold in the lava, and she followed close behind, the two of them squeezing through a narrowing tube deep into the heart of darkness that pushed up against them with granular edges until the air grew thick and she had to concentrate on refusing to panic. She could feel the lingering heat from his body as she moved into narrow spaces he left behind. She stopped, breathed deeply; with nothing to see, she tried to convince herself there was nothing to fear.

Rock pressed against her shoulders, her head bumped again and again against lowering protrusions. Her shoulders jammed. She could no longer sense that Ross was ahead, she could hear the throbbing of her blood, the rasping of her breath. She tried to move backward, but the rock caught her. She worked her arms out from under her body weight, walking her hands forward on clenched fingers until her arms were fully extended, and then she squirmed in a series of painful gyrations onto her side, her ribcage and her hip bone gouging into the floor. Her breath deflected back from the rock wall. She drew her legs up until her knees jammed, then, twisting her feet against the lava, she pushed, and, repeating this action over and over, she edged forward until the walls receded into black space and she was able to rise to her knees and crawl.

She recoiled as her fingers clawed into warm flesh. He had waited for her. She let her hand rest for a moment on his calf, then withdrew. They moved on, they seemed to squirm forward interminably; there were no cues to measure their progress. Then she reached forward and there was nothing. *Gone*, she thought. *Not again*! But when she waved her hand slowly through the fetid air, his hand grasped hers.

"We're here, now, love." As they both rose to an upright posture, he let go.

Love! An image of Ellen Ravenscroft danced in the dark before her eyes as a match suddenly flared and for a moment they were blinded, surrounded by the stench of sulphur.

He lit a candle, then a lantern.

"You can speak normally," he said. "We're deep in the bowels of the earth. They couldn't possibly hear us. And they wouldn't come in here even if they wanted to. Trust me."

"You keep saying that. Do they know we're here?"

"Certainly not you. You're dead."

"Did they kill me on purpose."

"Good Lord, no. At least, not with malice. They liked you."

"That's reassuring. By *they*, you mean Matteo and Te Ave Teao?"

"The other men, the three in uniform, they were government. The execution was their idea. They *don't* like you."

"*Didn't*, past tense. I'm dead. How do you know there were three of them?"

"There was a meeting last night at an abandoned farmhouse. We were picked up at the main road. The uniforms raided. All they found was a poker game. A little strange, considering we had no reason to be there. But there was nothing to charge us with. The three soldiers, they took our friends for a ride."

"And left you behind. That was convenient."

"Yes, it was. And several others. We played poker for a while, then left."

"And they came looking for me. Is it because of the book? They know about it, they know about me supposedly being a code-breaker. I'm assuming they don't know for sure about Matteo and Te Ave Teao."

"I doubt if they care much about the book, but they know you were sent by Maria. That makes you dangerous."

"I came to write a book of my own. Nobody sent me," she snapped, then looked into his eyes and smiled. "They can't hear us, right? Because we're inside a network of volcanic tubes? But even out there, the surf is smashing against the shore. Right? It's deafening. Then how come you stuck your tongue in my ear?"

"I most certainly did not."

"And groped my leg?"

"And pressed my shoulder blades into your breasts?"

"You noticed!"

"I most assuredly did not," he declared with insouciant authority, as if his status as gentleman was in peril.

"They couldn't have heard us out there if we'd shouted."

"If we'd shouted, they might have." In the lamplight his face was insufferably handsome. His deep brown eyes were pools gleaming in the flickering glow. "And I was rather frightened and did not want us to be discovered and whispering at the time seemed appropriate."

How, she wondered, *could I not be enchanted by a man who confessed to being rather frightened?* "You did not want *me* to be discovered. They knew *you* were staying here." She looked around. They were in a chamber the size of a kitchen, with shadows suggesting volcanic tubes leading off in a number of directions. There was a reed mattress, a table with a propane hotplate and some packaged foods, a number of ominously shaped wooden crates, and a tiny rivulet flowing from a crevasse near the ceiling into a crevasse in the rock floor.

"Yes, they know I stay here sometimes. The soldiers think I'm on their side, they leave me alone. I sometimes do favours for the government. But our friends, Te Ave Teao and Matteo, they know I am always with them. It is quite precarious, to be on opposing sides." He laughed at his own predicament, which was also, she realized, the source of whatever power and influence he had. "But you are on neither side, it seems — that would make you a threat if you were alive. You're better off dead. I have to leave. I'll be back."

"Are you going to give it to them?"

"The book? No."

"Tell them?"

"Yes. I may tell them about it. It might give me leverage."

"It's hard to tell, you know, if you're one of the good guys."

"There are no good guys."

"What if I know the code, does that change anything?"

"Miranda, you're bargaining with the wrong man. If you really do, once the government people realize the power of the book, you're done for all over again. They won't care what it actually says, only that it must be destroyed and you along with it. As for our island friends, they are convinced their holy bloody book will fuel the insurrection. They're almost as worried about having it fall into government hands as they are keen to have its secrets revealed. If they discover you're still alive and have actually broken the code, they will stop at nothing to make you share what you know. Not much of a choice. Stay here, be dead. Think of death as a reprieve."

"Between a rock and a hard place, still and again."

"Do not tell anyone about the code, do not tell me. Your secret may keep us both alive."

"Leverage?"

"Who knows."

He drew her to him and held her in a lingering embrace, and then he turned, and, sliding among the shadows, he disappeared into the rock. She stayed very still, not wanting to lose the residual warmth of his body, the sensation of where his body had pressed against hers. She wondered what his real name was. She wondered just which side he was on, or if there were sides at all, and not just a desperate idea smack up against an immoveable force.

She lay down on the reed mattress. It rustled when she moved, but was comfortable and the cave was surprisingly warm. She wanted to take off her dress and wrap herself in the light flannel blanket that smelled vaguely of Ross. The thought of being naked made her feel vulnerable. What if Matteo and Te Ave Teao turned up? The Santiago hotel room all over again. Ross assured her that islanders wouldn't come into the cave. She guessed it was somehow taboo. She got up and took off her underwear and rinsed it in the vertical flow of the rivulet, but put her sundress back on, lay down again, and covered herself with the blanket.

Her last thought as she drifted into a deep sleep was to wonder why she had lied about cracking the code. The last images in her mind were of Ross on the plane, Ross bleeding in her room, Ross at the farmhouse, Ross brooding over the smouldering ruins, Ross blinded by the darkness, slipping away. So many beginnings.

Miranda woke with a start, utterly disoriented in the pitch blackness. Bewilderment gave way to apprehension as she realized where she was and that the lantern had guttered and gone out, that she was alone, buried in the depths of a dormant volcano with no possible way to escape unless she had light. She listened and at first the only sounds she could hear were from her own hands as they moved slowly over her body, taking inventory. Reassured she was all there, she mentally followed the resonant splash of running water until she established direction. She had rarely experienced such profound darkness. She lay very still.

Sounds began to take on dimension as the chamber took shape in her mind.

Only a year before she had been locked in a cellar dungeon in the heart of Toronto. She had nearly died. The girl she ultimately took on as her ward had entombed her in a desperate struggle to bury horrors of the past, and had rescued her because it was a past they had shared. Death, then, had seemed seductive, but she had refused its entreaties and survived. *Damn it*, she thought, *absolute darkness doesn't mean death. He'll come back. And if he doesn't, if he's captured or killed, there are no doors, I'll crawl through tunnels until the end of time.*

She held up her left wrist with her right hand, not trusting the position of her arm without guiding it in front of her face. She squinted, trying to see the luminescent numbers on her watch. She felt for the watch. It was gone. A brief surge of panic subsided when she recalled having taken it off for her sponge bath at the farmhouse. It must have been consumed in the fire. She sat up, perhaps she could find the matches, but immediately she lost all sense of equilibrium and grasped at the mattress to allay the reeling sensation.

Had she been asleep for minutes or hours? Surely it was daylight outside. She had only the vaguest notion of where *outside* actually was, where they had walked in the darkness. Somewhere on Easter Island. Isla de Pasqua. Rapa Nui. *Te Pito o Te Henua*. Was she inside the volcano at Poike, had they made their way inland through the tunnels, somewhere beneath the quarry at Rano Raraku, or had they wandered around to the caverns past Anakena Beach? After they had left the main road she had stopped trying to inscribe their route in her mind; it was like dropping breadcrumbs among ravens. Ross rescuing her, he took her to his lair amidst a maze of volcanic tubes deep in the earth. He was hiding her in what might have been a burial chamber or a sacred refuge. He was keeping her prisoner. She sat bolt upright. Was he keeping her prisoner?

No, she thought. That was absurd. But nothing was absurd in such impenetrable darkness that she had to imagine who she was to be sure she was there. Thomas Edward Ross, was she his prisoner, destined to wither and die before he returned to deal with her remains and retrieve his book? *Did he take it with him*, she wondered? *Did he bother?*

She raised herself awkwardly to her feet and turned in the direction of the flowing water, but as she took a tentative step forward in the darkness, the floor of the cavern seemed to fall away beneath her and she collapsed to her knees. She crawled slowly to the rivulet and drank deep gulps of water from her cupped hands and then crawled back toward her mattress, sweeping her hands in the darkness ahead of her until with a great sigh of relief she found it.

Miranda lay back and composed herself as if she were a corpse laid out for viewing. She had done this before. It somehow, perversely, affirmed that she was in control. With her hands clasped across her breast, she stared open-eyed in the direction of the cavern ceiling, trying to imagine where it must be. The book! Her mind swerved to the present. Surely the revolutionaries knew as much as Miranda. But perhaps they were looking in the wrong place. They were trying to decode the handwritten marginalia, they were looking for hidden meaning in the cryptic notes. Maria had known how important the book was, but not what it meant. The book itself was the message, Miranda concluded. It was a key.

Miranda needed to know if Ross had left it behind.

She rolled over onto her side and slowly got up onto her hands and knees. She listened again for the running water to determine direction and then began crawling toward where she supposed the table to be, moving carefully to avoid scraping her bare knees, keeping low so as not to tip over from the vertigo that came with no reference points in the darkness. She found the book and holding it close she crawled back to the mattress where she rolled onto her back and balanced it on her stomach, feeling the reassuring pressure of its weight as she moved her hands back to the funereal position.

The air was heavy and perfectly still. Time endured; she endured. Then the air moved a little. She could tell she was no longer alone. Suddenly a beam of light surged between the lips of a crease in the rock. Miranda lay still. The beam swung wildly against the ceiling and walls as the bearer stood upright, then straightened as the intruder walked toward her, keeping the light out of her eyes. She watched as light settled on the dusty rubble floor and a face bent down to examine her more closely. Then his arms enfolded her in a powerful embrace.

"Matteo!" she exclaimed, pushing him violently back, trying to read his eyes in the flashing darkness as he fell from the light.

7

The Mysteries of Arctic Landscape

Gloria Simmons had arranged for a Twin Otter to carry them up the east coast of Baffin as far as Broughton Island, with a quick stop in Pangnirtung to drop off cargo and medical supplies. In Broughton they would be met by a company helicopter flown down from Pond Inlet. Landing in Pang, as Gloria called it, was exciting. The airstrip veered through the centre of the community in a harrowing effort to squeeze between mountains and the treacherous shore.

As the plane rolled to an abrupt stop, Morgan struggled to quell the butterflies in his stomach. Gloria Simmons emerged from the cockpit where she had spent most of the flight in the co-pilot's seat. She sidled in beside him on the other jump seat that had been fitted amidst the crates of cargo.

"The weather's closing in," she shouted over the roar of the idling engines. "We're just dropping the med stuff and going on; they'll come back to unload the rest. You okay back here?"

"Yeah," he shouted back. "You're a pilot, too!"

"I mess around a bit. If I'd wanted to I might have been very good."

Morgan looked up as the pilot emerged from the cockpit. She was younger than Gloria Simmons who had explained when they boarded that pilots in the North could manoeuvre these Twin Otters through the vilest weather and land on a gravel esker in the middle of a glacial stream without breaking a sweat. The woman exuded a jaunty confidence that seemed as much a part of her uniform as her flight jacket and bomber cap.

But she wasn't smiling as she bent down and shouted, "Control says Broughton's completely socked in. We might make the takeoff, but we couldn't land. Sorry."

Morgan and Gloria Simmons looked at each other. He could sense her desperation, although her facial expression remained unchanged except for a tightening around the eyes.

The pilot straightened, then bent down again. She started to speak, then abruptly stood up and clambered back into the cockpit. Suddenly there was silence.

"That's better," she said when she returned. "Gloria, there's no point." She said this not unsympathetically. "Your chopper won't be there. A bunch of hunters west of Pond are stranded out on an ice floe. Your guy was called in from Nanisivik for emergency evacuation. There are twenty of them out there, a couple didn't make it. Searching for the bodies of your people is second priority."

"He may not be dead."

"He's dead, Gloria. One way or another. Put it together. He has to be dead."

One way or another? That struck Morgan as a curious observation and as soon as the pilot moved away to supervise the unloading of cargo, he leaned over to ask Gloria Simmons for clarification. Neither of them felt inclined to leave the plane.

She glanced into his eyes and then away, speaking in a low voice without looking at him. "Inuit do not crash boats into whales. Whales do not attack boats."

"If there *were* whales?"

"There had to be."

"Why?"

"He wouldn't lie."

He might kill but he wouldn't lie. Again, Morgan felt locked in a parallel universe. *He couldn't swim, but he was picked up in the open water?* "You know him?" he asked.

"By reputation. He is a very powerful hunter. Pauloosie Avaluktuk. We do not swim, Morgan."

"The life jackets?"

"Life jackets, no bodies. They didn't have a chance to put them on, Detective. Perhaps he shot them and rammed the whales to cover his tracks."

"No," said Morgan, feeling more sure of himself. There was cultural difference and then there was human nature. "He wouldn't shoot them. Bodies have a way of turning up, even up here. He'd be afraid of that. And he wouldn't sacrifice his boat unless it was used as a weapon. Would he have known about the whales in advance?"

"Yes, probably. By radio."

"Two-way?"

"Or broadcasts. News programming up here includes the movements of whales."

Or, Morgan thought, *he might have smashed his boat on a shoal just deep enough below the surface to have sunk it without risking his own life. Then he wouldn't have needed whales.* He was offended to think this Pauloosie Avaluktuk would violate a cardinal credo of his culture, not by denying the truth, but by dishonouring such majestic creatures with his lie.

"They might have made it to shore," he said. "Avaluktuk could have been so busy rescuing himself he didn't see."

"Do you really think so?"

"No, but if there is the remotest possibility —"

While they had been talking, the plane was unloaded and the pilot slipped away. They were alone inside the empty fuselage. Morgan looked around. The seats had been removed in Iqaluit to make room for the cargo; there was a backpack shoved against a bulkhead. He could read the tag on the pack from where he was sitting. Lost baggage, destined for Broughton Island. He knew there was a remote federal park called Auyuittuq cutting across the peninsula, separating Cumberland Sound from Baffin Strait. Extreme hikers could trek from just south of Broughton Island to just east of Pang.

He had read it in a tourist brochure during the flight up from Toronto.

Gloria Simmons rose and walked to the exterior door, leaned out, and looked around, then pulled the door shut and locked it. With solemn deliberation, she climbed through into the cockpit and motioned Morgan to join her. By the time he was strapped into the co-pilot's seat, he knew there was nothing he could do to stop her. He was there as an observer, a witness, a hostage to fate, which he didn't believe in. She started the engines, revving the props until the whole fuselage shuddered, then abruptly the wheels jumped the blocks and the Twin Otter began to roll forward. With cool expertise she taxied toward a break in the thickening fog.

She pulled back full throttle, the plane lurched and rumbled as it accelerated on the narrow strip between the high school and the weaving co-op, and suddenly the earth dropped away and they were airborne, engulfed in swirling grey. Just as Morgan was beginning to unclench bowels and fists, a dark shadow loomed from the right, quickly transforming into a tumultuous wall of rock that sheared away as she banked over the frigid waters of Cumberland Sound and continued to climb.

To Morgan's astonishment she looked over at him and winked.

In the adrenaline surge they had momentarily forgotten their mission, but as soon as they broke into the clear, surrounded by infinite blue, they settled into their own private thoughts. He suspected fate was a euphemism for accepting what couldn't be stopped.

They were flying inland over spectacular alpine terrain that had broken through the cloud cover below them. The plane banked away from the Auyuittuq valley and skimmed low over glacial ice fields as they headed north through the relatively clear skies along the plateau. Gloria Simmons was flying like she'd been doing it all her life.

She leaned across and spoke in a voice loud enough that her words cleared the insistent drone of the engines: "So, Detective, do you think we'll be arrested?"

"Probably," he said.

"We didn't steal it, technically."

"Technically?"

"D'Arcy Associates has a major stake in the airline. Shareholder's rights."

"I don't suppose we were cleared for takeoff?"

"Controller was on his way home. I saw him duck off the runway when we took off. He and the pilot. They're a couple, I think."

Morgan looked over at her. She seemed ominously cheerful. "You fly well," he said.

"So far so good."

"You *are* licensed?"

"To fly?" She had to be enjoying this. It was a distraction from what lay ahead.

"Have you ever flown a Twin Otter before?"

"No, but I've watched very carefully from where you're sitting in the co-pilot's seat. And I've flown a Piper Cub, no, a Beaver, well, actually, I did the takeoff and my instructor did the landing."

"You are joking, aren't you?"

"I'm afraid I'm not. But I'm very good at reading the GPS and I know exactly where we are."

"About one thousand feet up."

"A little less at the moment. There's the Barnes Ice Field. We're right on course, except for the up and down part. We'll figure it out." She leaned forward and looked up, then to the side, and looked down. "I don't think it will be too hard."

Morgan shifted his gaze back and forth between the glacial terrain below and the glacial expression on her face. *If only she would smile*, he thought.

Once again, her uncanny sense of seeming to be able to read his thoughts kicked in and she turned, swinging in her seat to address him directly. Instead of words, she suddenly smiled. It was a radiant smile. Lines at the sides of her eyes projected unrestrained pleasure. She placed a hand on his knee and squeezed.

"Trust me," she said. "It can't be that difficult to land a plane. There's only one direction to worry about, and gravity works in our favour."

"Or not. Things fall. Copernicus, the Tower of Pisa."

"Galileo. And it probably never happened." She was still smiling. Her behaviour did not seem at all like a prelude to death.

Morgan took a deep breath and tried to smile back. She turned again to confront the instrument panel as if it were a code to be deciphered. She pushed and tugged and glanced and tapped, and he had to admit she seemed to have a stern command of the up-down thing and she apparently knew where they were.

"Inuk hunters read the land," she said. "They read striations in the snow, the patterns of wind, the contours of rock, they read the colours of white that record and anticipate weather, they read the colours of white." She repeated *the colours of white* as if she had just received a revelation.

While Morgan looked out the window, the world below abruptly disappeared and they seemed to be hovering motionless in a thick blanket of cloud.

"Broughton's socked in," he said. "Maybe we'd better head back."

"*Qikiqtarjuaq.*"

What Morgan heard was a cluster of dissonant syllables coming from the back of her mouth. He waited for an explanation:

"Broughton. We're taking back our country, word by word, Detective. *Qik-iqtar-juaq*. Means, 'the big island.' It's not a traditional name, it's a new name in the language of the people. This is the dawn of a new era, Morgan. Early morning, but it's happening. And we can't go back. Pang will be just as bad by now and, anyway, we're running low on fuel."

"That is not a good thing."

"It makes our decision easier."

"Our decision?"

"To land where they picked up Pauloosie. I think I can find the coast."

"We're flying blind — you can't see a thing."

"I'm calculating."

Morgan sat back in his seat, closed his eyes, then opened them again. He was not sure where to look.

She handed him a map.

"Can you read contours?" she asked. "Forget it. Hold it open for me. No, there, so I can follow along that fjord." An interminable pause. "We should be over it now. Hang on, we're on our way down."

Suddenly water appeared twenty metres below them.

"Yes!" she exclaimed. She pulled up just a bit, keeping the water in sight. She reached over and tapped on the map. "When we get about there, we veer left."

"We're landing on the water?" Morgan was acutely aware the sea looming up was filled with ice chunks, some as big as the plane.

"We've got tricycle landing gear, Morgan, no pontoons. Once we're directly off the north end of Aberdeen Island we'll cut diagonally back to the mainland, that's where they picked him up, and we'll try for an esker."

"What about snow?"

"Snow's too wet this far from the Barnes. Nothing glacial, just slow melting pockets. We'll find ourselves some solid gravel."

"Good luck," he said. "To both of us." He settled back against his seat again, his feet squarely on the floor, and waited for a summarizing explosion of flashbacks.

She flashed him another rare smile. "Hang on, we're going down when we can."

Cliffs loomed dead ahead, she pulled back almost into a stall, banked sharply, and dropped through the cloud swirling around them onto heaving terrain. As the plane fishtailed against gravel and slowed, it shuddered violently, but, true to its reputation, held together and came to an abrupt halt, swaying for a few moments as if finding its footing, and then subsided into stillness. Gloria Simmons killed the engines and there was an eerie almost deafening silence, broken finally by her nonchalant voice.

"According to my GPS, if they made it ashore, it would be about here," she said, unsnapping her seatbelt and standing up. "We're within shouting distance of the accident scene."

Morgan realized she was not referring to their present predicament — their own situation was not accidental and their survival was a remarkable achievement, which did not seem to surprise her at all. She opened the door in the fuselage and jumped out. Then Morgan heard a distinctly anxious shout. She had sunk into a gravel slurry up to her knees. He reached out and grasped her outstretched arms to haul her back into the plane.

"We seem to be on a small gravel moraine in the middle of a river," she announced. "The water looks treacherous, too deep to ford, we'll have to swim." She paused. "I don't swim."

Morgan gazed out the windows at the swirling torrent that flanked them on both sides. "Too deep, too fast, I don't think anyone's swimming anywhere. What time is it?"

"What difference does it make?"

"It's three p.m."

"You knew, why ask?"

"It was a rhetorical question." He bent low and looked through the windows on all sides as if taking measurements, and at last turned back to address his companion who, for the first time since he had known her, seemed uncertain and edgy. Her eyes had followed his perambulations and her mouth seemed poised to frame an inarticulable question.

"This is glacial runoff," he said. "We're sunk up to the axels in glacial debris."

"And?"

"This water was solid ice not more than a mile or two upstream."

"So far that is not reassuring. Keep going."

"We sit tight for twelve hours. The flow will die to a trickle during the night."

"There won't be much night, Morgan. We're north of the Arctic Circle. It's August."

"When the sun swings down across the northern sky, moving around from west back to east, even if it doesn't get dark it'll get colder, cold enough that the water flow will drop."

"You know this, how?"

"Explorers' journals. I read stuff. Between three and six in the morning, we'll be good to go. And given the weather I don't think Search and Rescue will be looking for us for quite a while."

Together they scoured every cranny of the plane interior, looking for food and extra clothes and found nothing more than a couple of chocolate bars in the cockpit and a rain jacket hanging in a bulkhead closet. They found a good first aid packet with bandages, splints, and a variety of patent medicines. As if they had tacitly agreed to save the best for last, they finally turned to the errant backpack and together they released its straps and fasteners like it was a shared Christmas present.

The temperature had dropped to freezing in the last hour and as they withdrew the backpacker's gear they put on what they could. Gloria Simmons slipped out of her wet pants and wrung out her socks and donned dry socks and a pair of pants that were too big for her. Morgan found a fleece pullover that was a little too small and put it on under his own clothes. There was a small gas stove, but no fuel. There was no food. The guy must have been planning to stock up in Broughton before setting out on the land. They found a ratty old sleeping mat with his gear, folded not rolled, and a down-filled sleeping bag that had seen better days.

They ate one of the chocolate bars, washed down with glacial water that Morgan had retrieved by removing his pants and socks, putting his boots back on to protect his feet, and manoeuvering through the slurry to the surging flow, which had not, as far as he could tell, diminished in the slightest. They rolled out the sleeping bag on the mat and sat on it close to each other, legs drawn up to their chests to preserve body warmth.

By about nine in the evening, when the cloud cover had descended to engulf them in its frigid, dull gleam, they were both trembling from the cold. Each seemed lost in personal thoughts; Morgan trying to imagine the subtropical warmth of Easter Island, and Gloria Simmons, perhaps thinking of the comforts of her life in Toronto, perhaps grieving in her peculiar quiet way for Harrington D'Arcy.

Abruptly, she stood up and started stripping off her clothes. At first Morgan thought she was simply redistributing them, trying to eke out maximum warmth.

"Come on, Morgan," she said. "Get naked."

As he watched her he wondered if she'd lost her mind, if her cool aplomb had finally collapsed. But she seemed inordinately calm as she unhooked her bra and dropped it beside him, then stepped out of her panties. His eyes filled with her, from her toes wrinkled with the cold to her honey-blonde hair that seemed to have just been exquisitely groomed. She was a natural blonde, tall and robust. His gaze stuttered, refusing to settle on her exquisite breasts as he tried to avoid gawking, and finally came to rest on her face. Lust, he had often imagined, was the last thing to go. "This must be me, dying," he mumbled to himself.

"Morgan!" She gave him a kick with the side of her foot. "You're defeating the point of the exercise." He tried to quell the brazen image of a naked Valkyrie and himself a slain warrior ready to meet Valhalla in her burning arms. She unceremoniously prodded him again. He got up; and she immediately squirmed into the sleeping bag. "Come on," she said. "It only works if we're both naked."

"What only works?" he said, as he stumbled out of his clothes, leaving his jacket, sweater, and shirt until last, then, with a great twisting heave, removing them as well, so that he stood before her feeling more exposed than he had ever been in his life. "Now what?" he asked, his hands cupping his private parts.

"Now," she said, holding the mouth of the sleeping bag open. "Now you climb in here beside me. Come on, let's not get any colder."

Morgan slid down into the warmth as she opened the space to receive him. Every nerve ending registered where he was touching her in astonishing detail as if his own body were a singular sensory organ. When he tried to twist away there was no room and she turned into him and pressed skin to skin so that their thighs touched, her breasts pressed against his chest, her breath streamed over his shoulder and against the crook of his neck. He could feel himself stirring and felt strangely embarrassed.

"This is how my ancestors kept warm," she said. "I suppose it's how they became ancestors."

Their hips ground in slow motion against each other. He could feel her breasts burn into his skin. Then she stopped. "Lie still, Morgan. Unless you think we can do it without sweating. If we sweat we freeze to death."

The material of the sleeping bag clenched them together so they could only make the smallest movements by consensus, but they were warm. "Have you noticed," she said, "that my people move with a lovely stillness. That is to avoid sweating." She was whispering in his ear. "If you sweat against furs in the winter, they lose their warmth. Same with down-filled sleeping bags. Do you think you can sleep?"

"No."

The Arctic landscape, surrounding with an immense austerity that was somehow felt deeply inside, this impossibly beautiful woman, the absurdity of their nakedness, invoked the poetic in Morgan's mind. Not evoked, he was no poet, but his sense of wonder brought out flashes of poetry inscribed in the depths of his mind and long since obscured, until now. This time it wasn't Hopkins.

"Have you ever read John Donne?" he asked.

"I was a chemistry student, Morgan. I'm a lawyer. *No man is an island*, that was Donne."

"*To teach thee, I am naked first.*"

"No you weren't, I was."

"*Full nakedness, all joys are due to thee.*"

"Is this what cops do in lieu of sex, recite dead poets?"

"*License my roving hands, and let them go behind, before, above, between, below.*"

"Lie still, Morgan. Count sheep."

Before long they drifted into a luxuriant sleep in which they both might have dreamed of exquisite and exploding orgasms in endless profusion and when they woke up they were entangled below in ways that made Morgan wonder if they had been lovers during the long warmth of the night.

"Morgan, what time is it? Can you get your arm out?" Their muscles had relaxed so completely they were almost atrophied; their bodies seemed to flow into each other. He wriggled his fingers and tried to snake his wrist up between them, but there was no room. With his right hand he reached over and delicately lifted her breasts to the side and unstrapped his watch, then slipped it upwards into her grasp so she could pass it hand over hand into the open.

"Four in the morning. Time to get up. Let's see if

this plan of yours worked, King Canute. And by the way, I prefer Leonard Cohen."

"To what?"

"Not to you, Morgan. To John Donne."

He started to shimmy upwards, then realized there was an impediment. He had a morning erection nestled tightly between her legs. As he tried to move, she responded by squeezing her thighs around the protrusion. Slowly, she began to grind against him. He exhaled with a drawn-out sigh as he realized what was happening. Her warm breath on his neck became more urgent as she swivelled her hips, searching for an unreachable position, it seemed, to accommodate their desire.

There was a ripping sound as the sleeping bag burst open, a shard of cold air, a shared shudder. She stopped abruptly. For a moment neither of them moved. Then she whispered: "Give it up, Morgan. There's not enough room. We'd better get going before the waters rise." Whether intentionally dismissive or merely an expression of her frustration, her words threatened to end their curious intimacy, but their renewed gyrations slithering free of the torn sleeping bag nearly brought them back to the edge until, suddenly, being exposed inside a giant refrigerator, their passion expired and they separately leaped for their clothes.

"Good," said Morgan, acknowledging the alacrity with which they cocooned themselves in every bit of clothing at hand. "However." He smiled and tousled his own hair into a semblance of order. Her hair was perfect. "Before we put on our damp boots, I suggest we strip off our pants and socks again."

"Morgan, you're insatiable."

"Just getting started," he said, stepping first on the toes of one sock, then the other, tugging them off without bending down, to avoid touching the icy inside layer of his clothing. Then he unbuckled his pants and dropped them, finally leaning over to scoop them up. "Give me yours," he said. "We'll need these dry when we get to solid ground. But put on your boots. That water will turn our feet into frozen stumps in seconds, so we'll need to protect them."

Gloria Simmons followed his directives as he packed up their dry clothes in the backpack and swung it over his shoulders before drawing the thick door open and lowering himself into the slurry. He turned, reached up, and lifted her down close beside him. She clearly felt assured that he knew exactly what he was doing, although Morgan was not comfortable with the role of hero — it felt like wearing a bearskin coat that was morally offensive, much too big, and very warm. He nodded his head in encouragement when she looked directly into his eyes, and, holding one of her hands in a tight grasp, he leaned away to draw first one foot and then the other through the sucking gravel.

Together, as an awkward quadruped, they manoeuvered the short distance to swift-moving water. Although flowing vigorously enough to make their footing uncertain, it was somewhat subdued from the roiling surge of twelve hours earlier, and it was crystal clear. Looking downstream, Morgan could see that the water flowing past the far side of their esker was as murky as curdled milk. *Lucky*, he thought, seeing his boots shimmer below him, *we chose the right side.*

As they sat on the rocky shore to empty their boots and get dressed again, they discussed the geological anomaly of clear water and murky water flowing from the same glacial face that filled the western horizon like a great bank of clouds in the clearing sky. They could feel waves of cold emanating from the ice and sweeping down in the early morning breeze.

"Okay," said Gloria Simmons, resuming command. "We walk in that direction." She pointed. "Just over that rise, there's open water. Let's see what we see."

With uncanny precision, she led them to the edge of the sea through boulders and clumps of moss and lichen up to their knees and over tiny blossoms of brilliant yellow and vibrant purple that seemed in valiant denial of the freezing temperatures and austere conditions. They walked along the smooth rock plane of the shore for a few minutes and then she turned away and he followed her over a rocky outcropping, where they came upon a cairn of boulders in the shape of a man, almost as if she expected it to be there.

"He'll be inside," she murmured, getting down on her knees to peer through crevasses among the rocks.

To Morgan, it was obviously an old grave, perhaps ancient. He lowered himself to his knees beside her and examined the minute strands of dried lichen particles on boulders that had been pushed askew. This grave had been dismantled perhaps only a day or two previously. Inside, there would be old bones, he had no doubt. But she was right, there would be a fresh body, as well.

Carefully, they lifted the rocks away, working slowly with a shared reverence understood between them for the skeletal remains of the original occupant. When the bones lay revealed in the open, they moved them gently aside, laying them out on a rock shelf in the proper configuration. There was a thin layer of frozen gravel draped over the body beneath where the bones had been, but there was no question from its contours about what lay concealed. They agreed it had been buried below to protect the flesh from foraging animals.

"This was not Pauloosie Avaluktuk who did this," said Gloria Simmons. "He would not violate the grave of his ancestor."

"His ancestor?"

"The dead are our family. We are human beings, Inuit; we are the People. He would not do this."

This would be the same man, Morgan thought, *who might murder but wouldn't lie*. He stood beside Gloria Simmons and watched as the first glints of sun spun waves in her hair. She was a denizen of Bay and Bloor, and a native of the North in her blood and her bones and her strange and strong set of mind. He was glad they had not made love. They might, he desired her with a fierceness that surprised him, but not now, this was not their time. Perhaps it never would be. But he doubted the desire would ever leave him, a desire inseparable from the solemn and breathtaking landscape, from the profound fear of crashing into it from above, and his perfect acceptance that whatever was to happen would happen. He was not a fatalist, but in this, his visceral passion for this woman, he felt at the moment completely resigned to forces he had no wish to rebuke.

A hushed whisper from the grave startled them both. They stared in wonder as the gravel shroud that was beginning to melt in the warming day began slowly to slide from the dead man's face, making quiet sounds like a human voice from far away. Without realizing it, Morgan and the woman had grasped hands as they gazed at the slowly revealing features, squeezing so hard their bodies trembled. Then, at last, Gloria Simmons spoke. "He's certainly dead. But it isn't Harrington D'Arcy."

"My goodness," Morgan declared, the inherent irony of his favourite expletive in this case being especially appropriate.

They stood in solemn silence, each trying to assimilate the implications of finding the wrong corpse in the right place. They had been so focused on D'Arcy that they had virtually forgotten the other two men who had gone missing. And as Morgan stared at the corpse, his bewilderment increased when he realized that under the gravel shroud that was disintegrating in the warmth of the sun the man was dressed in nothing more than briefs and a singlet.

"This gets curiouser and curiouser," he said.

She flashed him a look of annoyance that would have made the Queen of Hearts quaver.

"This doesn't mean D'Arcy's alive," he observed with a rueful smile. She seemed not to hear. He glanced over at the skeleton laid out on its stony bier and back at the frozen corpse that lay partially fused with the upper layer of permafrost, then let his eyes rest on his companion's face as he tried to fathom her emotional response. Wherever they were, he thought, here on the desolate coastline of Baffin Island, they were a long way off.

From what, he wasn't sure, but the rest of the world seemed exceedingly remote.

8

Guardians of the Cave

Miranda had shoved Matteo away with such force that he sprawled backward and his flashlight went clattering across the stony floor, flickered briefly, and expired. She scrambled off the mattress to the side and then crouched perfectly still. She could hear him moving about in the absolute blackness, searching for the light. He didn't seem to be getting closer. "If you're here to kill me again, you're in for a hell of a fight." She projected her voice in a low register and her words were fierce as they resonated against the enclosing walls.

There was a long pause, then he spoke, "I did not try to kill you in the first instance, or you would be dead. In fact, I made myself sure of your safety before torching the house where my grandparents lived their whole lives. You were hidden safely under the fallen *moai* with the bones of my great-uncle who disappeared when my father put his life to an end for betraying my wife. After a few years my father exhumed him and dismantled his skull and broke his bones. I told Te Ave Teao you were safe as I walked past him — he was going to stop me from starting the fire. When I went inside I saw the book was gone. I knew it was with you. You are all right, now."

"For a man who didn't speak any English until yesterday, you are surprisingly talkative," she said into the darkness.

"I am aware of how to distract you."

"From what?"

"Terror, perhaps."

"I was startled."

"You thumped me in the chest with astonishing force. There is no reason to be ashamed of that; you were terrified."

"I am not the least bit ashamed. Or terrified. I didn't thump you, I pushed you."

"Thumped." He was moving closer.

She stood tall, her equilibrium restored in the darkness by her will to survive, and edged silently away from the sounds of his breathing. He seemed to have stopped moving, listening perhaps, waiting. She reached out until her fingertips brushed against the tabletop. She slid them along the table then over to where the back of the chair should be and they closed around her damp but clean bra and panties, which she proceeded to put on, something that proved surprisingly difficult in the dark. *The shuffling rustling sounds must be baffling to him*, she thought. "There. Nothing at all to be ashamed about," she declared, as if the matter might still be in doubt and somehow linked to wearing no underwear.

"In the confusion I seem to have misplaced my flashlight," Matteo observed.

"You're very gracious, but I believe it smashed when I *thumped* you."

"There will be matches. You don't have a lantern without matches and I believe I noticed a lantern before the lights went out."

"You've never been here before?"

"Not in years. Our friend Mr. Ross seems to have set up housekeeping in a most unlikely place. Ah, here they are." He struck a match and a blast of light sputtered briefly and expired. He struck another more carefully and directed Miranda to bring him the red kerosene can sitting among the packing cases. Perhaps in the difference between darkness and light, they both seemed to have forgotten that only moments before they were adversaries.

"Now, this will be interesting," he said. "We will need illumination if I am to fill the lamp, but it would be better if we did not set fire to ourselves. You take the matches, but stand back a little."

"It's kerosene," she said as she lit a match and held it to the side while he filled the lamp. "It won't explode." She had worked at summer camps in Northern Ontario. She knew about kerosene lamps. They used to call it coal oil. It wasn't volatile, but the smell was evocative. Ontario loomed in her mind, like phantom sensations of an atrophied limb, and was quickly displaced by a more recent vision of the lamp at the farmhouse shattering into a blazing inferno.

"So," he said, standing back to look at her in the flickering lamplight. "You have now put on your undergarments."

Miranda instinctively clutched her breasts and then her crotch as if somehow she had been caught naked in public. She grimaced and dropped her arms to her sides with what she immediately recognized was a girlish gesture.

"I saw with my flashlight your little things on the chair and now they are gone," he explained.

"My *little things*. How long were you in the States?"

"Ah, one remembers the infinite rules of grammar, but one forgets quickly the proper names of unfamiliarities. *Kai i te au*. Some things slip from the mind."

"Your English is superb, Matteo. Now explain what is happening, how long have I been here, where is Ross, who is Ross?"

"You have been here two days."

"My God! No wonder I'm starving." She realized her appetite had been held in check by the tightness in her gut from suppressing panic. "And what about Ross?"

"Who knows? Mr. Ross is an enigma, that's what he is by profession."

"That's a profession?"

"In his case it is. The less we understand him, the better he is at his job."

"Which is what?"

"For us he is a delivery system and an agent of change."

"And what does he deliver that is so important?"

"Over the years, many things. Most recently, yourself."

"I am not a parcel to be handed about."

"This is not about you, personally."

"Apparently it is."

"I'm sorry you cannot understand your role in our affairs. Perhaps only Maria understood. But you were dispatched to serve the cause for which she died. We are not asking you to die, merely to co-operate."

For the moment her need for clarification was trumped by a desire to connect. Ross was an agent of chaos; he had left her in darkness. Matteo had brought back the light. They sat on opposite sides of the table, squinting as the lamp flickered in their eyes "I'd like to get out of here," she said in a firm, but conciliatory tone. "Preferably now, although God knows, where to?"

"The world outside this cave is still there, I assure you, and no less dangerous than when you departed it two days ago."

She gazed across the table at his beautiful features washed in the shimmering glow of the lamplight. They had nearly been lovers. She smiled a secret smile to herself. She felt a strong attraction to this cheerful, brooding man. The Englishman excited and repulsed her at the same time. Matteo seemed to connect with something deep inside that was constant and powerful, despite the bewildering circumstances. He caught her smile and smiled back.

She wished Morgan were there; he would understand. She had slipped into the role of romantic heroine in the novel of her own life, she had become the woman she suspected most women have a fear of becoming and dream they will become, her destiny darkly shaped not by will, but desire, fated to give herself, flesh, mind, and soul, to the man, exotic, or to the man, mysterious and impossibly urbane, either of whom would transform her ordinary life into something dangerously unfamiliar and important. *The hell with Morgan*, she thought, angry at him for intruding in her reverie.

"Matteo," she said, "this cave, it is a sacred place, *tapu* except for the *ariki*. Yet you are here. So taboo, or *tapu*, is no longer a factor?"

"Ah, but it is. Perhaps the sacred and forbidden are now cultural imperatives, not religious, but believe me, they count."

"Then you are an *ariki*?"

"My sister and I are of the blood. I am what we call *tiaki ana*, a guardian of the cave."

Miranda scanned the almost delicate and yet commanding features of this man across from her. She could not bear to use the past tense when she asked him: "Your sister? Is Maria your sister?"

"Yes. She was to marry Te Ave Teao, my brother."

"Your brother!"

"No, no, not my brother like that, not like you think. It is how in Spanish we say it, my age-mate, the friend of my life."

"But she married Harrington D'Arcy."

"Yes, she did. And Te Ave Teao, he did not marry another. Sometimes it happens like that."

Neither of them said anything for a few minutes.

"Let's backtrack a bit." Her tone was flat and rational. "You and your sister are descended from priests of the ancient times. Would this go back to the bird-man culture, the *moai* culture, to the culture of central Polynesia — didn't Hoto Matua bring your people from the Marquesas Islands, or was it Raiatea?"

"You have been reading, Detective Quin. No, we probably came from Mangareva. It is open to question. The anthropological subsets are still arguing. My sister and I are not holy people. But we are direct descendents of the final *ariki*."

"The final *ariki*?"

"The last. He was a man named Humberto Rapu Haoa who returned when the slave traders were persuaded by the Bishop of Tahiti to bring back survivors of the raids to the island. Over a thousand men had been taken away. Many died of smallpox while they were being transported home; they were stored in transit with the belongings of diseased American sailors. Fifteen made it back. My grandfather was the only *ariki* to return. He was the last human being in the world who could read *Rongorongo*."

"*Rongorongo*," said Miranda. A rare piece of wood incised with *Rongorongo* had turned up in Toronto, peripheral to a case she and Morgan had been involved in that was so horrific it had changed who she was — in some ways, for the better.

"You know about our writing?"

"Yes, a little." She had honoured in semiotics and linguistics at the University of Toronto. Most in the field knew about the writing of a people who could no longer decipher their own documents, writing that stood paradoxically between them and their past.

"Only men could write and read," Matteo continued. "They were like medieval monks in Europe. Generation by generation, they would re-copy our scripts because we had only slabs of wood to work with, which would deteriorate just like parchment and paper. We managed to develop writing, but never anything durable to write on. Men spent their lives incising script into wood for readings on formal occasions. Then the slavers came at about the same time as slavery was ending in the United States. They took away all the men. Of the few who returned, only my grandfather could still read the past, and when he died shortly after returning. Then the church enacted its own little Inquisition and ordered all remaining *Rongorongo* tablets to be gathered in a great fire. It was like the reversal of Genesis: God charged Adam to *unname* the world. The few pieces that survived were scattered throughout the world, and they remain, mostly in museums, a few with private collectors, a vital link and a terrible barrier between what we had been and what we might become. Perhaps there are more still undiscovered."

"Humberto Rapu Haoa was your grandfather?" Miranda marvelled at how incredibly articulate this man could be, this descendent of orators and priests.

"Yes, three times removed. He was my great-great-great grandfather, and it is because of him I come into this cave without fear. This is where the *arikis* would live, sometimes for years, to bleach their skin white. I believe that was something we did only after the Dutchmen and Spaniards and English and French appeared in the eighteenth century and passed so briefly and with such devastating consequences through our lives. Like a white cloud of death. Why would we want to be white?"

Miranda surveyed Matteo's handsome face and remembered thinking the moment she had arrived how beautiful the Polynesian complexion was, how perfect their features. Or was that Morgan who had told her to expect such beauty and she had only affirmed his judgment? Right now Morgan was probably sipping tea on the verandah of the Royal Toronto Yacht Club gazing over at the CN Tower, thinking of her. No, she thought, *with Morgan life is more complex than that.*

Morgan was in fact thinking of Miranda as he huddled on the shore of Baffin Island. He imagined his partner on Easter Island, basking in the Pacific sunshine, writing her mystery novel. He was trying to conjure an image vivid enough that he could feel the heat. He shivered and leaned closer to Gloria Simmons. Miranda wouldn't write romance, she wasn't romantic. She was rational, down to earth, a no-nonsense realist. Despite her location, she'd write about Toronto. It wouldn't be a thriller; it would be a police procedural. Her protagonist would be a woman, of course, who had a clever and annoying male sidekick. The woman would be beautiful in a subtle and provocative way. Gloria shifted and Morgan moved against her.

"What do you think?" she said. "The cloud cover is lifting a little. We might do better back at the plane. They'll see us there." She seemed to be gathering her spirits, perhaps having determined that her own partner might still be alive by virtue of the improbable equation that his associate was not. Not so improbable: someone had buried him.

"Do you think the plane's a writeoff?"

"Hell, no. Twin Otters endure." She had reclaimed her feisty aplomb, if not her cool serenity. "That should be the De Havilland motto. *We endure.*"

"Well, let's hope we're as durable. Yeah, we'd better head back. We left the sleeping bag there."

"Forget it, Morgan. We're not having another naked encounter just yet."

"Can we be sure Thomas Ross is an ally?" Miranda leaned conspiratorially across the table, searching for something in Matteo's dark eyes to affirm their connection. "Leaving the book behind in this cavern suggests it was a bargaining chip, in case he was bushwhacked by either side. He said it was for leverage with the soldiers, but it would be with you, even more. He didn't expect you to find me. He was sure you thought I was dead."

"Bushwhacked?"

"Ambushed — same difference — that's another Canadianism. It doesn't sound like he intended on coming back for me, does it? Why bother, if the damned book was stowed safely away in the depths of the earth? I was expendable. I told him I'd broken the code. He didn't care."

"Have you?"

"Not quite."

"Did you tell Ross what you think it says?"

"No, of course not. I don't even know if there *is* a code, for goodness' sake. But I suspect he actually believes the book has more value to you and your people if it remains a mystery." He looked at her quizzically and the lamplight flickered across the book lying on the table between them. "Matteo, I am sure he believes there is more power in the unknown than the known. Whatever the secrets of your holy book, they're not likely to change the world. A mysterious talisman in the present trumps messages from the past, no matter how stirring. He may have a point."

"He is a cynic, I am a zealot, you are somewhere between. A romantic, perhaps."

"A realist, maybe, caught between forces of history at play in someone else's backyard — where I happen to have turned up by pure chance." He gazed into her eyes, projecting dismay that she could possibly be so naive. "Believe what you will," she said. "Your faith is what's keeping me alive."

"Miranda Quin, we do not want you harmed. If you can help us, you will help us. If not, either way, we will try to protect you. The government agents who followed you from Santiago, they came to Rapa Nui to kill you. That did not happen. The soldiers came to my grandparent's house to kill you. That did not happen. You are among friends."

"The smoking man and his shadow, they were *Carabinaros*. What did you do with them?"

"You were there. You know."

"But what happened to their bodies?"

"They are now among the *desaparecidos*, the *disparu*," he said, without irony. "There are more places for the dead on this island than for the living."

"And Thomas Edward Ross, is he also among the *des-apare-cidos*?"

"Oh no, he is much too valuable. He is a man with very powerful connections in Santiago —"

"The Pinochet fascists?"

"Yes, but with the government, as well."

"And for you?"

"Yes, he is valuable for us."

"Where is he now?" she asked.

"Good question. There is a cruise ship anchored off Hanga Roa."

"Do you think he's gone?"

"Quite possibly he is in the process of leaving."

"So he can leave? Just like that! What about me? How would we go about the process of *my* leaving"

"Life is not fair. We need you for now."

"Look, maybe the book is just a book, Matteo. I'm not a literary critic. I can't interpret the ambiguities of a text and come up with the answer to life. I'm a homicide detective."

"And a novelist."

"Too busy surviving one bloody mystery to write another." The depths in his sympathetic eyes seemed to counter the grim set of his jaw. Saying nothing, he urged her on and she felt stifled by the pressure but compelled to continue.

"Okay, let's say the book really is a delivery system. We're looking for something hidden in plain sight. We have to figure out *what* the code is before we can figure out what it says." She smiled with a shrug of resignation. "Let's accept that the book is a map and I am the key."

"You *are* the key. It is a treasure chest and only you can open it."

Miranda shuddered at the preternatural implications, then suddenly realized the divergence in what they had each said. "We're singing in different keys, Matteo! I wonder, are we looking for a legend on a map that allows us to translate, or for an instrument that allows us to unlock some revelation?"

"Perhaps they are the same thing."

"You are a genius, Matteo." He beamed, but his forehead furrowed with lines of consternation. "We need a key," she continued, "a key that will reveal the message *and* allow us to decipher what it means. Meaningless messages won't help the revolution. We're moving, here, we're on the right track." Miranda was excited, she could feel her pulse rising, her heart beating through her entire system. "The book is in English, written by a Norwegian, and it's about Rapa Nui. The writings in the margin are in English, written in a very deliberate script. It's like someone copied the notes letter by letter.

I don't think it's about the words, they're just markers. Otherwise, why bother dropping them here and there throughout the text? So what do they mark? It could be phrases or passages on the marked pages. Maybe if we add up the letters in each snippet of wisdom and then count — count, Matteo? Numbers! That's it."

"Numbers?"

Miranda took a deep breath and opened the Heyerdahl book to the flyleaf. Her index finger quivered with suppressed excitement, she pointed. "What does it say there?"

"*Aku-Aku*. It refers to the spirits of our ancestors."

"No, no, you're looking at the title page."

"In handwriting it says, Thor Heyerdahl, I think. And a mathematical equation of some sort. Incomplete, nonsensical."

"Exactly. Mathematically, it makes no sense. So we read it metaphorically. $4/5 = 00$. If the parallel zeroes stand for infinity, the temporal version of space without end, then, okay, we have God! The Abrahamic religions are obsessed with the infinite and the eternal, correct? And what do they have in common? Muslims, Christians, and Jews all revere the first five books of the Bible. The Pentateuch."

"The Pentateuch?"

"The five books of the Torah, the Books of Moses: Genesis, Exodus, Leviticus, Numbers, Deuteronomy. The fourth book of the holy five is Numbers. The inscription directs us to look for the message in numbers, not words. Matteo, we've done it!"

"We have?" he said, a little incredulous.

"Yes, we have. Hand me the book. What sets of numbers are in a book? Page numbers. Illustration numbers. Chapter numbers."

"Where do we start? That is a lot of numbers"

Miranda turned the pages a few at a time, tilting the book to the lamplight. Matteo sat back, waiting for the revelation to unfold. Miranda fidgeted.

"Let's try looking at the page numbers where the marginal notes have been added," she suggested.

"You see, my sister sent you."

Miranda asked for a pen and some paper. He reached into his breast pocket and pulled out the stub of a pencil. No paper. Removing the dust jacket from the book she began inscribing numbers on the back. She made two columns. In one column she wrote *3, 60, 73, 294*. In the other she wrote *5, 20, 36, 95*. She stared at the columns. She wrote down the numbers again, but this time in horizontal lines.

Matteo leaned forward, watching her think. "Why are there two groups? How do you know one group from another?"

"Four of the statements concern enemies. Four do not. It seemed like a logical division."

"Why two groups? Why not three or four or five?"

"Because the first is a cluster of four. I'm guessing the others, which seem to have a vague affinity based on honour and beauty, would be the same."

"Why?"

"Because." She stared at the lines of numbers, then at the columns, then back at the horizontal lines. "Maps. Of course. Map coordinates. Do you have an atlas?"

"Not handy."

"No, of course not, we're in a cave." She looked up and smiled. "What we have here is a very specific location. So, the first set signifies northern latitude. The second is western longitude."

"How can you possibly know that?"

"It's my mushier side; I'm interpreting tropes of emotion."

"Tropes?"

"Something we used to say in literature class, years ago. It's me being a literary critic, don't worry about it. What I'm figuring is that if the person encrypting was an islander, or an outsider sympathetic to the islanders, the sentiments expressed about enemies and the dangers of allies might refer to Holland, Spain, France, and England. That is, Europeans, the emissaries of death and disaster from the northern hemisphere. The more positive sentiments in this scheme of things would be reserved for Rapa Nui, the island in the west. Okay! The numbers. Simple. Get rid of the divisions. Write them down, so."

She wrote down *36073294N* and below that she wrote *5203695W*.

"These numbers, they're not the same length."

"Therefore," she said, we move from right to left. We know for sure the final number in each case will probably be a four digit statement of seconds. That's the convention, seconds to two decimal places. Then the next number to the left will be two digits."

"Why not one, or three?" He leaned forward as if he were trying to hear her think.

"Not three because it will be a measurement of minutes, which only go up to sixty. And a single digit anywhere within the sequence would be expressed as two digits, with a zero added to avoid confusion, as in zero-one, zero-two, et cetera." She pronounced the word, *et kay teh rah*, her fractured Latin an indicator of the ebullience she felt in resolving what seemed an impossible conundrum ten minutes previously. "Since the middle number must be two digits, and a measurement of minutes cannot be more than two digits, the first number is whatever remains." She took a deep breath. "So now we have 36 degrees, 07 minutes, 32.94 seconds, north latitude. And we have 5 degrees, 20 minutes, 36.95 seconds west longitude."

"I hate to be, how should we say it, annoying, but ..."

"But?"

"There is no zero in front of the 5."

"It's implied. Catch up with me, Matteo. The zero is necessary only within a sequence. The degrees figure must be, like I said, whatever is left over."

"You are a mathematical prodigy."

"Smart cop from Toronto. And modest. Now, may I go home?" She knew her revelation had little to do with arithmetical skills or math, unless logic could be called a subset of mathematics, but she was pleased with herself.

"So where would this place you have discovered occur, if we had a map?"

"I'm guessing around Malta, maybe Gibraltar, maybe Casablanca or Tangier."

"And why would that matter to us?"

"Well, apparently it does. Whoever went to all the trouble to create the encryption must have thought it was a location worth dying for."

"On the other side of the world?"

"Yes, but conveyed in a book called *Aku-Aku*. Any book might have delivered the same message, but it seems your mysterious correspondent chose a book with a significant title. These are your ancestors speaking to you through Heyerdahl. I think you should trust them. Your quest is just getting started. But this is where I get off, I'm going home, now, Matteo." She paused, then said grandiloquently, for her own amusement, "My work here is done."

Unable to reach the plane, Morgan and Gloria Simmons sat on the rocky embankment and ate their remaining chocolate bar while boulders the size of basketballs worked their way downstream in the rushing torrent, grinding and jamming together to form new back currents and eddies that shifted the flow as they watched. They listened to the river roar like the rumble of faraway thunder.

The crystalline clarity of the water roiling at their feet, the turgid opaque water surging against the rocks on the opposite shore, the paradox struck Morgan as one of those natural anomalies that makes the world seem like an astonishing experiment. He considered a walk along the bank to see if the waters converged before reaching the sea. Instead, he turned to his companion and spoke in a voice loud enough to carry over the background noise of the river.

"Do you suppose we'll die here?" he said. It didn't seem a matter of much consequence. A conversational gambit.

"Quite possibly," she answered, looking up at the clouds that had closed over again and seemed to be descending rapidly, with rain lashing toward them in the quickening wind.

"If I go first, please feel free to eat my remains," he said.

"And vice versa," she responded. "You've already observed the choicest bits. But leave the face, I've always promised myself I'd go to the grave without facial surgery. Do we have a sharp knife?"

"Not even a dull one. Let's survive."

"Let's."

They lapsed into silence, huddled closely, but did not get out of the incoming storm until the first streaks of sleet-laden rain lashed at their cheeks. They rose simultaneously and scrambled over to a cluster of rocks set back from the embankment. By squeezing together they were able to crawl under a rock slab that effectively shielded them from the downpour. During a lull, Morgan tramped around, ripping up clumps of moss that were quite dry where they had clung in the lea of boulders, although patches growing in the sparse open soil were saturated. He threw the driest moss into their makeshift den and Gloria Simmons worked it around to make a viable nest. He crawled back in as the rains picked up and they fell into a sound sleep in each other's arms.

***

When Miranda and Matteo made their way to the mouth of the cave the sun was high overhead. They walked up a steep pathway that must have once accommodated caretaker servants of the *arikis* who inhabited the cave. At the crest of the precipice, she stopped to gaze around. She could see most of Rapa Nui from this vantage and as she followed the rolling landscape to the edge of perception she realized the possibility of a fondness for this small island, alone in the vast reaches of the South Pacific, that might be strong enough to arouse the most fierce loyalty in its people.

She reached over and grasped Matteo's hand and squeezed it with the passion of a compatriot. He had lost his wife and his sister and how many more to their cause, which in the larger world remained virtually unknown. If the attraction she had felt for Ross was the seductive reflection of his offhand indifference to morality, the attraction of this man beside her was his moral commitment. His unspeakable troubles he endured without fanfare through the strength of his character, the honour of his purpose. Beside him, she felt humble and yet proud. She was in love, she decided, but not with the man. Rather, with his quietude, his calm, and indomitable spirit.

Suddenly, she felt herself dragged unceremoniously off balance as her idol dug his feet of clay into the path and pulled her along. She could see a roostertail of dust swirling behind a vehicle moving in their direction and instinctively she wrenched free of Matteo and crouched, even though it was still a great distance away. Matteo shielded his eyes from the wheeling glare of the overhead sun, trying to make out who it was. Suddenly, he dove down and pulled Miranda over him into the low ground cover. Together they squirmed and scrambled into denser foliage and took shelter behind a small cluster of lava boulders. Another fallen *moai*, disguised by time as a natural outcropping.

"Who is it?" She whispered although the vehicle was still a long way off and its occupants could not possibly have heard them.

He held an upraised palm toward her face and shrugged. They waited. The sun beat down on them. They were hidden from view, but they were not in shadow. If the new arrivals strayed off the path, Miranda realized, they were completely exposed.

Doors slammed with the solid thud of a Land Rover. They heard voices. Without looking up, she knew Matteo could identify whose they were. She listened as the voices got closer. She could hear Spanish, snatches of Rapanui, and then Oxonian English. She exchanged a knowing glance of dismay with Matteo. Thomas Edward Ross was not someone either of them had wanted to hear. The cluster of voices moved over the edge of the cliff and out of range. Matteo slowly rose to his feet, surveying the scene carefully, in case they had left a lookout behind.

"Te Ave Teao is with them," he said in a low voice. "They have my brother, he is with them. He should not be with them. And your Mr. Ross, he is with them, as well, and I believe he is not their prisoner. I think he is leading them to the cave."

"He is not *my* Mr. Ross!" She paused. "He won't want them to find his boxes."

"And what do you suppose is in those boxes?"

"Armaments."

"No, I believe they are filled with artifacts."

"He's a collector?"

"An entrepreneur. He has visited our island a number of times. He has indeed brought arms, but they are not his to be stockpiled. He receives them from the Pinochet people, pays off the government people, and we have purchased them with our ancestral legacy."

"You supplied him with the artifacts."

"A few genuine. Most of them fake. We are very good at faking our past. It comes of not having access to how it actually was."

"So you have the armaments?"

"Hidden. And he had the artifacts hidden, as well. Rapanui wouldn't go into his cave and the Chilean soldiers didn't know it was there. It is not the boxes they're after. It's you."

"The bastard," said Miranda, with a grimace of embarrassment for being so easily betrayed.

"It would seem he is. Nothing with Mr. Ross is certain, even the circumstances of his birth. Once they find it, you know, the *federales* will have no hesitation about entering the cave. But my brother, he will cast himself onto the rocks below before he would violate *tapu*. He is a good Catholic, of course. He would not embrace suicide easily."

"Is that going to happen?"

"Yes, I think so. Your Mr. Ross will lead the Chileans into the *ariki*'s chamber. They will find you have gone. They will find the book."

"Yes," she said, "but they won't find the paper with our calculations." She pushed against the thin material at the waistband of her dress so that it crackled.

"Good," he said. "Somewhere between Malta and Casablanca or Tangier."

"Do we make a run for it?" she asked, looking around them, wondering where they would run to that was not even more exposed than their present position.

Without speaking, he took her hand. They walked not fifty paces before coming to a slight crevasse in the rock surface where two slabs of lava had thrust up against one another, leaving a space between. "Down here," he directed and disappeared into the earth. Miranda dropped to her knees and only then did she see where the crevasse opened at one end into a small cavern under the slabs and she crawled in after him.

Time passed neither slowly nor fast, but more like a feeling of warmth and security. Finally, voices in the distance moved closer, then away. Matteo climbed out of their lair and peered through the sparse foliage, following their movement. He sank back down into the shadows and stayed very still. They waited for the Land Rover doors to slam, then he spoke.

"Te Ave Teao is dead."

"No!"

"He was not with them. We must go now."

"No," said Miranda. "We need to talk. I'm so sorry. Your sister. Your brother." She did not know what to say. He smiled.

"My mother, she is alive in Toronto. Someday I must come and visit you both. Perhaps I will be a doctor as I was supposed to be and I will make my mother proud."

Miranda was speechless. This was a man. She reached out and touched his cheek with her fingertips. This was a man unlike any she could have imagined.

When Morgan woke up he was alone. He burrowed deeper into the damp moss, but could not get comfortable. A chill running shivers down his spine forced him to crawl out into the open where he felt almost cowed by the vastness of the Arctic sky. A vault of royal blue arced from horizon to horizon in every direction, including the west where the wall of glacial ice stood proud over the ragged landscape. As his gaze swung to the north, he saw a wisp of white that appeared first like a crack in the blue, then wavered, and he realized it was smoke.

Gloria Simmons approached him from behind and put her hand on his shoulder. "I see it," she said. "There was no point in waking you. We can't get across for a few more hours."

"Yeah, we probably can if we go upriver or down."

"Upriver, then, toward the glacier. It's narrower." She climbed onto a slight rise of rubbled rock. "No, downriver, it spreads, we'll find a shallow place." She jumped down. "I told you he was alive."

Close to the sea, they picked their way across knee-deep water, bracing each other in the surges, and stopped on the far shore to empty their boots and wring out their sodden socks, then trudged in silence over the rough terrain until they cut through a breach in the rocks and came out into a small open space in front of a granite boulder slide, and there in a natural cavern gouged out of the slope were two men reclined beside a smouldering fire of moss and dwarf willow twigs.

"Harrington D'Arcy?" Morgan whispered into the smoke.

D'Arcy raised his head slowly and seemed to be trying to bring Morgan into focus. His face showed a deathly pallor and his eyes seemed almost vacant, yet he spoke in a surprisingly clear, but tremulous voice. "I'm glad you are here, Detective." He shifted his gaze. "And you, Gloria, of course, you have come for me." He seemed to be trying to reach up as she leaned down to embrace him. "I don't suppose you've brought dinner?" he whispered. He reached an index finger up to his lips, then rubbed it against the bristle of his mustache in a small gesture of resignation before letting his hand drop back against his chest. "No, of course," he murmured. Then, rousing his spirits he declared with incongruous formality, "This is Miguel Escobar, we lost our associate, buried him by the shore, the cold got to him quickly, he was a smoker, his lighter has come in handy, we're lucky for that." He slumped back, exhausted by his role as host.

Gloria Simmons took off her jacket and wrapped it around him. Harrington D'Arcy was already wearing a layer of the dead man's clothes, as was Miguel Escobar. Morgan removed his own jacket and draped in over the other man's shoulders. The man forced a grim smile, but made no effort to speak. Morgan immediately set about gathering sticks of dried willow from ancient trees that had died having reached maturity at the height of his knees, after lives huddled close to the ground waiting for their brief seasons of growth and renewal. Gloria moved around with equal vigour to maintain body heat, gathering the driest moss in great clumps to build up their crude bivouac into something more comfortable.

"We need food," said Morgan and took back his jacket after they had moved Escobar closer to the blazing fire. "I'm going hunting."

Once he was out of sight, Morgan slowed his pace. He had never hunted in his life, except in the Don Valley Ravine when he was a kid, and then only for squirrels. With makeshift bows and arrows, and zero success. Dejected, he walked down to the river shallows where they had crossed and he sat on the embankment, staring into the water. The cloudy surface reflected deep blue shards of the sky, but it was ribboned here and there with streaks the colour of tarnished silver. He stood up to examine more clearly the unusual play between light and shadows that moved of their own volition.

"My goodness," he said aloud. In a few of the deeper pools close to the shore he could identify patterns that were facing upstream, with their tails to the sea, swimming lazily against the diminishing current. Morgan ran through the files in his mind. Arctic char was a freshwater and saltwater fish in the salmon family. Exceptionally hardy, thrived in the coldest waters, flesh a deep pink. Served occasionally in the same Toronto restaurants that also featured caribou and musk ox on their menus. He had never tried it.

He found a twisted branch among a thicket of dwarf willows the length of a walking stick. He broke it laterally and then sharpened the end on a rough piece of granite. He carried rocks to the bank and made a pile beside a submerged pool no bigger than a bathtub, then he waded into the water and hoisted the rocks into position to form a weir that gradually circled around to become an enclosure with an open segment in the downstream end. Periodically, he climbed out onto the land where he jumped up and down and stamped his feet and waved his arms wildly until feeling came back in the form of excruciating pain.

Surveying his work with satisfaction, he moved downstream until he spied a couple of char, then he made his way out into the flow and slowly closed in on them so that they lazily swam upstream and into his weir. There was enough water flowing through the rocks he had built on the upper side that the fish seemed content to linger in the current, oblivious to their fate. After another wild dance to warm his extremities, Morgan repeated the procedure, beating three fish, this time, upstream into the enclosure. Then he reached over and lifted rocks to block the downstream opening and proceeded with the slaughter.

Walking back to the encampment with five Arctic char strung through the gills on his warped willow spear, Morgan felt a strange sense of contentment and wonder. He seemed to have been working from a corner of his mind not previously explored. The notion of a survival instinct meant something different now than in his familiar world. He felt at home here as he never quite did on the streets of the city. Part of him hoped they would not be rescued for days. When he came over the rise into the open, he triumphantly held the fish out in front of him and tried to suppress a broad grin. His eyes watered as he peered at the other three through the fire's sweet-smelling haze that hovered over them like a nimbus signalling their salvation. Approaching closely, he set down his catch.

"Morgan," whispered Gloria Simmons, gazing up at him through the smoke with a sad smile. "Morgan," she repeated, her words barely audible, "Harrington D'Arcy is dead."

Matteo and Miranda approached the crowd of tourists seeking shade at the campgrounds below Rano Raraku. Dressed in safari clothes and Hawaiian holiday beach togs, the medley of European, American, and Japanese tourists had finished boxed lunches and were waiting to board buses back to their ship. Matteo and Miranda had been holding hands like wandering lovers as they ambled into view and on an island where everything seemed strange they drew no attention to themselves in their bedraggled state as they mingled with the visitors. Matteo spoke briefly to one of the drivers. They clambered into the back of a bus.

"I will get off before the bus leaves," he said. "Once you are on the boat and at sea, you will turn yourself over to the captain. He will make arrangements."

"Can't you come with me?" Miranda responded, realizing how small the island was, how limited his movements. "They will be after you, especially now."

"It depends whether Te Ave Teao jumped or pretended to slip."

She looked at him quizzically.

"They know we are brothers. If his death was an accident, they will offer condolences. If his death was by choice, they will kill me."

"Oh." She paused. "What about Ross, will he give you up?"

"He has nothing to gain. No, he would be well served by our revolution."

"How so?"

"It is only a rumour, but possibly, when it succeeds, the federal government would collapse."

"And this is a good thing? Isn't Chile a stable democracy?"

"Yes and no. For us it is immaterial, one way or another. And if other forces brought down the government, that might provide us an opportunity to slip away as collateral damage. It's a chicken-or-egg situation. It doesn't matter whether we're the cause or the outcome. Our interests and those of Mr. Ross's principal handlers represent parallel routes to perhaps much different ends."

"Handlers?"

"He is a puppet who thinks himself a free agent, and that is what makes him both dangerous and very useful."

"The strings are in American dollars?"

"Money, yes, but vanity, more."

"You admire him, don't you?"

"He is useful. And you, do you admire him?"

"I'm not sure."

"He is attractive, but expendable, remember that. Do not let him get close or you will go down when he does."

Whenever Ross appeared, he cast death like a shadow. "I hope never to meet the man again in my life." She wondered if this were true. "What would he gain if the government collapsed?"

"What would he lose if it doesn't?"

The tourists outside were slowly gathering into their separate groups, milling close to their buses, ready to leave. The *moai* at Rano Raraku were inspiring, but there was still time to get back for a stroll around the deck and hors d'oeuvres.

"When you get back to Toronto," he said, taking her hand, "look up my friend, please. His name is Rove McMan, he is a sailor. And tell my mother I love her."

Miranda did not ask how she would find either the sailor or his mother. His lack of specific directives reminded her she was a cop. She would find them, of course.

As he stood up she pulled him close over her without rising, and holding his face between her two hands she kissed him on the lips, a full lingering kiss that was neither sexual nor like family or a friend. It was a passionate statement of the connection between them. She would always carry that kiss with her, remembered with the whole of her being.

He was halfway up the aisle when she called him back. With as much discretion as possible, she squirmed around to retrieve from under her dress the dust jacket that had the mysterious coordinates written on the back.

"You'll need this," she said, holding it out to him.

"No," he said. "The numbers are inscribed in my mind." He leaned over and kissed her on the forehead, turned, and walked away without looking back.

As the bus rumbled over the road back to Hanga Roa, she memorized the numbers and shredded the dust jacket. Once aboard the cruise ship, Miranda kept to public rooms until Rapa Nui had slipped below the eastern horizon. Then she found a steward and after some insistence he agreed to take her to see the captain on the bridge. The master of the ship was a robust man with a beard, probably of eastern European origin, although his English was impeccable as he spoke to various others on the bridge before turning to her. Miranda suspected he came from Poland and wrote brooding, elaborate parables of the sea in his spare time.

Expecting the need to make a case for herself as a stowaway, Miranda was thrown when the captain addressed her with elaborate cordiality.

"Ah, Miss Quin. Mr. Harrington D'Arcy said you would come directly to me and so you have. Welcome aboard. I hope your flight, or should I say flights, from Toronto, yes, Canada, were not excessively arduous. Mr. D'Arcy asked me to give you this. You must have been rather rushed to leave your hotel empty-handed, so to speak."

Miranda opened the manila envelope as if it might explode and peered inside, looking for the trigger mechanism. Inside were the necessities of life.

Since the real D'Arcy was missing, there was a possibility that her mysterious mentor was actually him, but that seemed unlikely since he was last seen in the Arctic. More likely, Ross had reverted to an earlier identity. It must be him. She slowly withdrew a dark blue Canadian passport, convincingly worn at the corners, and opened it to see her own face staring back, looking wan and startled, and she realized what a clever forgery it must be, down to the unpleasant likeness. There was an Ontario driver's license and a health insurance card, both with the same picture as in the passport. That was a giveaway, should anyone examine these items too closely — the primary document was federal, the other two were provincial. There was no Toronto Police ID, but there were several credit cards tucked into the passport with unfamiliar numbers, both curiously ending in the same four digits. She expected they would be worthless, but the debit card from the Royal Bank, also with an unfamiliar number, she was equally certain would yield cash if she could find a bank machine on board. The PIN number would be the four digits the fake credit cards had in common. She wondered how much she was good for?

"Mr. D'Arcy will join us for dinner. I'll have you shown to your cabin."

"For dinner?"

"You will dine with me at the captain's table. It is not often we have the pleasure of Mr. D'Arcy's company. We must take advantage when we do."

"And where is Mr. D'Arcy now?"

"I expect he is in the casino. That is where he usually goes."

"Usually?"

"Mr. D'Arcy keeps a suite on board for his own private use and joins us from time to time as his schedule allows. A world-class sailor, you might say."

Miranda was more than a little bewildered. That did not sound like her sometime friend, Mr. Ross. To maintain a suite on a ship like this would be a major investment. Ross might be doing well in the world, but he did not seem inordinately wealthy. It did not sound like the reclusive Toronto lawyer, either. From what she knew of the real Mr. D'Arcy, he might be high-flying, but he wasn't jet set. She was shown to her cabin, which proved to be accessed through the D'Arcy suite and had a balcony of its own. As she devoured two bananas, a large papaya, and a piece of garnet-coloured passion fruit from a bedside bowl, she wondered if there could possibly be a third Mr. D'Arcy?

Only when she got up to dispose of the waste from her feast and wipe her hands clean did she notice a smaller manila envelope on the top of a dresser. She opened it carefully and withdrew another envelope, this one of clear plastic surrounding the brilliantly costumed figure of Wonder Woman from the April 1954 issue featuring the Stone Slayer of Easter Island. *Ross!* she thought. There was only one T.E. Ross, whatever his name really was.

9

Playing With the Dead

Morgan and Miranda agreed to meet at Starbucks on College at Yonge. She wasn't officially back from her leave, and he preferred to catch up away from the office. Both realized that much of what they had to say to each other was not police business, but personal. In the ten days since he had returned from the Arctic, Morgan felt at loose ends. He had wished his partner were around; he thought better when they were together. But when Miranda called from Tahiti to say she was on her way home, the first question that came to mind was not *why*, but *why call*? By the afternoon of the following day she'd be back. They talked for a few minutes about the stifling August weather in Toronto and the balmy weather in Papeete, and then she hung up and he realized how immensely relieved he had been to hear her voice.

"You're looking good," said Morgan as he rose to greet her when she came in. "A little pale around the edges." He wasn't about to ask why she had cut her sabbatical short. That would come when she was ready.

"Spent most of my time in a cave that was famous for bleaching skin white."

"No wonder I couldn't reach you. I thought you'd dropped off the face of the earth."

"And you didn't do anything about it?"

"I worried."

"Thank you, Morgan, but I can take care of myself."

He slurped his coffee to skim off the crema. She was back. She actually had the soft warm glow of a carefully acquired tan that made her hazel eyes sparkle. "Well," he said. "Well, well." He didn't know where to start.

"Tell me about Harrington D'Arcy," she said in a conspiratorial whisper.

"He's dead."

"The real Harrington D'Arcy?"

"As far as I know. What about your guy, the sleazy Englishman who borrowed his name, did he turn up again?"

"Actually, he did. Several times. I don't remember telling you he was sleazy. He was quite debonair, although he did try to kill me. Or to place death in my way. Or he saved my life. It was an odd relationship. Actually, I knew your Mr. D'Arcy was dead. I heard the news at sea. But I want to know the details, to catch up on your case. I take it you've been waiting for me to help sort out the complexities."

"I have," he said. "At sea?" His resolve to seem disinterested was fading. "Talk to me."

Miranda skimmed off her own crema with a spoon and savoured it with a lingering sigh, reached over and took the rest of his, then proceeded to tell him about her romantic cruise through the South Pacific, stopping off in the Marquesas Islands before travelling to fabled Bora Bora and then on to Papeete, Tahiti. She would tell him another time about the treacherous machinations of her Rapa Nui adventures. She would perhaps tell him about the suite kept on board the *Island Queen* in D'Arcy's name, and perhaps about the note that was on her silver salver when she sat down at the captain's table on her first evening aboard. But for the time being, she needed to find her way, to establish the right distance between herself and recent events in order to bring them into perspective.

She had stumbled, sprawling headlong into a culture in crisis. For Matteo and his cohort caught up in the heart of the maelstrom, their struggle was deadly serious. She did not want to diminish its significance nor overplay her role by turning it into an amusing adventure.

She had been right about the debit card and the PIN number that had given her access to enough money to get her home in comfort. She was curious about the source, but not anxious. It had seemed almost inevitable that someone else should be looking out for her interests. Before dinner she had bought a few clothes and toiletries and when she approached the captain's table she was quite confident that Ross would be waiting for her. Since she had again eluded death, he would be gracious. She was unable to decide whether her false papers and the money were from him in recompense for service rendered or, as she felt with a vague sense of foreboding, she was being maintained for purposes yet undeclared. If the latter, Ross would at least provide a touchstone so that she could anticipate what might be expected. Fate, she had thought, sometimes comes in the guise of an English gentleman of no moral suasion at all.

Instead of her false Mr. D'Arcy or another of the same name, there was only the note and a shrug from the ship's master by way of an explanation. It was he who had informed her before they reached the Marquesas Islands that Harrington D'Arcy had been reported dead in the Canadian Arctic, and he who had been only mildly nonplussed that the dead man apparently travelled from a semi-tropical island south of the equator into high latitudes above the Arctic Circle and managed to die of exposure, all in a matter of days, while his ship had steamed peacefully through the South Seas in its own separate world.

The note had been written in a familiar voice that she seemed to hear as she read. "My dear Miranda," it began. "Unfortunately, I am unable to join you. Please give my regards to Bora Bora. It is the most delightful island of any I know and I shall miss showing you its splendid charms to their best advantage. The suite is of course yours and you may sign for anything you wish. Do spend a few days in Tahiti before you return to Toronto. Papeete itself is a bustling port and you might want to pick up a strand of Tahitian pearls. You may charge to my account at the Pearl Market, a delightful shop on rue Colette, just up from the waterfront." The tone seemed casual and yet formal, like a sugar daddy not wholly convinced of his superior status. As an afterthought, he wrote. "I am very pleased you are alive. My friend, Te Ave Teao, distracted the *federales* —"

"Distracted!"

"I beg your pardon?" said Morgan.

"Sorry, I didn't say anything."

"I think you said *distracted*."

"I was thinking."

"Think away." Morgan liked watching her think. He had missed that.

Aware that her narrative had dwindled into silence and Morgan was sitting across from her in Starbucks, in Toronto, watching her think, Miranda felt a warm surge of camaraderie as she continued her mental reprise of the note from Ross. After dismissing the importance of the death of Matteo's brother, or perhaps diminishing his partisan sacrifice as a meaningless heroic gesture, he had continued: "I went ahead into the cave to assure you were hidden and was quite relieved to find you nowhere in sight. Enjoy your voyage. Yours T.E." And then at the bottom: "Don't pull the rug out from under yourself."

"Morgan," she said, leaning forward with a conspiratorial tilt to her head, "have you ever heard the expression, *don't pull the rug out from under yourself?*"

"Sounds Presbyterian. Or something done by the Cirque du Soleil."

"I don't think he meant it as theology. Nor as a bodily contortion."

"Who?" Morgan asked.

"Tell me about the investigation."

"Have you talked to Jill yet?"

Her ward, Jill Bray, was a student at Branksome Hall and presently on a fifty-two-day canoe trip across the Arctic with Camp Wanapitei.

"She won't be back for another week. Tell me about your investigation."

He wanted more of her story, but decided to forge ahead and let her fill in the gaps when she was ready. "Last time I talked to you I had one corpse to deal with, and now I've got two or possibly three, or four. D'Arcy virtually died in my arms."

"Really."

"No, not really. I was off hunting fish with a weir and a spear when he died. Of exposure. That's what the police report said. As for the wife, I'm still not sure."

"Of what?"

"What killed her. She seems to have died of exposure, as well."

"In Toronto … in August?"

"It's possible, apparently you can murder by weather."

"What in God's name were you doing in the Arctic? She must have been very alluring."

Morgan looked startled. Miranda flashed her teeth.

"Just a good guess, Morgan. But I'm right, aren't I?"

"How's your novel going?"

"Finished, polished, edited, in the bookstores tomorrow. If I'd known how easy it was, I'd have been writing mysteries for years."

"Devastating reviews," he said, projecting into the future. "Ignored by the public. Remaindered at a dollar a copy. End of writing career. Aren't you glad you didn't resign from the force?"

She leaned low across the table and looked up into his eyes. *He really is quite beautiful*, she thought. *Too many beautiful men in my life*. She slouched back against her chair and smiled dreamily.

Morgan had no idea what was going through her mind. "Did you ever read that book I gave you, Beverley Haun, *Inventing Easter Island*?"

"No, Morgan, I didn't. It went up in a fiery inferno that was meant to consume me."

He assumed she was speaking metaphorically.

She added, as an improbable addendum: "I watched from the grave, Morgan, cheek by jowl with a desiccated skull. Well, the cheeks and jowls were mine. He was on the gaunt side."

"It's a good book, I'm reading it now."

"Nice title." She tilted her head and a veil of auburn hair descended slowly across her field of vision. Exhaustion as an aphrodesiac was beginning to fade. She sat up abruptly. "Who was the woman, Morgan?"

"There have been several," he responded, and, much to his surprise, an image of Ellen Ravenscroft veered through his mind. Feeling self-conscious, he pushed back from the table and walked over to order two more coffees from the barista. When he returned, Miranda seemed to be lost in thought, barely smiling when he slid the coffee under her nose. He slurped at the crema and stared at the sun gleaming on the College Street windows. He looked back at her and then away, envisioning those final hours on the desolate, beautiful, haunting, disorderly shore of Baffin Island.

Gloria Simmons had been holding D'Arcy across her lap when Morgan returned with the fish. She had been holding his head against her body, almost as if she intended to nurse him before he expired. The other man, Miguel Escobar, was lying against her outstretched legs, curled up with his back pressed to her for the radiant warmth from her body. When she had looked up through the smoke and announced D'Arcy's death she hardly moved.

At the time he was dumbfounded and simply went about preparing the fish. He rolled them in layers of saturated moss and settled them into the embers. He had nothing to clean them with but expected the flesh would fall off in their fingers when they were cooked.

In retrospect Morgan realized how deeply he had been moved by the strange picture of the three bodies intertwined. There was something so primal about the scene that he had no words to describe it. In all his years in homicide he had never seen death and life so intimately connected; he had never seen a woman, a person, poised between them, so inextricably bound to both. The angel of life and the angel of merciful death.

When the fish was cooked he had helped to dismantle the tableaux, laying Harrington D'Arcy on a bed of moss close to the boulder face and propping the other man up so that he could eat morsels of char held to his mouth. After a little food and a few sips of water that Gloria Simmons carried to him in her own mouth and fed to him from her lips while Morgan tended the fire, the man seemed to relax into a deep sleep and she gently rolled him onto his side so the smoke wouldn't choke him.

The evening sky had cleared again to a deep blue; rescue would be on its way. Warm and satiated from succulent chunks of char, Morgan and Gloria Simmons moved to the edge of the smoke and were immediately inundated by clouds of tiny blackflies dive-bombing at what little exposed flesh offered itself up. The weather had been too cold during the night, then too bright and then too wet; now conditions were perfect and the scourge of the North attacked mercilessly until their prey moved back under the cover of smoke.

Without being prodded, Gloria Simmons had decided it was time for clarity. "You are patient, Detective Morgan, or very focused."

"Neither," he had responded

"Curious, then?"

"Very."

"There will be ripe blueberries close by. There always are when the blackflies come out."

He had expected something a little more illuminating, but as if she had just been warming to her own voice, she shifted perspectives and continued, "You know about Nanisivik on the north end of the island, Nanisivik is closing down." She adjusted her posture on their bed of moss and lichen. "A far bigger find has been made, running like a band across central Baffin. We are at the east end of it where we sit. Zinc, copper, lead, nickel, and, of course, immeasurable quantities of gold as a bonus. All of this is worth billions."

"In potential," he had said.

"Access will be relatively easy with global warming to help us along."

"Us?"

"There is us and there is them. You, I presume, are with *us*. Our side consists of the Inuit people who own the rights and a foreign investor."

"A foreign investor?"

"The government of Chile."

"And *them*?"

"A fascist cabal, also from Chile. People we do not like."

"Then why deal with them, if you have the rights?"

"They have much money, they are ruthless, they have a political agenda. All of that makes them a formidable foe, not easily dismissed. Some of our own people support them."

She had moved restlessly in their nest, her eyes were red from the smoke and tears were smeared on her cheeks. He reached up and touched his own face to confirm that he too had been tearing up. Escobar lay very still while Harrington D'Arcy seemed to dominate in death as much as in life. Morgan leaned toward Gloria Simmons in expectation. She complied. "You might call them Pinochet loyalists," she said. "They are a fascist junta who want to bring down the present government."

"Of Chile. Is Pinochet still alive?"

"Just barely. But they don't need him, they need his name. They already have a good part of the national treasury from the Pinochet years in offshore accounts. Chile is the world's largest copper producer.

With Baffin Island under their control, the Pinochet cabal could undermine Chile's control of the market, and destabilize the government. If the government falls, their investment here would assure their return to power — this time without help from the CIA, so far as we know. Two birds with one stone: destabilize this government; bankroll the next. Then watch the terrors begin all over again."

Despite spending time on Easter Island, Morgan was hazy on Chilean politics. It seemed obvious, though, that he would endorse the Inuit claim; he could not imagine being on the Pinochet side

"Their victory would be a very bad thing," she continued. "Pinochet was ruthless, thousands died. Thousands more simply disappeared."

"The *desaparecidos*."

"The *disparu*, yes. So, Morgan, our job, yours and mine, is to ensure that control of the Baffin copper belt does not fall into the wrong hands."

"Our job."

"You help get me out of here, we remain undead. We take Harrington D'Arcy back home for burial with his wife. We take our friend here, back for whatever awaits him. Then you get back to solving murders, and life returns to normal."

Life returns to normal. Pulling out of his reverie, Morgan looked across the table at Miranda and smiled shyly as if he were somehow embarrassed to have been so far away in his mind.

"Welcome back," she said.

"You, too," he said.

"It's good to be here," she said. "Morgan, once again, what the hell were you doing up there? You need me around to keep you grounded."

"It's a long story."

"I was sailing the South Seas on the *Island Queen* when I heard about D'Arcy. I checked him out on the *Globe and Mail* website and up popped a picture of you. Stock photo, not flattering. So I knew you'd been up there, and there were no survivors, apart from you and your lady friend. All three of the businessmen died, including Harrington D'Arcy. Tell me?"

"You knew about Gloria Simmons? And here I thought you were psychic. Yeah, we survived. The other three didn't. One of them was already dead when we got there. Then D'Arcy died. And the other one died after D'Arcy, it was like the breath had been sucked right out of him." Morgan remembered being shocked by the cruelty of the man dying at the point of rescue, but he also remembered feeling somehow his death was inevitable. "I went out into the clearing to meet the chopper that had zeroed in on our smoke. It was the D'Arcy Associates chopper from Pond Inlet. When I got back with the rescue team, the woman, Gloria Simmons, I'll tell you about her later, she was fine, but the man, *Señor* Miguel Escobar, he was dead. He'd seemed okay, he even ate a bit of the fish I cooked up."

"You hunted for fish, you cooked?" She tried to envision her partner in a primal mode, foraging in the Arctic, and she came up empty. She could imagine him on Rapa Nui easily enough, but not in the northern reaches of their own country.

"I fished with rocks and a spear. Arctic char. When we tried to move him, Escobar, we discovered he'd died."

"Three men died. Two after you got there."

"There's a lot to sort out. It wasn't really my jurisdiction. I was a bystander, a witness by no choice of my own. According to the RCMP report, all three died of exposure."

"Is that what the autopsies said?"

"There were no autopsies."

"Really! Doesn't that strike you as odd?"

"Miranda, the official version is they were in a boat that smashed into a pod of whales, the guide floated off and was rescued, they managed to get to shore, and we found them, but it was too late. They died of exposure, hypothermia, deprivation of the necessities for survival."

"But what do you think really happened?"

"They were out there for three days. No food. You just don't know how raw it can actually get, especially at night."

"In the land of the midnight sun?"

"Geography lesson: we were above the Arctic Circle, but by early August the sun dips below the northern horizon for a couple of hours during the night — it's like perpetual dusk only it doesn't go on forever, just seems like it, especially if you're wet from the sleet and cold without shelter. So, yeah, you could die in August in the Arctic, no problem."

"But you didn't die, you hunted and fished and shared body heat with a beautiful woman."

For a moment, Morgan was startled. "You realize we crash-landed in the middle of a river? At least we had the plane and a bit of gear. We were lucky. The others weren't."

"Lucky you crashed! Morgan, who was flying? The woman? How did you manage to land at just the right place? Was she the navigator, as well? And two people died after you found them! Some rescuers you turned out to be. Why no autopsies — no need? There's always a need when three guys die in questionable circumstances. Do you really believe they died of exposure?"

"Well, the first one did, for sure. Yeah, I do believe."

"Interesting answer from an atheist! Morgan, believing don't make it so."

"When I talked to the Mounties, they were adamant."

"Adamant?"

"That was that and the case was closed."

"Morgan, this is me. We're not buying their explanation even on a temporary basis. Whales don't attack boats. Boats maybe attack whales."

"You know this because?"

"Common sense. And nobody swims very far in the Arctic Ocean."

"Baffin Strait. Yeah, not for long."

"And what about the hunter, the report on the *Globe* website said he was wearing a survival suit. Really! And how come he was, and not them? And how come he was picked up and they weren't, if they swam ashore at the same time?"

"Nobody looked for them on the land. They found the guide floating, they found life jackets floating. They looked in the wrong place."

"Empty life jackets? Doesn't that strike you as strange? The guide got into a survival suit and they couldn't do up their own life jackets. Morgan, how did you cook your fish?"

"What? On a fire. Willow twigs, dead dwarf willows as high as your knees."

"And where did the fire come from, did you rub two penguins together?"

"Penguins live in the Antarctic. They already had it going, they lit it with their friend's lighter. The third man who had died earlier, he was a smoker. They buried him."

"Under the permafrost?"

"They piled stones on top of him."

"What kind of lighter? A Zippo?"

"How would I possibly know the name of a lighter?"

"Did it flare like a mini butane torch or snap open with a solid click like cocking a Winchester 73?"

"Yeah, the latter."

"It was a Zippo. Morgan, it had never been in the water."

"Or they dried it out."

"No. That wouldn't happen. The fluid would evaporate. Those men had never been wet, none of them, they wouldn't have lasted so long. They were dropped off on shore."

"So much for the RCMP report."

"The Mounties have a job to do, Morgan. It's bigger than resolving a single crime. I'm betting it was a judgment call and they decided to let things ride."

"You learned this at Mountie school?"

She didn't smile. Yes, perhaps not in so many words but it was drilled into them how to conduct the Crown's business in isolated communities. Mounties were expected to be cop and coroner, prosecutor and defence, judge and jury, social worker and therapist, confessor and friend. She had never been tested herself, but she knew others in the force who had, and she had great respect for them. In the field, officers are called upon to make calls that might be deemed inappropriate elsewhere.

"And the woman?" she said. "Gloria. Is she smart or just beautiful?"

"Gloriasimmons. Like it's one name."

"Quaint. So she's both."

Morgan explained who she was as best he could. He realized his description of her was sketchy and his attempt to account for her relationship with Harrington D'Arcy was devoid of humanity and his explanation of his own relationship with her was feeble. By the end, Miranda felt she had a pretty good grasp of exactly who Gloria Simmons was and where she fit into the scheme of things.

"Is she back in Toronto?" she asked.

"Yeah, she came back the day after I did. Haven't seen her, though. She's been looking after the D'Arcy funerals and trying to push through the deal between her people and the Chilean government cartel."

"Stop, stop, stop. *The funerals*? Have the bodies been released? *Her* people? You said she was *blonde*. What is she, a Laplander? And *cartel*? You just said the government of Chile runs a cartel!"

"You're cut off of coffee! You want to switch to hot chocolate or lemonade?"

"Morgan, I've been up for thirty hours straight except for a few naps on the plane. Get me a goddamn coffee. Please."

"Okay, but yes, she's a willowy blonde Laplander Inuk with a great style sense and the designated executor of both D'Arcys who have indeed been released, and I did say *cartel* because if the Chilean government closes the deal they'll have the next best thing to a world monopoly and they'll control world prices for copper and that will keep them in power, *them* being the individuals who will benefit from controlling said prices, and who are, therefore, in effect a cartel, a word also referring in the archaic sense to a co-operative arrangement among politicians. Now, let me get you a lemonade. It's on me. As were your first two coffees. Think of this as a welcome home party."

When he returned with a *grande* lemonade, known anywhere but Starbucks as a medium-large, and his third coffee, she was waiting with a question. "Does this mean you're on side with the existing government of Chile?"

"Apparently I am."

"Interesting," she said. "We're on opposing sides, Morgan. Not that it matters, but apparently we are."

"Do you want to explain?"

"I'll start at the end and work backwards."

"Why not start at the beginning?"

"Good stories never start at the beginning."

"You know this from your career as a novelist?"

Miranda glared across the table and forced a smile. "Yeah, there won't be a novel. I'm having enough trouble sorting out the divergent realities impinging on my life without imagining alternatives."

"You just said a mouthful."

"I did, didn't I!"

"*Divergent realities impinging* ... that's how I feel about my Arctic trip. It was all very real at the time, and this world wasn't." He made a sweeping gesture to take in the interior of Starbucks that also implied the city at large and, especially, Police Headquarters just up the street. "Now, *this* is real, that isn't. Know what I mean?"

"Exactly. We'll make it even more real, let's go to my place and order in pizza. But first, tell me more, tell me whatever comes into your mind. I've missed being there."

"Which do you want, the case or the odyssey?"

"Odyssey! That's rather grand. But, okay, skip back to the no-autopsy business. What gives with that, what really killed those three guys?"

"Like I said."

"Exposure? You said *the official report said*. What really killed them?"

"International commerce, I suppose. They went up there to sign papers on site, but that never happened."

"Who stands to gain by their deaths?"

"Your side. The Pinochet junta."

"How so — I'm not taking sides, Morgan — how do they gain?"

"D'Arcy Associates stood in their way. That's my

understanding. Gloria Simmons was his partner, they were representing the Inuit interests."

"There had to be Inuit on the junta side, Morgan. As the indigenous people, they hold the mineral rights."

"Yeah. *Inuit* means *the people*. I imagine the people as a whole would get a much better deal working with the Chilean government."

"The people, yes, but particular *persons* might benefit more from working with the cabal, what you call the Pinochet junta."

"Your side."

"For God's sake, Morgan. I'm not taking sides. It's just that the collapse of the present regime might be collateral damage if my friends on the island prevail. And vice versa. If the government falls, they might succeed. But believe me, we're not fascists."

"We? Miranda, what have you got yourself into? What's got into you?"

"You want an inventory of recent lovers?"

Morgan remained silent.

"Good, they're too numerous to mention." Miranda felt suddenly exhausted. She wanted to sleep in her own bed. She wanted to skip the pizza. She was about to propose they break off for the day when a thought occurred to her. "Morgan," she said, "when did they die?"

He stared at her, sympathetic with the exhaustion she must be enduring, trying to catch up or slow down to get on the same wavelength. "By *they* you mean the men in the Arctic?

"The last two, where were you when they died?"

"I was there. I was fishing when Harrington D'Arcy died. I was flagging the chopper when the other guy died, unless he died in our smoky little nest while I was there and I didn't notice. My goodness, what an ignominious way to go, without anyone noticing."

"And your new best friend, Msgloriasimmons, she was with them both."

"Miranda?"

"Yes." And then she added, as if clinching an argument, "His wife is regarded on the island as a martyr to their sovereignist cause."

"What on earth are you talking about?"

"Maria D'Arcy." Miranda watched the phases of incomprehension flitter across his features as he moved from bewilderment through annoyance to curiosity.

"She's from Rapa Nui! Of course she is. That explains the letters and her relationship with that guy, Te Ave something?"

"Te Ave Teao. What letters?"

"And her mother is from Rapa Nui!"

"You know her mother?"

"Yes," he said, pleased that he knew things she didn't; embarrassed that he was small enough to be pleased. "Maria Pilar Akarikitea."

"And a small-boat sailor called Ralph McMan, I suppose? You know him, too?"

"Rove McMan, as in rover. Yes, I do."

"Good, that makes my life easier."

He waited for her to explain, but she didn't, so he continued. "If Maria D'Arcy's island connection puts her in sympathy with the Pinochet cabal — and whatever you say, your side is on side with the fascists, even if it's only by default — and if Harrington D'Arcy's business connections were with the Inuit and the Chilean government cartel, that would put the D'Arcys very decidedly in opposite camps."

"*Cabal, cartel*, it's hard to tell one from the other without a scorecard. What about coalition and consortium. Too many c-words. Let's stick with Pinochet fascists on one side, I can't believe I said that, and the government in power on the other. Or better yet, the Rapa Nui interests and the Inuit interests. Chile's irrelevant."

"Hardly."

"Depends on your perspective, Morgan. Chile may be on centre stage but for us, at least, the real drama is off in the wings."

"And for the D'Arcys."

"Morgan, you don't think he murdered his wife just because you've come up with a motive?"

"No."

"Do you think he loved her?"

"Perhaps not in the conventional sense, but yes I do, very deeply."

"Then it seems to me a distinct possibility, Morgan, that contrary to your hormonal bias, the much admired and quite beautiful Msgloriasimmons, LLB, might not have been on the same side of this billion-dollar conflict as her partner, Mr. Harrington D'Arcy, LLB, OC."

"Miranda."

"I'm just saying."

"Miranda, she was the one who suggested the whale encounter was questionable. She even wondered if Pauloosie Avaluktuk had shot D'Arcy and the others, although she insisted the whales were real."

"And that kept your interest up, didn't it? She had nothing to lose by pre-empting suspicion, and you to gain as her sidekick. What the hell was D'Arcy doing out there on a boat, anyway?"

"Checking landing locations for ocean-going freighters, or so I was told. Seems reasonable. They'll have to build dockage to ship out the ore."

They sat quietly for a while, braced by the reassuring familiarity of Starbucks, Morgan deep in thought, and Miranda with a quiet sense of well-being and nothing on her mind but random images of Bora Bora settling into the tropical night.

Later, as they approached her building on Isabella Street, Miranda took his arm and leaned close to ask what seemed like the ultimate in arbitrary questions.

"No," he answered. "I've never been to Gibraltar. Why?

"Just wondering. Do you want to go? There's a cave I'd like to explore. St. Michael's. It looks like you can only get to it very high up, almost at the summit."

"Sure. Possibly next week. I'm kind of tied up at the moment with a murder, maybe several."

She rang her own buzzer. It was an old habit. He'd never seen her do it before.

"Do you want me to come up? Maybe you're too tired." He ran his hand through his hair, which seemed to her, somehow, a gesture of sympathy.

"For pizza, no, I've lost my appetite. But I want to hear more about what you've been up to in the ice and snow."

"And I want to hear about your South Seas adventures. But it could wait 'til morning, you know." He tousled his hair again. She smiled at the awkwardness of his gesture.

"Come on," she said. "Let's go up and tell lies."

10

The Tangled Web

As Miranda walked slowly up the worn marble stairs through the cool planes of dark walnut veneer, she finally felt at home. She had already dropped off her bags on her way to meet Morgan at Starbucks, and had hardly noticed where she was. Now he was traipsing behind her and, tired as she was, she felt exhilarated.

From Morgan's perspective, he thought she moved with deliberate grace, picking out each footstep in turn as she ascended through the muted light. He hung back a few paces, wanting to give her space to sort out whatever was swirling though her mind. By the time they reached her door on the third floor, he had taken the key from her hand and led the way inside.

"My plant's dead," she said as she walked into her living room.

"I watered it regularly."

"You drowned it, Morgan. My prized orchid."

"You bought it at the supermarket."

"I said prized, not prize. It was the only living thing in the world that depended on me completely and I let it down. Damn it, you killed it."

"Only by loving it too well. I'll buy you another."

"Not like Miss Grundy."

"Your orchid has a name?"

"Had. Now she's mulch. Sopping wet at the roots, desiccated up top. Morgan, I don't trust your relationship with Gloriasimmons."

"Pardon? I wasn't expecting that. We don't have a relationship."

"Exactly! With all you've been through together, and yet there's no relationship. Something's askew."

Over pizza, which they broke down and ordered, and a bottle of Châteauneuf-du-Pape, they talked well into the night. Morgan told Miranda everything he knew about the case. Of Maria's mysterious death and the story of how he ended up marooned on a remote shore of Baffin Island, disclosing every detail he could think of, but skipping over the sleeping-bag incident, which seemed graphic in his mind, but not relevant, and omitting any personal reference to Ellen Ravenscroft. His account was essentially linear and chronological.

Hers was a series of discontinuous episodes which she interspersed during his narrative as they came to mind. What she had experienced and endured was complex, not one story but many — layered and confusing. She didn't want reassurance or understanding and she certainly didn't want interpretations and answers. In the end, Morgan had a pretty firm grasp of what she had gone through, including an uneasy awareness of the dark romantic attraction she had felt for Matteo, which seemed understandable, and for Thomas Edward Ross, which seemed perversely destructive.

Eventually, she rose from the sofa and made a move toward her bedroom. "Do want to stay?" she asked him, turning her head to speak through an auburn veil of shoulder-length hair.

He smiled and rose to his feet. He felt very shy, as if he had been unfaithful. "No," he said, moving closer to her and touching her shoulder. "You need your sleep."

"I meant on the sofa, Morgan. It's late."

"Yeah," he said. "But you wouldn't sleep well on the sofa and I'd feel badly taking over your bed."

She walked into the bedroom so that he couldn't see her facial expression. "Let yourself out. See you tomorrow, love."

When Miranda woke up it was noon. It felt good to be in her own bed after a month of sleeping in bunks and berths, or curled up in chairs designed by committee, stretched out on rented mattresses, or in absolute darkness on a mattress of dried reeds. After a quick trip to the bathroom, she nestled under a sheet and luxuriated in being home. She tried to remember how much she had told Morgan about the divine comedy she had just emerged from. Or was she still in purgatory and her comfort was merely the calm at the heart of a storm?

Damn it, she thought. *He's the Presbyterian. If a person felt good, that wasn't bad. "Don't pull the rug out from under yourself."* She got up and made herself a coffee. To get back on track, she self-consciously reviewed what she knew of the Maria D'Arcy murder.

What struck her most about Morgan's summing up of the case had been how graphic some aspects were and how vague were others. She accepted that it was murder, but she was puzzled by the circumstances he had described. The body had been found exposed in the cockpit of the *Pemberly*. It seemed unlikely it had been brought on board post-mortem. The only indications of violence were scratch marks in the inside of a forward hatch, but D'Arcy himself seemed to have been below decks when she died and not a prisoner bent on escape. And he had apparently covered his dead wife's exposed breasts for the sake of propriety.

Miranda mentally moved to the morgue. She struggled to comprehend how a body could be compromised while in the coroner's possession. It had been washed down, eliminating the scent of Fleurs de Rocaille, which you couldn't get anymore, not the original blend she used to wear before they changed the formula. Instead of wildflowers it now smelled like perfume. No smell in a bottle should evoke only itself! Morgan insisted Maria had been wearing the original scent. And then, whoever cleaned her up left a hint of poisonous powder on the nape of her neck, but there was none found in her bloodstream.

The suicide note. It was in her handwriting, but Morgan was convinced it was written by a person in full possession of her faculties. This seemed to prove she did not die by suicide, but that she knew her death was coming. And why address the note to Morgan? Her husband had requested him as lead investigator into the possibility that he was the killer, that was strange enough, but for the wife to engage his sympathies with a note apparently intended to exonerate her killer, that was truly bizarre.

Miranda moved back to the yacht club. It was the only place where she could envision the real Harrington D'Arcy. And suddenly she shifted to the farmhouse where Maria grew up playing with Matteo in the long shadows of the *moai* on the slopes of Rano Raraku. She struggled to bring the two visions together and, curiously, the name Rove McMan came to mind. While Morgan seemed to find McMan a bit of a world-weary poseur, he trusted the sailor's judgment that the D'Arcys were enthralled with each other and completely in love. On the basis of McMan's apparent relationship with Matteo, Miranda trusted him completely.

Then Harrington D'Arcy — and here she had made one of those intuitive leaps that, once made, seemed inevitable — D'Arcy must have been working for the Pinochet cabal. Not because he believed in fascism nor for the money. For his wife, for her cause. To Miranda, this line of reasoning led inexorably to the conclusion that D'Arcy could not have murdered Maria. It struck her as equally certain that Gloriasimmons, representing the opposing interests, was therefore instrumental in the deaths of D'Arcy and his associates in the Arctic. The woman had used Morgan as her unwitting accomplice — and paradoxically, as a witness to her innocence. *Innocence be damned*, she thought.

Miranda moved finally to envision herself in the cave with Matteo, breaking open the secrets of the Heyerdahl book that had assumed the stature of a holy text, the early-morning harbinger of a new day for the island, the secret that he and his sister and friends were willing to die for. Miranda too had been an accomplice. She had been sent by Maria. This did not seem possible, and yet she had performed exactly as if her whole journey had been scripted in advance.

The telephone rang and she rolled onto her side to reach it, rolling back as she answered.

"Is this an awkward time," Morgan asked. "You seem to be breathing hard."

"Morgan, it's noon." She paused. "Two conclusions: Maria was murdered, but not by her husband. And two, if you're counting: we need to look into your relationship with Ms. Gloriasimmons."

There was a long pause coming from Morgan's end of the line. Finally, he said, "I'm on my way over to Rosedale to talk with her mother, do you want to come?"

"Maria's mother? For sure." She had already told him she wanted to meet her. "Can you pick me up."

"With what? I'm walking. I'll be at Bloor and Yonge in half an hour. We'll walk up together."

He clicked off and stared contemplatively at his feet thrust out in front of him on the blue sofa. One of his big toes was threatening to poke through his sock and he wondered if he should clip the nail before putting his shoes on, but decided the socks were done for, anyway. He figured if he left immediately it would take him half an hour to get from the Annex to Yonge. If he walked very slowly. He assumed that he thought more lucidly when he strolled, more in an approximation of rational coherence than in the usual concentric ruminations that sometimes rendered him brilliant and sometimes a little befuddled.

Turning east onto Bloor, he discovered he was still unnerved by Miranda's persistent reference to his relationship with Gloria Simmons. Linear thought was getting him nowhere.

He let his mind wander until random phrases and images coalesced, not around Gloria Simmons, but around Miranda Quin, and not sexually focused, but around the strange gaps in his comprehension of her unlikely escapades south of the equator. Morgan knew most of the places she had described in graphic detail, although the only caves he had been in while on the island were little more than weather-worn caverns gouged out of rock faces along the shore. Yet none of what she described seemed quite real to him, or perhaps it seemed too real to fully comprehend.

When she mentioned the village of Hanga Roa, the overgrown quarry at Rano Raraku, the beach at Anakena, it all came back to him, but as memories of his own experience. A woman's eyes, brown and green and golden in the tropical sun, traced out his imagined movements as he slipped from one place to another in response to Miranda's story, but they were not Miranda's eyes. He couldn't place her there, at all. He had fallen briefly in love with a woman on the island who wore sky-blue underwear and a battered Stetson. When he came home, she had merged in his mind with Miranda so that he hardly missed her, Beverley Weekes, because he felt she was with him, despite having returned to Wyoming or to her research as a paleo-ethnobotanist on Bora Bora.

Bora Bora! That's how he connected to an island he had never visited — when Miranda described it, he felt like he had been there already.

Her experiences on Rapa Nui were so beyond his own, which were cast in the afterglow of a romantic interlude, that they might have been in different realities. Her time on the island was a perilous journey; she had been immersed in revolutionary politics with brutal and horrific consequences.

This man who went by the name of Ross, he seemed to be the rather insidious factor connecting each of the separate episodes in her account. He was always there, first on the plane where he switched books, then bleeding all over her at the Hotel Victoria, later at the farmhouse, then at the cave providing rescue or betrayal, and finally as her invisible benefactor on the *Island Queen*.

Her friend Matteo. Maria D'Arcy's brother. Connections on so many levels. The friend of Te Ave Teao, who plunged to his death for an arcane belief about violating an *ariki*'s cave. Or, more likely, who died to create a diversion so Ross could go ahead into the cave and hide Miranda from the execution squad. Was that Ross's intention? Te Ave Teao may have read him wrong. Ross may have been giving her up to the soldiers and it was only through the good graces of Matteo that she escaped.

The book. He was fascinated by how she had broken the code, but at a loss as to what her discovery could mean. A cave on Gibraltar, halfway around the world? He had spent a few days on Gibraltar during his wanderings after university. It was simply a stopover where people spoke English between Tangier and the island of Ibiza, where he had worked in a bar and pretended he didn't speak English.

Morgan wondered about the book, how he had been the conduit between Maria D'Arcy and Miranda, except he had been given the wrong book to pass on. The right copy, introduced into the story by Ross, had somehow taken on scriptural significance and yet it wasn't Heyerdahl's text or the handwritten notes that were important. but what they obscured. *Not unlike the holy books of religion*, he thought.

The channels in Morgan's mind formed endless connections and he enjoyed wandering through them, but there was an urgency now, as he approached Yonge Street and could see Miranda in the distance. He was pleased she was working with him on resolving the murder of Maria D'Arcy, unofficially at least, and a little perturbed that she was seeing nefarious dimensions to the deaths on Baffin, but most of all, he was concerned for her safety. There was no way she could emerge from the carnage on Rapa Nui without a trail of blood in her wake. Her fare wasn't paid on the cruise liner or her flight covered from Tahiti without future consequences to which she seemed oblivious.

As soon as he reached the corner and she turned from gazing through her own reflection in a store window, he proclaimed, "You're compromised, you know."

She stared at him for a moment, trying to penetrate his thought process, then responded, "Morgan, he wasn't even on board. I wasn't on police business. We didn't have sex. And I can't pay back what he spent on bringing me home because, one, I don't know who he really is, and two, as far as the *Island Queen* is concerned he died with you in the Arctic and his account is closed."

When they came to the D'Arcy residence, she was surprised. He had described it as a seigneurial manor set among Rosedale mansions. But it was more like a medieval gamekeeper's cottage on a great landowner's estate that had been diminished over the centuries to a few metres of grass and some shrubs. The woman who opened the door was equally unexpected, not at all a ghost from the feudal past. She was handsome, dressed in black, and despite redness in her eyes that suggested weeping, she stood fiercely proud. This was not someone Miranda would have mistaken for a housekeeper. The woman nodded at Morgan, but as she stood back to let them in she fixed her gaze on Miranda's eyes so intensely that Miranda felt surely they had met before.

Morgan and the woman exchanged a few words and she led them into the library where the three of them sat down. Miranda recognized something in the room that suggested a strong but feminine presence, perhaps coming from the artfully haphazard arrangement of silver-framed photographs or the display of artifacts from Easter Island, set out not like they were trophies, but for their aesthetic effect. Among small carvings of volcanic tuft and *toromiro* wood, she recognized a narrow slab incised with *Rongorongo* glyphs. She could see through into a small study to the side that must have been Maria's special place, the inner sanctum of a descendent of the last *ariki*, so painfully far from Te Pito o Te Henua, the centre of the world.

Miranda became aware that the other two were waiting for her to finish her survey before speaking. Morgan knew his partner was responding to something in the study and library he had missed. What he had taken to be emotional austerity concealed behind a rich and impersonal decor, Miranda read as the expression of self-reliance, an ambience created by two people absorbed in one another's lives. She knew this perhaps from the sadness conveyed in these rooms by their owners' absence, reinforced by the old woman quietly grieving as she sat poised on the edge of a sofa, watching the rich play of emotion sweeping over Miranda.

At last, the woman in black spoke: "I am sorry to tell you, Miss Quin, Matteo, he is dead. I talk to him yesterday by telephone, he said you will come, *señorita*, and then after when I call back they say he is gone. I am sorry."

Miranda was stunned. She rose from her chair and sat down on the sofa, clasping the woman's old hands between hers, almost in a gesture of prayer. She could feel on her lips the kiss she had shared with Matteo on the bus in the lea of Rano Raraku. Her eyes welled with tears.

"There is so much death," said the old woman. She looked around the room, seeing perhaps more of what Miranda had sensed, a place haunted by absence. "I will go back, I will not die at Toronto. Perhaps I go back, *señorita*, I don't know."

Miranda drew in a deep breath. She wanted to hold and comfort the woman, but drew herself back. "Do you know what happened?"

"They kill him."

"Who?"

"He is dead, his sister is gone, *Señor* D'Arcy is dead. It is all over. They say Matteo die in a fishing accident, their boat smash on the rocks, Matteo and Te Ave Teao, his friend since they were childrens. But I speak to him only an hour before. He was not in his boat."

"And I know Te Ave Teao was killed falling on the rocks at the *ariki*'s cave," said Miranda. "They did not die together."

"Together, no, and their sister and *Señor* D'Arcy, Mr. Harrington D'Arcy, they all die for their island."

"Maria." Miranda said the woman's name. She simply wanted proof of continuity.

"Yes."

"Maria, I am so sorry." She leaned over and whispered in the woman's ear the message of love her son had asked she convey. The woman shuddered and squeezed Miranda's hand so firmly her fingers ached — almost as if they were sharing the pain.

Morgan stood up and moved away to give them privacy. In the small study, his eye was drawn to a gap in the bookshelves where a large book had been removed. He returned to the library and sat down on an ottoman in front of the two women. He knew Matteo had made a profound impact on Miranda and that she must be hurting deeply, and he was moved by how she was able to comfort the old woman.

Both women looked up at him in expectation. "Maria," he said, "*señora*, do you know what book is missing from your daughter's library?"

She gazed at him through glistening eyes, pausing for a moment to gain her bearings. "Yes, it was by Mr. Thor Heyerdahl."

"*Aku-Aku*, about Easter Island?"

"Yes, that book. Maria asked me to give it to the lawyer."

"Which lawyer?"

"To Mrs. Rufalo."

Morgan and Miranda exchanged glances. Miranda realized she needed to suppress her grief as Morgan continued.

"You gave the book to Mrs. Rufalo. This was because your daughter asked you to. Do you know why she would do that?"

"It was for you," she said, turning to Miranda.

"Do you know why?" Morgan asked.

"I know first I give to Mrs. Rufalo the wrong book. I walk over to her house, it is not so far. There were two copies." That explained the gap in the bookshelf larger than a single volume. "Maria was very unhappy I give the wrong book, but I told her the other copy was special from grandfather, her father's father, also Matteo, Matteo *Ak-ariki-tea*." She broke down the syllables a little differently than Morgan had, to make the word more accessible to her listeners. "That Matteo, he lived for more years than my husband, Maria's father, and he wrote things in the book which Mr. Thor Heyerdahl signed for him personally."

A rather austere signing, thought Miranda. *Very Norwegian, just a signature*. It seemed unlikely that the other notes were by Matteo and Maria's grandfather, a man who almost certainly didn't speak English. "My daughter," Maria Pilar continued, "she took the other one, the special book, and I thought she must give it to this lady, herself." She indicated Miranda. "Why do you want two books the same, I did not ask."

Miranda straightened. "Do you know a publishing company called Taggart and Foulds?" she asked. Morgan looked puzzled, but it did not surprise him when Maria Pilar responded in the affirmative. The room seemed to stir with a rush of fresh air — Morgan recalled someone explaining that wind is sucked into available space and not forced out of a space that is occupied. A troubling gap in Miranda's understanding had suddenly been filled.

He waited, but she said nothing more, beyond expressing her sympathy, until they were walking down the curved street under its leafy canopy of silver maples, the arboreal product of planning and privilege. The brick sidewalk stuck Morgan as wonderfully quaint, indulgent, and not very practical.

"There's no doubt now," she eventually said, as if they were sharing an ongoing conversation. "About the D'Arcys. They were on the same side."

"You know this because?"

"The house, Morgan. It's the home of adults in love."

He hadn't seen it quite that way, but trusted her instincts.

"And," she said. "it seems a reasonable assumption to believe I was sent to Rapa Nui by Maria. The D'Arcys had major shares in Taggart and Foulds, my overly generous publishers. When word got around I was going to the island, funds were made available to ensure I didn't back out. And then a very important book was given to me for delivery via you."

"But the wrong book," said Morgan.

"I actually ended up with the right book! Along with an inflated reputation for being very clever."

"Where would that come from?"

"Probably from you, bragging to Rufalo, and Rufalo bragging to his wife, and his wife bragging to Maria."

"Like a chain of evidence, a chain of ego."

"Probably from newspaper gossip, then."

"It's been in the papers more than once, you're the smart one and I'm just along for the ride."

"It's because you're so handsome, Morgan."

"Thank you."

"It's the fallout from dealing with higher-class murders, we sometimes appear on the society pages. Don't you remember, we're the sleuths of Baker Street, Sherlock and Holmes. The same columnist makes much of my capacity for rational thought. It's annoying, she's implicitly saying that women aren't very bright and I'm the exception that apparently proves the rule. I'm kind of stuck with *clever, logical, brainy, beautiful,* the way you are with *shambling, unkempt, dishevelled*. Whatever, we have to live with our own mythologies. Maria seemed to think I would be able to reveal the secrets of their sacred text. And I was! But, lest I become excessively smug, it should be noted I merely replaced an enigma with a conundrum, the coordinates of a cave on Gibraltar. St. Michael's. It is a place, from what I can figure out, that is quite accessible to the public at large."

"Maria Pilar passed on the wrong book, intentionally," Morgan repeated. "If she didn't know about the other one, that it was more than a family keepsake, how did they?"

"Matteo and Maria? Probably from their grandfather, Matteo Akarikitea. Although they had no idea what it said, they knew it was a message from the past. Not unlike *Rongorongo*, Morgan, a message of importance that no one could read."

"And given that you are a semi-famous forensic investigator, given that you're actually quite clever, and by your own admission relatively attractive, given that your trip to the island was assured, it was not that difficult to get you and the right book together."

"Someone sent my gentleman friend, Mr. Ross, to exchange copies, and to see that the book and I were safe until I'd delivered its secrets. Paradoxically, I think Ross believed the book was more valuable undeciphered, and probably with me either dead or safely out of the way."

"Someone sent him? Not the D'Arcys?"

"Someone in league with the D'Arcys. It wasn't the D'Arcys who paid for my exotic return."

"That sounds sinister, *in league with the D'Arcys*."

"It was, and it is."

The morgue was within walking distance. They lapsed into silence and moved along quietly together as Miranda struggled to deal with Matteo's death. At her side, Morgan occasionally rustled against her as he walked too close. When they got there, they went right through to the autopsy room. This was familiar territory, where their work and the coroner's merged.

Ellen Ravenscroft looked up from the corpse splayed open in front of her. "Miranda Quin! That's got to be one of the shortest sabbaticals on record. Bad trip?"

"And how are you, Ellen? Up to your arse in cadavers?"

"If you can't say *arse* with conviction, love, better say ears or ass. Good to see you're okay."

"Why would it be in doubt?"

"You're here, not there?"

"Just checking on your security system!"

Morgan interrupted, "We were just passing by."

"Good grief, love, surely you've got better things to do with your life. Any leads on the D'Arcy woman?"

"We were wondering the same thing," said Miranda.

"Well, on this end, there's not much to say. Her husband ended up in the drawer next to hers. They had to put him somewhere until clearance came through, then the lawyer turned up with the paperwork and off they went, the three of them, to the crematorium."

"Gloria Simmons?"

"In person, Miranda. For the mister, there was no reason to hold him. He came with a note from the Mounties, he was just passing through, a shipping clerk's idea of family togetherness. For the missus, the suicide note set her free."

"On whose authority?" Morgan asked.

"Your superintendent's."

"So we've come to a dead end," said Miranda, smiling at the medical examiner. Miranda felt indebted in a minor key for being let off the hook after saying *arse*. It was not a word she used, she didn't know why she had, and Ellen had graciously dismissed it as uncharacteristically vulgar. She wasn't sure why they were there.

Morgan wasn't sure why they were there, either. It seemed the logical next step as he introduced Miranda to the case. Yet there was nothing, he realized, that could not have been picked up in the coroner's report. He began to suspect he had wanted to bring the two women together; he was silently making a statement. To Ellen, that things were back to normal, Miranda was home. To Miranda, that nothing had changed. All this was manifest in his mind only as an uneasiness that he covered with a boyish grin that neither woman understood, since Miranda presumably knew nothing of what had happened, while Ellen seemed to have forgotten that anything had.

"Okay," he said abruptly, "we've got to go."

Miranda shrugged and followed him through the door. Strange, none of the usual flirting, no double entendres or risqué allusions. Maybe they had all grown up a bit. It was never too late.

"That was pointless," said Morgan as they cut over to Yonge Street.

"Your idea."

"Nothing is pointless," he countered, as if he had missed his own declaration.

"You sound like a Samuel Beckett monologue."

"Thank you."

They walked on in silence for a while, then Morgan spoke, "Why would D'Arcy's body end up with Ravenscroft?"

"Clerical indulgence, that's how she described it."

"No. I'll bet if we checked the papers — no, maybe she's too smart."

"Speak in whole sentences, Morgan. And yes, she is too smart, but you're coming on side, you suspect Ms. Gloriasimmons LLB. The Mounties released the body to her. I imagine they were happy to get rid of what amounted to material evidence in a crime they wanted buried, so to speak, and she organized the family reunion before she had them cremated. A corpse with papers is inviolate at the morgue; what better place to store him until she could make arrangements? No undertakers asking questions. Just Ellen, processing an *in transit* package. Then straight to the crematorium. Case closed."

"Cases, plural. We seem to be dealing with a proliferation of deaths."

"So you agree, Gloriasimmons killed D'Arcy."

"Miranda, we were there on a rescue mission. I was doing my Farley Mowat impersonation, I didn't see anything. Even if I was certain she did it, there's no proof. I'd be used as the primary witness for the defence. Let's take a taxi."

"Where?"

"To Harbourfront. You wanted to meet Rove McMan."

"What kind of whales were they?"

"Whales? Bowhead, I think. What difference does it make?"

"*If*, Morgan, if there actually were whales? I'm just wondering."

When they arrived at the RTYC ferry terminal, they were greeted by an eager young man in grey flannels and a blue blazer.

"Jacket and tie, sir? The lady is very well dressed, my compliments ma'am. But you, Mr. Morgan, are forcing me to bend the rules again. You are taking advantage of our relationship."

"Miranda," said Morgan, "this is Edwin Block. He is a mortician in the making."

"Death is our business," the young man said cheerily. "For Mr. Morgan and me, death is our business."

"Mine, too, I suppose," said Miranda.

"Are you a mortician, ma'am?"

Miranda grimaced.

"Oh gosh almighty, I'm sorry," Eddie Block exclaimed while looking over her shoulder to see that newer arrivals were appropriately attired.

"For what?" she said.

"For you, like, being a policeman. For my inappropriate compliments. We haven't actually started classes yet. I'm just practicing *how to make personal contact and be quietly gracious*. It's in the book."

"The mortician's book?"

"Yes. Mr. Morgan helped me get into the course. I would like to become very successful and buy my own yacht and sail out of the Royal Toronto. They take undertakers, you know."

"It never hurts to have one or two."

Once the ferry pulled away from shore, Edwin Block sidled up to Morgan, grinning sheepishly at Miranda, who stood beside him.

"Mr. Morgan, you told me to keep an eye open and I have."

"Good man, Eddie. What's to report?"

"Well, Mr. McMan has been taking things of great interest to his boat, he's outfitting his ketch for an ocean voyage."

"He is?"

"Self-steering gear, an antique binnacle. Backup for all the electronic devices. A bolt of sailcloth. A case of Scotch. If you're a sailor, you just know what he's doing."

"Thank you, Eddie."

"And that woman has been over several times. You know, the supermodel, high heels, perfect hair."

"Gloria Simmons."

"Mr. D'Arcy's friend and associate."

"Thank you, Eddie."

When they disembarked at the club wharf, Miranda caught the young man's eye as she walked past. "Good luck with the undertaking school," she said. She mouthed the words so he could understand, despite the shuffling noises of other passengers who were squeezing by where he was poised at the gangway like an apprentice Charon on the shores of Hades.

"And good luck to you, miss, in all your endeavours," he responded with a solemn and practised smile.

11

Murder is Sometimes Necessary

The *Tangata Manu* rocked gently on a surge that worked its way up the narrow channel from a passing freighter. Weeping willows draped over the water, screening out the sun except for a few random slivers falling like light through a shaken mantilla. Ducks squabbled along the embankment. The hollow slip-slap of halyards against masts rattled up and down the column of boats moored in parallel with sterns to the shore.

"Long way from Mission Control," Miranda observed. "If it were me, I'd never untie from the dock. The clubhouse is soulless, pretentious, and architecturally derivative. This is nice, right here. Ducks and willows. Beautiful boat. Why go to sea?"

"Like Mallory said about Everest, because it's there," said Morgan.

"Everest, of course, killed him."

The words drifted up from an open stern hatch, followed by a determinedly affable Rove McMan. "Detective Morgan, I was expecting you. Do come aboard and bring Detective Sergeant Miranda Quin along with you."

"My fame precedes me."

"I don't follow crime in Toronto unless it's exceptionally lurid. I'm Rove McMan."

"I suspected as much," she said as they clambered aboard, taking off their shoes without being asked when they stepped onto the weathered teak deck.

Morgan leaned comfortably against the tiller, and, gazing up at the club burgee fluttering gently in the shrouds, he thought perhaps he had followed the wrong calling.

"You're not surprised that I knew you were coming, Detective Morgan, Detective Quin?"

"I expect our mutual friend let you know," said Morgan.

"Gloria Simmons, yes."

"She's not my friend, I've never met her," Miranda protested.

"She gave the impression you were all acquainted," said McMan.

"Did you know Matteo is dead?" Miranda asked him directly, apparently drawing the question out of the blue.

He seemed suddenly distracted. He stared at his own distorted reflection in the gleaming brass binnacle that had been newly mounted in the cockpit, then slowly looked up into her eyes and allowed a gentle smile to move across his face before lapsing into an inscrutable expression of apparent indifference. "I don't think I know anyone by that name," he said, glancing over at Morgan, then back to the binnacle.

"New equipment?" Morgan asked. "You're planning a trip?"

"I am."

"To Rapa Nui," said Miranda, as if the destination was not in doubt.

"Are you a sailor?" he asked her.

"Nothing smaller than a cruise ship," she said. "Do you know the *Island Queen*?"

"I've heard of her."

"Matteo asked me to come and see you."

"Why?"

"So you do know him."

"I did."

"And?"

"And nothing. He's dead."

"He said to give you his best."

McMan caught her eye and smiled sadly. "Too late."

Morgan shuffled over to the companionway and gazed down into the interior. Then he turned and addressed Rove McMan, "Tell us about your relationship with Gloria Simmons."

"No relationship. She was Harrington D'Arcy's law partner. Not much of a sailor."

"Which is the ultimate criterion of good character."

"Something like that."

"She's been over to see you twice since Maria D'Arcy's death," Morgan declared with casual certainty.

"Three times, if you're actually counting."

"Waving money?"

Rove McMan sat back against the warm mahogany of the cockpit combing. He leaned forward again. "I don't need money."

Morgan left his unspoken question hang in the air. In Morgan's eyes the teak and mahogany, the bleached cotton sail rolled on the mizzen boom, the sheets and halyards, lines and shrouds, all seemed to be arranged around the man as authentic extensions of his personality. If ever there was a sailor, this was him.

McMan responded to the question Morgan's silence implied. "She does want something, no question, and I certainly don't have it. But apparently *you* do." He turned to Miranda. "You have something she wants very much and she is determined to get it. At any cost."

"That's a bit dramatic," said Miranda.

"You tell me Matteo is dead," he said. "Te Ave Teao is dead. The D'Arcys are dead. Doesn't that tell you how serious this is?"

Morgan interrupted. "Whatever happened on the island, that island, you're saying it threatens us here?" With a sweeping shrug of his arms he took in the idyllic setting around them.

"Only Ms. Quin. She seems to be the only person alive who knows the secret."

"My God," said Miranda. "It's not a distinction I relish."

"Ms. Simmons has a way of getting what she wants," said the sailor. "She wanted you to know she wants whatever it was you found in the book."

"That sounds like an open threat. You understand what she's after?"

"I do, more than most. That's why she came to me. I'm not threatening you. I'm warning you."

"And if I told her, then what? Nobody seems to know its significance."

"I do," said McMan.

Miranda and Morgan both leaned toward him in the cramped cockpit, waiting. Rove McMan, however, seemed no more inclined to share his own secret knowledge with them than he had been with Gloria Simmons. Instead, he issued a directive, "If you have it written down, I would urge you commit it to memory. Have someone you trust with your life do likewise. That's your insurance."

"You think she'd try to kill me?"

"In the flicker of an eye."

"And what would she do if she got it out of me, though God knows she won't."

"Kill you. Either way. She will destroy the message, erase it, and eliminate the mind that knows what it is. You are familiar with her, Detective Morgan. You can confirm that she is an indomitable force."

"Not that familiar." Fragments of memory and conjecture were flying off in tangents in Morgan's mind, and an entirely different set of memories and their implications were swirling in Miranda's, avoiding resolution in both.

"So, this is what I want you to do," said McMan. "I want you to tell me."

"Tell you what?"

"The coordinates. I know that is what the book revealed to you in the cave.

"The cave. So you *were* talking to Matteo."

"Now, I do not want to know the coordinates just now. If it were to be known that I knew, I might be made to disappear, myself. It's all too easy to be swallowed up at sea without a trace. No, what I want is for you to tell me, do I sail east or do I sail west?"

Miranda stared at him, dumbfounded. The *Tangata Manu* rocked gently against the tension of spring lines, creaking with personality.

"You're a likeable man," she said. "But we're not best friends. I might have told my partner the coordinates, but why you?"

"Because," he said. "It is important. You were sent to Rapa Nui on a mission."

"I went there to write a murder mystery set in Toronto."

"And you were successful in your mission, and you came home safe and sound. But the struggle is not over. My friends have died. There are others. I don't know what those coordinates signify, but they are important enough to die for, or to kill. It seems it is up to me to go there, to find whatever is hidden, and return it to the island. So, this is what I want. Tell me, do I sail west to Rapa Nui or do I sail east? When it is time, you will direct me more precisely. If the *Tangata Manu* goes down, you will have to take my place."

"No," said Miranda. "I can't imagine why. But yes," she looked at Morgan who seemed to be on side, "you should sail eastward."

"Damn," he said.

"What?"

"West would have made for an easier voyage. You're taking me through the Suez. The Gulf of Aden. All those damned pirates."

"Why not around the Cape?" said Morgan.

Rove McMan looked at Miranda for direction.

"No," she said. "Not around the Cape."

"Through the Strait of Gibraltar, then, that's all I need for now."

"And if I don't get in touch?" Miranda inquired, immediately revising her query. "How am I supposed to reach you?"

"I'll let you know where I am," he responded, then turning to look at Miranda straight on, with an intensity she found unnerving, he said, "I suggest you find Ms. Simmons before she finds you."

Morgan had revised his earlier judgment of Rove McMan. He had seemed likeable, but feckless, a charming drifter. His boat was a repository of incalculable treasure, but he had seemed hardly impressed. He had described the *toromiro* tablets as the Rapa Nui *Domesday Book* and Constitution and Charter of Rights rolled into one, yet he had seemed not much concerned with what would become of them. Now he was setting out to sail to the other side of the world to deliver them home. Single-handed. The long way around. And in the process he would retrieve whatever was hidden in St. Michael's Cave and return it, as well.

And he seemed genuinely concerned for Miranda.

He wondered what one would do with the *Domesday Book* if no one knew what it said? Why return the *Rongorongo* to Rapa Nui when their value's out on the open market? Take them to Sotheby's or Ritchie's or Christie's. Use the money to pay for the funerals of Miranda's friends on the island. Start up a scholarship fund. Buy the whole island a trip to the Arctic.

"Could I see the *Rongorongo*?" Miranda was saying.

Morgan suddenly realized the other two had been talking while his mind was avoiding the brutal realities where his odyssey to the Arctic and her excursion to Easter Island converged. McMan and Miranda descended into the main cabin. Morgan remained in the cockpit, trying to reconstruct from random details of memory exactly what he had been through with Gloria Simmons, and what he had missed.

Miranda carefully unwrapped a slab of wood and held it up to the light. "This is *toromiro*, isn't it? It has a lovely swirl to the grain; very dark, almost ebony, with auburn streaks. I saw a few pieces on the island. Used for carvings, though, not *Rongorongo*. It looks very old."

"Yeah, I'm guessing these are among the very few that survived the bonfires."

"When the priests came?"

"In the mid-nineteenth century." He took a deep breath, attracting Morgan's attention. "We brought lethal diseases and gave them an alien God to forgive them for dying. We erased their memory, you know, and filled the emptiness with our own cultural cast-offs. We taught them to be ashamed, to be humble, to cower in fear of the Lord. Can you imagine ennobling a God who demands your fear, for God's sake. How pathetic we really are."

Morgan listened from the cockpit, slack-jawed in amazement but gratified to hear so clearly articulated the sailor's disgust with the world that drove him to wander. Miranda, who had no expectations, merely smiled. The weight of the colonial legacy driven home by his repetition of the word *we*, curiously made her feel strong. She did not carry a burden of guilt for the past, but she did feel empathy for the people who were struggling out from under the oppression of the imperial project, a phantom kinship with people like Matteo and Te Ave Teao and Maria and the rest.

"Are they all *toromiro* wood?" she asked him.

"Yes."

"What about the ones up front?"

"In the bow?' He seemed offended by her ignorance of nautical terminology. "I really don't know."

"Let's take a look."

Squeezing forward with Miranda peering over his shoulder, Rove McMan extricated a wrapped bundle from its vault beneath the fo'c'sle floorboards and passed it back to her. Braced between lockers and the door to the head, she peeled away outer layers of plastic as the pungent scent of oils and wood filled the cramped spaces around her. Moving back into the main cabin, she carefully unfolded the oily coverings from the first two slabs in the bundle and held them to the light, then she called Morgan to come down and see what she had. She proceeded to unwrap the other pieces and lay them out on a berth as he backed down the companionway steps.

Miranda contemplated the pieces, but let them lie where she'd placed them. Morgan watched her thinking. McMan glanced back and forth between the other two. He was a man used to waiting.

Many of the pieces showed curious notches and channels cut into wood which didn't have the density or depth of colour she had expected. "They're smaller than the others," she observed. "The ones back here." She nodded to the gaping hole by their feet, and then to the single dark piece streaked with light that McMan had set carefully on top of the chart table. "These aren't *toromiro*, are they?"

"No," said McMan. "It looks like *mako'i* wood."

"Does that mean they're more recent?" Morgan asked. He had been impressed by McMan's knowledge of island woods.

Rove McMan shrugged. "I haven't given it much thought."

Miranda began fiddling with the slabs, handling them with deliberate care as she arranged notches and tabs, channels and edges, until they took the form of a small cabinet the size of a breadbox. "There," she said. "Now if we only knew what treasure it used to contain."

The two men had been watching her in astonishment, and each in turn lifted the box when it was fully assembled and turned it over and over in his hands, testing its heft and solidity.

"It was like a Chinese puzzle box," she said. "I'm good with puzzles."

The box gleamed from *tamanu* oil, which had been rubbed into its pores to preserve the wood. Miranda recognized the scent from shops in Hanga Roa and Tahiti. Sold as an oil and an elixir, exported for some ungodly reason in bulk to Utah. When the lid was held in place so that the upper edges of each side were lodged in corresponding grooves, the box had a soundness that proclaimed it a marvel in cabinetry and engineering. And in artistry and perhaps scholarship, as well. Incised on every plane, inside and out, were lines of intricate glyphs, some tiny figurative renderings of birds and humans and sea creatures, and others geometric and abstract. But, while the exterior was somewhat scuffed, the interior showed no markings scratched or gouged by lost treasure. It simply was what it was.

Rove McMan seemed as surprised as Miranda and Morgan that the pieces came together in such perfect accord. The three of them stared at it, sitting on the chart table like a holy relic. McMan's urgency to return it to the island now seemed to make sense, perhaps even to him, although he appeared to be driven by wanderlust more than commitment, content to sail over the horizon in either direction, westward or eastward as Miranda's revelations would determine.

It was Morgan who broke the silence. "*Aku-Aku*, the book," he said. "It was a delivery system, right?"

Anticipating where he was going, she realized the same could be said for the *Rongorongo* box. "The treasure isn't missing," she declared.

"Exactly." Morgan turned to McMan. "When do you figure this was carved? Maybe the 1880s?"

"No, earlier. It's not *toromiro*. And *tamanu* nuts didn't grow on the island. The oil would have come in from the Marquesas, maybe brought by traders or whalers."

"But you've never seen anything like this box, right?"

"Never seen, nor heard, of anything like it."

"You said the wood might be *mako'i* from Rapa Nui. That means it might not be. Could it be Peruvian?" Morgan was on to something. The pieces were falling into place.

"Yes, for sure. A rosewood of some sort."

"A wood that might remind a Rapa Nui exile of home."

"Morgan?" She wasn't questioning him, she was urging him on.

"The last king of the island died as an indentured servant in Peru. His name was Kaimoko. Most of the people sold by the slavers into servitude didn't die in guano mines. That's what anthropologists and historians used to think. Most died as household slaves, many from disease. Over a thousand. All men. Some of those men were *ariki*, they could read *Rongorongo*; they knew how to write it. Perhaps one particular *ariki*, in the fragments of time he could claim for himself, maybe he made this."

"You've been reading again."

"Yeah, I have." He paused for dramatic effect. "There was a Chinese population in Lima at the time. And, let's say, an *ariki* enslaved in Lima studied their boxes and decided to build his own. And he inscribed each piece so that together they make a book of his people. This is their history, their collective memory, their ancestral past. This," he turned directly to Rove McMan, "this is their real *Domesday Book*. The information on the other pieces is incidental. Relatively speaking."

"But it found its way back to the island, it was given to us on Rapa Nui," McMan protested.

"I'm coming to that. A handful of men returned. Miranda, you talked about Matteo and Maria, they are descendents of the last *ariki*. He brought it home, freed from slavery by order of the same Church responsible for erasing his heritage. He was dying with smallpox. Freed from bondage, he brought hope for the remnants of his people. But it had to be hidden, it had to be protected. It had to outlast the powers of alien gods and foreign governments. And so it has."

"His name was Humberto Rapu Haoa," Miranda said. "Who gave it to you?' she asked, turning to McMan.

"Matteo's mother. Not to me, to the D'Arcys for safekeeping."

"When did the D'Arcys meet?" she asked, trying to understand their shared connection to Rapa Nui.

"On the island. The first time we sailed there. Harrington and I, nearly twenty years ago. I stayed for half a dozen years. He stayed for six months, then flew off to Tahiti and back to Toronto."

"With Maria?"

"Yes. Back home, his law practice thrived; they prospered. Several years ago, we returned, the three of us, on the *Tangata Manu*. That's when Maria Pilar gave us the bundles. She did not understand their significance, but she knew the elder Matteo, the father of her children's father, Matteo Akarikitea, he was what they call a *taiki ana*, literally a guardian of the cave, he had treasured them. When her husband died, the old man told her these were the gift of the last *ariki*. Later, she flew to Toronto. I pity the poor woman, her children are dead and she is alive, it must seem unnatural. She has only her grandchildren and they are at school in Chile."

"Grandchildren!" Miranda exclaimed. "I didn't know the D'Arcys had children."

"They didn't, but they paid the school fees, they are the godparents."

"Matteo's? Are they Matteo's?"

"They are Matteo's children, a boy and a girl. Twins, nearly ten."

Miranda tried to assimilate what he was saying. Matteo had never talked about children. He talked of the future, but always as a cause, a commitment. Why would he need to protect them from her? No, he was protecting himself. Their mother was dead. They were safe. If anything happened to him, they could be moved to Toronto. He was protecting himself from the pain of having to leave them.

Morgan looked across the cabin and shifted around to shield his eyes from the sharp rays of the afternoon sun streaming through the portholes. Miranda, triumphant only moments ago, now looked forlorn. He wanted to say something to reassure her, but there was nothing to say. She had to work through her relationship with Matteo. Relationships don't stop when someone dies, not for the living.

"Your plan is to take this back, then?" Morgan asked the sailor.

McMan looked at him and reverted to his ancient mariner guise. "Aye. It's time to move on. I've no more stories to tell. I need to stock up in the enchanted islands and for sure on the open seas."

Morgan couldn't tell if the man was joking or really believed he could juggle personas without being seen as a misfit or a fool. Or if he cared.

"Via Gibraltar."

"There's no other way," he said, nodding toward Miranda, who seemed distracted by her private thoughts. "I might take Maria Pilar with me, if she wants to go."

"The old woman? I'd think she'd have all she needs right here," said Morgan. "Especially if she brings the twins up from Chile. And if she went, certainly she'd fly?"

"She'll go back, eventually. She will take the children back to the island. She really has no choice. Historical inevitability, you know."

"Nothing is inevitable until it's over. History is written in the past tense."

"History is never past, Detective Morgan. Before it occurs, we call it fate, but fate's just history getting ready to happen. Dead reckoning, detective."

Miranda picked up the last few sentences in their conversation and turned abruptly to McMan. "Do you know Thomas Edward Ross?" In her mind, the question had something to do with fate and the manipulation of history.

"I've met him. He used to spend time on the island while I was there. I didn't know him very well." He paused, then volunteered, "I didn't like him. I didn't trust him, but I gather he was useful."

"To the cause?"

"The cause, yes, the independence movement, if you can call a handful of dissidents a movement."

"You don't sound impressed."

"On the contrary. They were my friends. I admired them tremendously. More so because they were doomed to fail. As for Ross, I would describe him as whatever I'm not."

Miranda knew just what he meant. She had met people who could best be explained in no better way, they were what she was not. "His interests paralleled those of the movement, but he was working for the Pinochet faction," she suggested.

"Faction? The fascist junta! No, not really, he works for himself. He apparently does quite well. A few million stashed away here and a few million there. A villa with a view looking over Lake Cuomo in Italy, a suite on the *Island Queen*. He would occasionally bring a case or two of armaments to the island, courtesy of his patrons in Chile, and he would trade them for artifacts. The *movement*, as we're calling it, posthumously, had little money. The authorities kept close tabs on Matteo to see that no funds came through from Toronto. These small shipments were Ross's way of keeping in touch with the revolution. He may have been working for the government, as well. He's a fake, you know."

"His personality or his credentials?" she asked

"Everything. His class. Borrowed, he has none of his own.

"Oxford?"

"He was born in a village on the outskirts of Cambridge. Abington Piggotts. Charming name. Never completed his A levels.

"Sloane Square?"

"Earls Court."

"Washington?"

"Highly unlikely, although I'm sure he is monitored by the CIA, and probably CSIS, MI6, Mossad, and possibly the KGB. He might even do the occasional odd job spying for one or the other. But he's too high profile to be much use. Spoiled by his own success as a scoundrel, you might say. Mostly, he's a pawn who thinks he's a knight on the chessboard of life."

"Very poetic," said Miranda. "And what piece are you?"

"I'm the sailor, of course."

"There is no sailor."

"Exactly my point."

Miranda liked Rove McMan. He apparently had the privileged background that Ross claimed to have, and he chose to go his own way. She looked around the cabin of the *Tangata Manu* with renewed interest. Almost everything of real importance in this man's world was nearly within arm's reach. She looked over at Morgan. His eyes were almost closed, he seemed to be enjoying the gentle rocking of the boat, the murmur of voices as she talked with McMan. She didn't know if he was following or not.

"Tell me about Maria. She was betrothed to Te Ave Teao, wasn't she?"

It took him a moment to assimilate the shift in conversational direction. "On the island? No, there was nothing formal. It was something they grew up with. He was desperately in love with her. Everyone knew that. But for Maria, he was like Matteo, they were her brothers."

"He must have been crushed when she went off with D'Arcy."

"No, he wasn't."

She waited for an explanation, but none came. "Perhaps he was pleased for her good fortune."

Rove McMan again indicated no response was forthcoming.

"D'Arcy described her as wanton," said Morgan. He had been thinking about the packet of letters tied in a faded blue ribbon. He had not had them translated. He would return them to Maria's mother.

"As they say in Rapanui, *kai i te au*. I wouldn't know about that."

"You sailed with her for weeks at a time, you knew her when she was barely out of her teens. What do you think, was she promiscuous?"

"Like I said."

"What about D'Arcy?" said Morgan. "He described himself as bisexual."

"I doubt it."

"Homosexual?"

"We lived in cramped quarters for months on end."

"You have a high opinion of yourself. What about asexual?"

"Not interested? Possibly. Likely, I guess."

"Do you think his wife was promiscuous?"

"You asked me that. And no, I did not have an affair with her. Nothing, not so much as an exchange of lascivious glances. And not with her husband, either."

"I had the impression they were on the verge of divorce," said Morgan.

Rove McMan stared at the floorboards and shrugged noncommittally.

"Is there any chance D'Arcy was having an affair with his partner?" Miranda asked.

"Gloria Simmons? Hardly." He straightened and looked resolutely first at Morgan and then at Miranda. "You don't get it, do you? With Maria and Harrington, it wasn't about sex or money or privilege. They were passionately, deeply, romantically, wholeheartedly in love. I just don't think sex had much to do with it. Or money. Or privilege."

Romance and passion without sex. Miranda spun the notion around in her mind, looking for traction. Morgan recalled his strange affair on Easter Island, the woman with eyes like Miranda's, brown and green and golden. They had shared an exquisite romance and never had sex. It was perhaps the most intimate relationship he had ever had and they never did more than hold hands in the moonlight. *I get it*, he thought. But for Miranda, the concept seemed as dreary as sex without passion. Maybe without romance, but not without passion. Why bother?

"One thing they shared," Rove McMan continued, unaware of their divergent personal responses, "was a profound connection with Rapa Nui, *Te Pito o Te Henua*, it was the centre of the world for both of them."

"Understandable for her, but why for him?" Morgan asked.

Miranda thought the answer was obvious, but it was not what she expected.

"Revenge. How long have you lived in Toronto, Detective Quin?"

"Me, I came as a student, went to U of T. Nearly twenty years."

"And you, Detective?'

"Just over forty, I was born here. Why?"

"Then you will remember 999 Queen Street West. And you, Ms. Quin, may not."

"I've heard of it," said Miranda. "Notorious asylum, palatial on the outside, mayhem and squalor within."

"We used to go over from Cabbagetown just to scare ourselves when we were kids," said Morgan. "We'd boost each other up to look over the wall, or jump around on the north side of Queen Street, yelling at inmates peering out through the windows. With the huge dome and the columns and porticos, it looked like a cathedral — of the damned, I suppose."

"It was a majestic building," said Rove McMan.

"Yes, it was," said Morgan.

Miranda remembered her parents telling her that when visiting Toronto was a big thing for people from Waldron, before the 401 was put through with a cloverleaf right on the edge of the village, they used to do three things: they went to the Royal Ontario Museum, they went to the top of the Bank of Commerce Building (this was before the CN Tower), and they strolled past the hospital for the insane, *999 Queen*, as it was universally known, which had once been the grandest building in the entire province of Upper Canada, surrounded by a wall twenty feet high. Egyptian mummies with their toenails showing, a modest skyscraper, and being literally a stones-width from bedlam, these were the thrills of the city, punctuated for the more sophisticated by an elegant lunch in the Georgian Room at Eaton's College Street store, or rounded off with a magic show at the Royal Alexandra Theatre.

All this came flooding back on a wave of nostalgia for times before she was born. She smiled wistfully at Morgan. She knew his memories of the past were of a different city, a city of streetcars and sirens, of rules to be tested and strangers to be taunted. She painted him an almost Dickensian childhood that somehow had fallen away like an old set of clothes when he entered university — just like her village childhood and the trappings of a small-town high school had fallen away.

"My sister died there," said McMan.

Morgan had been anticipating this, but Miranda was horrified, and in part for the depths of emotion she had forced the unfortunate man to suppress while she pursued her own meandering thoughts about the asylum. It was not at all what she had expected to hear.

"I read about it," said Morgan. "In a fire."

"She was older, she looked out for me after my father died." McMan's voice was dispassionate and yet carried utter conviction. There was no room for argument or interpretation. This was how it was. "My mother was focused on finding my father's replacement, upgrading to a superior model, which she did. My sister was there for me. And then she went mad. Just like that. I went to visit her once, but she didn't know who I was. I never went back. She wouldn't have wanted me to, or so I thought. My mother pretended my sister had eloped with a princeling leftover from the Austro-Hungarian empire and several years later she announced her death by Porsche in Provence. She was pleased Princess Grace crashed her car in Monaco — it gave her own story validity."

He paused, then asked Morgan, "Where did you read it? My mother kept it out of the papers. There was a small news release saying two inmates had perished and their names were being withheld until the families were notified, which they weren't."

"They weren't notified?" Miranda exclaimed.

"The names weren't released. My mother saw to that. She paid for both funerals."

"It was in the coroner's report," said Morgan. "There were two of them. The other woman was somebody Sinclair."

"Somebody." Rove McMan repeated the word with a wry smile. "Her name was Kaitlin Sinclair."

Now Miranda was anticipating where the story was going. If the death of his sister was only a prologue, then what was to come was going to be big.

"Harrington D'Arcy and I lived parallel lives in a number of ways," McMan continued. "His mother also married twice, also after the suicide of his father. She married a man by the name of D'Arcy."

"A man who adopted him. His birth name was Harrington Sinclair, wasn't it?" exclaimed Miranda.

"And he had a sister," Morgan observed, catching up with the story.

"He had a sister and she was an inmate in 999. She was a younger sister. His sister and Elizabeth —"

"Your sister?" Miranda was now leaning close and the closer she leaned the quieter McMan's voice grew so that Morgan had to lean forward, as well, until the three of them were huddled like conspirators in the light that was now quite luminous, the sun having sunk below the leaf-line to glimmer off the water surface and shine into the cabin.

"My sister Elizabeth and Kaitlin Sinclair, they shared a room. Harrington used to visit them, they'd sit out on the great pillared verandah at the end of the broad corridor and they would order tea to be served and the nurses would bring tea and biscuits, it was a lovely and loving domestic scene. Except Harrington's sister forgot who he was. But still he went to visit, especially in the spring and the summer when the silver maples outside the verandah would shut out the city."

"It sounds perversely idyllic," Miranda observed.

"It was the worst of times and the best of times," said McMan, distorting the Dickensian allusion with an ironic smile.

"And what was the worst?" Morgan asked. "The fire?"

"The life. They were inmates in a notorious madhouse, a palace for the insane. They were madwomen who recognized only each other. According to Harrington, they were blissfully happy and entirely out of touch with the world. It almost sounds like a nice way to be, islands unto themselves. In retrospect, I wish I had gone in to visit, to see Elizabeth."

Rove paused to let his emotions catch up with his narrative, and then he continued. "I have often wondered if they were lovers. I don't know. They were smokers. They were not allowed to smoke in the corridor, and not in their room. They were only allowed to smoke on the verandah. One day in the winter, they barricaded themselves in a linen closet and they lit up. The nurses couldn't get them out. A resident doctor was called. His prescription was time. They would get bored or hungry or need the toilet. Lock the door from the outside, cause them sufficient distress so they wouldn't do it again. So he locked the door. Doors in an asylum are thick, all doors in an asylum lock. He pocketed the key and left.

"A nurse telephoned Harrington and he came onto the ward. He talked to Kaitlin. He talked to Elizabeth. He asked the nurses to release them. That wasn't so long ago, but back then the psychiatrist was God. They needed his authorization. He was nowhere to be found. They didn't have a key. Harrington was insistent. The only person more powerful than God in most people's eyes is a well-dressed lawyer. They sent for a janitor, someone with a master key. The doctor had gone home for the night. The janitors couldn't track down the right key.

"Harrington talked to the two women through the door. The girls, that was the affectionate name among the staff for them, *the girls* talked to him. They went through stages of panic, and then they seemed calm, quite cheerful, he explained when we met at the funeral. Then smoke began seeping out from under the door. Elizabeth and Kaitlin had lighted the linens on fire and they sang an indecipherable hymn and burned themselves to death in a fierce embrace, their bodys clenched together so that it was impossible to separate their remains. They had a common funeral, as I said, courtesy of my mother. At D'Arcy's insistence, what was left of them was placed in a single casket. With cosmic absurdity, they were buried, not cremated, and the empty casket and the shared casket were laid in the ground side by side. That was something negotiated between my mother's lawyer and Harrington D'Arcy."

"And the doctor?" Miranda asked. "Was there an inquiry?"

"Essentially what the Brits call 'death by misadventure.' No charges."

Morgan had not forgotten where McMan's story had begun. With the D'Arcys' mutual love for Rapa Nui. He asked Rove McMan to explain.

"It was where his wife was from. That was important. But, it was where he abandoned his conscience. In what to him was the ultimate moral act, he transcended morality. It ceased to be a factor in Harrington D'Arcy's life although he acknowledged morality in others. That's what made him such a good lawyer, apparently."

"I can understand this as a response to the fire," said Miranda. "He listened through a door while his sister died. But how does the island fit in?"

"We met at the funeral. He became a sort of mentor, but in some ways we were alter egos. You've met us both, Detective Morgan. You'll know what I mean. In so many unexpected ways our lives had merged. We sailed together. We went to Rapa Nui. We —"

His story came to an abrupt halt. Neither Morgan nor Miranda said a word. He needed time. He was on the verge of exonerating his mentor for unspecified crimes or condemning him to the judgment of the morally righteous. That's what they guessed he was thinking, although his face seemed curiously impassive.

"The doctor's name was Levesque," he continued. "Quite young. Apparently he was shaken up by the *misadventure*. His marriage broke up. He drank. He disappeared."

"Disappeared!" Miranda exclaimed.

"He turned up doing good works in a very remote part of the world. Putting his medical training to use, seeking redemption. But redemption is not absolution. No one on earth or in heaven could absolve him of those deaths at the asylum. No one."

"He went to Rapa Nui, to work as a volunteer in the island hospital." Morgan didn't ask this as a question, but offered it as a link, for narrative continuity.

"And you and D'Arcy went after him." Miranda, too, offered this as a statement of the obvious, the inevitable.

"I am a sailor. We sailed to Isla de Pasqua. Dr. Levesque was still drinking. Many on the island feared him. He was careless, but worse, he was angry. An angry doctor is dangerous." He stopped talking again, this time as if his story had come to an end.

Morgan and Miranda both wanted more — Morgan, to illuminate his investigation into Maria's death, possibly into D'Arcy's death, and Miranda, to round out her knowledge of the island, itself, to shade in the grey areas with colour.

"Were you there when Dr. Levesque died?" Miranda asked.

He had not expected such a direct question. He looked into her eyes. He smiled. "Yes," he said, "I suppose I was."

"But you didn't kill him?"

"Not as I remember."

"Maria knew about this?"

"We were close friends with her family."

"D'Arcy killed him?"

"Yes."

"Strangled him?"

"Yes," he said.

"At the farmhouse. You buried his body under the ruins of a *moai*. I believe I have met the late Dr.

Levesque. In trying circumstances. We didn't have the opportunity to become well acquainted."

Neither of the men knew what she was talking about. Somehow McMan's story had merged with her own.

Strangulation? Because D'Arcy wanted revenge. Only his bare hands would do. Murdering a man might have broken a civilized person, no matter how much he felt morally obliged, or it might have cast him free from morality forever. The latter, she assumed, was the case. She had gazed into the empty eye sockets of the man whose cavalier judgment had condemned two creatures so vulnerable and innocent to a terrible death.

"Rapa Nui was Harrington's Calvary," McMan murmured and proceeded to clarify. "The person he had been died there. What remained was something quite different."

"Not a god," Morgan protested.

"No, not at all. Nor the Devil. A hollow man with a great heart and no soul."

"A man with a great heart and no soul," Miranda repeated, turning the phrase in her mind like a spindle on a very slow lathe, trying to smooth the words into something she could comprehend. "A man who could love deeply or despise, but could not endure the consequences of either."

The two men said nothing.

Shifting abruptly from the abstract to the concrete, she said, "Matteo and his sister, even their mother, Maria Pilar, they were all there at the farmhouse."

"Not in the room. Matteo, myself, and Te Ave Teao, we were witnesses. Later, the women prepared the body. The men, the brothers, they disposed of it in a makeshift crypt that islanders would never disturb. It was a pile of rubble, really, where another burial had taken place following retribution for a crime that was only of concern to the family. It carried its own sort of unofficial *tapu*. Police sometimes know when to let things lie, even dead things."

Miranda thought of her explanation to Morgan about why the RCMP chose to close the case on the deaths in the Arctic. "What was your connection with Matteo's family?" she asked.

"I'm not sure. Ironically, it was Dr. Levesque who introduced us to them. We met him at a hotel bar in Hanga Roa, a tiny hotel, there wasn't much there for tourists at the time, and he knew immediately who we were but he said nothing, we said nothing. We shared tapas with him over drinks. Matteo came in and the doctor introduced us. We didn't see much of Levesque after that. He worked slavishly at the hospital or drank in his small house by himself. Young Matteo and D'Arcy warmed to each other. We spent many evenings in their compound in town, and they showed us around the island, they showed us the old farmhouse out by the quarry, Rano Raraku, we spent evenings out there, talking. Sometimes I stayed on the *Tangata Manu*, but Harrington seemed driven to connect with the island, with the remnants of its lost past, with this place he knew he would not leave before committing murder.

"And when he was ready, we did it. We all participated. He left the island with Maria. I stayed until I could forget the look in Levesque's eyes." He paused, then resumed. "While Harrington's fingers choked the life out of him, Levesque gazed at his killer with a sort of affection that still haunts me, as he embraced his own death. When I see those eyes in my sleep, I dream of my sister, when we were young and she was my refuge, and I wake up lonely, but happy she died with someone she loved."

Miranda wondered if Rove McMan had ever opened up so much to anyone in his life. *It's not us,* she thought. *It's because our stories merge.*

She recalled vividly how she had felt as she stared into the gaping eye sockets in the dead man's skull, but she couldn't have summoned the words to describe those feelings if her life depended on it. And Morgan knew, now, with a certainty that Gloria Simmons had murdered Harrington D'Arcy, he knew why, he just didn't know how. She had sucked the life right out of him. The phrase lingered in his mind as they prepared to leave.

It was almost dusk, the ducks were raucous, the channel was rippled in anticipation of an evening breeze, halyards clattered restlessly against hollow masts and the willows had turned a deep green as sunlight on the western horizon seemed to shine up on their leaves from below. The *Tangata Manu* dipped gently under their weight and rocked gently away as Miranda and Morgan stepped off.

Lost in their own thoughts they made their way to the ferry, leaving Rove McMan alone with his. "*Kai i te au*," he had said when they left. "Whatever the question, *kai i te au*, the question cannot be answered. I can live with that. *Ia orana*, Detectives. Goodbye."

Neither expected they would see him again.

12

Things That Go Bump in the Night

Eddie Block was still on duty and welcomed them aboard with a deferential clasping of their hands in his own, then ushered them across the gangway with unnerving solemnity. Once they cast off, he tried for congeniality, pointing out to Miranda how Lake Ontario itself could be reached through the Eastern Gap to the east and the Western Gap to the west, and when they were well across the harbour he directed her to look south, away from the city, where she could see the lighthouse at Gibraltar Point towering over the low terrain.

"I wonder did you know the city's first murder happened there in 1815? Mr. Rademuller, he was the lighthouse keeper, he died and they didn't find his skeleton until years and years later."

"Possibly, it was the first *unsolved* murder," said Miranda, amused that he felt murder was the politic topic of conversation with a homicide detective.

"Nobody got hung, anyway."

"Hanged, Eddie, not hung."

"Like I said, Mr. Morgan. They didn't catch the scoundrels."

He was quoting a tourist brochure. Miranda doubted Mr. Rademuller was Toronto's first murder, solved or otherwise. The city had been ravaged, with killing and plundering, by American forces in 1812, treachery that necessitated the burning of Washington in retaliation, two years later.

"At least we showed restraint and only burned down their public buildings," she said. Eddie Block smiled and retreated to pursue other duties. Morgan went off in his mind on tangents of his own until they docked.

Curiously, Eddie followed them ashore and made a point of stepping squarely into their path. Morgan tried to move around, but Miranda sensed an urgency in the young man's awkwardness and stopped right in front of him.

"Detective Quin," he said with a scowl intended to convey the high seriousness of his mission. "A man asked me to give you a message."

"Really," she responded. "And why would he ask you to do that?"

"He saw you go over, I think. He made it seem pretty important."

"We've been there for hours, Eddie. Why didn't he just come over if he needed to see me?"

"I suppose because I'm the person in charge and he wasn't a member."

"Or he wasn't wearing a jacket and tie," Morgan suggested.

"Eddie, why didn't you tell me before?"

"I was working," he explained.

"Well, now that we're on dry land —" She stopped herself. "Who was this guy and what did he want?"

"He didn't say. His name was, I wrote it down but I remember it, Terrace Rattigan."

"Terrace or Terrence?"

He pulled a neatly folded piece of paper from his pants pocket. "Yes, Terrence. We're supposed to keep notes to help us get the names right. It's always better for the aggrieved if we call them by name."

"The grieving," said Morgan.

"Eddie, did this Mr. Rattigan leave a card? How am I to reach him? Did he say why? Police business or personal?" Miranda turned back to Morgan. "I'm still on sabbatical. It must have been personal. Eddie, was he attractive?"

"Yes, ma'am, he was. I don't know, maybe not, I didn't notice. He said to tell you he is not staying at The Four Seasons."

"He's *not* staying at the Four Seasons? He said that?"

"Ma'am, he said you'd figure it out. He didn't say what he wanted, but he was an important person. You could tell. I see a lot of important people in my line of business. He said you met on the *Ireland Queen*."

"In your line of business?" Miranda couldn't help admiring his spunk. "Important people die in the end, Eddie, the same as the rest of us. And work on your note-taking. It's the *Island Queen*, not *Ireland*."

"I think Eddie was referring to his present line of work," said Morgan as he edged around the young man, grimacing at Miranda in a bid to have her follow. "I'm sure Terrace Rattigan will track her down, Eddie. He sounds like a determined sort of fellow. Semi-determined, since he didn't get past you. Good man. G'night."

"Good evening, Detectives," said Eddie Block, with a hint of a bow, or perhaps it was a tentative genuflection, it was difficult to tell in the fading light, but there was no question about the slight quiver of deference in his voice as he called after them, before turning back to the ferry to resume his sea-faring duties. "I was pleased to be of service."

Morgan tapped the refrigerator for a beer and the remains of a day-old submarine sandwich. They had decided not to have dinner together. Miranda's system was struggling to sort out the difference between being awake and asleep and Morgan was feeling cranky. They walked up to Union Station and caught the subway, Morgan going west and Miranda going east, which was an illusion since the lines arced north and ran parallel only a few blocks apart.

She had talked about her mysterious visitor with an offhand lack of interest that surprised him. He figured it was either because she had no idea who he was or the exact opposite, that she knew exactly who he was and chose not to disclose his identity. Morgan watched television for awhile and went to bed early. At three a.m. he woke up. Precisely at three. It unnerved him how that happened. He wore an old Bulova that had been his father's retirement gift. The gold was worn through on the back, but it kept perfect time. The movement inside was absolutely silent. Yet somehow, it woke him to the exact second measured by the sweep second hand at the top of the hour. Not every hour, just hours deemed important by the watch, or by his mind as it blindly monitored his progression through time.

If he set his alarm, sometimes he would wake up five minutes before it went off. Not four minutes before or six but five. It seemed the timepieces in his life showed an uncanny prescience.

He stared at where the ceiling would be if he had been able to see it in the diffuse light coming in from the street through his broken blinds. He might have been dreaming about sex. He had that same uneasy feeling, although no images came to mind. He tried to focus on his case, which seemed after their afternoon with Rove McMan to be simultaneously coming together and in even more of a shambles. He wondered if Miranda was awake. He decided not to call her. It was three in the morning, after all.

When he woke up again a few minutes later, he had been unmistakably dreaming about sex. He lay very still, waiting for the ache to go away, but each time he relaxed the perfect naked body of Gloria Simmons presented itself as a vision, while at the same time she seemed to be snuggling her warmth close against him within the narrow confines of a down-filled sleeping bag.

To distract himself he focused on Ibiza, when he had been in his early twenties, and indulged in recollections of his greatest humiliation. He was trying to take his mind off the natural blonde beauty of Gloria Simmons in what he hoped would be an inversion of the Cialis effect. Two English girls had taken him home for the night. He was working in a bar on the harbourfront. The girls had been smoking pot and drinking beer. When the *taverna* closed, they asked if he wanted to see their room, which was like a small outbuilding on the flat rooftop of a larger building. When they got to the room, the girls did their minimal ablutions and took off their clothes and motioned for him to do the same and crawl into bed between them. The three of them lay side by side, naked under a sheet. He was totally ready. After a while one of the girls fell asleep and then the other girl fell asleep. He stayed awake all night, baffled by what he might have done or should have done or could have done and didn't do. In the morning, the three of them got up at the same time, used the toilet affair on the roof outside their door, and went back to the harbour area for breakfast.

Their names were Mandy and Christine. He could remember the exact shape of their breasts in the lamplight, the exact warm, clean smell of their bodies. When he met them for drinks back in London, they seemed exotically ordinary, and he realized they didn't have much interest in him, either. Years later, he had a somewhat sordid tryst with two women from headquarters, a one-time thing, but that, he thought, was another story.

As he had anticipated, his ruminations led to self-judgment which extinguished his yearnings. The aching had subsided. The whole threesome thing, he thought — he supposed every man had been through similar experiences — suggested an inability to sustain a relationship. He thought of Lucy, his ex-wife, he thought of Miranda, he thought of Beverley Weekes on Rapa Nui, a swarm of memories in jagged fragments raced through his mind.

Suddenly, he knew who Miranda's friend was and where he was staying. When they had walked over to the subway from the Harbourfront, she had expressed irritation at the man's cryptic behavior. "There were a surprising number of eligible men on board," she had said. "I dined and danced for a week, Morgan. How am I supposed to remember them all. Terrence Rattigan? No, maybe Terry. There might have been a Terry. Who pays attention to names on a cruise ship? Everyone is *buddy* or *mate* or, you know, those instant nicknames travellers use so they don't have to remember real names. Politicians do the same thing. Your funeral friend said he's attractive."

"Only because you asked," Morgan had said.

Squirming around in his bed to make himself comfortable, Morgan drifted on the edge of sleep. Amidst the flurry of women's faces and body parts that he seemed to have amputated in a frenzy of objectification, a theatre front in London loomed in his mind. Columns, portico, billboards. The Haymarket Theatre. He had met Christine and Mandy for drinks in a pub opposite the Haymarket Theatre in London, just down from

Piccadilly Circus. That's where he'd seen the revival of a play about the later life of Lawrence of Arabia, after Lawrence changed his name and joined the R.A.F. The play and T.E. Lawrence were both called *Ross*. The author was Terrence Rattigan. Of course, the name had seemed familiar. And Rattigan-Ross was staying at the Haymarket Hotel, a boutique hotel off Bloor Street frequented by lesser celebrities. *Not* the Four Seasons. Terrence Rattigan had challenged Miranda to figure it out. This Terrence Rattigan, not that one. The Haymarket, hay, market, one season, when hay was brought in after stooking to dry on the fields of Sussex and Kent. And who else but Ross would define Miranda in terms of her ability to solve puzzles?

She had told Morgan quite a lot about T.E. Ross. The man seemed to thrive on maintaining a precarious balance between the treacheries of sedition and incidental grace, with only his charm and good looks to help distinguish between them. Morgan suspected he also travelled under the name of Peter O'Toole, the actor who had brought Lawrence and Ross so memorably to the screen. Or his real name was Peter O'Toole and that was his incentive for plundering Lawrence for his nominal disguises.

Morgan got up and walked into the bathroom. It was only a little past three, too early to shave. He dressed in yesterday's clothes, which were still draped over the chair by his dresser, put on a windbreaker, anticipating the chill of a late August morning, and headed out at a brisk pace for the Haymarket Hotel.

There was only one man on duty behind the desk

and no concierge in sight. Morgan asked for Terrence Rattigan's room number.

"It's 3:48 in the a.m," said the man, looking at Morgan like he had materialized on the spot. "Didn't hear you come in."

"I know the time. What room is he in?"

"You'll have to come back." The man was about Morgan's age, clean shaven, but red-eyed. Probably wary he'd screwed up too many jobs in the past, he wanted to avoid trouble. "Sorry," he added.

Morgan flashed his police ID. "Homicide," he said.

The clerk stiffened. "You guys carry Glocks?"

"Yes we do," said Morgan, glaring. He was wondering whether his handgun was in his gun locker at headquarters or at home in his underwear drawer. "I'm here unofficially." He said this in a Clint Eastwood whisper. He read the man's nametag. "Jeffrey, I need your co-operation. A key card. I'd like to surprise Mr. Rattigan." Morgan suspected the clerk had previously had run-ins with the police. He was trying to turn his life around. Morgan had little use for bully cops, but he felt a gut-driven urgency to connect with T.E. Ross before Miranda did.

Once outside Rattigan's room, Morgan slipped the card into the lock and gently pressed down on the handle. He entered silently and stepped into the darkness, closing the door quietly behind him. By the light of the clock radio, he shuffled his way to the bedside. He leaned forward and immediately realized the absence of warmth emanating from the bed signified trouble. He straightened; too late.

"Checkmate, Mr. Morgan." Morgan flinched at the pressure of cold steel against his right temple. He guessed a .44 Magnum semi-automatic. This guy wouldn't use a revolver. "I'm assuming I paid the desk clerk more that you did, Detective. I was expecting your partner. She told me about you. Do sit down. Oh, you can't see. Well here's what I want you to do. Very slowly, unbuckle your belt." The barrel of the Magnum bit into Morgan's flesh. "Good, now drop your pants. To the ankles. There. I do apologize for the awkwardness. I assure you my interest is not libidinous in the least. Now, turn, slowly, sit down on the bed. Sit back. It's very soft. And quite low. There now, comfortably off balance, feeling rather silly? Let me turn on the light."

Morgan felt like a fool. It was an old trick. He'd read about it in spy novels. He felt even more foolish when light flared from the bedside lamp and he could see his captor's hands even though his face was still shrouded in darkness. Ross was pointing toward him with a travel-sized canister of shaving cream. Morgan had been rendered powerless, not by Remington, but by Gillette.

"You are Mr. Morgan, I presume? Otherwise, I will have to kill you and deposit your body piecemeal in the mail chute."

"Was this really necessary?" said Morgan as he struggled awkwardly to his feet and drew up his pants.

"Probably not," said Ross, moving toward the door and turning on the overhead. "It's all part of the game. And if you had been someone else — but I knew you were not. I could smell the absence of a sidearm. Do you realize guns emit odours, even when they haven't been fired in a very long time? Of course, by the time I figured you were unarmed, you were disarmed. Nice to meet you."

Ross thrust his hand forward as if he were at a class reunion. Morgan took the proffered hand and gripped it for a moment as he contemplated his advantage, then shook it firmly. So much of what he had heard about Ross suggested a professional: cool, very clever, sophisticated, elusive, ruthless, a man unencumbered by passion or moral integrity. Ross in Toronto struck Morgan as more amusing, even charming, and more dangerous than he had expected. A gifted amateur, treacherous and unpredictable.

"We have a lot to talk about, Detective Morgan. Let me call room service for coffee. The kitchen opens at four. We're already well into the day."

Miranda had gone directly home after she left Morgan at Union Station. She had not managed to pick up groceries since she had returned so she opened a tin of Spam and sliced off a piece which she slathered with strawberry jam, washing it down with a room-temperature can of Canada Dry. When she was a girl her favourite dinner, and her father's favourite, as well, was Spam fried in butter with tinned pineapple slices and a sprinkling of brown sugar and cinnamon. Years after he died she realized this concoction wasn't her father's favourite at all. It was something they had invented together when her mother and sister were out. She still kept Spam in her kitchen as comfort food.

Despite the exhaustion, after her dinner she turned on her computer and explored for a couple of hours, made a few phone calls and, satisfied, collapsed on her bed and was asleep in minutes.

She awakened in the middle of the night at virtually the same time as Morgan. Her system insisted she was feeling sluggish after an excessively long afternoon nap, Tahiti-time. She stared into the depths of the shadows moving across her bedroom ceiling as her curtains played with the ambient light of the city that was filtering through.

The name Terry Rattigan bounced through her mind aimlessly. He said they had met on the *Island Queen*. Maybe he was the guy she had spent a day with on Bora Bora, sourcing the best buy for Tahitian pearls. She had already been given carte blanche for a necklace at the Pearl Market in Papeete, although she wouldn't allow herself to be compromised by accepting something like that on Ross's account. It was one thing to exploit his hospitality on the ship — she figured he owed her — but jewellery was something else.

The man she was remembering as Terry had shared free taxis with her for the short hops from pearl shop to pearl shop, offered as a courtesy. Most of the shops on Bora Bora were actually within walking distance in the village of Vaitape, but some were ensconced in the lobbys of luxury resorts. They'd had fun, checking out strings of pearls in the $10,000 range, deciding that that was their fantasy limit, and finally buying a grey luminescent pendant for him, $300, and smoky-blue earrings for her, also $300. They had lunched extravagantly at the Intercontinental on Matira Point and dined at the famous Bloody Mary's in the evening, but saw no celebrities. She recalled every detail. But they didn't use names. They had felt too close during the entire day to ask, then back on the ship at night, they had been shy with each other and next morning they sat at different tables for breakfast before disembarking with a handshake in Papeete.

She wasn't sure she wanted him to find her. Rapa Nui had been one world, Toronto was another, but her Polynesian sojourn between them connected to neither. Here she was a homicide detective on leave, on the island she had been an aspiring novelist snared in espionage and armed insurrection. On the ship, she had been someone else. Thoughts of Terry Rattigan slipped out of her mind.

She reconstructed conversations of the previous afternoon. With Maria Pilar, then Rove McMan. She had forgotten the interlude with Ellen Ravenscroft at the morgue. In retrospect, one figure dominated through the entire day like a shadow brooding over their visit to the seigneurial cottage and then on board the *Tangata Manu*. Miranda had never met Gloriasimmons, but she felt she knew her in some ways better than Morgan did, and Gloriasimmons was a dangerous woman to know.

She suddenly decided it was time to meet her potential nemesis. She got up and walked into the bathroom where she had a quick shower and meticulously applied minimal makeup before dressing in the best summer suit in her wardrobe. She adjusted her holster harness under her jacket so that it wouldn't bulge, picked up her cellphone and called a cab, then dropped it into her purse.

Entering Police Headquarters through the main entrance, she signed in at the night desk and took the elevator up to her office. The desks in Homicide were empty, except for a couple of people in the shadows at the side of the room where one guy was writing up a report and another was hunched over, asleep. But Superintendent Rufalo's light was on and she could see him through the glass, busy with paperwork. She waved. He did a double take, then came out to greet her.

"Morgan didn't tell you I'm back?" she said.

"Morgan who?" said Rufalo. "I never see Morgan. Without you around, he's counter-social."

"*With* me around he's counter-social. Did you just make that word up?"

"What are you doing here? Did you finish your novel?"

"Life overtook fiction. I couldn't make notes fast enough to keep up. I'm here for my Glock."

"You're on leave." He recognized the determined look on her face. "Okay, you're back on duty."

"Thanks, Alex." She unlocked her desk and dug out a key, then walked to the gun locker, and, removing her scaled-down Glock semi-automatic, she tucked it into its holster. "One thing? Did the book you gave Morgan to pass on to me, did that come from Maria D'Arcy?"

"Yes," he said. "From her mother."

She could tell by the look on his face that he was struggling to resist asking why she seemed to be confirming something she already knew. He felt vaguely complicit in the murder Morgan was investigating. Miranda knew this, just as she knew the answer to her query. She also knew how to keep him from asking too many questions about what she was doing there in the small hours of the morning.

He shrugged, walked back into his office, and closed the door.

Miranda realized he didn't want to be questioned about why he was there, either. During marital difficulties he was known to seek occasional refuge in the comfort of the one place in the world where he was sure of himself. He closed the interior blinds and opened the exterior blinds to anticipate the earliest traces of morning light.

Walking briskly to ward off the morning chill, Miranda cut down University Avenue to the gigantic steel-and-glass edifice in the financial district which housed D'Arcy Associates on an upper floor. The revolving doors were locked, but she attracted a security guard who let her in after she flashed her ID through the glass. Taking the elevator up, she stepped out into a lobby appointed with opulent austerity calculated to be intimidating, mysterious, and in its suggestion of brute force under restraint, either daunting or reassuring, depending on which side you were on.

"Welcome," said a cool voice off to the side, as Gloria Simmons stepped forward through an office door. "You must be Detective Sergeant Quin. I've been expecting you. Not, perhaps, at 5:30 in the morning. How did you know I'd be here?"

"Because it's 5:30 in the morning. I take it that the security guard announced my arrival."

"He did. But I knew you'd be coming sooner or later. From what your partner told me about you, it was inevitable."

They looked at each other. Miranda had expected a beautiful blonde, but not the self-possessed icy demeanour. Gloriasimmons looked absolutely at home in this soulless place, inseparable from the extravagantly manufactured materials surrounding her. Miranda could not imagine her in a city park, never mind the Arctic. She was a perfect specimen, perfectly turned out, robotic in her sexual, sensual perfection. She could not imagine this woman committing a spontaneous act.

They both wore suits, perhaps in deference to the early hour. Miranda's was her best. The other woman was wearing Armani.

Miranda wondered, how had she known that Gloriasimmons would be there at this time in the morning? Cyborgs and Cylons don't sleep. A chill ran through her. When they do, they count electric sheep. Morgan might see her as the alluring fusion of a *Vogue* supermodel and a *Playboy* vixen, but for Miranda she was a magazine layout, two dimensional, air-brushed, and her staples were showing. Gloria Simmons, meanwhile, gazed unabashedly at her. She seemed puzzled by how beautiful Miranda was. Hazel eyes and auburn hair. Morgan had talked warmly about her, but with the kind of casual admiration usually reserved for an unruly sister.

Miranda knew instantly, this woman who was apparently fearless was afraid of her. This surprised them both.

"Come into my office," said Gloria Simmons, stepping back and inviting Miranda to walk by her into a large room with one wall of glass and another of leather-bound legal books. "We'll be more private in here." Given that there was no one else around, Miranda couldn't tell whether this was meant to be ominous or ironic. "Have a seat," she said, indicating an exceptionally low-slung Swedish-design sofa. "Please."

As soon as Miranda sat down she was aware of the disadvantage. She struggled forward to get up and found that Gloria Simmons had placed herself so close in front of her that she would literally have had to push the woman aside to get to her feet. She settled into the leather cushions, feeling her semi-automatic press reassuringly into her spine. Gloria Simmons moved back a little and leaned against the edge of her very large desk, lifted slightly, and relaxed so that her weight was supported, but she was poised to spring. Miranda crossed her ankles then uncrossed them carefully, ready to rock forward and break free from the sofa's indelicate grasp if the occasion demanded.

This would be where she'd seat her adversaries, Miranda thought. Clients would get the chairs, also Swedish, but higher and more firm. Meanwhile, she would stand as she was, her perfect bottom on glass, her shoes firmly on the oriental carpet. The day-lit window would cast her features in shadow while offering a sharp silhouette with a glaring corona, and it would spotlight the faces of her audience. The forbidding darkness of her law books to one side was counterpoised with a wall of prints and sculpture on the other.

"Detective Quin?"

"I was just admiring the Inuit art. "

"No, you were not."

Miranda knew enough from browsing through high end galleries in Yorkville that she recognized original prints by Pitseolak Ashoona and Ovilu Tunnillie from Cape Dorset, but the sculpture was what she thought of as *corporate generic*. The best soapstone art was by artists who lived the life; men who hunted, women who turned polar bear fur into *kamiks* to keep the feet warm at minus fifty. These women and men carved pieces small enough that a single carver could handle them. The sculptures artfully placed in Gloria Simmons's office were massive polished stereotypes.

"Have you ever noticed?" said Gloria Simmons. "Carvings by men show the muscles beneath the surface, the spirit within. Women tend toward mythic representations, the spirits at work."

An interesting distinction, Miranda thought. This woman assumed she was now in complete control. Miranda smiled the smile she saved for occasions when she intended to imply the smile was unwarranted. "You must be busy, winding up your Arctic project," she said in a tone that gave her the conversational initiative. "Your side won."

"My side? I'm a lawyer, Detective."

"You're also an Inuk. Your side won. Which means D'Arcy lost."

"We were partners, Detective."

"On opposing sides."

"You don't understand."

"Edify me."

"No."

It was difficult to argue with an unqualified *no*. Miranda thought of a term she had once heard for relentless interrogation: *an interview without coffee*. She decided to speed up the process, to go for the jugular.

"I did some checking around. You don't have a license, but you're an experienced De Havilland Twin Otter pilot."

Gloria Simmons said nothing. The window behind her was slowly transforming in the dawn light from a wall of mirrors reflecting the room to a vista of the harbourfront punctuated with office towers, a crowding of condos, and mist rising off the water. Miranda slipped forward on the sofa. "You've studied navigation, haven't you?"

"I took a course."

Miranda smiled enigmatically

"You're not actually on duty, are you?" said Gloria Simmons. "You just got back."

"Actually, I am."

"And you're carrying a gun."

"I am, actually." Miranda rose to her feet a little awkwardly and moved around the room until she stood in front of the window, forcing Gloria Simmons to twist uncomfortably sidewise to maintain a perch against her desktop, and to squint to keep her in focus.

"Nice earrings," said Miranda. "Tahitian pearls. Are they new?"

"A little gift. And yours?"

"Would the donor be Terrence Rattigan?" Miranda assessed the pearls without moving closer or into the woman's direct line of vision. Her own were small, 8 mm. These were maybe 14 mm, apparently flawless and with astonishing lustre. Probably worth ten or twenty times what she had paid for hers.

"Thomas Ross gave them to me a year or two ago. A business associate."

Thomas Ross! Terrence Rattigan? The man Miranda had spent the day with on Bora Bora was Thierry! There was no Terry, no Terrence Rattigan. The man looking for her at the ferry was Ross. Of course. *Not* staying at the Four Seasons. The Haymarket. That was the only seasonally related hotel name that came to mind. She didn't make the connection between the names Rattigan and Ross. She had never been to London.

Miranda moved back around the desk, closing the space between herself and Gloria Simmons who rose to her full height, which was formidable. Morgan had not said she was tall. Although Miranda's semi-automatic had not been discussed again, its presence was a factor in the dynamic of their curious *pas de deux*. As Miranda pressed closer, Gloria Simmons took small steps backward until her calves pressed against the soft leather sofa cushions. She settled gracefully into the depths of the sofa, crossed her long legs so that they showed to best advantage, and dangled one of her Louboutins so that the red leather sole displayed a disconcerting lack of wear.

Miranda now perched on the edge of the desk. "I

ran a navigational check," she said. She did not know enough about navigation to have sufficient vocabulary for what she had discovered, but she needed to convey its ominous significance. "The coordinates, you know, they don't match up …" She let her words hang in the air.

"I have no idea what you're talking about."

"No, of course. You don't know how to fly. You're a novice with maps. You crash-landed safely. Turns out you landed within shouting distance of the three men who were lost in an offshore accident, only they were on shore. I'd call that precision flying. Your friend with the boat, the whale hunter who lost them, he was found floating in the water fifty kilometres away. Interesting, isn't it? Fifty kilometres. You crashed so deftly on a coastal incline along Baffin Strait, one fjord to the south of where your friend was picked up, yet, by the most amazing coincidence, that was precisely where the three missing men happened to be stranded."

"If my coordinates were out by so much, then weren't we lucky to find them? But, no, they all died, so perhaps it wasn't lucky after all. For Morgan and me, yes, we got out relatively unscathed. Very lucky. But there was no nefarious plot, Detective, just amateur navigation and fate with a twisted sense of humour."

"A cosmic joke. You rescued corpses." Miranda threw her a quick smile. "Fortunately for Morgan, you needed him to vouch for your heroic intentions. Otherwise you might have returned with four corpses, not three. You did bring the body back from the burial cairn, didn't you? No, I suppose the Mounties did."

"It was your partner's idea to be there."

"Where? In the Arctic, on the Twin Otter, at the death scene? I believe he was invited. By you. And compelled of course by his investigation into the death of Harrington D'Arcy's wife, something about which you may be able to shed a little light. No? Not now? Perhaps later. You must have been pleasantly surprised, when you got there, and one man was already dead."

"He had been for several days."

"That must ease your conscience. You only murdered two."

"Do you really expect me to confess? Why would I want to continue this conversation? I have a lot to do." She started to slide forward on her strategically designed sofa and found herself clasped in its indifferent embrace. Without squidging sideways, she was stuck.

"I'm sure you have a lot to do," Miranda wryly observed. "Wrapping up the details for Inuit control of the mine in league with the government of Chile — that has all worked out as expected, I assume."

"It will take years to finalize. I'm sure you must be disappointed. Your friends on Easter Island were hoping things would go the other way. They were on the fascist side."

"No, they were on their own side."

"Everything is connected, Detective. Collateral damage from one perspective is a direct hit from another."

"The men who died with D'Arcy, they were connected, right? Miguel Escobar, the other man. To the Pinochet bunch."

"Apparently they were; it is public record."

"So from your perspective, their deaths were another stroke of luck. And Harrington D'Arcy? He was up there to swing the deal in their favour. Not yours. So his death was fortuitous, as well."

"He was my partner."

"But he was on the other side, so you killed him."

Gloria Simmons flashed a chilling smile.

"You work out at the Toronto Women's Club on a regular basis, don't you?" Miranda continued, as if this were the most logical question in the world. There was no response. "You run on the treadmill four days a week, an hour at a time. Never out of doors, always inside. You're a big woman, and I mean that in the nicest possible way. Big rib cage, good set of lungs. Robust. Your oxygen intake must be enormous."

"Are you a runner, Detective?"

"No, I'm a detective." Miranda paused. "The two survivors, when you found them, were in very bad condition. Morgan went off to be a hunter-gatherer. When he came back, one was dead. Morgan went off to guide in the rescue chopper. When he came back, the other was dead. Very efficient, Ms. Simmons. You sucked the air out of them. You're smiling? You placed your lips over their lips, you sucked them empty. You're still smiling. I'm warm, but not quite on the money. You didn't suck, you blew air into their lungs, rapid, deep breaths. I remember from scuba diving, it's called latent hypoxia. You reduce the carbon dioxide in the blood by blowing in and the body thinks there's enough oxygen when there isn't — it's counterintuitive, And bang, blackout. Then you prevent air intake. Bang, death. They were suffocated with the help of their own autonomic systems. I may not have the science quite right, but the smile's gone!"

Gloria Simmons adjusted her facial features and her posture into a professional mode, as if she were going to square off with an adversarial counsel. Then she slumped back comfortably into the leather cushions. Miranda was trying to determine whether this move was strategic when her cellphone rattled inside her purse. Gloria Simmons reached over and handed the purse to her. Miranda fished out the phone.

"Morgan, not now."

"You'll never guess who I just spent the morning with?"

"It's only six a.m. The morning's not over. Morgan, I'm tied up at the moment."

"You'll never guess."

"Thomas Edward Ross, a.k.a. Terrence Rattigan," she proclaimed. The disappointment coming over the silent airwaves was palpable. "Morgan, can I call you back? I'm with Gloriasimmons right now."

"Give her my regards. Be careful."

"Yeah, sure. How'd you know to call my cell?"

"You didn't answer at home. I figured jet lag and that you'd be out drinking coffee somewhere to get back into your normal irregular sleep pattern. It's nothing that won't keep." He paused for effect. "Ross seems to know the Gibraltar coordinates."

"That's impossible, Morgan? Are you sure? He must have been bluffing."

"I don't think so."

"Maybe I should let McMan know."

"He's already at sea. At lake. He left late last night."

"How do you know that? Your apprentice mortician?"

"No, your Mr. Ross."

"I'll talk to you later."

"For sure," he said and clicked off.

"Morgan sends his regards."

"And mine to him." Gloria Simmons straightened against the back of the sofa again. "This is quite interesting. I have numerous questions, but since it's all very clever conjecture, I think I'll pass. My support staff are arriving out there. I really must get to work." She rose awkwardly to her feet and immediately regained her poise. "If you'll excuse me," she said, placing her hand on the door without pulling it open, in subtle acknowledgement that Miranda was still in control.

"Of course," said Miranda, "but in deference to the principles of full disclosure, let me illuminate the case for prosecution."

"Are you a lawyer, Ms. Quin?" Miranda smiled.

Gloria Simmons smiled.

Miranda proceeded. "With his wife's death, Mr. Harrington D'Arcy did a serious about face, I believe. She was more persuasive in death than alive. And you needed the Canadian government to see that D'Arcy Associates was completely on side. *Were* completely on side, all of you, not just the corporate entity. When D'Arcy flew north to undermine your deal, he had to be stopped. You made arrangements. The hunter, his name is Pauloosie Avaluktuk, he's active in politics on Baffin, he stranded the two Pinochet guys and Harrington D'Arcy on a remote shore, then he went off in search of the whales. The more absurd the account of the missing men, the less likely it would be to arouse suspicion. Absurd things happen, especially in the Arctic, it seems." Miranda paused. "I have to wonder, is Chile paying you as well? Of course, they are. Why ask. You are Inuit, apparently, but you are a lawyer for hire. The problem: there was no guarantee that D'Arcy was dead. A billion-dollar deal, the future of your people, and a goodly commission were riding on his death. When you heard he had only been reported missing, you flinched. You needed to be positive. So you went north to make sure the job was done, and you took Morgan with you to vouch for your innocence. Anything else you'd like clarified?"

"He is a very pleasant travelling companion. Not my style, but a lovely man."

"And what is your style?"

Gloria Simmons smiled. The exchange of enigmatic smiles was beginning to wear Miranda down. She was ready to leave.

"Are you a lesbian?" Miranda asked in a sudden fit of inspired confusion.

"Sometimes."

The interview without coffee was over.

13

Killing People is Wrong

Morgan and Miranda agreed to meet at the open end of Trafalgar Mews, where it retreated from a leafy side street off Avenue Road into its own little realm of subdued good taste. This was a hard place to find, even if you lived in the neighbourhood. What had once been rows of carriage houses standing close to the street had been converted into chic private residences for people who found ostentation superfluous. Every building was the same, although each front door, opening directly onto the pavement, was a small work of art, painted and repainted to a high gloss like the doors of Dublin. Like Morgan's front door, the only part of his home in the Annex on which he had ever expended effort to upgrade.

Miranda arrived first. She had changed into a summer dress after she woke up in the heat of the day, but in the late afternoon she could already feel a chill gathering in the air. She had not thought to tuck a sweater into her handbag. She gazed down the Mews, at first bewildered by what seemed out of place. Then she realized that there weren't any cars. Since there were no yards in the front or back, and no passageways or alleys behind, people there must keep their cars in a valet-serviced parking garage. *Ironic*, she thought. *These very buildings would have been carriage houses for mansions several blocks away, the carriages to be summoned by messenger.*

She smiled as Morgan approached. He seemed deep in thought and appeared not to notice her until he was within whispering distance.

"You know the menace in Clint Eastwood's voice?" he whispered. "It was something he picked up watching Marilyn Monroe movies."

"I expect that's a rumour, Morgan. He probably watched her movies for other reasons."

"Maybe so," he said, reverting to his normal voice, "but the point is, you never know the source of illusions."

"If you did, they wouldn't be illusions. You're thinking of Ross?"

"And of Gloria Simmons. Maybe Ross is not as dangerous as he seems. He works at it, like Eastwood. It's his stock in trade. And maybe she's more dangerous. Not the voluptuous waif, more the ingenuous femme fatale."

Msgloriasimmons, ingenuous? Doesn't that mean innocent? Not likely, Miranda thought. *Around that woman, death is contagious.*

Miranda had only spoken briefly to Morgan since their phone conversation in the early morning. Both had spent the day catching up on sleep. Thomas Ross had called Morgan after lunch to suggest a meeting with Gloria Simmons at her place in Trafalgar Mews. It seemed inevitable that the four of them would get together, since they had much to sort out. Morgan called Miranda and they agreed to the meeting. Gloria Simmons's place seemed a reasonable locale.

Whatever the connections between the gorgeous blonde Inuk and the stunning Englishman, the D'Arcys were at the heart of the matter and the D'Arcys were dead. It was possible that Ross might somehow reveal the extent of Gloria Simmons's involvement, if only through his compulsive need to play centre stage. The beautiful people were on different sides of the Baffin project, supported opposing factions on Rapa Nui by virtue of their conflicting interests in Chile, and had a history that involved pearl earrings. It was worth a try, meeting together. Normal procedures didn't seem adequate. Better they keep things social and avoid Police Headquarters for the time being.

"I suspect you're partly right about Gloria Simmons," Miranda cheerfully conceded. Morgan was not the best judge of women, especially beautiful women. "As for Ross, trust me, he's dangerous." For an instant, it crossed her mind that she was not always the best judge of beautiful men. "Morgan, the only way he knows about the Gibraltar coordinates is if Matteo told him before he died." She shuddered with dread at the horrific possibility that Matteo had been tortured, and then shuddered with rage to think that Ross might have been present.

But if Matteo broke, the *Carabinaros* would also know the coordinates. Most likely Matteo took Ross into his confidence. "Matteo would have counted on Ross to track down whatever is hidden in St. Michael's cave. Not because he gives a damn about island sovereignty, but because he's paid by the fascists and they want the insurrection to succeed."

Morgan protested. "What difference would it make? Whatever's hidden on Gibraltar is probably irrelevant by now. Ross found the coordinates too late."

"I don't know," she responded. "I imagine Baffin is only a setback for the Pinochet bunch, not the end of the line. The junta might appreciate an insurrection now more than ever." She paused. "I really am not a fascist, you know. I shouldn't feel the need to tell you that."

"No, you shouldn't."

"Shouldn't feel it? Or shouldn't need to?"

Morgan smiled. Miranda's hazel eyes gleamed. He knew she was conflicted as much by her role in translating the island's secret as for the repugnant political bedfellows her intimate connection with the rebels implied. He wanted to reach out and touch the auburn highlights in her hair, but tousled his own, instead.

They walked along to number 19. The door had a deep blue sheen and imposing brass fittings. Morgan knocked. They waited. He tried the doorbell and they could hear chimes inside. The snapping sound of an electronic lock clicking open welcomed them in. The foyer was small and immediately in front of them were narrow stairs leading up to the principal living area. They opened the door at the top of the stairs and were confronted by a smiling T.E. Ross, who faced them from behind a counter separating the kitchen from the living room. Despite the time of day, the curtains were drawn and several lamps were on, casting a mottled patchwork of shadows and light.

With Morgan by her side, Ross didn't strike Miranda as quite so outrageously handsome.

"Come in, come in," he called out to them cheerfully.

Both of them slipped off their shoes and parked them neatly inside the door. Canadians did that. Miranda sighed, looking at her wedge-heeled, open-toed slingbacks whose architectural design carried her weight with felt grace. It was midsummer and there was no slush or snow to track in, but northern habits had become custom, a mark of respect distinguishing friends from other visitors. Professionals on duty, whether doctors, morticians or police, kept their shoes on; service people usually carried slip-overs with them. Friends walked about in socks or bare feet. Canadians were notorious for clean floors.

In spite of the motley gloom, it wasn't until the door closed behind them that they both sensed something was wrong, followed immediately by the resonant clickety-click of oiled steel as their host's arm flashed a lever-action Winchester 73 and jumped a cartridge into the firing chamber. They found themselves staring down the barrel of a loaded gun.

Out of their line of vision when they had entered, Gloria Simmons was seated with material of some sort bunched around her ankles. She seemed inordinately still.

"I'm glad you could make it." Ross motioned them into the centre of the room and spoke in a quiet, conciliatory voice. "Detective Morgan, you know the drill. Drop your pants. This time it's not shaving cream."

Miranda looked from one man to the other, bewildered by their private joke, angry that her partner seemed at a disadvantage.

"Miranda, I'm afraid I have to ask you to do likewise. Place your purse on the table. Just so. Now, since you're wearing a dress it will have to be your underwear pants."

Underwear pants, thought Miranda. *Canadian childhood redundancies like bare-naked, or great big huge and little tiny wee. Not very menacing.* But Morgan, exasperated, started to unbuckle. Miranda glanced over at Gloria Simmons and recognized the material around her ankles as the skirt to the Armani suit she had been wearing that morning. As her eyes adjusted to the gloom, Miranda could see the woman's hands were bound. Her demeanour was determinedly stoic, verging on contemptuous indifference to their common plight.

"No," said Miranda. A *no* without qualifiers is difficult to argue with. Morgan zipped up his fly.

A suppressed grin spread across Ross's face. "First time I've been refused. Well, sit down, the both of you, over by Ms. Simmons. Let me turn up the light, but I believe I'll leave the drapes closed for now. The four of us have a lot to discuss."

Miranda and Morgan both remained standing.

Miranda made eye contact with Gloria Simmons, who showed no sign of recognition. She looked around the room. It was filled with soapstone sculpture, some were stolidly solemn and highly prized, dating back to the 1950s, and some were recent acquisitions that verged on abstraction, all of them small enough for one person to handle. There were carvings made from segments of caribou antlers and a pair of glowering two-faced carvings made from bowhead whale vertebrae. Miranda was impressed. She glanced back at Gloria Simmons and realized her assessment was being monitored. The woman permitted herself a hint of a smile.

"Don't you think perhaps Ms. Simmons might be allowed a little more dignity?" said Miranda, and without waiting for an answer she placed herself between Ross and the woman and helped her with her skirt. Then she turned to face Ross and scolded, "You're a silly bugger. If you were going to kill us, there would surely be better ways than using an old hunting rifle. I imagine you found it here, you didn't even come armed, and this business with the dropped trousers, that's childish in the extreme. God, Thomas, I have no doubt you're capable of murder. And by the way, thank you for the *Island Queen* vacation, thank your people for that, and thank you for the Wonder Woman comic, I'll return it to Morgan, it was his in the first place. But what is it you're after, Thomas? Morgan tells me you already have the mystical coordinates. What more could you need?"

Thomas Ross compliantly lowered his head. Then he raised it and suddenly jammed the Winchester barrel into Miranda's gut with such force that she doubled over and dropped, and in a continuation of the same movement, he swung the barrel up sharply and across, catching Morgan on the side of the head.

Gasping for breath, Miranda crawled to Morgan, who had collapsed against a sofa and slid to the floor. She pressed the heel of her hand into his jaw, stemming the spurting blood. She took her hand away tentatively. The blow hadn't opened the carotid artery; the spurting was from the pressure of the blow itself exploding an ancillary vessel. She glared up at Ross and slowly rose to her feet. She squared off with him, just out of range if he decided to use the Winchester as a club again. It had not occurred to her to carry her Glock in a body holster. It didn't go with the outfit. She glowered, then shrugged. Expect the unexpected. Of course. The last thing she had anticipated from Thomas Ross was violence of his own accord; therefore she should have known it was coming.

"How very predictable you are," she said, conceding the opposite.

He seemed momentarily confused, then replied with an air of refined condescension, "Restrained brutality, my dear Miranda? Think of it as a social necessity. Instant clarification of where we all stand."

"I expected better."

"You presume on our relationship."

"I didn't know we had a relationship."

"Friendship, my dear, but friendship does have its limits."

"I'll try to remember that, should I ever be holding a gun on a friend."

He turned away, restraining a hint of an appreciative grin. "Detective Morgan, sorry, old man, that was rather abrupt, but as you can see I'm quite serious."

Morgan had risen unsteadily to his feet; the three of them were now positioned in a curious standoff, given one had a gun, but a gun he had used as a club.

"Morgan," said Miranda, "hand me my purse."

"Not bloody likely," said Ross.

"For goodness' sake, Thomas, I have to go to the bathroom. Your gun butt has prompted activity in my lower region, if you know what I mean."

"Sorry," said Ross. "No purse."

"Well, I'm going to the bathroom. What do you suggest I do, improvise?"

"No purse, no bathroom. No handgun, Miranda."

"Oh, dear, is that where I put it. In my purse. Well, never mind."

Ross swung the rifle barrel slowly back and forth between the detectives, then suddenly cranked the lever action open and closed, spewing a live cartridge onto the carpet. "If I have to, I will," he declared.

"You're not on home territory, Thomas Ross. I'd be very careful about what my next move was, if I were you."

"Let us sit down and be civilized about this," he said, motioning her to help Morgan, who was struggling to remain standing. "It is home territory, actually," he said, and his Oxford accent wavered and collapsed into a flat Torontonian inflection. "I grew up in Parkdale. Did you know that when they built the insane asylum, 999 Queen Street was set among fields and orchards? Parkdale grew up around it."

"Rove McMan said you grew up in England, in a village called Abington Piggotts near Cambridge."

"That's where he prefers to imagine I'm from. Just as you'd like to think I'm an Oxford graduate from Sloane Square. Mr. Morgan would prefer I'm from Parkdale, I think." He turned to Gloria Simmons and caught her attention with a wave of the gun barrel. "Where would you like me to be from, Ms. Simmons? No, you don't care. That is your problem — you really don't care."

Morgan tried to focus against the pain swarming through his head. In small, tearing movements he tugged his shirt collar away from his neck, breaking the bond of congealed blood binding cotton to skin. He could feel a warm trickle from the newly opened wound. "So, Thomas," he said, wincing as he suppressed the pain. "Should we call you Thomas? You seem to have surrounded yourself with a tumble of names. Personally, I like Terrence. I saw Terrence Rattigan's *Ross* in the West End years ago. You have the floor. Where should we start?"

Thomas Ross sat down opposite the other three and laid the Winchester across his lap. "I saw the Rattigan play, also, a revival, at the Haymarket," he replied, balking at letting Morgan take the lead.

"Down from Piccadilly Circus."

"Yes, of course," he said peevishly, reverting to his Oxonian demeanour. As he continued, his words took on the pained enunciation of the educated English who swallow their vowels. "Communed with the fellow at his tomb in St. Paul's. I don't suppose you've read *Seven Pillars of Wisdom*?"

"Which edition?" Morgan asked. Pressing his advantage, he said, "Lawrence isn't buried in St. Paul's Cathedral, you know. You were communing with an empty crypt. His body fetched up in a little village called Moreton, in Dorset."

Ross smiled in begrudging admiration and changed the subject. "You must be wondering what I have against Gloria Simmons and why I am destined to be the instrument of her ultimate undoing."

"Are you?" said Morgan. "Destined?"

"Yes, on this otherwise very fine evening."

"Retribution?" Miranda suggested, as she struggled to reassess his position in the moral universe — if there was such a thing as a moral universe, or a moral position in relation to Ross.

"Indeed, you might easily call it retribution. I would call it justice. Ironic, isn't it, a renegade like me meting out justice to a member of the bar?"

"She screwed up your Baffin deal," said Morgan. "Is that something to die for?" He wasn't sure whether Ross was threatening for rhetorical impact or playing the role of amiable assassin.

"Yes, she did do that." He turned to Gloria Simmons. "Please feel free to interrupt at any time. It's your life under review."

"You can take back your earrings," she said.

"Really. They're quite lovely, you know. Very expensive."

"I prefer the subtlety of Detective Quin's."

He turned to Miranda. "Now, Miranda, you must wonder why I did not join you on the *Island Queen*. How awkward, had the news made its way to the bridge that I was both dining at the Captain's table, a bon vivant with a beautiful companion, yourself, and dying or dead in the Arctic wasteland."

"How in hell can you afford your own suite on a cruise ship?" Miranda asked him, not unappreciative of her own small benefit from the demise of Harrington D'Arcy, nor surprised that he knew about it as a story in progress.

"It's not as expensive as you might think. About the same as a Manhattan condo, and it's a tax write-off."

"You pay taxes?" she asked incredulously.

"Here and there, as the occasion demands." Ross looked over at Morgan who seemed to be uncomfortable with their banter. "You were up there yourself. In the Arctic wasteland."

"It's actually very beautiful," said Morgan. "You ought to visit someday. And go whale-watching."

"With Pauloosie Avaluktuk," said Miranda. "The outcome is preordained."

Morgan smiled, then his features hardened. There was something in her voice that caught him off guard. She could see he was puzzled by her insinuation that the Inuk guide might be part of a larger conspiracy. She gazed at him though lowered eyes, feeling awkward but a little bit pleased. "You don't know, do you?"

"Please explain for us all," said Ross, happy to be in the midst of shared revelations.

"Yes, do explain," said Gloria Simmons, as if she were inviting Miranda to pass the biscuits and tea.

"Morgan, Msgloriasimmons is a trained pilot and a trained navigator."

When Morgan realized that was a statement, complete in itself, he turned his gaze inward. Like a collapsed house of cards in reverse slow motion, the episodes of his shared adventures with Gloria Simmons reformed as a narrative that was both shocking in its diabolical complexity and painfully simple in retrospect. He had been in grave danger, not only from the crash landing, physical deprivation, haunting isolation, and summer sleet, but from the woman who had made it all seem an exhilarating adventure.

"Morgan," Miranda continued, "your lovely friend crash-landed the plane precisely where Pauloosie Avaluktuk had stranded the three men. Think about that. It was fifty kilometres distant from where he was picked up, where his boat supposedly rammed the whales." Miranda watched Morgan as he assimilated her revelation, then glanced back at Gloria Simmons, who seemed imperturbable.

Morgan rose to his feet and moved close to Gloria Simmons. He leaned over to whisper in a voice loud enough the others could hear. "You knew exactly where they would be. You would have killed me, too, if I had caught on."

"But you didn't," she said.

"You didn't!" exclaimed Ross. "I'd love to know how she did it, with you right there on the spot." Miranda, Morgan, and even Gloria Simmons glowered at him, the menacing interloper. "Do carry on," he said, glancing at Miranda. "It seems we may all be on the same side, after all. Not you, of course, Ms. Simmons.

Miranda felt more tentative as she proceeded, "To understand what went on, you need to know that your Gloriasimmons, Morgan, she and Maria were lovers."

Again, cards splayed at random in Morgan's mind began in slow motion to assume the shape of an edifice, only this time it was not a new reading of old events; this was the original narrative, seen clearly for the first time.

Suddenly, he was ahead of her. "You remember," he said, addressing Miranda as if the other two were a negligible presence in the room, despite one being bound at the wrists and the other holding a Winchester 73 poised to explode in their direction, "you remember McMan said Maria left the island with D'Arcy, she deserted her betrothed —"

"Te Ave Teao."

"Yeah. And heartbroken as he was, the man accepted it all with good grace. He knew she was a lesbian, they had no future together, and they both knew that D'Arcy was essentially asexual and was very fond of her, a wealthy man already, a good contact with the world beyond the borders of Chile, a man whose soul was already embedded among the ancestral bones of the Rapa Nui."

"What, what?" Ross interrupted.

"What does that last bit mean?" demanded Gloria Simmons, suddenly eager to be more than an audience and astounded to find herself on side with her potential executioner.

"You didn't know?" Miranda asked Ross, while including Gloria Simmons with a sidelong glance. "I'm surprised."

She had expected there was little Ross did not know about events on the island, especially ones as morally ambiguous as the murder of Dr. Levesque. It was disconcerting that she could describe murder as morally ambiguous, even to herself. She briefly related the story about the execution of the man who was responsible for the death of D'Arcy's sister. It seemed somehow urgent that Thomas Ross and Gloria Simmons have the fullest possible understanding of the D'Arcys.

"In Matteo's farmhouse?" Ross exclaimed. "My God, I'm astonished."

"I'm not," said Gloria Simmons, who seemed to have no trouble assimilating this new aspect of Harrington D'Arcy's personality.

"I thought you'd be interested," said Miranda to both, in a tone that let Morgan know this was as much information as she felt the need to share.

"Ms. Simmons," said Ross, who seemed determined now to take their discourse in another direction, "the lesbian thing, does that mean our little dalliance two years ago was an aberration? I suppose it does. Pity I didn't know. How humbling. We might have had a jolly good threesome."

She smiled with icy condescension. "How fickle men are. Don't you agree, Detective Quin?" Miranda did not disagree. "Thomas, you seem to forget. Our *dalliance*, as you so pathetically describe it, endured for two days and the one night between, and it was never actually consummated." She turned to catch Miranda's eye. "I have been a reborn virgin through much of my life." She turned to Morgan. "I have not been penetrated, with respect to male members, since I was raped at fourteen."

Morgan thought of their sleeping-bag encounter, how ambiguously intimate they had been, and with an eerie absence of passion.

"For the record, the man who raped me died the same night." She looked from Morgan to Miranda, then to Ross, and continued. "In his sleep." She smiled almost wistfully, which sent a chill through the room. "I went into juvenile detention in Ottawa. It wasn't tuberculosis. My record was expunged, of course. I studied chemistry. After due diligence, I graduated near the top of my law class. University of Toronto. Articled for D'Arcy, fell in love with Maria, and my rebirth as a virgin was complete."

"Why law?" asked Morgan, in what might have seemed an extraneous question.

"Because religion no longer holds the power. And because I am a woman."

Miranda realized these two still had a connection, even though Morgan knew she might have rendered him very dead had things not worked out so well, from her point of view, on the desolate shores of Baffin Island.

Ross seemed nonplussed to have been caught out having forgotten such an awkward gap in his sexual prowess. He ceded control of the discussion, apparently confident he still held the upper hand cradled across his knees. Miranda was happy to relinquish control as well, for the moment.

"The three of you," Morgan said to Gloria Simmons, "you, Maria, and Harrington D'Arcy. A perfect *ménage à trois*."

"A curious idea of perfection, Detective. No, we were bound by the tensions between us as much as the passion. Maria and I were romantic partners. Harrington and I were business partners. He and his wife were domestic partners. There were three separate pairings, each excluding the third person. You can see the complications. Not jealousy. None of us was inclined to jealousy, God knows."

"Perhaps the same passions that held you together eventually destroyed you."

"Perhaps." She seemed to be contemplating the fatal paradox of what they had been in each other's lives. "Perhaps you're right," she affirmed somewhat sadly.

"But you made a choice that changed everything."

The room filled with silence.

Thomas Ross rose to his feet. "And that's why I'm here," he said. The others looked at him as if he had been rude, interrupting a conversation that wasn't his concern. "Ms. Gloria Simmons killed them both."

"Yes," Morgan agreed, "I believe she did. Miranda can explain how Harrington D'Arcy died, apparently." He watched Gloria Simmons for a reaction, but she betrayed nothing more than passing interest, like someone mildly annoyed that the end of a novel she had already finished was about to be revealed.

"Blowing into the lungs," Miranda explained. "Excessively oxygenating his blood. Too much oxygen forced into the bloodstream creates a deficit of carbon dioxide necessary to trigger the impulse to breathe. She doesn't suck, she blows. The empress of ice cream blocks passive intake of air. Death follows."

"Empress of ice cream?"

"Would you prefer succubus? Like I said, she doesn't suck. Morgan, this is not a nice woman." Miranda glanced over at Gloria Simmons who seemed to have lost interest again and was staring in the direction of her soapstone carvings, looking as if she were trying to access which ones she might eliminate from the collection.

"For that to work, the blow-block thing, victims would have to be cooperative," Morgan observed. "Or weak from exposure,"

"Or a little bit drunk on Dom Perignon," said Gloria Simmons. She had been listening, after all.

"Thank you," said Morgan. Then, turning to Ross, he proceeded with his summation, "We discover Ms. Simmons strangled a man when she was fourteen. We postulate that she killed again on Baffin Island, behind my back, so to speak. It is reasonable to surmise that she murdered Maria D'Arcy in much the same way." Shifting his focus to her, he noted with an interrogative lift at the end of his observation, "Perhaps there have been more?"

"Morgan, with the man in Apex, I used a pillow. Smothered, not strangled. I was only fourteen."

"Sorry. Did you murder Maria to force D'Arcy's hand or to prevent her from playing her own?" Morgan was back on track.

"These were two people I loved very deeply," she said. "It was not a pleasant thing to do, when they had given me so much."

"But you did kill them?"

"Yes."

"Continue."

"They both knew of my commitment to the Baffin project — whose success would bring their own project to a crashing halt. After Maria sent the message to Matteo —"

"The message?"

"The book, Morgan. Me!" Miranda had been following while her thoughts raced back and ahead. The fascist junta had wanted her kept alive in case the insurrection sputtered out. That explained the luxury cruise. Her knowledge of the island's secret might just be incendiary enough to start it up again. But Ross knew the coordinates, now, so she was expendable. Miranda suspected he wouldn't hesitate to eliminate her if the need arose, and Morgan, as well. With regrets, of course. But at the moment, he was hunched forward, listening intently, and he had set the rifle, almost as a challenge, casually on the floor. Clearly he was trying to get a stronger grasp on his own role in the unfolding story.

Gloria Simmons continued. "After connecting Detective Quin with the encrypted message, Maria knew I would have no choice."

"You realize she wrote me a suicide note?" Morgan asked.

"To exonerate me."

"Not D'Arcy?"

"Not at all."

"Why not, if she loved him?"

"Morgan, she wasn't a stupid woman. She knew you'd see through the suicide gambit. She also knew Harrington would be devastated by her death and would swing his open support to the Rapa Nui side, no matter what the cost. But D'Arcy Associates were, and are, committed to maintaining the stability of the Chilean government and underwriting the interests of the Inuit people. It would not be politically correct to do otherwise. This is Canada, you know. The conflict of interests nearly destroyed him before this all blew up. Our side was the right side. But his devotion to his wife and his commitment to Rapa Nui had reduced him to a painfully passive role in our negotiations. The trauma your partner explained makes his situation that much more poignant. I didn't know about that."

"By *trauma* you're referring to his execution of a human being with his bare hands."

"It can be quite traumatic killing someone, even someone who deserves to die. My own people were not excessively offended when I killed my attacker in Apex. It bothered me at the time, though. And of course it bothered the so-called authorities who brought me to law — and taught me its uses."

"The uses of the law?"

"Of the legal system, yes. It is arbitrary and dispassionate and its powers are almost without limit. The perfect model for a lost little girl ..." She looked deeply into Morgan's eyes and for the first time, ever, allowed him to see the human within. A girl desperately in search of something to connect with, who found only the law. And its uses.

The woman blinked, glanced at Miranda, and back at Morgan. "I am a very good lawyer," she said.

"Very successful," said Miranda. "They're not the same thing."

"Sometimes they are," said Gloria Simmons, and then continued as if she were completing an earlier thought, "I did not want to kill Maria, but she knew I had no choice. It was difficult."

"The choice? Or the killing?" Miranda genuinely wanted to know.

"Both."

"So she knew you would kill her because she was vitally important to the insurgency, more so having sent the book. Didn't you play into her hands, though, making her a martyr?"

"The *planned* insurrection. It hasn't happened. She and her family were a powerful force on the island. But I'm sure when her brother heard of her death, he knew it was over, he prepared in his mind for his own death."

Miranda flinched. Matteo was not a fatalist.

"You were nearly finessed," Morgan observed. "She knew her death would force her husband to oppose you. But why would she want to make him a suspect?

"Because that would bring *you* into the story."

The room had filled briefly with silence before, now it seemed drained of air. Morgan said nothing.

"I've been through this, Morgan," said Miranda. "It gets you wondering whatever happened to free will.

She sent you the suicide note. But also, she would have suggested to her husband that, should anything happen to her, he was to get *you* involved. And he did get you involved. That wouldn't have happened if he had not been a suspect."

"Why me, for goodness' sake?"

"I asked the same question about myself. The answer is, *we were brought in together*. Separately, but as a team. It was a good call: we're here, sorting it all out. The flaw in their plan, unfortunately, is the guy holding the gun."

Almost casually, Thomas Ross leaned over and retrieved the Winchester. "It's a beautiful piece of hardware, isn't it. My compliments, Ms. Simmons, on keeping it clean and well oiled. Have you ever used it?"

"Not recently." She smiled.

"The D'Arcys' master plan seems to be in disarray," Miranda observed.

"If you mean the Rapa Nui part, things will work out," declared Ross. "Independence is a pipe dream of course, but as they rise from the brink of annihilation, they yearn to be recognized as a people. And that, trust me, will happen. And it's worked out well for the Inuit, something that would please Harrington D'Arcy, in spite of himself. I think Ms. Simmons might agree."

Gloria Simmons responded as if they had been sitting on opposite sides of a seminar table. "Maria believed with all her heart that the Rapa Nui need historical sovereignty to survive. Possession of their own past is the best guarantee of a future. Political independence would be a bonus. As for us, we simply want to control our resources. That gives us all the autonomy we need. The Inuit were never conquered, you know. Canada joined us. We don't need independence, simply the powers to be who we already are."

"Well said, Ms. Simmons." Ross rose and touched her lightly on the shoulder with his free hand, his other being occupied with maintaining a grip on the Winchester.

"Whose side are you on?" Miranda exclaimed.

"There are no sides," said Ross, then turning abruptly to Gloria Simmons he whispered, as if exchanging confidences. "Speaking of poison —"

"Were we?" exclaimed Gloria Simmons, as if they had been.

"It was more than a rumour, then?"

"What?" said Miranda.

"Ms. Simmons has a certain reputation, enviable in some circles, as the Catherine de Medici of the corporate world. Apparently, it was more than a metaphor for the appalling brutality of international commerce."

"You've got the wrong Medici," said Morgan. "Poison was epidemic among the Medicis. Catherine wasn't the worst."

"The wrong Medici, but the right Ms. Simmons," said Ross.

Morgan turned to Gloria Simmons. "Speaking of poison, then, why the perfume, the break-in, the wash-down? Were you afraid of losing me on the case?" That sounded strange. It made him uncomfortable, not through modesty, but to think he'd been so easily manipulated.

"Fleurs de Rocaille," she said. "A lovely scent. The original, not the faux version. No, that was Harrington's idea, I imagine. The perfume was Maria's own, the poison was apparently mine. I mixed up a batch of the nasty mixture a few years ago from a recipe I devised as a chemistry student. Harrington had his own small portion stored for emergencies, possibly for blackmail. Of course blackmail worked both ways, should either of us have actually used it."

"But you did use it," Morgan argued.

"Killing people is wrong," she responded with a smile.

"But sometimes apparently necessary. In Papua New Guinea, on Madagascar, in Dublin! Places where D'Arcy Associates did business. As Mr. Ross indicated, in some circles it was apparently not a secret."

"Perhaps not. I believe Harrington and Rove, Rove had his own bit, remember, I believe they accomplished the morgue caper all on their own. It might have been Rove by himself, but it would have been Harrington's idea, he was afraid you wouldn't think it was murder. I heard about it from you."

"Really," said Morgan. "It had the opposite effect. It convinced the medical examiner that the only felony was desecration of a corpse; it convinced her that the death itself had been suicide. A conclusion affirmed by the suicide note."

"But not you, you knew it was murder."

"I *felt* it was murder, there's a difference."

"And you suspected Harrington? You felt he was guilty."

"On the contrary, I *felt* quite strongly that he was innocent. I believed he could point me in the right direction, if only I could figure out why he was trying to lead me on. It was important for us to talk. I think he was relieved when he saw me on Baffin. I felt in some ways that he'd arranged for me to be there. What I did not feel, or comprehend, was that *you* were a threat to his survival. I realize now, he must have recognized his predicament the moment you appeared like a Valkyrie in the mist, ready to spirit the slain warrior away, only he wasn't dead yet. He wanted to die. Not that that absolves the crime."

"That's a lot of feeling," she said. "I never trust a man in touch with his emotions."

Miranda's jaw dropped. These two were flirting, for God's sake. This woman was in extreme peril, Miranda and Morgan were in jeopardy; this woman had killed at least four people, probably more. "Morgan," she said in a resonant voice that he recognized immediately was loaded with unspecified meaning. "I think it's time we deal with Mr. Ross."

"Mr. Ross is holding a loaded Winchester 73 with the safety off," said Thomas Ross.

"That appears to be the case," said Morgan.

"It's rapid-fire," said Ross. "Given its vintage, it's remarkably fast, less than half a second between shots. I adore the lever action. Listen." He flashed through the lever action, ejecting another live bullet and snapping a fresh one into the chamber. "Fast, isn't it?"

"Then let us proceed with our discussion," said Miranda. "We might as well make the most of our time."

"Whatever is left of it," said Gloria Simmons with a sardonic flick of her perfect eyebrows that might have led into a shrug, had her arms not been bound.

Now there, Miranda thought, *is a fatalist, a Calvinist to the core*. No wonder she and Morgan were drawn together in spite of the fact that she was a cold-blooded killer and he, well, he was Morgan, a lapsed Presbyterian.

"Thomas. What's your real name? Are you really from Parkdale?"

"Miranda," Morgan remonstrated, "this isn't a coffee klatch." He paused. "Maybe we need a break. I could use a double-double about now."

"A what?" Ross demanded, afraid they were speaking in code.

"He's not from Parkdale!" said Morgan, grinning. "Or he's been out of the country for a very long time."

"And yet he knows the terms *bare-naked and underwear pants*! So, next question. Real gentleman gone bad or sophisticated fraud?" Miranda queried, trying to lighten the gloom.

"You make them both sound rather appealing," Ross responded with a wry smile. "I'm afraid I'm with your partner, though, I don't see the relevance."

"It will make it easier to track you down when we're finished our present business."

"You're quite remarkable, Miranda. Do you see this rifle?" He slapped the lowered barrel against the side of his leg. "It's very real."

"I'm trying to determine if you are."

Morgan stifled a chuckle.

"Or if you're from Abington Piggotts? I wouldn't mind if you were, you know. Thomas, you really did give me a knock in the gut? Could I go to the bathroom for a minute? Now I really have to. Glock's in the purse."

"No."

"Right, then. I'll wait." She gazed at him, trying to find something in his facial expression to connect with. He was inordinately handsome again, but revealed almost nothing. Chameleon good looks, it must have something to do with danger and the unknown. "So you're here in relation to the deaths of the D'Arcys?"

"Did I say that?"

"A few minutes ago."

"Then I am. Yes, *in relation to*, that's the best way of explaining it. Okay, go to the bathroom, leave the door open, if there's any funny business — what a curious expression — I will shoot your partner through the head, And when you come back, hand me that lovely pigskin valise by the door."

When Miranda returned with the valise, Ross sat down and set it carefully on his lap, leaning the Winchester against his chair within easy access. Morgan had remained contemplative while she was gone, aware that smouldering just beneath the awkward civility of their bizarre little gathering was the potential for revelation or bedlam, possibly both. He was intrigued by his own inability to anticipate how it would all work out.

"Now then," Ross said. "I am in Toronto for two reasons. One, as she is well aware, is to deal with Ms. Simmons. The other is more interesting."

14

Come Away, Death

T.E. Ross slouched back in his chair, and, instead of explaining the valise, or clarifying his enigmatic pronouncement, he gazed about the room, apparently examining the array of Inuit carvings as if he were seeing them for the first time. Miranda sidled closer to the table where she had set her purse. If she was quick, and if Ross hesitated, she might retrieve the Glock in a single lunge. Morgan, who at this point was conducting an inner monologue on conflict resolution, caught her eye. He shook his head. She glanced at Ross. He smiled. The moment had passed. She was grateful.

"Why *deal with* anyone?" she said, returning to the sofa. She wasn't at all sure he was capable of murder. He was not unfamiliar with violent death. *Hell*, she thought, *it seems to follow in his wake.* And he was obviously not beyond meting out violence. She turned to look at Morgan — despite the initial spurt of blood, his wound was little more than a scratch. Morgan squinted at her, trying to guess what she was thinking. He was waiting for her to take the initiative. Despite their compromised situation, he considered Ross to be primarily her problem, as Gloria Simmons was his. Miranda suspected as much. She found his obtuseness absurd, even dangerous, but oddly endearing.

"The D'Arcys are dead," Ross said. "There are people who wish them avenged. I am being paid with these," he said, opening the valise and extracting a pair of *toromiro* slabs incised with *Rongorongo*. "They should fetch a fair price. I'm very interested in Easter Island antiquities, you know. There is a huge black market for the very best artifacts, and they don't come better than this."

"Exactly how much are they worth?" Gloria Simmons spoke up quite casually. She might have been negotiating the price of a hat. "How much is my life worth, Mr. Ross? I'm sure I could double it."

"No doubt," he said. "But that isn't the point, is it? I am not a man without feelings and you have murdered my friends. Well, you're a friend, too, but you see what I'm getting at. It's about Easter Island, Gloria. I really do wish the best for the island."

"To enhance your investment, I imagine. I wouldn't be surprised if you had a few more artifacts squirreled away. Whatever the state of island sovereignty, you need to maintain your connection. Is your treasure trove still there?"

It is, thought Miranda. *Deep in the bowels of an* ariki's *cave. Te Pito o Te Henua. Stored in munitions boxes.* "You are a morally corrupt man," she muttered with suppressed indignation. In spite of everything she would have preferred to find something admirable in Ross apart from his roguish good looks.

"Morality isn't what it used to be, my dear Miranda."

"Was it ever?" said Morgan.

"Your partner is making a very good point. Certainly, in my case, it never was," said Ross without bothering to look at Morgan. "I am somewhat rootless, as you have observed. A man without a history by choice. I am condemned to be free, to make it up as I go along, you might say."

"Your values?"

"My life."

"Talk about illusions of grandeur."

"Were we? I would think it humility, to confess being a man unsustained by conventional morality."

"Unencumbered."

"But keenly aware of the morals of others," said Ross.

"Which makes him a dangerous man to know," said Morgan as if only he and Miranda were talking.

"Which gives me power, Detective Morgan."

"The gun helps," Miranda observed.

"Indubitably."

"I don't think anyone has said *indubitably* since Arthur Conan Doyle turned from making fiction to believing in it."

"I am tempted then to say it again, then. Indubitably. But more to the point, being morally aware means I am not a psychopath, and that must be a relief to us all. But ethical — I do believe I am an ethical man. If I am indeed condemned to be free — I believe Jean Paul Sartre said that before I did — then what I am is a matter of choice. And what I choose is self-respect. I have been bought and well paid for, yes. Matteo made the arrangements; Rove McMan delivered. Now I am honour-bound to comply with my end of the bargain, even if it means my life."

"Or mine," said Gloria Simmons.

"Indeed, or yours."

"Then let us proceed," said Gloria Simmons. "I'll be interested to see which it is."

"Do you care?" said Ross, then, distracted perhaps by his own lack of gallantry, he engaged her in what from his tone might have been a casual conversation. "How did Maria die exactly? The same way as Harrington and the gentleman from Chile?'

"She died in my arms."

"Quite literally the kiss of death?"

Miranda watched as Gloria Simmons struggled briefly with emotion, but responded with detachment. "Our causes conflicted. She was prepared to die for hers. I was prepared to do what was necessary."

She turned to Morgan. If anyone deserved an explanation, it was him. "We made love in the *Pemberly* cabin. A bottle of Dom, it was a perfect encounter. A few tears. We lay in each other's embrace. Harrington came on board, he looked down into the light. He knew she was dead. He locked us below. I fixed her makeup and covered her naked body with a blanket. The air was getting cool. I tried to get out. Used a screwdriver, but it didn't work. Harrington was on deck, contemplating fate, I suppose. I talked to him through the wood. Fate relented. He opened the hatch. We lifted her out."

"Did you put on her bikini?" Morgan asked.

"Not the top. She had lovely breasts, rather voluptuous. Harrington insisted we cover her. I left him to fuss and work out his strategies. I had my own to consider."

Miranda was mesmerized, listening to this woman who was guided by the strength of conviction to commit the most heinous crimes, a cold-blooded and passionate, fearless and sensitive, arrestingly beautiful monster. She glanced over at Morgan who seemed to have drawn a line under the accumulated details as he switched his attention back to Ross.

"You said you were in Toronto for two reasons?" Morgan phrased his words as an incentive for their captor to continue. *As long as he's talking*, Morgan thought, *there is the possibility of a resolution to our situation without further violence.* He was intrigued by Ross's definition of himself as a man of principle without principles. This made him dangerously unpredictable, but not vicious, nor capricious, and not necessarily adversarial.

"There is the matter of Ms. Simmons, yes. And to connect with Rove McMan. Which I have. It's about bringing the parts of the puzzle together, you know," said Thomas Ross. "There's something I want to show you. You will enjoy this. I know you have seen the cache on the *Tangata Manu*. On Matteo's authority, I have taken my small cut." He glanced at Miranda and picked up the two pieces of *Rongorongo* from the floor where he had casually set them and returned them to the valise. He then proceeded to pull out another slab of wood incised on both sides.

"This will interest you," he exclaimed with a note of triumph. "This is from St. Michael's in Gibraltar. *On* Gibraltar. It's a false island, you know, just an outcropping of rock on the Iberian peninsula."

"That's it!" Miranda exclaimed. "You found the Rapa Nui treasure."

"The key to their treasury, I would call it. The coordinates were right on the money, although, I must say, there was a bit of a puzzle to be resolved; you would have liked that Miranda, I nearly missed out."

"It wasn't *inside* the cave, was it?"

"You knew!"

"Not until now. But I did wonder how anyone could conceal something in such a public place. The coordinates don't pinpoint the height above sea level."

"Exactly," said Ross, quite pleased with himself. "It was hidden among the rocks on top of the cave, not inside at all. And incidentally, Rove knows I have it. That's part of the deal. Now he can sail west, into the setting sun, and avoid the Somali pirates. A much better course, don't you think, for our ancient mariner in the making?"

Morgan reached out and Thomas Ross surprised both of them by handing the treasured piece of wood across to him. Morgan turned it over and over, then chuckled and handed it to Miranda. She tilted it to the light this way and that, turned it over a couple of times, then set it down carefully on the table beside her.

"Astonishing!" She exchanged glances with Morgan, but addressed Ross. "It's not just another piece of *Rongorongo*!"

"No," said Ross with a smirk that threatened to swallow him whole. "It is not."

"What?" Gloria Simmons leaned forward, trying to determine what it was that had so easily relegated her fate to the margins. "What is it?"

"It is very important," said Morgan.

"The Rosetta Stone," Miranda declared.

"The exemplar of translation machines," Gloria Simmons observed without seeming to pick up the excitement. "British museum. Ptolemy the fifth." She smiled wanly before reverting to casual indifference, and Miranda recognized her energy was flagging; there was much more going on in Gloria Simmons's head than the mysteries of *Rongorongo*. It took disciplined concentration to maintain her cool demeanour.

"The Rosetta Stone has three kinds of inscription on it. Egyptian in hieroglyphs, Egyptian in script, and classical Greek," mused Miranda. "All say the same thing. It was used as a decoder."

"And that's what this is." Gloria Simmons declared before closing her eyes. A small smile spread from the edges of her mouth and fanned out from the corners of her eyes, giving her face the kind of radiance Miranda had occasionally seen on the dying just before they lapsed into final stillness.

"It is," said Miranda. "It is," she repeated. She picked up the piece of wood again. It felt different from the Chinese box, but she was certain the stylized pictographic incisions were by the same hand. "What do you think, Morgan, what kind of wood?"

"It's not *toromiro*." He took it from her. "It doesn't look like the Peruvian rosewood the box is made from. What's the island wood they used when they ran out of *toromiro*?"

"*Mako'i*. Yeah, that's what I think. Take a look on the back."

"I know. It makes sense. Latin."

"The person who carved this was Humberto Rapu Haoa. I'm sure of it. Before being shipped off to Peru in chains, he studied Latin with the priests, and he studied Rongorongo as an *ariki*. He carved the history of his people into the sides of the box while he was in servitude, and when he returned to the island, a dying man, he realized he was the last *ariki* and he carved this, the key to the sacred text. He used the only wood available. What an utterly astonishing gift to his descendents."

Miranda realized as she talked that Ross was no longer a shadowy figure in the Rapa Nui story, but central to how it played out. Her treacherous handsome Englishman was the designated chamberlain, the keeper of the key, as Rove McMan was the guardian of the treasury. Whatever else was happening here, for weal or woe, Ross held the future of a people in his charming perfidious grip.

"This is *mana*," she said, "the best of good fortune. Humberto Rapu Hoa has given his people their past. The rest is up to you."

"Actually," Ross corrected her, "*mana* is more about power, usually with supernatural origins." At that moment he seemed benign, and a bit of a pompous prig. "My Rosetta slab and Rove's Chinese box have a magical affinity. Don't you worry, the rogue and the sailor, we'll both play our parts."

Miranda marvelled at the strange integrity of those two men, both of whom lived outside the pale. Each knew the other had an invaluable treasure that would be immeasurably enhanced by his own, yet there seemed no question of stealing or extorting to gain access to both. *Honour among scoundrels*, she thought — except Rove McMan was neither scoundrel nor thief. She glanced at Ross. Perhaps he was both, but he was still, in his own way, a man of honour.

She stood up and walked over to Gloria Simmons with her back to Thomas Ross. She untied the woman's wrists. "It's over," she said, turning to face their captor. "Your call, you can shoot us, but why bother? It would be a nasty distraction. Or you could leave now, return this amazing gift from the past to the island, as you say you're going to, and slip into another persona. I'm sure you have a few lives left in you yet. Vengeance will be through due process. We'll call it justice. Gloria Simmons will be dealt with. You told me something, once. Actually, you wrote it in a note. *Don't pull the rug out from under yourself.*"

Morgan had quietly risen to his feet. Ross seemed to be mulling things over. Morgan leaned down to take the Winchester. Ross tightened his grip, then released it with a shrug that asserted he relinquished no power by giving it up. Morgan hefted the rifle tentatively, letting his fingers curl around the unfamiliar rhapsody of cold steel and darkly polished wood, admiring its functional perfection. So this was the gun that won the West. And revolutionized the North. It was heavier than he expected. He stepped back and held the rifle at an angle between himself and Ross, with the barrel poised to slash down across the other man's face.

"Morgan," Miranda cautioned.

"Miranda, I am not a violent man."

Ross stared up at him with an annoying sense of bravado and made a gesture with the back of his hand as if to push the gun barrel away, but then thought better of it and let his hand drop. *"One cannot die in the middle of Act Five,"* he declared.

Morgan leaned the Winchester against the shelves at the back of the kitchen counter, then picked it up again, aimed it to the side and pumped the lever action in rapid succession, spewing the remaining live cartridges onto the carpet. Equanimity restored by this small act of controlled violence, he lay the rifle down on the floor and moved into the centre of the room, then moved to flank Gloria Simmons on the other side from Miranda.

Gloria Simmons leaned forward in her chair. She turned her head to address Ross as if she were clarifying matters of litigation. "I have two questions. One, to you. How did your magical Rongorongo piece end up in a Gibraltar cave? And two," she glanced first at Morgan and then at Miranda, "how do you expect to convict me for anything more than flying a Twin Otter without a license and misleading a cop in a sleeping bag?"

Morgan flinched, Miranda tried unsuccessfully to suppress a grin.

Ross turned to look at Gloria Simmons, then began to walk around the room, touching things as he talked, moving around Miranda and around Morgan. He ran his hands over a number of the Inuit carvings and seemed to settle his interest on one in particular. "I have visited Easter Island a number of times, you pick up the stories," he said. "Foreigners took away many valuable things, but this special piece was sent away for safekeeping." He retrieved the Rosetta slab from the table and turned it in the muted light, running his fingers gently over the runic incisions then set it back, Latin side down. "There are *moai* wrenched out of their place as ancestral guardians now sitting in major museums of the world."

He reached into his pocket and extracted a Swiss Army knife. "This carving, Ms. Simmons, it is a beauty." He held the knife absently in one hand and with the other he caressed the smooth green stone of a raptor caught in a brilliant instant of violent motion. "A Peregrine falcon, I presume. You can tell by the owlish face. Do you know these devils murder at two hundred miles an hour?"

Morgan looked over at the soapstone raptor, a beautiful piece with wings arced sinuously to arrest his sudden descent as he swooped on his prey. Talons like razors spread for the kill, flared eyes glaring yellow against the green-grey stone, pupils murderously black.

Morgan couldn't resist: "Not Maltese?"

"More deadly, I think. I'll bet I know how the stone-carver did the eyes. A clever innovation. I understand Inuit sculpture is a recent phenomenon."

And then, while Morgan was anticipating an irritating monologue on Dashiell Hammett and Inuit sculptors not being bound by tradition, Ross launched into a different discourse entirely:

"An Englishwoman by the name of Katherine Routledge mounted an expedition to Easter Island just before the Great War." He spoke softly, but his eyes kept flashing deliberately from one of them to the other. "Routledge was an historian, a spiritualist, an incipient schizophrenic, and a pioneer in the field of anthropology. Quite a beauty in her day, although somewhat faded by the time she arrived on the island. Incidentally, her armada consisted of a single schooner she named *Mana*. Ironic, isn't it? Routledge and her enterprise were invested with the unseen powers of empire: her *mana* had the strength of the imperial enterprise behind it while the *mana* of the islanders had been diminished almost to extinction. She meant well, I'm sure."

"So did the Spanish Inquisition," Miranda observed with wry exasperation.

"It is all a matter of perspective," Ross responded. While speaking, he had kept one hand on the polished head of the stone falcon, seeming to absorb the smooth coolness through his open palm. He withdrew his hand, stooped and stared directly into the brilliant eyes. He opened his knife, exposing a small allen wrench. "The eyes are magnificent, aren't they? The artist has cut cross-section slices from a yellow screwdriver handle, do you see, and embedded them in hollows in the stone. Ingenious!" He straightened and looked around almost as if he expected applause.

"Simply ingenious," he repeated. "Reminds me of the eye sockets in *moai* on Rapa Nui. They filled them with red scoria set into white coral. It was done after the statues had been hauled to their final destinations, I believe. The ancestors only resided in the stone once the eyes were installed. Living stone, you know, and why not?" He seemed pleased with his level of erudition. "You see, I have studied a little. I like to know about my investments."

He shifted his position so that the other three seemed to be arranged about the room as his audience. "Now Katherine and her husband, did I mention he was on the expedition, something often overlooked by her fans. Scoresby. A delightful name. They had a very close friend on the island, a handsome devil by the name of Jean Akarikitea." The syllables flowed like he had been born to the language. "The three of them, Jean Akarikitea and the Routledges, remind me of what I've been hearing about the D'Arcys and you, Gloria. Much the same dynamic, I expect. But that is another story, isn't it?"

Despite being freed, Gloria Simmons had not moved from her chair. Miranda and Morgan had made themselves comfortable, leaning against furniture, but remained on their feet.

"Now then," said Ross. "The pupils, you see, appear to be deep because they're empty. That might almost be a lesson in life! But not to digress. The holes are where the steel shaft of the screwdriver went through the plastic handle. This little do-hickey on my knife seems to fit the hole quite precisely. Look, when I twist and pull, the whole eye comes out. Both eyes. Isn't that haunting, those big empty black eye sockets. Now it looks like the angel of death."

He twisted around to gaze at Gloria Simmons who sat perfectly still, her own eyes fixed on him with a pitiless stare.

"I don't know for sure if this Jean Akarikitea was a grandson of Humberto Rapu Haoa, the last *ariki*, but he might have been," continued Ross. "It doesn't matter, he was the father of Matteo Akarikitea, the grandfather of my friends, Maria and Matteo, and great-grandfather to Matteo's children in Chile — they were, and are, all bound to the same *kainga*, the land claim of their ancestors. It may surprise you to know that on such a small island there are territorial divisions, but they still exist."

Thomas Ross bent forward and poked an index finger into each of the raptor's eye sockets, dislodging from a hollow within a small packet that he drew out through one eye, pushing it through from behind.

"But the Routledges, yes. After sixteen months of collecting and collating and speculating and, oh, becoming very much involved in the distant war effort as it impinged on Chilean politics and the sovereignty of Easter Island — at one point they had to hide their plunder from a ragtag contingent of the German fleet — they left. Stopped at Pitcairn and the Gambier Islands, then doubled back to San Francisco, stopped at Gibraltar, and arrived home in time for Christmas."

Ross appeared to pace aimlessly as he talked but he ended up behind Gloria Simmons, placing one hand on her shoulder. "Lovely earrings," he said.

"What a shame."

"What's that?" Morgan asked, indicating the packet.

"Ms. Simmons will explain in due course." Ross shrugged. "Whatever Katherine Routledge may have plundered, sanctioned by archaeology, the imperial science — or is that anthropology? No matter — I believe Jean Akarikitea freely gave her the magic slab for safekeeping."

"Because it wasn't time, yet," Miranda explained, unable to resist speaking up.

"Is it ever?" Ross retorted somewhat testily.

Miranda thought she detected an edge of despair within the cynicism. "The island population was far too small," she went on. "The Rapa Nui had been reduced to just over a hundred and were increasing slowly. The authority of the Church, reinforced by the government of Chile, was soul-destroying. It was time to wait." As she spoke, she felt a connection with Matteo and his brother, Te Ave Teao, and images of the dusty streets of Hanga Roa, the majestic *moai* of Rano Raraku aslant in the sun, the farmhouse still standing as if there had been no fire, all flashed through her mind. She lapsed into silence, inviting Ross to continue.

"Katherine had a spot of trouble over the next few decades," Ross declared. "Delusional paranoia. Her papers are with the Royal Geographical Society, but some of them took a long time getting there. Scoresby had her kidnapped and locked in an asylum, where she eventually died. Madness had taken over their lives and he ended up living in Cyprus. Died in 1939. Various documents, photographs, and letters turned up over the next few decades. A woman by the name of Van Tilburg is making great headway on the story as we speak. Among their papers was a copy of Katherine's book, *The Mystery of Easter Island*. It was originally published in 1919 but this copy was special. It was inscribed to Jean Akarikitea of Rapa Nui, but, according to Matteo, it was never sent, not until Scoresby's things were being tidied up. By the time it reached the island, Akarikitea had died, but Matteo Akarikitea, his son, was there to receive it. The book contained strange notations by Katherine herself. She had devised an intricate code to record where in the world their Rosetta piece was hidden. I don't think Scoresby was much interested. The whole thing smacks of paranoia, doesn't it? Of course it does. Katherine was paranoid."

"About Rapa Nui, perhaps for good reason," said Morgan.

"One does have to wonder why she didn't simply drop Jean Akarikitea a note explaining her encryption." Ross seemed genuinely perplexed.

"Better yet," Morgan concurred, "a note telling him that the translation slab was hidden inside Gibraltar."

"No!" Miranda protested. "Katherine Routledge must have known it could take generations before the island came into its own; she needed to protect its past until a future was possible. There's nothing delusional about that. Hopeful, maybe. She was an historical determinist, she believed the code would be broken when the time was right."

"And it was," said Ross.

"Possibly," Miranda acknowledged, enjoying a tingle of satisfaction. "But? How do we get from *The Mystery of Easter Island* to *Aku-Aku*? That doesn't make sense."

"I have no idea," said Ross. "Matteo suggested Heyerdahl took the Routledge book away with him in the 1950s. It's probably with his papers in Oslo, or been sold to a private collector."

For a moment suspended in time, the four of them might have been friends. Whatever else they were thinking, each was also engaged with resolving the problem of transference: how could a secret embedded in the particular pages of one book end up in another if the person transcribing didn't understand the system of encryption?

"Perhaps whoever copied it actually did know the code," Morgan suggested.

"Then they wouldn't have needed me," said Miranda.

"All right," said Ross, smiling at her with a warmth that ignored the fact he had jammed a rifle butt into her abdomen only a short time before. "You solved the primary puzzle — why not this one, as well?"

Miranda glowered at him without conviction, looked to Morgan for support, and then into the expectant eyes of Gloria Simmons who had been following everything closely since the focus had shifted away from her. For reasons Miranda could not quite comprehend, all this seemed vitally important to the woman from Baffin, the Toronto lawyer whose lethal activities had so casually sabotaged Rapa Nui interests as collateral damage to her own.

Morgan was thinking about navigation through time by dead reckoning. The future is determined by assumptions about the past. If your calculations are wrong, you end up lost or on the rocks. There's a reckoning — you're dead.

"You're sure Heyerdahl took the Routledge book?" he asked.

"As a latter-day artifact, yes, according to Matteo."

"Why on earth would those people give up their treasures?" Gloria Simmons spoke up suddenly, shaping her words with a mixture of exasperation and despair.

Morgan wondered why she did not seem to comprehend the powerlessness of the exploited. Ross raised his eyebrows in surprise and let them droop to a furrow of reluctant respect. Miranda resisted the urge to plea for empathy, the one faculty she felt certain Gloria Simmons did not possess.

"*We* were never defeated," the blonde Inuk declared in a sort of refrain, leaving it to the others to make the connection. There was an emphasis to her pronouncement that left no room for argument.

Miranda stared. Gloria Simmons's defiance of Ross was beginning to take on larger dimensions.

And then, out of nowhere, Miranda conceived a scenario to explain how the transference of the coded message had occurred. Sometimes people fulfilled their destinies without understanding what it was they were doing. Not, she reminded herself, not that she believed in destiny.

"Maria's grandfather copied Routledge's message into the Heyerdahl book," she explained. It all seemed self-evident. "The handwriting in *Aku-Aku* is very deliberate. Now I realize why. It was copied letter for letter by someone who didn't know English. Thor Heyerdahl gave Matteo Akarikitea an autographed copy of his own book in exchange for *The Mystery of Easter Island*. Before parting with the book that Routledge had inscribed to his father, the islander laboriously transferred her notations. If he had understood English, he might have copied her words onto a flyleaf or a scrap of paper. But because he couldn't read the words, their context must have seemed as important as the script itself. He replicated, page for page, Routledge's original."

"*Rongorongo* all over again," said Morgan. He was touched by the image of an elderly Rapanui urgently copying messages from the past without knowing what they were saying. He remembered the bittersweet feelings he'd had, seeing intricate but unintelligible inscriptions on slabs of imported wood for sale in the markets of Hanga Roa. How poignant to replicate copies in the hope that someday someone might know what they meant.

"A lovely irony," he said. "Heyerdahl's 'acquisition' forced a new interest on the island in Routledge's coded message. *Aku-Aku* displaced the Routledge book as the sacred text. A new testament displacing the old: same message, different text. And it ended up with the D'Arcys, who brought the secret full circle through you, Miranda." Morgan was both pleased and wary that the details were coming together. "With help from you, Mr. Ross. Even you and I, Ms. Simmons, we all seem to have played our parts in the drama. We must be nearing the end of Act Five."

Miranda shuddered at the implications. She looked at her partner, flashing acknowledgement of his astute if unnerving summation, looked at Ross, seeing him as both a relatively benign enemy and a dangerous ally, and looked at Gloria Simmons. "Are you okay?" she said.

Gloria Simmons permitted herself a small smile. "As well as can be expected under the circumstances." She paused, as if searching for some sort of closure. "Maria's ashes and Harrington's ashes, I mixed them together. They're in a sterling silver casket on board the *Tangata Manu*, on their way to Rapa Nui. When things change on the island, they will be there. There will be time for waiting," she said, enigmatically, "no matter how long it takes."

"One of the few benefits of death," said Ross.

The small sack in his hand rustled in the shadows behind Gloria Simmons. She remained perfectly still. He extricated a tiny bottle from the folds of cloth and twisted open the cap. A copy of *Maclean's* magazine lay on the coffee table. He picked it up, and, giving the bottle a quick shake he tapped out a sprinkling of fine powder, which settled lightly on the cover picture, obscuring the eyes of a world dignitary. Morgan had expected it to be a potion. Ross handed the vial over her shoulder to Gloria Simmons who grasped it between thumb and two fingers as if it were a butterfly and she had to be careful not to damage its wings.

"I always thought it might end like this," she said. "Poetic justice." She held up the bottle as if to catch traces of light in the butterfly's wings. "It's a mixture of coniine, pancuronium, talcum powder, and ground glass, none of them very difficult to procure. I ground the glass myself."

The tension in the room was palpable, although each must have felt it in a different way. Miranda and Morgan edged closer to Gloria Simmons, but as they reached out to restrain her before she did something foolish, Ross held the magazine at arm's length in front of his face and issued what seemed like a controlled but explosive sneeze. Morgan's hand shot to the wound on his neck in a small act of self-preservation. Swirls of lethal powder took to the air in a cluster of tiny exploding tornadoes and with virtually no time passing, a thin layer of powder settled on their exposed skin. Instinctively, they stopped dead still. Morgan throttled the urge to brush it away from his eyes, the stronger urge to reach out and wipe the powder from Miranda's cheeks and chin and upper lip and blow it away from the exposed curve of her breasts peeking above her summer dress.

"Freeze!" said the ice queen emphatically, if unnecessarily. A fine residue on her forehead caught the lamplight like face powder on an old woman's face. "Do not move," she reiterated. A slight tremor crept into Gloria Simmons's voice that left no one in doubt about the urgency of her command. "Neither of you. Morgan, think like an Inuk, remember the sleeping bag, movement will kill you."

Ross carefully set the magazine down and stepped back a pace. "Stay very still," he echoed, his voice was insistent, reinforcing her directive. "I have no interest in seeing you die, Miranda, nor you, Detective Morgan, but she's right, you will indeed die if you try to interfere. Hobson's choice — witnesses to justice, you *are* police, after all, or collateral damage. You *were* police, past tense. Either way. Ms. Simmons is dead."

They might have been figures in the gloomy tableaux of a master sculptor, their arrested movement caught at the moment of death. Only Ross seemed alive as he proceeded with uncanny stealth to move through the shadows until he could see into everyone's eyes, but he said nothing more, satisfied for the present to observe. He had set something in motion that was inexorable and unholy, and he was determined to watch it play out.

"Listen to me, Morgan." Gloria Simmons was speaking to him like an intimate friend. "If you move, if you sweat, the ground glass, the slightest abrasion, will allow the poison access to your system and it's over. Keep your hand over the open wound on your neck. Trust me. Even a facial expression will kill you. Trust me," she repeated. Her features shifted into a curiously wry and possibly lethal smile. Not sardonic, no cynicism, just wry, apparently in response to her admonition of trust. "Stay very, very still."

After an interminable wait — Morgan felt his Bulova watch silently strike the hour — Ross became impatient and shifted his strategy. "It is now indeed the end of Act Five, Ms. Simmons," he said. "Your move."

"No!" Miranda exclaimed, rocking on her feet but remaining otherwise motionless. "You have a choice," she declared through clenched teeth.

"No, Miranda, I do not. But you do."

Morgan shuffled slightly, trying to inhale through his mouth, but exhale through his nostrils, to avoid taking wisps of the poison mixture into his body or spreading it around on his face. He could feel Miranda's stillness beside him the way he could sometimes feel the stillness of death on a homicide case. But he could also feel the warmth emanating from her body and he knew she could feel his. He looked at Gloria Simmons and they made eye contact, then her eyes shifted focus to Ross.

"Is this what you want, Thomas?" Her voice was steady, a little threatening, almost seductive. "To murder a couple of cops? Not a smart move for a very smart guy."

Ross raised an eyebrow. "Gloria Simmons," he said, "I truly wish we could have been chums and lovers."

"Chums, perhaps."

"Do you ever consummate any of your affairs, Mr. Ross?" Morgan's eyes flashed to the side. This was Miranda talking. The enunciation was slurred as she struggled to keep her features immobile, but, damn it, no jibe was worth the risk. He hoped she could feel his censure.

The women exchanged a knowing gaze. Everyone, even Ross, stood motionless. Morgan was sure he could hear the hum of a light bulb on the verge of expiring. Miranda felt a bead of sweat gathering between her shoulder blades and involuntarily twitched inside her clothes. Morgan sensed her movement and glowered without looking at her, then felt an intolerable itch in the clenched hair of his groin and focused with excruciating effort until it subsided. Miranda cleared her throat, admonishing him to remain still.

Gloria Simmons spoke, "Miranda Quin, David Morgan, here's what I want you to do."

Good God, thought Miranda, *the woman is directing her own death scene.*

"I want you to move very slowly — remember David how we refused to sweat — just shuffle, I believe Mr. Ross will not object, it is not to his benefit, move together, and when you get to the bathroom turn on the shower very gently so the flow will not drive the poison into your skin, and let warm water flow over your exposed skin, and gently, very carefully, remove each others' clothes. Some powder will float free into your clothes and onto your skin, do not use soap directly, create a lather, and let it rinse across your skin. Do it for one another, and then dry each other gently under the radiant light. You may survive. I hope you do. In another life, David, we could have been lovers; more likely, in another life, Miranda, you and I would have been lovers and your partner and I, we could have been close friends."

She gave the bottle a shake and a fine dust drifted across her collarbone and down into her cleavage. "Think of this as Nemesis, my friend, restoring order to the universe." She addressed Morgan with a whimsical glint in her eyes. Gloria Simmons rubbed the powder languorously into her exposed skin. "I'm sorry it isn't Fleurs de Rocaille." She smiled in Miranda's direction, then shifted in her chair to try and bring Ross's face into focus, but he stepped back into the cavern of shadows formed by the drawn curtains.

Miranda, poised to move closer, hesitated, hovering, immobile, ready to spring to the other woman's aid, constrained by an overwhelming instinct to remain motionless, to survive.

"Please, Miranda. There is nothing you can do." Their eyes met. "I only get one crack at this. I'd like to do it right."

And as she composed her face and posture for maximum dignity, Gloria Simmons looked ethereal. She tilted her head slightly and gazed at Morgan, then she winked and slowly her eyelids drooped and she closed her eyes, accepting her execution with a kind of beatific forbearance. "Come away, death," she whispered. The words were an invitation, distinct, conspiratorial, quietly triumphant. Her eyelids fluttered. Minutes passed, then, with a convulsive shudder, she slumped and settled back into the chair. A smear of discoloured moisture darkened her lower lip.

Morgan stared in sustained horror; he had expected rage. He felt sick, suffocated, bewildered. Why embrace death like an act of self-love, of devotion, a caress, speeding it on its way? He felt close to her, angry, intimate, understanding, almost. It was to determine her own moment of dying. Power and grace in the face of the absolute, the utter inevitable inescapable immanence of death.

She had rendered Ross impotent.

Or was it Ross, in the shadows, a gracious assassin, who allowed her the illusion of power?

Morgan could feel Miranda's anguish. It was never easy to watch someone die, even a self-professed killer like Gloria Simmons. *And there was no one like Gloria Simmons*, he thought. He began edging toward Miranda with such imperceptible movements it felt like he was creeping inside his shoes.

As she began turning toward Morgan in ultra slow motion she felt a disconcerting mixture of wary compassion for her partner's predicament. Poor man, it must be confusing, his survival skills may have saved Gloria Simmons in the Arctic, she resisted murdering him when she could have, and now he was the helpless witness to her death.

When they touched each other, avoiding skin contact, fabric gently brushing against fabric, they focused single-mindedly on what they were doing. Neither looked at Gloria Simmons and Thomas Ross was irrelevant. Their survival depended on complete concentration; one quick move, sweat, or the slightest abrasion, and either might die or, what would be worse, might kill the other.

Morgan slowly held his free hand up to eye level and scrutinized his thumb and forefinger for evidence of the poison. Satisfied they were clean he reached over and pulled the neckline of Miranda's sundress away from her breastbone. When she realized what he was doing, she hunched slightly forward, allowing the weight of her breasts to draw her flesh down to avoid abrasion. Then, awkwardly, without straightening, she reached across and returned the favour, tugging the blood-saturated cotton of his shirt away from the back of his other hand, which was still clutched over his wound, holding it clear of his skin. When he pulled his hand away from his neck he felt a sudden stinging pop, but no blood flowing.

As they shuffled in their excruciatingly sluggish dance toward the bathroom, silence reinforced the stillness and they moved with a quietude that surprised them. No quips, no commentary. They progressed in unison with such little overt effort that no air stirred. They could hear their clothes rustling. As each moved, the other followed in a shuffling four-foot quadrille until at last they were in position to enter the shower. She had left the light on. Slowly, gently, she opened the glass door.

Morgan reached cautiously into the stall, which was custom built and extra large, and turned on the water at low pressure.

When the water was lukewarm they stepped in, fully clothed.

Like a soft tropical rain, the water washed over their exposed skin and soaked through their clothes until they were drenched. Both began to relax, they seemed in their own small intimate world. As she felt warm water pooling in tepid pockets against her skin, Miranda realized the poisonous blend might have been driven through the fibres. Diluted, still lethal.

"Careful," she slurred between clenched teeth, "It's not over."

Morgan had come to the same conclusion. Their sopping clothes were like instruments of medieval torture, hair shirts made from poison fleece. "Did you ever read about the Inquisition?" he asked, jaw rigid, lips unmoving. "Or is that just something you talk about?"

"Shuddup," she muttered, then looked up at

Morgan without raising her head and risked a small smile as she began to unbutton his shirt, making slow progress because the material was saturated. Item by item, they removed one another's clothing until they stood face to face, warm water streaming over the contours of their naked flesh, the pile outside the open shower door with twin peaks of baby-blue panties and underwear pants, as Morgan persisted, with endearing conviction, in calling his most personal apparel.

Miranda knew they were still within a flick of death's finger, but she was enjoying their prolonged intimacy, the languid pace and sensual movements of their ministrations to the needs of the other. They were so close it would have been equally as awkward to observe his body as her own without craning her neck. And possibly lethal.

Morgan could sense every pore and nerve and plane and contour of Miranda's body, which he would have thought was familiar territory; they had worked so closely together for over a decade, had skinny dipped together, had even been lovers in one brief flurry of erotic abandon that they had immediately contained and set off to the side as if it had happened to two other people who were only vaguely recognizable, but now he was intensely aware that neither *familiar* nor *territory* were adequate to describe the sensations her nakedness worked on his own body and on his mind, which was also concerned with impending death and strategies for survival.

Slowly, with caressing motions, they created lather, and gently they soaped one another's bodies, allowing the lather to slide delicately between hands poised like petals over intimate curves, capturing errant particles that might have stuck to their skin or clothing, and washing them away. They didn't touch, letting water and gravity slide the poisons away. As they moved so they were almost in profile to each other Morgan caught a stardust shimmer along the upper plane of Miranda's breast closest to him. He felt a deep thudding in his chest and his breathing constricted. Visible powder had been washed off, but there might be residual poison adhering to glass. When she handed him the soap he worked up a foam that he let slip from his hands over each breast. In the flow of the water over their taut contours, the foam skirted her nipples before sliding down into the shadows on the underside of her breasts.

Morgan let the soap bar drop on the pile of contaminated clothes and they stood still, lost in the enfolding warmth of the water. He thought *she* drew him to her and she thought *he* drew her to him because they moved at the same time. Their arms circled one another and with his head tilted down and hers tilted up, their cheeks touched and their hair formed a drowned medley of auburn and dark brown flecked with grey. Time stopped.

When it started again, Morgan leaned back and gazed into her eyes. Miranda glanced down.

"Morgan," she declared, "That is most inappropriate."

"Consider it a compliment."

"You know what we used to do when our old stallion did that? Whack it with a flyswatter."

"You never had an old stallion."

Hearing one another laugh, simultaneously it came to them, the death scene in the other room that they had blocked out in their efforts to concentrate on survival. They suddenly became aware of their nakedness. Wrapping towels around themselves, they walked gingerly into the living room, both of them glowing with a sheen of water. Morgan moved close to Gloria Simmons's side and Miranda squatted down in front of her and wiped the discoloured moisture from her lips with a bit of tissue, careful not to touch the powder still on her forehead. Morgan remembered her on Baffin, poised between the living and the dead. Miranda touched Morgan, letting her fingers rest against his arm, thinking that sometimes the arc of a life was brief but full, and this woman, whom she reviled and admired, but did not judge, had lived a full life and taken her leave with class.

In slow motion, Morgan shifted his focus to scan the room, knowing Thomas Ross would not be among the shadows. He exchanged glances with Miranda. "The valise is gone. He took the Rosetta piece with him," he said.

"That's good."

"What do you think?" Morgan looked down at the dead woman. He shuddered and looked away.

"Gloriasimmons got what she wanted, Morgan. Baffin wins. Your side, Morgan. Sometimes bad people do good things." She gazed down at the dead woman. "Sometimes good people do very bad things. Because they have to."

Morgan tightened the towel around his waist, and, in an instinctive response to his modesty, she tucked the top edge of her towel more firmly in place.

"Your friends on Easter Island are farther ahead without the junta," he said. "Fascists aren't generally sympathetic to splinter groups. If McMan and Ross follow through, maybe within the legal framework of a Chile revitalized by the Baffin investment, the Rapa Nui will get to control their future."

"Crimes of the early morning, that's how Matteo described the new era in his people's history, the twilight just before dawn. Ross will end up doing the right thing, even if it is for the wrong reasons." Miranda felt certain of this. "And ultimately, Matteo's children will come into their own. They will, it's inevitable."

Morgan, who had his doubts about fate and the inevitable, nodded assent. "We'd better call this in. We've got a dead person, here. And we've got a fugitive on the loose."

"Tell me about the sleeping bag, Morgan."

Feigning nonchalance, he smiled. "There's nothing to tell. We were just keeping warm." To reveal the naked part seemed inappropriate, given the lady was a corpse. "It's from Shakespeare, you know. *Twelfth Night*."

"What?"

"What she whispered. *Come away, death*."

"It's from *Twelfth Night*."

"I just told you that. It's a lament for lost love."

"It's about consolation, Morgan. We studied it in

high school. *Not a flower, not a flower sweet, On my black coffin let there be strown.* We took it in grade eleven as the absolute zenith of romantic despair."

"And for Gloria Simmons, it meant exactly the opposite."

"You think? So, you figure her death was, how could we put this, self-inflicted? I mean, Ross was, well no he wasn't, he …"

"If you were going to say innocent, he's anything but!"

Miranda grimaced. "Not, exactly. Guilty."

"Except for assaulting two of Toronto's finest, kidnapping, aiding and abetting a suicide, fomenting an insurrection, impersonating a lawyer —"

"Maybe he went to law school."

"It wouldn't surprise me in the least." Morgan was concerned by how vulnerable her ambivalance toward Ross made her seem. "You know," he said, "W.B. Yeats once explained his disdain for Wilfred Owen by saying, 'There is every excuse for him but none for those who like him.'"

"His poetry, not the man. Yeats didn't know the man."

"Exactly, and you don't know Thomas Edward Ross."

Miranda gazed down at the dead woman, then back at Morgan. "The kidnapping charge wouldn't stick. Forcible confinement, maybe. Except after the bonds were removed, she didn't budge. I mean, this was her home, Morgan."

"Was it? You should have seen her on Baffin."

"You know what I mean." She paused. "You should have seen Ross on Rapa Nui. He was even better-looking there — if you like the type. We won't catch him, you know. He'll become whoever he needs to be and slip through."

"Catch him, no. Find him, yes. Back on Easter Island, sooner or later. But agreed, why bother? I've got my killer."

"She's dead."

Morgan looked down at Gloria Simmons. Death had leached the lustre from her complexion, the contours of her skull pressed against her face from the inside, through the flesh, in shadow her eye sockets seemed empty beneath the skin, but with her cascade of perfect hair, and the dignity of her expression in final repose, she looked less a cadaver than a wraith, a Valkyrie slain. Morgan felt an odd sense of relief that it was over, and an odd sense of loss. "Know what's interesting?" he said. "It's all speculation. It might be hard to convict Ross, but imagine trying to pin anything on Gloria Simmons. I'm in for endless paperwork, or very little at all."

"I suspect the latter, although Ross had no problem finding her guilty."

"More to the point, she accepted her sentence as just."

"And death, inexorable. She embraced it."

"Yes, she did." He ran his hands through tendrils of his own damp hair. "I suppose it is for us all." She had never heard Morgan sigh, but he exhaled with an audible hiss through his teeth that might have been a stifled sigh. He reached out and touched her cheek with the back of his hand and his dark brown eyes seemed unfathomably deep. "Inexorable," he said, as if he had just coined the word.

"Morgan, you're standing here naked with a beautiful woman— myself — who is also standing here naked. Admittedly, the other beautiful woman on the scene is deceased. But let's get over the mortality thing." She reached up, grasped his hand took it away from her cheek, and let it drop to his side. "Let's cover ourselves up, call this in, and go out for dinner. I want to tell you about a novel I'm thinking of writing."

Morgan walked back into the bathroom and in a short time she could hear the dryer whirling. *Oh God!* She barged in, but their clothes were still in their twin-peaked heap.

"I didn't know how to pick them up," he said. "So I didn't."

"O-kay," she said slowly, drawing each syllable out with an exaggerated pursing and flexing of her lips. "We'll have to make do with the towels."

"My shirt's ruined, anyway."

"We need it for evidence. We need all our clothes, unwashed, as is, for evidence."

"Is that a push-up bra?" he asked, nodding toward the baby-blue swirl of cotton in the clothing pile.

"Morgan, why don't you go into the bedroom and see if you can rustle up something for us to wear that's not laced with residual poison. Make do — I don't expect that she had many overnight visitors your size. And don't worry about finding a bra," she said, arching her back just slightly. "I can do without."

When Miranda walked back into the living space, she looked at how graciously Gloria Simmons had settled into death and she reached over with a fresh tissue and dabbed a bit more moisture from her lips. Then Miranda picked up her purse and withdrew her cellphone. As she punched in the number for headquarters, she rummaged around for her semi-automatic. No Glock! The bastard had gone off with her gun. She blanched with outraged embarrassment. Morgan came out, still wrapped in a towel, he glanced over at the kitchen counter. Her Glock was lying beside the breadboard, racked and ready to roll. Ross had just wanted to show them he could.

Miranda's hazel eyes and auburn hair glistened as they stepped out into the evening sunlight. She was wearing a rumpled pantsuit, the legs and one sleeve were rolled up precariously, the other sleeve had followed the natural inclinations of fabric and design to engulf her fingertips in a flapping tube of smoky green. She wore it with the assurance that an Armani looks good even when it doesn't fit. Class buys clothes a life of their own. Morgan looked different. His pants were a soft, grey linen and excruciatingly tight, and he moved very awkwardly since the crotch was not cut for a man. He wore a most curious sort of swashbuckling blouse, white silk with cuffs flared below the elbows, and a broad swooping collar that caught the air as he moved; only the buttonholes, off-centred down the front, betrayed its borrowed status not from a dashingly effeminate Caribbean pirate, but from a woman of quite different proportions. They both wore pale blue silk scarves, one sheer and one opaque, flung casually around their necks, and they wore their own shoes, without stockings or socks.

"Dinner?" she said, taking his arm.

No one arriving at the crime scene had uttered a word about the green garbage bag full of their sopping clothes on the bathroom floor, nor about them walking off wearing what might have been considered evidence for the Crown, and everyone fastidiously followed instructions to touch nothing, especially the corpse, without thick, protective gloves.

"Dinner," he affirmed. "You look lovely tonight."

"And you," she paused, biting her inner lip. "You do as well."

They walked slowly down Trafalgar Mews, past an assortment of police cars and a Black Mariah from the city morgue. Despite the gathering coolness of evening, their body warmth pooled between them like an ineffable bond. The moon in the first quarter was a pale crescent against the August sky. Morgan was smiling. He looked at Miranda. She was smiling that radiant inscrutable smile that could mean just about anything. He wondered if she would make him a character in her novel that would never be written. She wondered if he had slept with Ellen Ravenscroft. She shrugged. It was good to be back in Toronto.

Acknowledgements

In the decades before writing *Reluctant Dead*, I backpacked and canoed extensively on Baffin Island and through vast reaches of the Canadian Arctic. Among my publications from these adventures was the book *Enduring Dreams: An Exploration of Arctic Landscape*. I also had the good fortune to accompany my wife, Beverley Haun, on research trips to the South Pacific. Her book *Inventing Easter Island* has proven to be a model, a source, and an inspiration. My daughters have taken time from busy schedules to offer invaluable insights: thanks to Julia Zarb, Laura Moss, and Beatrice Winny. Thank you also to Shannon Whibbs for her sensitive and intelligent contributions. And for his fearless candour and concrete suggestions I'd especially like to express my indebtedness to an old friend who understands that it matters, Jack Morgan.

More Quin and Morgan Mysteries by John Moss

Still Waters
A Quin and Morgan Mystery
978-1-55002-790-7
$11.99

This psychological mystery introduces David Morgan and Miranda Quin, two maverick and culturally sophisticated Toronto police detectives. When a man is found dead in a garden pond in the wealthy heart of Toronto's Rosedale neighbourhood, Morgan is led into speculations about Japanese ornamental koi fish, and Quin into a chilling sequence of revelations that could destroy her. But the real mystery begins not with the deceased, but with a woman who walks onto the crime scene and without emotion declares herself to be the victim's mistress. From that point on everything changes, even the past.

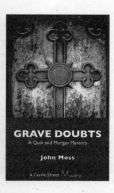

Grave Doubts
A Quin and Morgan Mystery
978-1-55488-405-6
$11.99

The discovery of two headless corpses dressed in colonial clothing and locked in a grisly embrace draws Detectives Miranda Quin and David Morgan of the Toronto

Police Service into a Gothic mixture of sex and death that ultimately threatens their survival. Beginning with morbid curiosity, they get caught up in a story of inspired depravity. Through revelations in such diverse locations as a Toronto demolition site, a lonely farmhouse on Georgian Bay, the crypt of a derelict church, and inside the murky depths of a shipwreck, this perverse account of love, lust, and murder builds to a horrific crescendo. Seduced by their own personal demons, Quin and Morgan might not find their considerable skills and strong bond enough this time to help them overcome the terrors that await.

Available at your favourite bookseller.

DUNDURN PRESS
www.dundurn.com

What did you think of this book?
Visit *www.dundurn.com*
for reviews, videos, updates, and more!